Paladologies

Paladologies

PHILLIP CAMPBELL

Cruachan Hill Press
Grass Lake, Michigan

Second Edition

ISBN: 978-1-957206-09-7

Cover artwork by Chris Lewis of Baritus Catholic Illustration Mapwork by Luca Coppola. Illustrations by Lucy Campbell.

TABLE OF CONTENTS

MINOR PALADOLOGIES

APPENDICES

Foreword to the Second Edition
Phillip Campbell

So, you've decided to read *Paladologies*. My friend, I applaud you. *Paladologies* is a work of considerable length and density, requiring an attentiveness and commitment modern readers sometimes find distasteful. When it was first published, I used to autograph copies of this for young readers with the note, "I dare you to finish this book." I suppose the dare holds today for those who undertake the journey through *Paladologies*. Yet, for the persevering, it is an endeavor whose effort yields its own reward.

I hope with this modest forward to introduce you to the *Paladologies* so you know what to expect as you dive into the deep lore of the peoples of Manissé.

Origin and Influences

I wrote and published *Paladologies* in 2010, the year after the publication of *Tale of Manaeth*. But, like the *Tale*, the origins of this book go back much earlier, to short stories and concepts I created when I was a boy. To this day I still have a crumpled, moldy piece of notebook paper from around 1992 outlining the extensive family tree of the seven houses of Manissa. I also still have an old print out of a Word file from that time with summaries of some of the stories, such as Belar, Elifanora, Oros, and more.

Unlike *Tale of Manaeth*, which is a war epic, *Paladologies* was always conceived of as a series of short stories. The structure of the work was deeply influenced by Edith Hamilton's

Mythology, in which the Greek myths are organized as a series of tales about particular gods and heroes. I first encountered Edith Hamilton's masterpiece in the library of my seventh-grade classroom. It is difficult to exaggerate the influence the work had on me; indeed, I was so enamored with it that (sorry to say) I stole the book from the library. Hamilton's organization of the rambling corpus of Greek myths into a cohesive narrative spanning multiple generations was the prototype for the structure of *Paladologies*.

The content of *Paladologies* was the fruit of many influences. The name itself is reminiscent of the Roman *Martyrologies*, the traditional list or catalogue of martyrs of the Roman Church. Just as the *Martyrologies* is a list of martyrs venerated in the Latin rite liturgy of the Catholic Church, so the *Paladologies* provided a catalog of venerated "paladins," ancient heroes of the houses of Manissa.

Like *Tale of Manaeth*, both the Hebrew Old Testament and the myths of ancient Greece shaped my creativity as I weaved the stories of *Paladologies*. *Paladologies* is very much the "Old Testament" of the peoples of Elabaea; that is, a national history spanning centuries and featuring a multitude of characters, yet unified in the transcendent destiny of a specific people who are instruments by which divine power is wielded. But it is also deeply Greek in its overarching sense of tragic fatalism; in tale after tale the flaws of protagonists lead to their own destruction.

How to Read the Paladologies

Paladologies is unique in that there are numerous ways to read it. You can, of course, read it beginning to end like any conventional book. However, given that the *Paladologies* is a collection of thirty-six short stories with varying degrees if interconnectedness, reading cover to cover may not be the best approach for beginners. *Paladologies* is broken up into three sections of "books": the "Chronicle of the Days of Hadrior" (*Iniön éla Hadrior*), the "Deeds of the Sons of Manissa" (*Nöm etha Manissé*), and the "Paladologies" (*Anridion*), which is subdivided into two parts, the so-called Major Paladologies (*Anridion Aior*) and the Minor Paladologies (*Anridion Inoré*). Each of these books has its own internal chronology which may or may not link with the chronology of the others. For example, the Minor Paladologies begins with a story (Pilux) that takes place over a thousand years *before* the story that immediately precedes it (Mantarax). If you would like to avoid these sorts of time jumps, consult Appendix D for a recommended chronological reading.

As for the content of the three books, this is covered in greater detail in Appendix A for those who want to understand the *Paladologies* the way the ancient Manissans did. But, in brief, the first book, "Chronicle of the Days of Hadrior," is principally concerned with the events of Hadrior's reign. It is the immediate sequel to *Tale of Manaeth*, picking up only two years after Manissa's disappearance. The second book is "The Deeds of the Sons of Manissa." This text contains six stories about the seven children of Manissa, plus the records of a great census taken around two generations after her reign. The third book, "Paladologies" is divided into twelve stories deemed "Major" and twelve deemed "Minor." Both the Major and Minor Paladologies concern the more remote descendants of Manissa's house; the Major are tales are longer and more involved, dealing with the grand development of Manissan history, while the Minor are entertaining shorter stories that are much smaller in scope. The entire work from cover-to-cover spans just over 1100 years; those interested in understanding the exact chronology should consult Appendix C on the calendars of Manissé.

Finally, readers interested in world-building and the lore of Manissé should absolutely make use of Appendix B, "Glosses and Commentary." This was the most enjoyable part of *Paladologies* to write. Inspired by my own love of medieval glosses and patristic commentary, Appendix B is a fictionalized collection of how later generations of Manissans interpreted the *Paladologies*; it is essentially their version of patristic commentary. Appendix B draws out allegorical and mystical meanings from the *Paladologies* that the reader would never infer but which would have been important within the world of the Manissans. Appendix B is my love letter to the venerable tradition of Catholic patristic and monastic commentaries on the Scriptures. Throughout the text, when you see an asterisk* at the end of a phrase, it means there is a gloss on that passage in Appendix B that can be consulted for further insight into the text as it was understood by the Manissans.

All this begs the question, "Why not just write a normal book? Why make it so complex and challenging to sort through?" The answer is simple: *Paladologies* is not meant to be a "normal" book. It is supposed to mimic the intricacy and garbled nature of mythic anthologies, like the Norse *Edda* or the Ulster Cycle of ancient Ireland. The national histories of ancient peoples were usually amalgams of stories written and collected over centuries—consider the Hebrew Old Testament's 46 books! This genre is the mold for *Paladologies*.

The Themes of Paladologies

Paladologies is a story of disinheritance, promise, and redemption. The gradual disinheritance of Manissa's children follows their own failure to live up to the lofty example set by their remarkable mother. We see this in Baldor's hesitance to press the claims of his house, the rashness of Elphas, and the unbridled rage of Perior. Manissa's descendants share all the marks of classical heroes of tragedy: imbued with extraordinary power and prowess but doomed to fail due to their inability to overcome their own flaws. There is thus a profoundly tragic element to the book.

Nevertheless, the grace of their mother abides with them from across the mysterious veil of the otherworld. For every failure, there is strength and promise of redemption. Guiding her house from beyond the world, Manissa scatters seeds of promise that will germinate in the final redemption of her kin, the restoration of her house, and the overthrow of their enemies.

Though she is scarcely in the book, the shadow of Manissa looms over all the tales of *Paladologies*. She sometimes acts directly through supernatural manifestations, such as the opening apparition in the Temple of Mironna to Hadrior, her appearance before the walls of Dretia in the paladology of Oros, or the mystical vision narrated in the Book of Cyllinus. But beyond her direct appearances, we see her role within Elabaean society develop over centuries, as she becomes less a historical personage and more an object of veneration. By the middle of *Paladologies*, it is clear that the Manissans view her in religious terms. She has joined the ranks of deified founders; even as the Romans deified Romulus, the Manissans find Manissa "among the immortals." She thus serves as a sign of unity for her people—no longer simply Asylians or Cadarasians, but "men of Manissé," those who call upon Manissa.

Paladologies is a notably tragic work, exemplifying the folly of human arrogance and the snares that so often beset those in power. Yet it is not without optimism and certain faint glimmers of beauty. It is my sincere hope that through the cycles of glory and defeat, victory and disaster that befall the House of Manissa throughout the centuries that one can get an appreciation, however dim, of the beautiful saga that comprises the origin and growth of the Manissan kingdom.

Phillip Campbell
September 1, 2022

Maruda

Lamlash

Elam

Ambrè

Zurlina Forest

Gihon

Epidymia

Epidyne

An Hered

Ganas

Debir

Cadarasia

Cadaras

Iturian Highlands

Ituria

Lissus

Thòn

Gela

Kobarth

Sehn

Avlos

Eftap?

Nearer Asylia

Molossia

Paros

Asylia

Farther Asylia

An Erras

Dindumon

Elos

Nimru Pass

Bados Mountains

Than

Cyrenaica

Cyrian Highlands

Wilds of Enna

Hill of Cruachan

Eidyllion

Aucoria

Adarwood

Lugaria

Manissé

At the Death of Hadrior

Asylia

Erriad

o Elos

o Cadaras

Cadarasia

Greystone

Betulia   Aldor

Nimru

Cadar

o Ganas

Galmura

Bay of
Norn

o Halicor

o Engor

o Bados
(Ardilla)

o Anentora

■Manis

Teruel

Cumala

Isle of Dretia

Emeric
o o
o

Illyrana

o Badoa

Corbalund

Western Manissé
At the Time of Oros

RAHAN

Tabia

Tabés

Lygon
(Nargobaith)

Ligar

Adarwood

Oracle of
Orale

Lugaria

Thán

Cyrenaica

Arcoria

Cyrian
Highlands

Karanak

Asylia

Eidyllion   Enna

Northwestern Manissé
(Casias, Pelinos and Adrias)

Inión éla Hadrior
(*"Chronicle of the Days of Hadrior"*)

Of the Murder of Erogel

৩৯৯ ৩৯৯ ৩৯৯

It came to pass in the days when Hadrior was king of Asylia reigning from white-walled Cadaras, the City on the Plains, the whole kingdom being at rest, that the king went forth in the second year of his reign to the Temple of Mironna in the Citadel to offer the yearly sacrifice for the well-being of the peoples of Asylia and Cadarasia, as had been the custom of Blessed Manissa in days past. Therefore he put off his finely embroidered garments and his crown of delicately wrought silver and donned the white linen ephod of the priests of Mironna. After performing the customary ablutions and waiting for the oracles of the augurs, he went forth into the sanctuary of the temple in the shade of its great cedar beams. The priests of Mironna handed him the golden censer, and after blessing the king, sent him into the sanctuary alone. As Hadrior stood in the sanctuary in the heat of the day before the altar offering the customary incense, a thick darkness and a trembling fell upon him so that he was struck with great fear. Then the censer fell from his hands and crashed upon the flagstones of the temple floor, and a cloud of smoke dense and fragrant came forth and filled the sanctuary.

Then, behold! It seemed to him that the voice of Manissa called forth out of the smoking cloud, and he knew not whether he was having a vision. Then the voice of Manissa seemed to call his name, saying, "Hadrior, my kinsman."

Hadrior fell upon his face and did obeisance, daring not to lift his eyes to the vision. But the voice said, "Arise, Lord of the Asylians," and Hadrior arose. Then he peered into the smoke and the form of Manissa came forth, wreathed in clouds, treading upon mountaintops, glorious and terrifying in her apparel. In one hand she held a branch of the terebinth tree and in the other she seemed to wield a great spear made of lightning, out of which issued forth flames and a sound like the roaring of voices.

Hadrior trembled violently, but she said, "I come to bring you consolation and the victory of thy people. Therefore have no fear but be bold. Heed now my words: go forth into the south, into the lands of the Illyrs, the Badoans, the Dretians and the people of Emeric, and there make war upon them and subjugate them, for in doing so you shall surely prevail and win glory for thyself and for Asylia. If you do this, victory shall never flee from you, nor shall anyone raise up sword or spear against you all your days."*

Then Hadrior tried to call out to her and said, "My lady, come again and reign among us!" But he found himself alone in the sanctuary in the midst of the cloud. King Hadrior was much perturbed because of the vision, but when he came forth from making the sacrifice he did not tell anyone the vision (though he did in later days). This he did because he was wroth with the King of Cyrenaica, for Hadrior had set his face to the north, to go thence to make war on King Endumion. This King Endumion had some years prior done a great evil to Hadrior, during the war against Caeylon, for he had taken Hadrior forcibly and thrust him into the den of a certain beast named Ochu, thereby hoping to put him to death. But Hadrior escaped and fled from Endumion, though his leg became crippled and Hadrior was lame to that day. As he fled from Endumion he had sworn an oath, saying, "By the beard of Manx and all the gods of the sky and earth, I shall be avenged upon Cyrenaica and Endumion for my leg and for the wickedness they have conceived against my queen. I shall return again to Cyrenaica and surely lay this city waste and put Endumion to death." Thus he would not go south against the nations of that land, as Manissa had spoken to him in the vision, but rather sought to go into the north to chastise King Endumion.

But the servants of Hadrior brought word to him in Cadaras that Endumion was no longer reigning, for the throne had passed to his son, Imbrossé, who was reigning in his stead, as Endumion was advanced in years and had been ill for some time. Then Hadrior rejoiced, saying, "Now I shall be avenged on Endumion and his house, for the king is ill and the throne in the hands of a stripling." Therefore, he summoned his generals, Arummnax of Orioön and Toranoss of Cadarasia, and bade them call forth the men of Asylia to war.* Also among the captains of Hadrior were Erogel, son of Arrax, and Baldor, son of Manissa, both strong and in the glory of youth. Baldor was in possession of the great spear of Ioclus, which he had inherited upon the passing of Manissa. Hadrior called forth the men of Asylia; forty thousand who drew the sword came and mustered for war on the plains outside Cadarasia. Then Hadrior entrusted command of the army to Toranoss, and Toranoss in turn apportioned the men according to their thousands and their hundreds and set over them captains of his own choosing. And Erogel son of Arrax and Baldor son of Manissa were crestfallen, for they were given but small commands and in the rearguard.* But Hadrior said, "If you would be entrusted with command then prove thy worth, for boasts of a man untested by the fires of war are as useless as the gossip of midwives."

Baldor was consoled and determined to prove his valor by glorious deeds, but Erogel was offended and went around the camp railing against Hadrior, saying that the honor of his house was slighted, and demanding justice. So Hadrior came out to him and said, "Thou base knave! Ever are you rash and full of foolishness like your father. Will you sunder the army on the very eve that we march forth to war with your useless words? But if you do well, will you not be approved also?" Then the companions and kinsmen of Erogel agreed that Hadrior had spoken wisely and counseled Erogel to make peace with the king. So Erogel agreed to Hadrior's words and renounced his challenges.

Yet Hadrior was a somber and brooding man and did not forget the slights of Erogel, nor the ease with which he had stirred up the army against him. Therefore, when the army set forth to the north for Cyrenaica in the spring of that year, Hadrior waited until they were some ways from Cadaras, in the environs two days west of the Sehu as one goes up towards Ituria. There he called Erogel to him by night to confer with him. Then he summoned Toranoss and said, "Toranoss, what should be done to a man who dishonors the king and insults his pride before the warriors of Asylia?" Toranoss said, "Such a man should die." Then Hadrior said, "By your own words, so shall it be done. Therefore, conceal yourself behind the drapes in my tent until Erogel son of Arrax calls upon me. When I shall speak the word, you come forth and strike him dead." Toranoss was grieved because of the greatness of the house of Arrax, but he feared Hadrior and had condemned Erogel by his own words. So he said, "It shall be done."

Then Erogel called upon the tent of Hadrior and was shown in. He greeted the king, saying, "Is all bitterness past?" But Hadrior said, "Now, Toranoss! Strike him!" So Toranoss came forth from hiding and thrust his sword into the side of Erogel. Erogel groaned with a cry of grief and sunk to the ground, uttering curses against Hadrior and Toranoss. Thus perished Erogel, son of Arrax.

But Toranoss was greatly unnerved, and his conscience troubled him, for he knew Erogel to be a righteous man.

Hadrior said, "Yes, 'tis tragic noble Toranoss, but it must needs be done." Toranoss said, "Even so, now the kin of Erogel, the brothers of his wife Analissa, will be hot for your blood, for they are all fierce and vengeful men like Arrax in days of old, in the days before his heart was tamed by Erissa, that dark beauty of Caeylon. They shall rise up and slay you; though you are king, for this will not stop them."

So Hadrior brooded in his tent and said, "Ever hateful has been the house of Arrax to me, for he was always a braggart and took delight in speaking ill of me before Ioclus and Manissa. Are the brethren of Erogel among our numbers?" Toranoss said, "They are." Hadrior said, "Go, then, and strike them as you have struck Erogel and put them to death." Toranoss said, "It shall be done, my king."

Then Hadrior drew Toranoss close and said to him quietly, "Also, send some of your most desperate men, true rogues, back to Cadarasia to the house of Analissa, wife of Erogel, and have them slay all they find there, that the house of Arrax might be utterly blotted out from under the sun." Toranoss was overcome with great sadness, but he nevertheless carried out the commands of Hadrior, King of Asylia. So Toranoss took some picked men and went to the tent where the kin of Arrax, the brethren of Erogel (that is, the brothers of Analissa), were reclining at table. Toranoss called them and said, "Come forth, my lords, for Hadrior summons thee to dine with him this evening." The kin of Erogel came forth from their tent in festive garments with goblets of wine in hand but were greeted by cruel spears. Thus Toranoss had them speared to death as they came forth, so that their blood mingled with their wine spilled out upon the earth.* Then a band of rogues was sent back to Cadarasia and came unto the home of Erogel, and bursting through the gates, went throughout his house and slew all whom they found, both servants and kinsmen. Also slain was Anareth, youngest child of Erogel and the only son born to him. But Analissa, wife of

Erogel, escaped and took with her young Anaxandra, the eldest child of Erogel and his only daughter. They fled eastward and dwelt in Anentora among the people of Caeylon and were there until the days of Hadrior King of Asylia were completed.

Of the Siege of Thán

After Hadrior had satisfied himself with regards to Erogel and the kin of Arrax, he called for Baldor, son of Manissa. Now Baldor was craftier and wiser than Erogel and had heard how Erogel had been treacherously slain and his family killed. Therefore he took heed not to offend the dignity of Hadrior or give the king any cause to suspect him. So he came to the king cheerfully and said, "Is it well with you, my lord?" Hadrior arose and greeted Baldor and blessed him, and said, "Fear not, son of Manissa, for thy life is held sacred to me and no harm will befall you, on account of your mother and the kinship I bore to her by virtue of my marriage to her sister, Saraeth, who was slain at Lissus. Therefore, be not anxious regarding me."

Baldor knew not what to make of Hadrior's words and said, "Thus did you make overtures of reconciliation to Erogel before his murder. Come now, what surety will you give that you speak the truth and that you will not slay me? For I am the eldest son of Manissa, and how could you regard me as other than a bane to your throne?" Hadrior said, "Let us make a covenant together." So they went out into the camp in the midst of all the warriors of Asylia, and there Hadrior swore an oath to Baldor in the sight of everyone, entering into covenant with him and swearing by Manissa and all the gods to do him no harm and in all things be as a father to him.* Then Baldor confirmed this in the sight of all with many oaths, and Baldor son of Manissa and King Hadrior poured out libations and swore many oaths of kinship. From that day forward Baldor was like a son to Hadrior, and Hadrior was like a father to him and increased Baldor's command. And Baldor feared for his life no more, though he still grieved the killing of Erogel. Then Hadrior had a great standing stone erected in that spot and called it *Eiriniétha*, which means "Peace among sons."*

When these affairs had been settled, the army was mustered on the lowlands west of the Sehu on the fifth day of the third month, when the frost still lay upon the grasses of the Asylian meadows. Hadrior gave the command to march forth into the north, skirting the forests of Zurlina to the west and proceeding into Ituria. The roads from Eiriniétha were few, and the armies of Hadrior made slow progress, for the thaw of spring was upon the land and the Asylian horses fared poorly in the mud. They spent many weeks traversing those lands until by and by they came out of the lowlands into the rugged regions around Ituria and Thon, which are peopled by the Iturs, a race hardy and fierce. The lords of the Iturs had been vassals of Manissa for many years and greeted Hadrior when he passed into their land. But Hadrior was haughty with them and demanded provisions for his army, for they had depleted them coming north from Eiriniétha into Ituria. So Marmelos, chieftain of the Iturs said, "How is it that you Asylians make such arrogant demands of us to provision you? What did the men of Cyrenaica ever do to harm us, or when did Endumion or Imbrossé raise up sword against us that we should aid you in their destruction? Did not your own rulers, noble Ioclus and Blessed Manissa of happy memory, fight bitterly against the Caeylonics for the same very outrages which you now place upon us? How is it then that you have turned the oppressor?"

But Hadrior laughed and said, "You have ever been a stubborn and disagreeable people. You hang back when the battle is hot and then rush in to claim the spoils when the fighting is done, just as you did to Blessed Manissa, whom you would not aid in lifting spear against Adaran but reaped the fruits of peace she won with blood. Now will I take what you have long owed to us." So he led his army up past Thon and raided the Iturian villages in that region, seizing cattle and grain for their provisions. They did not harm the people, but only plundered them.

So the anger of the Iturs burned fierce against Hadrior and the Asylians, and the chieftains of the Iturs said, "So, the Asylians want to see our spears wielded in battle? Let us wield them against Hadrior!" But Marmelos calmed them, saying, "We are severely insulted, my brethren, but let us bide our time and see what becomes of the Asylians when they march against fair Cyrenaica. Our time to be avenged is not yet come." So the Iturs buried their anger for a time but did not forget the insults given them. Ever after were their faces set against Hadrior.

The march from Ituria into the realm of Cyrenaica was a little more than a fortnight. The nation of the Cyrenaicans lay upon the northernmost coast of Elabaea, where the sun ever shines and the winters are mild. The buildings there were stately and strong, white and glistening in the northern sun, built of marble quarried and shipped from Lamlash and made splendid with Lysonian alabaster. Now the people of Cyrenaica trace their ancestry from the offspring of Cyréa, the lovely wife of Anrothan, grandson of Laban. The sons of Cyréa and Anrothan settled the northern coasts of Elabaea and there raised up the great city of Thán, which grew strong and propersous through trade with Lyson and the other cities in Caeylon. It was for this reason that, in days past, King

Endumion of Cyrenaica would not aid Manissa against Belthazre, for every year the amount of gold he received in trade from Caeylon was two hundred talents, and about three hundred talents of silver besides.

When Endumion was told that Hadrior was near, he rose from his sickbed and summoned his eldest son, Prince Imbrossé, who was cruel with the spear and a swift runner; he also summoned his other two sons, Bassio and Entharion, and gave his sons these words, "My sons, I am old and at the threshold of death. I thought to live my days out in peace and prosperity, beholding the glory and power of my sons and delighting in the beauty of my daughters. But Hadrior of the house of Manissa of the Asylians has come north to make war on me and bring me down to the grave in bitterness. Resist him, my sons! He is crafty and bold; trust him not if he comes out to you and says, 'Let us make a treaty,' for know that in days past I did him a great evil and that he will stay his sword for nothing less than my blood and thine. Therefore, resist him to the end, I say! Win glory for yourselves and for the house of Endumion your father. Do not let him bring my gray hairs down to the grave in blood."

So Imbrossé, tall and grim, said, "Father, why are you anxious? You know the white walls of Thán have never been breached. Furthermore, though they should besiege us, is our harbor not broad and deep? The Asylians are a landbound people from of fields and hills; what do they know of the sea? Though they should bring all their spears to bear against our walls, they cannot stop us from going forth and receiving succor from our allies abroad, for they have no ships and can do nothing to block our harbor. Therefore, we will not go forth to engage Hadrior upon the plains but will maintain ourselves within the city walls until they weary of the siege and return south."

Endumion said, "Perhaps it shall be so, but I fear this Hadrior. May the gods bless your endeavors." So, Imbrossé,

21

Bassio, and Entharion went forth from their father's presence and made the city secure. Every able-bodied man they armed with spear or bow, and when every preparation had been made, the mighty gates of Thán were drawn closed and sealed. Prince Imbrossé himself stood guard at the gates keeping watch for the coming of Hadrior.

Soon after Hadrior came into the region of Cyrenaica, and with him ten thousand mounted riders of Asylia, wild men who roamed the Asylian plains west of Erriad after Manissa's removal to Cadaras and who were ever fierce in war or peace. These ten thousand were entrusted to two brothers, Ixindor and Oruseth, distant kinsmen of Hadrior. He also had with him five thousand horsemen from Cadaras, of whom he rode at the head, as well as three thousand riders from the eastern Asylians, all hearty and loyal men whose aim with the spear was flawless; these were commanded by Arummnax of Orioön, who had been with Manissa in the Arcorian Wood. Of infantry he brought twenty-two thousand stout Elabaean warriors of Asylia and Cadarasia, each armed with a great shield, an oaken spear, and a sword of bronze. Toranoss the Cadarasian was made commander of these, but after the dispute with Erogel and Baldor, Hadrior separated out three thousand of these warriors and entrusted them to Baldor, son of Manissa. These three thousand he set in the center of the army where the fighting would be the hottest.

The Asylians encamped on the broad plain about the city of Thán and encompassed it round about. Some of the captains wanted to attack the city at once and throw up siegeworks, but Hadrior said, "Let us not assault the city yet, for it is very old and marvelously wrought. Let us rather lay siege to it in hope that they will deliver the city to us of their own accord without causing us to destroy its defenses or its buildings." So the Asylians surrounded the city and forbid any Cyrenaican from leaving or entering, but they did not attack it or bring up their battering rams.

The city of Thán was under siege for four months, until the time when the summer constellations are at their zenith, at the full moon of the eighth month. The men of Asylia brooded in their tents in the stifling heat, for they perceived that though the city was surrounded, the people of Thán were supplied from sea by ships that were constantly coming and going. Toranoss and Arummnax came before Hadrior and said, "My king, the Cyrenaicans show no signs of wearying though we have besieged them for four months, for their men are still stout and confident and their womenfolk still plump and jolly. There is no shortage of food nor have their spirits dampened, for they are constantly resupplied from sea by their harbor! Unless we can cut off their allies from sending ships into their harbor, our siege avails nothing."

Hadrior was downcast and said, "You have spoken wisely, my lords, but what shall we do? We are people of the plains and do not possess any man skilled in ship making nor any sailors to man them. How shall we block the harbor?" Then Arummnax of Orioön said, "My lord, in days past when Blessed Manissa walked the earth, did you not have allies among the people of this region who sheltered you from the rage of Endumion when you fled Thán after escaping the pit of Ochu?"

Hadrior's countenance lifted, and he said, "Indeed it is true, Master Arummnax, for I was sheltered by the people of Baris to the west for some time while I rested myself and regained my strength after my leg was torn by Ochu. They took compassion on me and reckoned me as one of their own and named me 'Achanor' in their tongue.* Therefore, let swift riders be dispatched to the town of Baris, bringing them tidings that Achanor has returned to the land at the head of a mighty host and calls upon them once again for aid." So Toranoss sent his swiftest riders west to Baris bearing these tidings.

Now Baris was some ways northwest of Thán, in the more distant regions of Cyrenaica that are seldom visited by the Asylians. The people of Baris rejoiced when they heard that Achanor had come again into their land, and they sent a grand delegation back to Thán with the men of Toranoss. The men of Baris loathed Endumion because he had in the recent year taken some of the men of that region and fed them to Ochu. They were therefore willing to aid Hadrior against him. When they came unto Hadrior outside Thán, they bowed and did obeisance to him, hailing him as Achanor. Then Hadrior said, "Men of Baris, I shall not forget the kindness you showed to me years ago when, bloodied and near death, you took me in and treated me like one of your kin until I was restored to health, though my leg is forever crippled by reason of my fight with the beast, for which you have honored me by calling me Achanor. Now I am again in need of thy aid, this time to win vengeance against the tyrant who wronged me so long ago. Tell me, have you any knowledge of the art of shipbuilding which is practiced among the people of Cyrenaica?"

Then the men of Baris said, "Great king, though we are not situated on the coast, we do have among our people many who have knowledge of such skills and have worked at the docks of Thán constructing ships for Endumion's fleet." So they sent and brought these men to Hadrior's camp on the plain, and from the eighth month until the end of the ninth month Hadrior set men to work hewing wood, shaping it, and constructing ships on the shores of the sea in accord with everything told him by the men from Baris, so that by the end of the ninth month the Asylians put forth ten ships into the water, all sturdy and made after the fashion of Cyrenaica, as the men of Baris directed. These ships came into the harbor so that when supply ships from Caeylon or Lamlash or the distant lands to the west came near, the Asylians drove them off. Thus merchants were afraid to come to Thán any further, so that the city of Thán began to suffer.

When the Asylians had thus blockaded the harbor for two months, Imbrossé, Bassio, and Entharion, sons of Endumion, went to their father and said, "My lord, the ships of Hadrior have cut off our supplies this second month and our people are weary and deprived of food." Endumion said, "Did I not tell you he was crafty? Now you have no choice but to meet the Asylians in battle, for if we wait longer our men will not have strength left to wield sword or spear. Therefore, muster your men for war and go forth from the city to give them battle on the plain." Valiant Prince Imbrossé said, "It shall be done, father. I shall bring back the head of Hadrior as a trophy to you, for the Asylians have had rest from war these many years. Arrax and Eridax, their captains of old, are gone, and Hadrior is out of his prime. Who will be their champion now?" Endumion said, "May it be so, my sons. The gods be gracious to thee." So they went out from him eager for war.

Then the sons of Endumion called forth all the men in the city able to bear arms, fifteen thousand in all. Bassio was entrusted with five thousand men to march on the left; to Entharion was given five thousand to march on the right, and Prince Imbrossé took for himself five thousand men and marched in the center, for he was the eldest and skilled at war. Each man was armed with a round shield of beaten bronze after the Cyrenaican fashion, as well as a throwing spear. Each arrayed himself in a tunic of white bound with a crimson sash, and upon each man's head a helm of copper that glittered in the sun. Thus the army of Thán came forth from the gates and began to muster themselves upon the plains south of the city, beneath the shadow of the walls.

Toranoss told Hadrior, "Behold, their army comes forth from the gates! Let us charge them and make a rout at once!" But Hadrior said, "Nay, for if we charge them now, they will retreat within the city and shut themselves in again. Let the entirety of their force come forth and muster upon the plain; I care not. Whither shall they go? It is better to finish them all here in one strike than to prolong this tedious siege." So the Asylians held back while the men of Thán arranged themselves upon the dusty plain outside of the city. Then Hadrior gave the command, and the men of Asylia gathered themselves together for battle, some forty thousand strong.

When the Asylians were mustered, Bassio sent word to Prince Imbrossé, saying, "We are greatly outnumbered, at least two to one." Imbrossé said, "It matters not. The Asylians have not been to war since the days when Adaran came into the west. They have grown slothful and timid. Furthermore, the Asylians do not fight together, for each man fights alone for his own glory. But we Cyrenaicans fight together, so that the soldiers all move together as one man, and because of this they will be routed before us, and their numbers will count for nothing."

Then Hadrior sent forth the mounted warriors under Ixindor and Oruseth to harass the flanks of the Cyrenaicans, but the men of Cyrenaica stationed on the flanks bore great spears seven cubits long. These they turned toward the cavalry so that the Asylians rode upon a wall of blades and were unable to break up the legions of Bassio or Entharion. Many of the Cyrenaicans hurled javelins or slung stones at the riders of Ixindor and Oruseth and slew a great many of them, so that the ranks of the riders were thrown into confusion. When Imbrossé perceived that the cavalry attack of Hadrior was faltering, he cried, "Forward! Trample them underfoot and run them from our land!" So the ranks of Cyrenaica moved forward with great speed, each man girt in white with glimmering helm of copper and brazen spear poised for death.

Then Arummnax and Toranoss moved their troops forward, and there was a great clashing of shields and ringing of arms upon the field. But the men of Cyrenaica prevailed everywhere, for they did not break ranks, nor did they give ground, while the Asylians sometimes lunged forward recklessly, sometimes pulled back, sometimes stood their ground, and sometimes gave ground, so that the Asylians were rolled back. The spears of the Cyrenaicans were cruel and sharp; the field was pierced with the cries of wounded and dying men. Then came Bassio, son of Endumion, and with his spear slew Manreth, Ebullax, and Illoss, all lords whose fathers had rode with Manissa. He also threw a javelin and struck Laios, son of Eridax, in the back as he was fleeing. He stripped the armor from Laios, saying, "Thus have I brought down the son of renowned Eridax in his first battle." Entharion the brother of Imbrossé also brought death to the Asylians, for he killed Imbus and Ioreth, sons of Andaramas, a lord of great fame in the west. But of all the Cyrenaicans Prince Imbrossé was most feared, for his arm was strong and his aim sure; he brought down to death Arrius, the page of Hadrior, a young man, who had drawn close to the battle that he might bring a report back to the king. He also slew Ornace, brother of Toranoss, and Minnox, a Badoan warrior of great renown from the south lands.

Arummnax sent word to Hadrior saying, "The day is lost, my lord, for we have given the field to the Cyrenaicans and have lost many slain and as many wounded." So Hadrior gnashed his teeth and cursed Endumion and his sons, pounding his fists upon the ground and saying, "Will I never be avenged for my leg and the infamy of the pit of Ochu? By the beard of Manx and the blood of Manissa, who will avenge me upon Endumion?"

Then came forth Baldor, son of Manissa.* Seeing the rout of the Asylians, a trembling and fierce rage fell over him, and he was filled with strength untamed and fought as one possessed. He roared fiercely and hurled himself alone into the forces of Bassio, thrusting this way and that with his spear and downing scores of men. The warriors of Bassio came upon him in vast numbers hurling their spears at him, but all of them missed and landed harmlessly in the sand, while every thrust of Baldor hit its mark and felled some man of Cyrenaica. Then

Baldor cried out with a deafening cry and dashed into the very midst of the Cyrenaican army, thrusting and swinging the spear of Ioclus about him, ripping flesh, severing limbs, and cutting a swath through his opponents. No weapon wielded against him prevailed; no shield raised against his fury held. The men of Cyrenaica quaked and turned before him, and the ranks of Bassio began to break while Baldor stained the sand with the blood of the Cyrenaicans. Bassio tried to rally his men, calling them cowards, but Baldor dashed across the sandy earth with remarkable swiftness, covering great strides with every leap, and striking down men with his spear until the legions of Bassio were in full retreat.

Bassio called and said, "Come unto me, Baldor son of Manissa, and let us see if the Fate which favored thy mother will favor thee before my spear!" Baldor called out in reply, "Let us prove it, then!" The two warriors closed in on each other, shields glaring in the burning sun, spears poised and ready to strike. Bassio lunged at Baldor but found him too quick to hit, and seeing he could not strike, in desperation hurled his spear at the son of Manissa, aiming to pierce him through the belly. But Baldor held aloft his mighty brazen shield, upon which the spearhead clanged and crumpled. Bassio drew his sword and closed with Baldor, but Baldor thrust with the spear of Ioclus and pierced Bassio straightaway through the heart. Bassio cried out and fell to the dust in death. When the Cyrenaicans saw this, they wailed aloud, and many fled back to the city.

But then came forth Entharion, son of Endumion, on the right. He wore upon his head a great crested plume of dazzling white horsehair and was carried in a mighty chariot car gilded with gold. He gave the sign, and his men advanced upon Baldor, who stood alone someway out in front of the other Asylian troops. Yet again a great rage fell upon Baldor, and he leapt mightily and thrust the spear of Ioclus with such force that it punctured shield and armor alike. No weapon cast was able to hit him, and Baldor wrought great destruction among the ranks of Entharion. Then Entharion ordered his driver to make for Baldor, and Entharion hoisted his spear to cast. But Baldor charged the chariot of Entharion, and with mighty strength, heaved the chariot car above his head, as if it were but a wicker basket, and hurled it to the ground. The costly chariot shattered, and the bones of Entharion were broken. Then Baldor took the spear of Ioclus and slew Entharion, son of Endumion, and with him his driver, a fellow named Bannus. Then he called his servants and had them detach the horses of Entharion's chariot team and return them to the camp for trophies. When the Cyrenaicans saw that Entharion had been slain and that Baldor had heaved the chariot over his head with little effort, scores dropped their weapons and fled.

But the center legion under Prince Imbrossé held. When the prince saw the men under his brothers fleeing, he cried, "Is there no man left in the city of Thán or the kingdom of Cyrenaica who will stand up to these barbarians?" Baldor's eyes raged with a mighty fire, and he dashed towards Prince Imbrossé with strides greater than those of any man, nay, even greater than those of the Asylian steeds of old. Prince Imbrossé said, "Come and die by my sword, son of Manissa." Baldor closed with Imbrossé, spear ringing against sword, and the two buffeted each other with many blows. But Baldor was tireless in his strength and swifter in his movements, and Prince Imbrossé soon grew weary—even more so because they fought not upon solid earth but upon the sandy plain, which borders the city to the south. Imbrossé felt his strength failing, and so turned to flee back towards the city. But Baldor took aim and let fly the shaft of his grandfather, striking Imbrossé in the small of the back and giving him a grievously painful wound. Then the men of Cyrenaica, both those upon the plain and those in Thán watching from the walls, wailed, "Imbrossé has fallen before the son of Manissa! We are doomed!"

Baldor overtook Imbrossé on the plain and found him lying in the dirt. He lifted him and said, "Who is mightier now, boastful son of Endumion?" Imbrossé scowled and said, "I saw you leaping upon the plain, son of Manissa, and the way you hurled your spear with fire in your eye. Our contest was far from even, for some god or sprite has bewitched you and given you victory, a victory greater that any in memory, for you have slain the three sons of Endumion in but a single day, yea, in a single hour. Thus is Hadrior avenged! Dispatch me as you will."

Baldor said, "Choose you fate, son of Endumion, will you embrace death at my hands, or servitude in my house among myself and my kin?" Imbrossé scoffed and said, "Slay me here upon the hot sand under the eternal blue sky." So Baldor drew his sword and thrust it into the neck of Imbrossé, leaving him to bleed his life out on the sand just out of bowshot of the city gates.

Then the men of Hadrior ran up straightaway, and taking the city, smote it with a great destruction. But Hadrior had compassion on the people of Thán and did not have them put to death, but imposed upon them a heavy tribute, for the city possessed much wealth by virtue of its harbor and the trade it carried on with Caeylon. But he allowed his men to plunder the city for three days and had its defenses demolished. Then he came to the pit of Ochu in the gardens outside the palace of King Endumion and had it filled up with stone and mortar, so that no person should be thrown into the bubbling jaws of the creature ever again.*

But never had anyone beheld a warrior fight with such zeal and might as did Baldor, son of Manissa, before the walls of Thán, so that in later days the proverb was said of any great warrior that he "fought like Baldor before the walls of Thán."

The Spear of Ioclus

֍֎ ֍֎ ֍֎

At the time Hadrior took the city, Endumion was laying ill upon his sickbed. A servant ran to him, saying, "My lord, woe upon us! Thy three sons, Bassio, Entharion, and Imbrossé, have all fallen in a single hour before Baldor son of Manissa!" While he was still speaking, another servant came in and said, "My lord, woe to us, for Hadrior has brought his Asylians up and taken the city and they are even now on their way to the palace!" So Endumion raised himself up and tore his garments, and weeping, said, "Thus Fate has brought me down to ruin in my old age. I see now that I cannot escape the curse of the vow which Hadrior uttered against me the day he fled from my city, invoking the beard of Manx and all gods in vengeance for his leg! Come, servants! Clothe me in my royal garments once more and support me on my left and on my right. Let us go out to King Hadrior and do homage to him. Perhaps he will be merciful to us." So the servants of Endumion arrayed the old man in his royal vestments and lifted him up, supporting him as he left his chambers to do homage to Hadrior.

After he had finished destroying the pit of Ochu, Hadrior came to the threshold of Endumion's palace. There he was told that the king was coming to do obeisance to him and pledge fealty. So Hadrior awaited Endumion at the threshold of the palace. But when old Endumion was brought forth and beheld Hadrior standing beyond the door as a mighty conqueror with his captains round about him, he grew angry and indignant at Hadrior. Refusing to be brought out to him, he shook with rage and shouted insults, and neither could his servants persuade him to come forth. Therefore Hadrior grew impatient and ordered his guards to seize the old king and bring him, but Endumion struggled and refused to come out of his house. Then one of the Asylian soldiers, a young man, took an oaken cudgel and struck Endumion on the head, intending to knock him senseless drag him out to Hadrior. But the blow cracked the skull of Endumion, and he died upon the threshold of his house in the presence of Hadrior. Thus Hadrior became master of Thán, and all Cyrenaica fell under Asylian dominion.

Yet though it was due to the prowess of Baldor, son of Manissa, that the city was taken, Hadrior did not reward him or give him honor. Instead Hadrior gave the city and its environs into the hand of his captain, Toranoss of Cadarasia. But Baldor he did not honor, neither in praise around the council fire, nor in giving of gifts and largesse. So Baldor grew downcast and brooded about the camp, drinking wine, gambling, and indulging riotous living. And his countenance was dark.

Baldor was in possession of the spear of Ioclus, the mighty spear which had been gifted to Ancyrus, King of Asylia, by the sons of King Dyans of Epidymia. It was this with spear that Ioclus, father of Manissa, had in his youth slain a great boar in the region of the Gihon. With it Manissa had driven the Marudans from the west; the spear was the last thing touched by Blessed Manissa while she was upon the face of the earth. Therefore it was highly coveted among the warriors of Asylia, especially since Baldor, who possessed it, idled his days away in dissipation and gambling and seemed unworthy of its glory. But it was Arummnax of Orioön who coveted the spear most, for he had once retrieved it for Manissa at the battle in the Arcorian Wood when she had slain an enemy with it and lost it among the Caeylonic ranks. Ever after he had coveted that which his hands once touched.

Thus, in the days after the taking of Thán, when the Asylian army was still encamped upon the sandy plain outside the city awaiting orders to return home, it came to pass that Arummnax summoned his brothers, three worthless fellows, and said to them, "Do you see how the son of Manissa disgraces his house and his people by brooding about the camp these past many days? Indeed, he is unworthy to wield the spear that his mother carried into battle." Then he instructed his brothers in the following way: "Since Baldor is given to drink and games of chance, you shall go unto his tent and drink with him in the evening time. When his eyes are heavy with drunkenness, you shall compel him to play a game of chance with you, some game of dice perhaps. In his drunkenness you shall cause him to wager the spear as a bet and take it from him. Thus shall Baldor be shamed, and the spear come to our house and redound to our glory."

So the three brothers of Arummnax came to the tent of Baldor that evening and found him already drunk with wine and well-disposed to their plan. So tables were set up, the dice brought forth, and the four men began to gamble and drink into the late hours of the night. But when Baldor was weary and would have retired, the sons of Arummnax chided him and said, "Is this the son of Manissa? Surely you know that the choicest wagers come in the late hours of the night, when lesser men have retired. Come, let us make a man's wager, something of exceptional value." Then the brothers of Arummnax brought forth three sacks, each containing a hundred gold coins, saying, "Let us wager all our spoils we have taken from this campaign against the spear of Ioclus, which stands beside you struck into the ground." Baldor would not have gambled the spear, but he was overcome with wine and wished to silence the mocking of the brothers of Arummnax. So he consented. But while the table was being set for another round of gaming, the brothers of Arummnax brought forth their own dice, weighted, so as to ensure that Baldor lost the wager. More wine was brought out, the dice rolled, and Baldor lost. Then he trembled and said, "Alas! In a moment of drunkenness, I have lost my senses and gambled away the most valued treasure of my inheritance!" But the brothers said, "Come now, bring forth the spear of Ioclus and give it to us, as you swore."

Baldor began to weep, and he took the spear of Ioclus and gave it to the brothers of Arummnax; it was so mighty that none of them could easily hold it. So the brothers departed, exultant that they had cheated Baldor son of Manissa and won the spear of Ioclus from him. Yet in their elation and haste, they left behind the loaded dice with which they had won the game.

Baldor thrashed about his tent weeping, overturning his furniture in regret for his deed. Then he laid eyes on the gambling tables, threw them down, and smashed them. But he noticed that the dice, when cast upon the earth, came to the same number that had caused him to lose the spear. He took up the die and cast several more times, and each time it came up the same number. Then he boiled hot with rage, realizing that he had been tricked. He quickly donned his cloak and stormed out into the night after the brothers.

The brothers of Arummnax were not far from Baldor's tent when he overtook them on the path through the camp. He gnashed his teeth and said, "This evening you have offended the wrong man." Then a rage came over him, and he seized the mighty spear of Ioclus from them, and wielding it with marvelous quickness, fell upon the brothers of Arummnax. He slew all three of them upon the path, piercing them each through the heart before they had a chance to raise their swords in defense. The brothers of Arummnax fell to the ground, gasping as their blood and fluids drained out upon the sand.

The next morning the Asylian camp awoke and saw Baldor standing over the bodies of the brothers of Arummnax with the spear of Ioclus in hand. He cried out, "If anyone wants to possess this spear, let him come wrestle me for it in open combat! These fellows tried to take it by treachery, and thus have they paid for their foolishness. But why resort to such deceit? Behold, I declare before you all that I will freely give this spear, the heirloom of my house, to whatever man can throw me in wrestling." So the whole camp of the Asylians went forth from their tents and came down to the seashore, about a half league north of the camp, and there upon the sand Baldor wrestled men from sunup to sunset without rest. But no man was able to prevail, for Baldor threw every man who came against him.

The following day, Baldor challenged them again and said, "I shall give the spear of Ioclus to any man who can outdistance me in the throwing of javelins." So again the men of Asylia went down to the beach and threw javelins against Baldor all day long. But no javelin thrown by any man came within even a bowshot of Baldor's javelin, for his throws were mighty and his aim was sure. Thus he retired on the second day without having been bested.

On the third day, he again challenged the camp, saying, "Any man who can down me in boxing, to the same man will I give the spear of Iolcus." So the whole encampment went down to the beach and Baldor boxed from sunup to sunset. But nobody brought against him could stand, for Baldor became like one possessed in his fighting, so that many men retired at the end of the day with bloodied faces or broken noses. But Baldor seemed unwearied; indeed, his might seemed even greater at the going down of the sun than at its rising.

On the fourth day there was considerable excitement when Baldor announced that he would again accept challenges

for the spear of Ioclus. So all the men of the camp went down to the beach, among them all the captains, Arummnax, whose brothers had been slain by Baldor, and Toranoss, newly created Lord of Thán and Cyrenaica, as well as King Hadrior himself. Then Baldor took up the spear of Ioclus and said, "Who among you would desire to have this trophy?" Then scores of men cried, "Yea!" for many of them had been pummeled by Baldor the day before and were angry with him. Many also were from the region of Orioön, kin of Arummnax, who wanted to revenge themselves upon Baldor for the lives of the brothers of Arummnax. Then Baldor said, "This will be the final competition. Who is willing to come down on this beach and fight me to the death in single combat for the glory of possessing this spear?" Then scores of men cried out and came forward to engage Baldor, full of rage and brandishing swords glimmering in the morning sun and ready to kill. But seeing this, Baldor took the spear of Ioclus in hand, and turning, hurled it into the sea with a mighty throw. So far did he hurl the spear that only those with keen eyes could see where it fell into the water. After it went under there was a grievous sigh from the camp. Then Baldor said, "Any man who would kill the son of Manissa in order to have her spear is not worthy of it." Then he returned to his tent and brooded no more. But the Asylians wept, for the spear of Ioclus had been the greatest heirloom of all Asylia, and ever has it remained lost under the blue sea since that day.*

Of the Rua Calidé

✦✦✦

After several days of feasting outside the walls of Thán, when the affairs of the region had been set in order and the government of Cyrenaica established in the hands of the Asylians, King Hadrior left Toranoss in command of Thán with all its environs and people, some seventy thousand souls, and sounded the call to break camp and return unto Cadarasia. He left with Toranoss three thousand Asylian spearmen to keep garrison in Thán and appointed Arummnax as commander of the king's armies in place of Toranoss.

Now Arummnax hated Baldor, because Baldor had slain his kin over the spear of Ioclus, but also because he resented the influence of the sons of Manissa in the court at Cadaras. Toranoss also resented Baldor, for Toranoss had slain the son of Arrax, Erogel, and feared that Baldor would one day take vengeance upon him for the killings. But Baldor held not grudge against either man and went away again south with Hadrior, without breathing any threats or maledictions against Arummnax or Toranoss.

But on the first night after the Asylians and Cadarasians broke camp and were making their way south from Cyrenaica, something marvelous happened. In former days, there was a great portion of the northern sky which had been vacant of any stars or luminaries and formed a sort of void between the northwest and northeast regions of the heavens. The

Cyrenaicans called this void the *Rua Calidé*, which in their tongue means the "Empty Quarter." From the beginning of the habitations of men in the west unto that time, no star had appeared in that part of the sky. To sail beneath it on open waters was considered an ill omen among the seafarers of Cyrenaica.

Yet at dusk of the first day after departing, when the Asylian army camped for the evening, Baldor, son of Manissa, was seated upon a great stone overlooking the road gazing to the north as the sun was falling and the sky darkening. He summoned to him his servant Indor and said, "Indor, run north up the road a distance and tell me what you see in the sky." So Indor did as he was told, and returned saying, "My lord Baldor, the sky is vacant, for it is the Rua Calidé where no star shines. Surely you know this, my lord?" But Baldor gazed up the road and said, "Run north again to the crest of yonder hill which overlooks the plains south of Thán, beyond which is the blue line of the sea. There look again into the sky and tell me what you see." So Indor ran again to the crest of the hill and gazed into the Rua Calidé and behold! A single star shimmered in the firmament! So Indor rushed back to Baldor and said, "Master! A single star shines forth in the firmament!"

Then Baldor stood and gazed north, and when the sun had fully set and the sky became darkened, he said to Indor, "Return again to the crest of the hill and look into the Rua Calidé and tell me what you see." So Indor ran again some ways up the road, and gazing into the northern sky, saw that three more stars had appeared beneath the first with the darkening of the night, arranged like a belt beneath the first star. Indor ran with great haste back to Baldor and said, "My lord Baldor, a great marvel! Three more stars have appeared in the firmament beneath the first! How is that my lord knows of these things?" But Baldor answered him not.

By now night had fully fallen, and more Asylians noticed the new stars and were marveling at the night sky. When it was nigh unto midnight, Baldor called Indor to him again and said, "Indor, run again yet once more and tell me what you can see from the crest of the hill." So Indor went forth again and stood upon the hill and saw a fifth star, some ways beneath the other three by the horizon, blazing brightly in the dark blue firmament. So he ran back to Baldor and said, "How is it that these stars come forth in the Rua Calidé, which henceforth was called empty? And how is it my lord knows of this?" So the whole camp marveled and a great fear fell upon them.

Then Hadrior summoned Baldor to his presence and questioned him concerning this sign. Baldor said, "Why is it for me to interpret the signs of the heavens? Manissa herself has come unto you and told you what you are to do, yet you have hidden her words and followed your own will. Yet know this: in this sign is established that Blessed Manissa is indeed among the immortals and lives ever more, for her spear has appeared in the heavens." So ever after the new constellation was called *Laoön*, which means "Lance" in old Asylian. And ever since has the sign of Laoön filled the Rua Calidé as a hope to the people of Manissa.*

The rock where Baldor sat and gazed into the northern sky is called *Lapidoth*, which means "Stone of Gazing" and the hill crest from whence Indor gazed upon the Rua Calidé has ever been called *Anaímsir*, that is, "Hill of the Stars." Indor himself was called *Indor Aíroth*, that is, "Indor the Star-Gazer," for he was the first of men to see Laoön.

The Final Days of Hadrior

H adrior returned from Cyrenaica with great power, for the King of Cyrenaica had been vanquished, Thán subdued, and the king's ally Toranoss established in the lordship over all Cyrenaica, subject to Cadaras. But King Hadrior feared Baldor, for the son of Manissa had done mighty and terrible things before the walls of Thán, and Hadrior trembled for his throne. Therefore he confirmed Baldor in the lordship over the city of Asylia in the far west, where Baldor's mother had reigned in the days before the Hall of Orix was burned by Adaran. Thus Baldor took his place as Lord of Asylia and of the Western Asylians, but Hadrior ruled as King of All Elabaea from Cadaras. Baldor was established far from Hadrior in the wilds across the Erriad. There Baldor took to wife Oxanna, a fair maiden of Asylia, and by her begot a son, Belar.

Hadrior was unnerved, however, when he was told that the wife and daughter of Erogel, son of Arrax, had escaped the sword and were dwelling in safety among the Marudans, for he feared the house of Arrax and would have slew Analissa and Anaxandra if he could. But they remained in safety in Caeylon and did not return again into Elabaea until the days of Hadrior were ended. Yet throughout his kingdom he extended his power, so that everywhere he appointed as captains and lords men who were favorable to him. In Cyrenaica he set one

Toranoss, a kinsman from Cadaras, and Toranoss in turn divided his realm into three kingdoms, bestowing them upon his sons, worthless men who were wild and cruel. The house of Arummnax of Orioön the king established in the regions just west of the Erriad, for Arummnax bore a great hatred towards Baldor by virtue of Baldor's slaying of his brothers. Thus Hadrior settled Arummnax as a shield against Baldor and his people should the son of Manissa ever rise up in revolt. He also exalted his kinsmen Ixindor and Oruseth, great warriors and men of renown, and set them over all the armies of Asylia and Cadaras. Ixindor and Oruseth also bore hatred towards Baldor and the house of Manissa, for Baldor had won glory and defeated the Cyrenaicans when these two could not prevail against Imbrossé and his brothers. So everywhere throughout the kingdom the friends of Hadrior were strengthened while the allies of Baldor and the house of Manissa weakened.

When Hadrior was established in the kingdom, he again mustered his armies in the sixth year of his reign to go to war against the Iturs in the north, who served under Marmelos. Ever since Hadrior had come up against Cyrenaica and ravaged their villages they had been cold towards him, and all commerce between Ituria and Cadarasia had ceased. So Hadrior called Baldor and said, "Will you come out to war with me?" But Baldor refused, saying, "Far be it from me to raise my sword against a people who aided my mother against Adaran. Go, if you will not be turned, but I fear it will come to no good end." Hadrior scoffed at the words of Baldor, determined nonetheless to prosecute his war. In the spring of that year he summoned to himself thirty thousand men of Cadaras and Nearer Asylia who drew the sword; but those from Western Asylia, the regions near the Cyrian Highlands and the lands under Baldor, did not come out to go to war with the king.

So Hadrior went forth at the head of his army, taking the northeast road into Ituria, whereupon he hoped to make war against Marmelos and bring the Iturs into submission. But Marmelos roused his people, and they took to the hills of Ituria, where they remained in the wilderness and would not engage Hadrior in open war. Hadrior spent the better part of the summer purusing the Iturs about the wilderness with little success. It then came to pass when summer was at its peak that the Iturs laid an ambush for the Asylians at a place called the Yellow Forks, where three roads came together in the midst of some low-lying hills. When the Asylians were passing by the crossroads, the Iturs rushed upon them from the hillsides and struck them. Now the manner of the fighting of the Iturs is not like other nations, for before they go to battle, the men strip themselves of all their clothing and dance about in a great circle for the better part of the morning, until they work themselves into a great frenzy. Then the womenfolk of the villages come forth and whip the men with rods until blood streaks down their backs, but rather than unnerve the men, this only incites them to battle all the more, so that they act more like rabid animals than men. They then cover their faces with white and yellow dye and charge upon their foes with furious shrieks, attacking with spears and mattocks.

And so, while the force of Hadrior was passing by the Yellow Forks, thousands of Iturs fell upon them, pressing them from all sides and decimating their ranks, for they fought with such fury that the shield-walls of the Asylians were unable to throw them back. Very soon there was confusion and panic among the Asylians—more so since their way of escape had been cut off. The Iturs besieged them all that day and hacked at them with great fury, splitting skulls and hewing off limbs with their mattocks until Hadrior broke through at dusk and managed to withdraw his forces to the south, taking refuge on a small hilltop about a league off. The Iturs pursued and surrounded them on every side, assaulting them through the night and into the next day. They would have overrun them utterly had not Toranoss come down from Cyrenaica with six thousand warriors of the north. When Marmelos saw Toranoss approaching, he called a retreat and the Iturs fled, turning off into the wilderness again. Toranoss approached and gave succor to Hadrior and his men, and when the following morning came, they reconnoitered the hill and the road up to the Forks and found that twelve thousand had fallen slain with as many wounded. So Hadrior returned home disgraced, for it was the worst defeat ever suffered by the Asylians since the burning of Cadaras by Arahaz.

In his final days Hadrior grew bitter and cruel. He put to death some of the sons of Arummnax for treason and hung their corpses on the wall of Cadaras to rot. If he desired anything or property from anyone he took it by force. He pilfered the inheritances of many of the nobles and perpetrated many other evils. So the Asylians and the Cadarasians groaned, counting the days until his death, but he lingered on until he was advanced in years. In Western Asylia, however, in the realm of Baldor, there was peace and prosperity, for every Asylian was secure in his field and among his flocks, for Baldor ruled with justice and mercy.

In the fourteenth year of his reign Hadrior again mustered the men of Asylia and Cadarasia for war, now going west to assault the Lugars. The Lugars were then dwelling under Cygnus, son of King Karanus, who had in former days pledged loyalty and aid to Manissa when she came west fleeing Adaran. The coming of the war with Lugaria, the envy of Hadrior, the grief of Baldor over Belar his son and the defeat of Asylia, are they not all written in the Book of the Deeds of the Sons of Manissa?*

So the Lugarians defeated the Asylians with a great slaughter and overthrew the armies of Hadrior, so that Toranoss was slain along with all his sons; so were Arummnax of Orioön, Ixindor, Oruseth, and all the lords loyal to the king, for their destruction was total. But these things are written of in another place and do not enter this tale.* Then last of all

Hadrior fell ill, and shaking violently, gave up his spirit on the third day of the eleventh month in the fifteenth year of his reign. Then Anaxandra, daughter of Erogel and granddaughter of Arrax, was brought back from Caeylon and made Queen of All Elabaea, being at that time only about twelve years of age. And she reigned with Analissa her mother until her fifteenth year, when she ruled in her own right.

Nöm etha Manissé

("The Deeds of the Sons of Manissa")

Mariammné and Baldor

❦❦❦

Blessed Manissa brought forth seven children while she was upon the earth: Mariammné, a daughter; then followed six sons: Baldor, who afterwards became a mighty warrior, exceeding even Arrax in fury; then Hazer, who was a composer of poems and songs; Necho and Elphas, twins and men of renown; then Secum, who was celebrated in all lands for his wisdom, for he was wise and gave counsel to many great men; finally was born Perior, who roamed the countryside like a wild man and had a mighty strength that rivaled the giants with whom he warred in the hill country of the west.

In those days the sons of Manissa began to be great upon the earth, for some were mighty with the strength of many men and did great feats across Asylia; others were found to be of exceptional beauty and wisdom, like the Holy Ones of old; still others spoke prophecies in riddles and foretold the future, while others dreamed dreams and had visions.* Many also became warriors of renown, fighting countless battles for the glory of Manissa and her house, so that from Asylia as far away as Epidymia and Caeylon people marveled and said, "Who are like the sons of Manissa? Wherever they go, marvels follow!"

Now in the days when Hadrior grew old, Mariammné came of age and was known as the most beautiful of all maids

49

of Asylia. Her hair was straight and fine, tumbling down her back lightly; her eyes were of a brilliant, deep blue. Her form was comely and pleasant to look upon, and her voice and laughter were light and cheerful, like the songs of old Asylia in the spring, when the virgins go forth in flowered troupes to sing and welcome the coming of the thaw.* In her it was said that the divine beauty of her mother lived on, but those who were old and could remember said she was more like Osseia in appearance. But she was also fierce, for in her youth her mother had trained her to throw with the very spear of Ioclus, though that relic later passed to Baldor. So blue-eyed Mariammné was also renowned as possessing the prowess of her mother and was therefore considered altogether lovely.* She was but a girl when her mother was taken, and so was adopted by Hadrior to be brought up in the court of Cadaras as his adopted daughter.

But Hadrior, who was grey haired and cold hearted, brooded about his palace by night in fair Cadaras in lament, saying, "Alas, that I came to the kingship in such a state, that my wife should have perished in my youth while I grow old alone, with no son or heir to succeed me, save Mariammné, daughter of Manissa, who is beautiful but unfit to rule." This he said partly because he thought Mariammné too young to bear the burdens of state, but also because he desperately hoped for a relative of his own blood to succeed him.

It came to pass one day, as Hadrior was brooding about the halls of his chambers, that he caught sight of the Lady Mariammné reclining in the gardens outside the Citadel with her maidens, her hair done up in tresses, her lithe footfalls gliding over the flowered terraces, her light gown of whited linen falling behind her gracefully, and her laugh spilling about the courtyard as water tumbles over rocky bed of the Erriad. Then was his old heart set aflame; he realized that the young girl was no longer a youth but a fair maiden, and he began to nurse wicked thoughts in his head regarding her.

Thus, day after day he watched his niece in the gardens making merry with her maidens, and day after day grew enflamed with passion for her, until he exclaimed, "Though this thing I conceive be against custom and law, I will make my mind known to fair Mariammné and compel her to accede to my desires to become my wife and bear me a son and heir." So he came unto her in the gardens and she kissed him upon the cheek, saying, "Hail, uncle and king!" But when he made his mind known to her, she recoiled in horror and said, "Uncle, in former days it was said that you were the cleverest of all men of Asylia, most renowned for devising stratagems with all manner of cunning.* Therefore, take hold of your senses and see that the thing you propose is abhorrent to me and hateful to the gods, for though it has been heard in times past, in primitive times, that an uncle has been wed to a niece, I am also thy daughter by adoption, and the laws of our people forbid such a union." So Hadrior withdrew sullenly.

But as day followed day, he pressed her on the matter unyieldingly, until she became sorely troubled by him. When she continued to rebuff him, he began to treat her harshly, imprisoning her in a tower until she should agree to be made his wife. Yet all was not lost, for among the people of Cadarasia were many who saw what had become of Mariammné and pitied her.

It came to pass shortly after she was imprisoned that an envoy of Baldor, Indor by name, was visiting Cadaras from the west. Upon inquiring of the Lady Mariammné on behalf of Baldor her brother, Indor found how she was being cruelly treated. When blue-eyed Mariammné was told that a friend of her brother was in the city, she sent a message to him by stealth and besought him to come and deliver her. Indor accordingly came to the tower by night and spirited Mariammné away out one of the tower windows, fleeing with her westward. They fled Cadarasia by night, traveling by horse

many days until they came unto the hall of her brother, the lord Baldor.

When Mariammné told Baldor of all that befell her and how Hadrior had pressed her for an unnatural union, Baldor tore his clothes and vowed, "Had I not sworn an oath of loyalty to him, by the gods I would ride to Cadaras and cast a spear into his belly this very night! But though I cannot slay him, I swear by heaven and earth that I will never again offer any aid to Hadrior all his days, neither to succor him in battle, nor to send him men or supplies, nor even to make known unto him what his enemies may do in this region, for I am resolved to do everything save the shedding of blood to redress this insult and to oppose this tyrant." Then Mariammné was given the hand of fellowship and dwelt with her brother Baldor in Asylia for six months. It was while Mariammné was dwelling there that King Cygnus of Lugaria, son of Karanus, came unto Asylia to bring gifts to Baldor, for the two men were close by virtue of the alliance of Cygnus's father with Baldor's mother. There at the court of Baldor was Cygnus of Lugaria smitten with love for light-footed Mariammné, and she for him. Baldor rejoiced in their love, and the two were given to each other in marriage. So Mariammné was wed to the King of Lugaria and became queen of that people. After seven days of feasting she bid her brother farewell and departed for Lugaria with her husband King Cygnus.

Hadrior was downcast at Mariammné's flight. The king sent a deputation to Baldor, saying, "Baldor, son of Manissa, it has been reported abroad that Mariammné thy sister has fled unto thy kingdom. Therefore, hand her over, that she may be sent back to Cadaras to become wife to King Hadrior that he may raise up heirs by her." Baldor said, "I do not deny that the Lady Mariammné was at my court as of late, but she has been given in marriage to the young King Cygnus of Lugaria and has returned with him unto that land to be queen of the Lugars and dwell in security."

When this was communicated to Hadrior, he was filled with wrath and said, "The house of Manissa will not thwart my will in this matter!" Then he summoned Arummnax of Orioön and said, "Muster the army, for we shall go forth across the Erriad and bring back Mariammné from wherever she has fled to." So Arummnax came to Cadaras, bringing twenty thousand mounted Asylians who threw the spear. Toranoss also came down from Cyrenaica, and with him his three sons, bringing eight thousand men in all. Inxindor and Oruseth, kinsmen of Hadrior the king, also came at his call, and each brought with them three thousand warriors. Hadrior mustered from Cadaras five thousand riders, so that the total number mustered for war was forty thousand men. From every corner of Elabaea, every lord and captain who was loyal to Hadrior or had a grievance against the sons of Manissa came unto him, swelling his army until its numbers were vast.

Then Toranoss said, "My king, are we to make open war upon Baldor, son of Manissa?" Hadrior said, "Nay, at least for the time being. Rather, we shall march into Lugaria, chasten the young King Cygnus, and retrieve Mariammné. If affairs go well and the land can be subjected, we will also chastise Baldor and the western Asylians for their arrogance, for he will then have no ally to call upon. But if we attack him first, it may happen that Cygnus and the Lugarians will come to his aid." Toranoss said, "But could not Baldor come to the aid of Cygnus if we first attack the Lugars?" Hadrior said, "No, for Baldor swore a solemn oath never to lift his sword against me, and thus he will be compelled to stay out of the fray, lest he become an oath-breaker, which he will never do."

And so the army of Hadrior set forth west across the Erriad in the early spring of that year when the frost was still upon the ground at daybreak. He brought his company into the wilds of Enna, betwixt Asylia and Lugaria to the southwest. There he found the Manruthim dwelling, the sons and grandsons of those Marudans who had been granted refuge in Asylia by Manissa. He hassled and slew some of these, but the better part fled north into Asylia. These Manruthim gave word to Baldor that Hadrior was marching a great army to the south. Some of his captains urged him to ride out and strike Hadrior, but Baldor said, "I have sworn neither to raise my sword against him nor to help him, therefore I will not aid his march nor hinder it, but we shall leave it to Fate to determine his end. Yet I say this: the last time any man came from the east seeking to remove a maiden from hither by force it came to no good end for him!"

But young Belar, the son of Baldor, was put out by his father's words, for he was youthful and rash. He came before his father in his hall, in the presence of the lords of the west, and argued that it was not fitting that the loyalty of Asylia should be with a foreign king over their own rightful lord, Hadrior, who had ridden with Manissa. Baldor said, "My son, I have sworn an oath regarding myself only, but I bind no other man. Let every man do what seems best to him." So Belar mounted his horse and rode off to the south to join forces with Hadrior. Hadrior was gladdened to have him, for Belar was a renowned artisan and craftsman of fine armor.

Baldor thus reclined in his hall, eating, drinking, and entertaining his lords, awaiting news from the west, though concern for Belar his son weighed heavily upon him. But one of his servants, Indor, he who had rescued Mariammné from Hadrior, was sorely troubled and thought it foolish to leave the outcome of the campaign to chance. Therefore, Indor secretly fled the city of Asylia by night and rode without rest into Lugaria, five days journey, and from there was brought into the presence of King Cygnus at Karanak. There he told the king of Hadrior's march and how he intended to subdue Lugaria and seize Mariammné. Cygnus wept and said, "Alas that one to whom Blessed Manissa entrusted so much has turned his hand against me, whose father Karanus gave aid to the Asylians in days past, even hiding them from the Marudans and deceiving Adaran so that he foolishly entered the Arcorian Wood! And alas that Belar son of Baldor rides in his company!" Then Cygnus sent criers throughout his domains, mustering the Lugarians for war upon the plains outside Karanak. Within five days he had summoned more than thirty thousand, for the Lugars were very populous in those days. Then Mariammné came to Indor and said, "Will you return to the court of my brother in Asylia?" Indor said, "Nay, now that I have abandoned him and fled here without his permission, I shall remain in Lugaria, come what may."

King Cygnus remained behind in Karanak for another two days, his forces swelling to near forty thousand, equal to those of Hadrior. Then, in the midst of the spring of that year, the armies of Lugaria marched east into Enna, seeking to block the entry of Hadrior into their land.

The origin of the people of Lugaria is very ancient. When Laban came into the west, he took to himself a wife named Uta who was a Lysonian maiden of exceptional beauty. Uta bore him four sons: Machor, Enusath, Samnor, and Ramah. Machor was wed to Vara, and they begat Anrothan and his brothers, who became the fathers of the peoples of Asylia and Cadarasia; meanwhile Ramah, the youngest, dwelt in the wilds west of Zurlina and became the father of the peoples of Ituria. Enusath did not follow his father Laban all the way into the west but settled in the fair regions east of Zurlina. There he became the father of Elnasir, who in turn established his house there and became the founder of the kingdom of Elam. But Samnor, the third of the sons of Laban, wandered furthest of all, until he settled in the farthest reaches of the uttermost west, where the sun descends in the evening. There upon the coast of the endless sea founded his kingdom and raised up many sons. It is told in their genealogies how the youngest son, Lagés, traveled into the wilderness and became the progenitor of the race of the Lugars, a folk vigorous and fierce. Desiring to raise up a powerful kingdom, Lagés took for himself a hundred wives and by them bore four hundred seventy sons. When those sons came of age and needed wives of their own, he led them south, and they took for themselves by force women from the Moguls, a primitive and hardy folk of the south, of whom it is said that their women all give birth standing up. Thus the sons of Lagés begot children by the Mogul women, and so rose up the race of the Lugars, hardened warriors and skilled craftsmen all, and their rulers both wise and fearsome. Ever since Lagés their women have borne many sons, so that Lugaria in those days was a powerful and populous nation. As it is sung in the lays of that land even to this day:

Sing of Lagés, comely and fair
Who gathered wives to himself like the very stars
Who spawned sons like the sand of the seashore a far
And dwelt in the lands yonder there

The land of Enna going towards Lugaria is wild and rugged, full of tall field grasses and scattered stones that make it dangerous for horses. Therefore the army of Hadrior was impeded in traversing the region. But Cygnus, who knew the land well, sent out runners to scout the forces of Hadrior coming through Enna, taking note of their numbers and positions so that Cygnus knew in advance from whence Hadrior came. Cygnus marched his army east for a day and a half, positioning them on a broad plateau at the westernmost edge of the wildlands of Enna as one comes into Lugaria. There he drew up his men according to hundreds and thousands and set them upon the plain. But Hadrior did not emerge from the wildlands for another two days.

When he saw the army of Cygnus arrayed upon the plain, Hadrior was wrathful that he had lost the initiative and ordered Arummnax to proceed to attack as soon as possible. But Arummnax said, "My lord, we have only recently come out of difficult terrain and the men and horses are tired. Let us camp and assault them at first light on the morrow." But Hadrior said, "No, for they shall vanish into the wilds like the Iturs, only to beset us in some ambush later. It is here and now we must give battle." So Arummnax gave the word and the Asylians and Cadarasians went forth to battle.

King Cygnus called his men to war and they advanced towards the Asylians, weapons drawn and ready for blood. Great was the crashing of shields and the din of battle; many men fell in the first engagement. For a time, the shield wall of the Asylians held against the advance of Cygnus, but by and by they started to falter, and the Lugars began to break the Asylian ranks. Then panic ensued, for the Asylians feared another entrapment as at the Yellow Forks. The Asylian captains could not keep charge over their men, for terror had fallen upon them. Then King Cygnus advanced and overthrew Hadrior's army with a great slaughter. The Asylians began to flee; the Lugarian spearmen advanced and hurled their javelins, piercing many Asylians through the back as they fled. Nor did the horsemen of Asylia avail anything, for Cygnus kept near him a great contingent of archers who rained missiles upon the Asylian cavalry, decimating their ranks.

Hadrior led his army in retreat, back to the stony wilds of Enna. But when he saw that Cygnus was hot in pursuit, he cried, "Let us give battle here, my lords, for this is where Fate has decreed that we must stand." So they fought all that afternoon with their backs to the wilderness. The Lugarians slowly encircled them and cut them down, smiting them all that day. By night Cygnus called off the slaughter, and the Lugarians rested from their killing to recline at warm fires and drink wine.

The next morning King Cygnus viewed the battlefield before him and said, "Praised be the gods of Lugar who have given us a great victory," for the plain was littered with Asylian dead. And who was overthrown there in Enna? Who among the mighty men of Asylia left their corpses to rot in the wilderness? There fell that day twenty thousand men of Asylia, and all the great lords of Hadrior's court, for Toranoss, Lord of Cyrenaica fell slain, an arrow through his eye. Around Toranoss were the bodies of his three sons who fell defending their father, pierced with many wounds. Who else was among the dead? Ixindor and Oruseth, kinsmen of Hadrior who had fought at Thán, both had fallen in the rout. Also killed was Arummnax of Orioön, who crossed swords with Cygnus and was pierced through the gut. He tried to withdraw to recover and leaned upon the shoulder of his only living son, Eburax by name (for his other sons had been killed by Hadrior). But Cygnus gave him no respite, and falling hot upon his heels, he first struck Eburax, son of Arummnax, at the nape of the neck and slew him. When Arummnax perceived that his son was dead, he fell upon his body, but Cygnus descended upon Arummnax and struck off his head. Many other captains of Hadrior fell; some warriors who had been with Manissa in the Arcorian Wood in their youth were slain as well. Also among the dead was Belar, son of Baldor. Cygnus wept upon the finding of the body of Belar, for he had wished no ill upon the lad. He had the body washed, anointed, and dressed in new robes of linen.

The battle being won, Cygnus returned to Karanak and summoned his wife and Indor, servant of Baldor, and told them of the victory. But Mariammné and Indor wept when they heard of the death of Belar. Then Cygnus sent Indor back to the court of Baldor with a letter asking Baldor's forgiveness for Indor's desertion and told how his servant's actions had saved fairest Mariammné his sister. He also charged Indor with bringing the body of Belar back to his father as a token of the esteem of Cygnus. So Indor returned unto Baldor and was forgiven by him and restored. But Baldor wept bitterly when he heard of the death of Belar, his son. His lords stood by and marveled at how he wept for his son, but Baldor said, "I foresaw it would come to no good end." Then the customary rites were performed for Belar son of Baldor, and he was buried in the tombs of his fathers in Asylia.

Yet not all the Asylians were overthrown in the wilderness; many returned east and made their way back to Cadarasia, among them King Hadrior, who had fled as soon as the battle turned foul. After his return to Cadaras he began to be pained by gout in the leg and grew obese. Then, when many of the lords came to Baldor and inquired how he knew the campaign would end in disaster, Baldor made known to them the vision which Hadrior had seen in the first year of his reign bidding him to make war in the south, and how he had kept the vision secret and not heeded it.* Then all the lords of Elabaea were very wrathful with Hadrior for disobeying the vision. They came upon him in Cadaras and wanted to hold him accountable for the disasters of Enna and Yellow Forks, and for the murder of Erogel and the house of Arrax, as well as the vile plans he had for Mariammné. But Hadrior fell ill and died upon his bed before they could do justice upon him. He was sixty years old and had reigned fifteen years at the time of his death.

Then Baldor remembered his friend Erogel, son of Arrax, who had been treacherously murdered. He sent word to Erogel's widow, Analissa, who was dwelling in Anentora in Caeylon, and said, "Bring again into this land the maiden Anaxandra, daughter of Erogel, for Hadrior and his entire house are dead." So Analissa rose up and returned unto Cadarasia with Anaxandra her daughter, who was twelve years of age. When the people of Cadaras came out to welcome her, they were struck by her great beauty and the semblance she bore to Arrax, her grandfather. Anaxandra was lovely in appearance and wise in speech, and the people were so overcome with joy at the safe return of the descendants of

Arrax that they began to cry with one accord, "Long live Queen Anaxandra! May her days be blessed! May she reign forever and be unto us like immortal Manissa of happy memory!" And the people pressed for Anaxandra to be made queen.

So the lords consulted together and, after obtaining the blessing of Baldor, proclaimed Anaxandra queen and rightful successor to Hadrior, crowning her in the Temple of Mironna with great festivities. As she ascended her marbled throne, it was Baldor who held the train of her skirt on the right and Mariammné on the left. But Hadrior's body was tossed into a common grave for the poor.

After blessing Anaxandra and giving her many words of wisdom, Baldor son of Manissa returned west to Asylia with his retinue. He ruled justly for many years, and though he grieved ever for Belar his firstborn, his wife Oxanna conceived and bore him many other sons and daughters, and thus was he blessed. He was again called upon to lead men into war and won great glory for Anaxandra in her wars in the south. When he came to old age he was surrounded with many sons and daughters, though also with grief. Thus Baldor, son of Manissa, perished in his hall in Asylia, being about sixty-two years of age. He was buried in Asylia near the tombs of the sons of Ioclus, and his grave can be seen there to this day.

Blue-eyed Mariammné, after residing some time with her kinswoman Anaxandra in Cadaras, returned by way of the south to Lugaria and her husband, King Cygnus. She conceived and bore him five sons, stout fighting men, noble grandsons of Manissa, and her house won great renown in Lugaria and Asylia. In her old age Cygnus preceded her in death, and Mariammné left the kingdom of Lugaria to her eldest son, Ancus, and returned unto Asylia. She dwelt again with Baldor and attended his bedside when his spirit departed. Then Mariammné fell ill and took to bed, and after some time gave up her spirit, being nearly sixty-four years of age. Thus perished Mariammné, firstborn of Manissa. She was buried in Karanak in Lugaria where her son Ancus reigned as king. Her house is numerous among the Lugars to this day, for her offspring were blessed with health and fecundity.

Hazer

ꙮꙮꙮ

In the days of her glory, Manissa gave birth to Hazer, who was next eldest son after Baldor. Baldor was a man of great power and prowess in battle, in whom the rage of Arrax was reborn; his foes trembled before him when he wielded his spear or clashed his shield in war. But Hazer was a gentle man and delicate; he preferred the trees and rills of Asylia to the distant battlefields of Cyrenaica or Illyrana. He was handsome and comely to behold, but quiet and distant, so that in his youth many said that he was mute or dumb. But Manissa stroked his curled yellow locks and said, "Nay, he speaks and shall speak yet, for he speaks naught but what his beautiful." Her words proved true, for when he came of age he became a poet, the composer of splendid songs and melodies, and wrote much prose and verse.

At the time when Baldor went west to take lordship over old Asylia, Hazer came with him as far as the region of An Erras-by-Erriad, where once, many years earlier, his mother had won a glorious victory over Tegleth the Baazite. There the company of Baldor and Hazer encamped, for there was yet several days journey ahead of them. But in the morning when Baldor awoke, Hazer his brother was nowhere to be found. So the men of Baldor scoured the region and found Hazer some distance off, seated in a poplar grove atop a hill a little way to the south, reclining and taking his supper.

Baldor was incensed and said, "You foolish and thoughtless youth! Do you not know that we have been searching all day for you? Yet here you are reclining in the grassy poplar grove taking your meal!" But Hazer said, "It is my intention to remain behind here. Do be at peace and go on to Asylia without me." Baldor attempted to prevail against his wishes, but Hazer would not be moved and insisted on remaining behind in the poplar grove. So Baldor left him with rations for three days and then departed.

Hazer made for himself a rough home out of reeds and stone, packing it together with clay. Thus he dwelt in the poplar grove, eating nothing but seeds of the cattails that grew along the Erriad, the mulberries which were abundant in that place, and the ants of the ground. In the morning he would come forth from his hermitage and stand upon the apex of the poplar hill, gazing to the northeast. Before him stretched the fair fields of eastern An Erras as far as the hill country of Dar Gelion and the environs of the Sehu to the north—a breadth of green all the way to the horizon, cut by the Erriad that wound through the wilderness like a silver ribbon, spotted with clusters of poplar and oak throughout. He lifted his eyes and saw that it was a pleasant land, and when he came forth in the morning and felt the cool of the day in his nostrils, he would begin to sing in verse, mostly composed in honor of his mother Manissa, but some of which praised the glory and beauty of the land. He would sing from sunrise until about the third hour, and this he would do on the first day of the month. On the eve of the new moon, he would again come forth and sing to the valley from the twelfth hour until the setting of the sun. So he came forth and sang his poetry twice each month.

Before long it happened that persons passing over the Erriad noticed Hazer dwelling in the poplar grove upon the hilltop and began to turn aside to see him, and as many who did marveled at his songs and the power therein. Word spread from Asylia all the way to Cadaras that the son of Manissa was dwelling in a hut in An Erras, and many more people came out to behold him. His brother Baldor scorned him and sent servants imploring him to return to Asylia, for he was shamed by his singing. "You, the son of a queen, live in a hut like a common a pauper! You embarrass the house of Manissa by your manner of living. Return, therefore, to Asylia and your kin," he said. But Hazer would not desist.

Then, when it became widely known that Hazer sang on the first day of the month and at the new moon, crowds flocked to his hill on those days from all around, so that many thousands spread themselves out on the hillside and in the grassy fields nearby. When Hazer emerged from his hut to sing the praises of his mother, all the people fell silent and listened in awe. And it happened that marvels happened as people listened, for women who had been barren suddenly conceived after hearing Hazer, and sick horses or beasts that were brought with their masters recovered in the presence of his singing. Reports concerning the miraculous songs of Hazer traveled swiftly all about Asylia, and even as far as Caeylon and the Southlands. So many people flocked to see him that the entire plain of An Erras was covered with multitudes on the first day of the month and at the new moon, so much that they spilled over onto the eastern banks of the Erriad. And many cures were wrought there: the blind had their eyes opened, persons with various diseases were healed, animals restored to health, seeds that were brought yielded bountiful harvests, flagons of wine tasted richer; some even brought their dead out on biers, and many who did so had them restored to life by the singing of Hazer. Even the land round about was blessed, for the flowers blossomed fragrantly, the grass seemed fuller and more alive, the animals bred plentifully, and the crystal waters of the Erriad have never before or since flowed as brightly or with such vigor as in the days when they were graced by Hazer's songs. The trees seemed to stretch forth gloriously and grew with a verdant swiftness, and everything around was bursting with life. All that drew near to Hazer and his singing was blessed, so that people constantly marveled, saying, "What can these things mean? Behold the marvels worked by the son of Manissa!"

King Hadrior heard the reports of the marvelous things going on over the Erriad and came in person to question Hazer about these matters. The king came with a small retinue of soldiers, and after banishing everybody else from the hill, ascended to its summit and called upon Hazer to come out. So Hazer came forth from his dwelling, arrayed in rags with a mighty beard and disheveled in appearance. Hadrior said, "How your appearance has changed since the days when you sulked about the court of your mother, silent and dressed in finery, with your mother's blessed fingers constantly intertwined among your golden locks!" Hazer said, "Have you come all the way from Cadaras to comment on my appearance?" Hadrior replied, "Nay, but to inquire from whence comes the power with which your songs heal the lame and bless all the land." Hazer said, "I know not whether it comes from myself or from some spirit, nor do I understand its working, for the song wells up in me like a fire and issues forth from my mouth." Hadrior was angry and said, "Can you tell me nothing more about this marvel? Have I come so far to hear so little?" Hazer said, "I can tell you only that it comes as a sign, as do the deeds done by all the children of Manissa, and this of certainty."* Upon hearing this, Hadrior went away somewhat contented. After this he always sent scribes to the hill of Hazer on the days when he came forth and sang, so that the words he uttered might be recorded. On this account many of the songs of Hazer are recorded in the Temple of Mironna at Cadaras to this day.*

So Hadrior returned to his court at Cadaras and brooded upon these things. While reclining at table one evening, he told his lords and attendants about the marvels he had seen and heard with regards to Hazer. One of the maids of his court,

Iyla, the daughter of one of his captains, listened with rapt attention. She was filled with wonder and resolved to go and see Hazer for herself. Yet all the days of Hadrior she was prevented from going, as the king grew suspicious of any person who went west to consult with the sons of Manissa. But not long after Hadrior died and Anaxandra returned from exile to take the throne, Iyla saddled her horse and rode forth alone to the west, to the land of An Erras-by-Erriad to find Hazer and hear his marvelous singing.

This Iyla was a lovely maiden, slender but strong, with skin that was pale like the snows of Mount Eriar, with golden hair that tumbled down her back in a multitude of curls. Her father was a cavalry captain for Hadrior, a kinsman of Ixindor (who later was overthrown by the Lugarians in the last year of Hadrior's reign). She had been brought up in the court at Cadaras, where she had heard of the exploits of Baldor and the marvels that followed the children of Manissa. Thus Iyla purposed to gaze with her own eyes upon Hazer and hear his gracious melodies with her own ears.

Coming into the west, she found the hill of Hazer in An Erras and beheld with her own eyes the son of Manissa singing the glories of his mother to the surrounding lands in the splendor of the morning upon the first day of the month. After she heard him sing, she panted with longing and said, "Truly I was not told the half of the truth about this man! His song fills my heart with delight and blesses my spirit with joy." So she returned twice every month to hear him sing for many months, for the singing of Hazer filled her with contentment and gave radiance to her appearance, so that she grew in beauty day by day. After several months she said, "I must go and speak with him." She thus remained in An Erras after the multitudes had departed at the closing of the first day of the month and ascended the poplar hill to converse with the son of Manissa.

Hazer came forth and said, "Why does a fair maiden of Cadarasia linger here to converse with me?" She prostrated herself before him and said, "Your maidservant has been coming to hear thy words for many months now and has seen their power and grace, for they have awakened life within me and blessed me with joy. Therefore do I love thee, Hazer son of Manissa, and humbly beg thee to take me to wife."

Hazer laughed and said, "My fairest lady, look upon me! I go about in rags and dwell in a rude hut of mud and stone. My beard is long, my hair disheveled. How could I make a fitting match for thee? Furthermore, I have vowed to remain on this hilltop ever more and compose poems and songs in honor of my mother, which I sing out on the first day of the month and at the new moon. Therefore, I could not leave here, despite thy beauty and gentleness." But she persisted and would not be silenced until he should take her to wife, so that finally Hazer said to Iyla, "Your beauty and devotion are very great indeed, and so I will take thee to wife, but upon this condition: that you stay here with me and we live as husband and wife for seven days out of every month, and for the remaining days of the month you shall return to Cadaras and leave me in solitude to bless the land with my songs." This was agreeable to Iyla, and so she was wed to Hazer son of Manissa and dwelt with him but seven days out of each month, the other days returning to Cadaras to the house of her father. Nevertheless, the happiness of Hazer and Iyla was great, for they loved each other intensely and were devoted to one another, and never were the songs of Hazer more joyful and lovely. Their times apart made them long for each other more, so their love was swet and never grew stale.

But unbeknownst to Hazer, Iyla had been wed to him clandestinely, for her father had been a captain of Hadrior who detested the sons of Manissa and would not approve of the union. Thus was the marriage kept secret from her father. It soon came to pass, however, that Iyla conceived, and when her father perceived that she was with child, he berated her and demanded to know by whom she had become pregnant. At first she would not say, for she feared the wrath of her father; but he pressed her all the more, until she said, "The life in my womb comes by Hazer, son of Manissa, and furthermore I have been lawfully wed to him and am his wife." When her father heard this, he was beside himself with rage and took her forthwith to the Temple of Mironna in Cadaras. There he brought her before the priests forced her under many threats to repudiate her marriage to Hazer. In fear she repudiated Hazer with many tears and was afterward confined to her house and forbidden to leave. Then was Iyla given into the hand of one Andross, a captain and friend of her father, and forced to become his wife. So the sorrow of Iyla was very great. Before long she conspired to send a servant to bring word to Hazer of all that had occurred.

When Hazer heard that his wife was with child and of all that had occurred regarding her father and the marriage to Andross, he was stricken with grief. His heart ached and his knees trembled so that he was unable to rouse himself to praise Manissa on the first of the month and at the new moon. Instead, he came forth and sung dirges and somber songs of lamentation, tragic and melancholy in tone and melody. And as much as the land had been blessed before by his singing was it now cursed.* The grasses dried up and blew away from the hillside, and the poplars began to rot. Many of the persons who came to hear Hazer sing became ill when they heard his lamentations, and if any traveler passed through An Erras by cart when Hazer happened to be about, the wheels would fall off, or the oxen would stumble, or some other misfortune befell them. The Erriad became muddied, and the fish died. Quickly the crowds that had gathered to marvel at Hazer and bless him turned to cursing him and came no more. Thus Hazer came forth twice a month as he had done previously, but only to wail dirges, and as much as he wailed did the land suffer. So An Erras became a desolation, a frightful place that people avoided by all means.

This endured for ten long years, for Iyla gave birth to not one but two children, twin boys, whose names were Erras, from the land where Hazer dwelt, and Pelarus, from the Asylian word for poplar. Andross her husband treated the two boys badly and frequently beat them about the back and sides with a thong of cords, for he knew they were sons of Hazer and wanted no part of them. He was further angered that, try as he might, Iyla conceived no children by him. "You give a lord of Cadaras no heirs but to that rat Hazer you bear twin boys?" he raged. Yet by night Iyla would comfort her sons and tell them of their father Hazer and of the glories of the house of Manissa.

It came to pass that when the boys were ten years old that their stepfather Andross beat them so severely that they fled together from Cadaras in the night, and making their way west by way of Molossía, came unto the regions of nearer Asylia by the Erriad. Then Erras and Pelarus skirted the banks of the Erriad for a day until finding a spot to ford, and upon crossing, came into Asylia and the region of An Erras where they knew their father Hazer dwelt, whom they had never seen. But they were taken aback, for the land round about was desolate and wasted. Then Erras and Pelarus lifted up their eyes and saw the lone hill of wilted poplars someway off and knew it to be the hill of Hazer. Trembling and with much trepidation, they ascended the hill and made themselves known to Hazer. Then Hazer wept when he saw them, for Erras and Pelarus bore the semblance of Iyla, their mother. So Erras and Pelarus abode with their father and ministered to him on the hill of poplars in An Erras.

It was not long until Andross, husband of Iyla, learned of the disappearance of Erras and Pelarus. "They have fled west to that rogue Hazer!" he cried, and saddling his swiftest horse, went off west to find them. This he did not because he cared about the boys, but because it was not widely known in Cadaras that he was not their true father, and he desired to keep this knowledge from the people. It was not two days before Andross approached the land of An Erras and came to the hill of the poplars where Hazer dwelt. Erras and Pelarus saw Andross approaching on horseback and cried, "Save us father, for this is the one we told you about who berates us daily and beats us cruelly." So when Hazer saw Andross approaching he was filled with rage and seething anger and came forth from his hut trembling.

Andross called out, "Hazer, son of Manissa, be not stubborn and obstinate, but deliver to me my children who have fled to thy hill for protection! For I am their lawful father and have come to claim them." At this Hazer boiled over with fuming vengeance and said, "I will deliver the children up to thee, as you request. But first it is dusk, and I must sing as I am accustomed on the night of the new moon." Andross was pleased by this and said, "Recite thy verse! I have earnestly desired to hear the fabled songs of Hazer and will grant you this boon before I take my sons and return east." Hazer turned to his sons and said, "Go within the hut and stuff thy ears with wax from the candles. If you do not do so, I am guiltless of what becomes of thee." The boys went within and did as Hazer commanded, stuffing their ears with soft wax.

Then Hazer stood upon a stone facing north and began to sing from atop the hill of the poplars. And the song he sang was so woeful, so bitter, so filled with despair and lamentation, more so than anything Hazer had ever sung before, that the color of Andross left him, and he fell down dead upon hearing it. Then Hazer summoned his sons, saying, "Take him and bury him at the foot of the hill." So Erras and Pelarus, filled with awe and wonder, buried Andross their stepfather at the foot of Hazer's hill.

Then joy returned to An Erras, for after this Iyla came again unto Hazer and dwelt with him as his lawful wife. Erras and Pelarus lived with Hazer their father and ministered to him. They wrote down the songs and words that he composed, compiling them in a great tome. Iyla came as before to dwell with Hazer seven days of the month and returned also on the first of the month and at the new moon to hear his song, and again did he praise and glorify his mother and bring back blessing and bounty to the land, so that An Erras again grew fruitful, and the people again flocked to hear Hazer the Beautiful sing his songs to the valley and the plains. In those days Iyla again conceived, and bore to Hazer his third son, Asaph, who in later days became a prophet.*

So Hazer dwelt upon the poplar dotted hill and blessed the people of that region for twenty-five years until his eyesight failed him and also his voice—and this by the wickedness of the men of Cadaras, as is related in the tales of Perior. Then, when he was old and advanced in years, he laid down upon the floor of his abode and fell asleep in death, being near sixty-five years of age. Then his wife Iyla and his three sons, Erras, Pelarus, and Asaph, along with their children, buried him on the hilltop upon which he had dwelt. His wife Iyla erected a shrine in honor of Manissa atop the hill, and ever after was it a destination of pilgrims who came from afar to venerate the place from whence the marvelous music of Hazer, son of Manissa, went forth.* Therefore did that place become known as *Ar Pelaroth*, that is, Hill of the Poplars. The sons of Hazer raised up families for themselves and settled down in the region of An Erras, and their kin became known as the house of the Hazerites.

Necho and Elphas

ome time after giving birth to Hazer, Manissa again conceived and brought forth the twin brothers, Necho and Elphas. Necho came out of the womb first, and the maidens who were attending upon the queen said, "Here is a brave young lad indeed who has opened the way for his brother!" But Manissa said, "First coming into the world and first leaving it shall he be. Therefore his name shall be called Necho," from the Asylian word *Nechor*, which means "first." Then came forth his brother, and he was given the name Elphas, which means "might and power." Necho and Elphas were but youths when Hadrior ascended the throne of their mother and were sent west to Asylia to be raised in the court of Baldor, their brother. As the lads grew, they were trained in all manner of weaponry and war, so that they became warriors of renown like their elder brother. Necho was quick on his feet and most accurate in throwing the spear while Elphas was most dexterous with the sword and shield; yet to the eye both brothers were of similar countenance, tall and light haired, and only with great difficulty could one tell them apart. Both of their faces bore a great resemblance to their glorious mother.

When Elphas came of age, Queen Anaxandra entrusted to him the shield of Ioclus, which had been an heirloom in the house of Arrax, since it was bequeathed unto that house by Manissa in the days of her glory. A mighty shield it was, four layers of hide overlayed with beaten bronze and rimmed with delicate silver ornaments. When Necho saw that Elphas had been given the shield of Ioclus, he was crestfallen, for no gift was made unto him. His brother Baldor said, "I would have given you the great spear of Ioclus, but it rests at the bottom of the sea until the ending of the world." So Necho was consoled by this honor.

The boys grew into young men and became restless, aching to go forth and win glory for their house. Then it came to pass in the second year of the reign of Anaxandra, daughter of Erogel, that Asylia and Cadarasia went to war with the two great kingdoms that bordered them to the south, Illyrana and the kingdom of Emeric, for these had united in a league and vowed to put the people of Cadaras under tribute. The Illyrs and the people of Emeric were of similar stock, but they bore no relation to the people of Asylia or any of the western tribes, for the Illyrs and the people of Emeric did not descend from the sons of Laban but were more closely related to the Zhinkanthans and the peoples of western Caeylon. They dwelt in great cities in the plains south of Cadaras that sit east of the Bados Mountains, mighty cities built atop mounds which loomed like fortresses upon the grassland. Their regions were populous, for their capital of Illyrana was larger and better fortified than any city in Cadarasia or Asylia. Moreover, they were fierce in battle, for they fought in bronze chariots like the Marudans, and their infantry were formed into great phalanxes of spearmen who could not easily be broken up or overwhelmed. The peoples of Illyrana and Emeric had made their cities supreme in all the south by reason of their prowess in war and their cruelty in victory. They were vile and wicked in their religion, for they had it as a custom that the prisoners of the peoples they conquered should be made human sacrifices in their temples, for which reason they were especially feared and detested among the other tribes of the south. In the final years of Hadrior the Illyrs had extended their power further north, coming into conflict with the peoples of southern Cadarasia, whom they had put under tribute with the threat of destruction if the amount was not paid. Queen Anaxandra sent envoys to pacify the Illyrs and make peace, but they and the people of Emeric would have none of it and provoked Anaxandra into war through their thirst for strife and conquest.*

When it became known in Asylia that Anaxandra was mustering an army to make war in the south, Necho and Elphas were eager to join the campaign, as was Baldor, for he had chastened Hadrior for not making war on the wicked nations of that land and now rejoiced that Anaxandra was carrying out the will of Manissa in this matter. So Baldor left his wife Oxanna in charge of Asylia and came east with his brothers Necho and Elphas, passing over the Erriad by the northern road so as to avoid An Erras, where then Hazer was singing his dirges for the loss of Iyla. When they came unto Cadaras, Anaxandra received them with joy, and by common consent of all the lords of Elabaea made Baldor commander over all her armies. Under him were set two other men of renown, Gilgax, one of Baldor's vassals from the west, and Athoss, a proud war chief from Kerion who had been an ally of Hadrior and Toranoss but now pledged fealty to Anaxandra. Necho and Elphas were made captains in the legions of Baldor and set over a thousand men each, for inasmuch as they were inexperienced in war, Baldor wanted to reserve the higher commands to men of greater skill.

When the armies were mustered outside Cadaras it was found that they had less than twenty-five thousand men of war, for many men had fallen in the battle at Enna against Cygnus and the people were not yet recovered. Then some of the older lords, those who had served Hadrior, grumbled and said, "This is folly, for twice in the last ten years have we suffered disastrous reverses, and this shall be more of the same." But Baldor said, "Nay, this time it shall be our enemies who perish, for we do as Fate decrees." So the armies set forth for the land of Illyrana that year as soon as the snows were melted.

The war was bitter and long, enduring for three and a half years. If the Illyrs or the people of Emeric prevailed in battle over the Asylians, they took the prisoners and wounded back to Illyrana and offered them up to their detestable gods as sacrifices. When it became known among the Asylians that their foes were sacrificing their comrades, the Asylians likewise beheaded any Illyr prisoners that fell into their hands, so that the battles became very desperate, for men fought to the uttermost end of their strength, knowing there would be no quarter if they faltered.

Finally the Asylians and Cadarasians laid siege to the city of Emeric, taking it by storm after four months. Ascending the great mound, they raged throughout the city pillaging; it was lit on fire and burned with an unstoppable conflagration for four days. When the fire receded on the fourth day, the entire city was reduced to ash and rubble and the King of Emeric was slain by Elphas, for Elphas came face to face with the King of Emeric in combat and slashed his belly with a sword, so that his guts came spilling forth. Elphas won much glory for this, because the King of Emeric had been guilty of a great crime against the house of Manissa, as is told in other tales.*

After this victory, the Asylians began to prevail over the Illyrs and laid siege to Illyrana, and after some time took that city by storm. The Illyrs fought savagely from house to house, yielding ground only very slowly. Their resistance compelled the Asylians to torch Illyrana as well, so that it was destroyed utterly. Any Illyrs that fell into the hands of Baldor or the Asylians were slain, so that by the third day there remained none living in Illyrana.

Then Anaxandra said, "Go forth into the countryside and root these Illyrs out of the land utterly." So Baldor and the armies of Asylia and Cadarasia spent all that summer scouring the lands around Illyrana, burning the villages, overthrowing their abominable altars of sacrifice, and scattering or slaying the people, until in the sixth year of her reign Anaxandra recalled the armies from the south, for Illyrana and Emeric were no more. And upon the ruins of Illyrana the queen ordained the building of a new city, which she named Annete, after one of the queen's most trusted companions, a valiant maid of Asylia. So the armies of Asylia returned north to rejoicing and mirthfulness, for these notable victories and the destruction of the southern kingdoms had made the people forget about the defeats under Hadrior. Even more, the survivor of the Illyrs and the people of Emeric were made vassals to Anaxandra, and the dominion of Asylia and Cadarasia was doubled. Many Elabaeans came into the south to dwell, and they brought with them the tales of Manissa and their peculiar devotion to her.* Thus it was in the south among the conquered peoples of the Illyrs that the Asylians and Cadarasians were first called *Manissans*, which means "people of Manissa."

Baldor returned to Asylia and dwelt in peace in his great hall, but Necho and Elphas remained in the south. Elphas was hungry for more glory, and when he saw that the war was over in Illyrana he resolved to go east into Caeylon and sell his sword there. But Necho said, "As for me, I repent of the blood I have shed in Illyrana and resolve to take up war no more." Elphas mocked him for this, but Necho would not relent, and warned his brother, "You mock me for choosing the way of peace, but before the end you, too, shall repent of the blood you have shed." Thus they argued, until when each saw he could not prevail they at last agreed to part ways, and so they were separated by the oak tree at Gemurath, Elphas departing into the east and Necho remaining in the plains. Necho then founded a city called Engor and there and took to wife Engelé, a maiden of that region of noble birth. The house of Necho became fruitful, for Engelé bore to him six sons and two daughters, and his house became great in the south and dominated that region, so that Anaxandra created him Lord of Engor in the twelfth year of her reign. All throughout that region Necho was known for his justice, wisdom, and humility in all his dealings. He prayed three times a day, ascending a great hill to the west of Engor called Mimmoth, and there looking out over Engor and the plains, invoked the gods and besought the protection of his mother in all his undertakings. Always in his prayers he faced north, and his longest and most pious prayers came at eventide, when Laoön, the sign of the spear, arose in the skies of the distant north.

But Elphas wandered east into Anentora, where Anaxandra and her mother, Analissa, had dwelt during the days of Hadrior. Anentora was in those days a vassal of Caeylon, and from there he proffered his sword to the armies of Caeylon. His renown had reached the ears of Caeylon, and he was offered a great sum of money to go to the capital and become captain over a command of Caeylonic fighters. In those days Caeylon was waging war against the Epidymians (whose dominion is north of Cadaras in the Sehu-Gihon Valley) and were assembling mercenaries from all over their empire. So Elphas joined with a caravan traveling east from Anentora and came into the domain of Caeylon, and as he went east the plains gradually fell away to dry steppes and finally to arid desert. Elphas was many days upon the desert until he lifted his eyes and saw the mighty city of Caeylon rising from the orange sands. When he beheld the city, he said, "I did not know that it was possible for men to build such things," for Caeylon was bigger than any city of the west by many times. He thus came into the city and became a captain of a troupe of Marudan soldiers, learned the ways of Caeylon, and became in all respects like one of the men of that country in his dress and mannerisms. Then he went forth into Epidymia at the head of five hundred men and made war on the Epidymians who served under King Juna. There he won much glory, for the Caeylonics pursued the Epidymians westward to Poar Maxum and set fire to that city.

Then Elphas and the men of Caeylon attacked the Epidymians by the Brook of Eschar and forced them to take a stand in the field south of the stream. There Elphas did great deeds, for in the midst of combat he crossed swords with one Nuba, a great captain of the Epidymians and a friend of their king. Nuba ran at Elphas and hurled his great shaft at him, but the spear crashed against the heavy shield of Ioclus and shattered uselessly. Then Elphas let fly his sturdy spear at the finely armored Epidymian, but the head only grazed the flesh of his arm. The two men locked swords, each pressing upon the other and seeking for a chance to strike a fatal blow, until finally Elphas pressed upon Nuba with his shield and threw him to the ground. Before Nuba could arise, Elphas fell upon him and thrust his sword through his belly, so that Nuba howled and doubled over. When the Epidymians saw their captain slain, they fled in disarray, some across the Brook of Eschar and others to the wilderness of the north. Because of this victory, King Juna sued for peace and sent a great many gifts to the Caeylonics. Elphas was given ten talents of gold in reward for his victory over Nuba.

Elphas was in the service of Caeylon for fourteen years and was renowned among all the armies of Maruda. But as the years passed he became puffed up with pride and treated the men under him roughly, so that they grumbled and said, "Who is this son of Manissa to order us about so? Do we not have fathers and kin who were slain warring against his mother?" Nevertheless, Elphas continued to treat them poorly and abuse them, so that they became determined to kill him as soon as they had the chance. The leader of this plot was a man named Zupha, a captain whose father had been slain in the Arcorian Wood. He was tall and strong, popular among the men and dangerous to offend, for he himself had a son among the soldiers who was known as a great swordsman and was zealous for the pride of his father and of his house.

One day, when Elphas was berating his men and disciplining them, the son of Zupha stood up and challenged Elphas, calling him a barbarian and a braggart and with many such insults tried to shame him. But the son of Manissa grew hot with anger and in an instant drew forth his sword and struck off the head of Zupha's son as he stood before him. When the men saw this they grew mutinous and took up arms to assault Elphas, but Elphas fled the Marudan encampment and hid in the reeded marshes along the banks of the Gihon in eastern Epidymia. When Zupha heard that Elphas had beheaded his only son, he wept with bitterness and swore an oath by Mardu that he would not rest until he had hunted down Elphas and killed him. And all the companions of Zupha's son who had witnessed the killing vowed the same.

Elphas thus became a solitary man, dwelling alone in the wild, eating the fish of the Gihon, and hunting the boar that roamed in that region. After many months he made his way north, to the ascents near Zurlina, where in days past his mother Manissa had come in pursuit of the stag of Agenor. By and by he came unto the tomb of Ruah, steed of Manissa, and there venerated his mother and offered sacrifice in her honor. But when he had finished offering sacrifice and lifted up his eyes through the smoke, he noticed a great stillness upon the land. Behold! There before him on the hillside in the shadow of Zurlina stood one of the noble Lamassu, the great stags of Agenor. Then Elphas recalled a song of Asylia which sang of these great creatures and their lord, and he sung:

Greatest of the Great Ones, ah, Agenor!
Who splitteth the oak and sunders the hills
Who tears the rock open and sings at dawn
Whose call the sea heeds from the farthest shore

> *Ah Agenor, ah Agenor! Lord of wood*
> *The great stags thou hast set in the green north*
> *In Arcoria, thy delight and gem*
> *And of thy creatures most wise and most good*

But a great arrogance came over him, and he thought to bring the creature down and carry it back to Asylia in triumph, saying, "My mother pursued the Lamassu and caught it not, but I will triumph over it." So he raised his spear and cast it at the beast, striking it in the hind quarters above the hip, drawing dark blood from the creature that trickled down its whited coat upon the bedewed grass. Immediately a great light blazed all about Elphas and he was thrown to the ground. He lifted his eyes and saw not the stag as it had previously appeared, but now a creature glorious and full of splendor, of which no man could write or sing of.* Its glory covered the hillside and its eyes burned like a furnace, so that Elphas was sorely afraid and hid his face from the stare of the creature. Then he lifted up his head and found himself alone on the hillside by the tomb of Ruah, all signs of the Lamassu gone, save for the bloodstained grass upon which it had stood. Then Elphas quaked and said, "Alas, I have committed a great sin." And he carefully picked the bloody grass and kept it as an heirloom.*

But in the surrounding countryside it became known that something was amiss, for the peasants of that land had looked up at midday and beheld a glorious white light coming forth from the hilltop, so that rumor soon spread all around of the strange occurrence by the tomb of Ruah. It was not long before Zupha the Caeylonic got word of this. He said, "By Mardu, the son of Manissa is behind this, for marvels follow that house to the ends of the earth! Let us turn aside and hunt him." So Zupha took ten men and rode north towards the sources of the Gihon and the tomb of Ruah, for the Caeylonic army was passing back east and was not far from the region. It was not long after the encounter with the stag that Elphas was waylaid by Zupha and his men while wandering along the westerly course of the Gihon. A great rage came upon Elphas, and he trembled with fury; then, rising up from the rushes, he drew his sword and slew several of the men who came against him before fleeing south along the river's edge. Zupha pursued Elphas on horseback and cast a javelin at him that struck him in shoulder, wounding him grievously. But Elphas turned to face Zupha and struck off the leg of his horse, causing the Caeylonic to come crashing into the dust. Elphas would have slain him there, but several more Caeylonics came upon him, forcing him to flee into the woods, from whence he made his way south towards Cadarasia.

Then Zupha returned to the main body of his soldiers, who were encamped some distance off. He gathered a great force of men, almost one thousand, saying, "The son of Manissa has betrayed us and slain some of our own, my son among them. Arise! Let us pursue him into the south where he has fled." So Zupha mounted a bronze chariot and led his one thousand men southward, passing into Cadarasia from Epidymia two days later.

Elphas came into Cadarasia ahead of Zupha but did not pause there, for he hoped to reach the city of Cadaras and take refuge at the court of Anaxandra. While passing through the hill country north of Cadaras, Elphas came upon Athoss, one of Anaxandra's commanders. This Athoss had fought beside Hadrior in olden days, and also beside Baldor in Illyrana. Elphas said to him, "Master Athoss, I am fatigued and sorely wounded by a Marudan spear, I beg thee, take me into the City on the Plain that I might be succored and receive protection from my queen, the Lady Anaxandra. For there is a multitude of Caeylonics hot upon my path, how many or when they shall be here I know not, only that their captain is driven on by fiery vengeance, for he seeks my death in retaliation for the life of his son, whom I rashly beheaded in Epidymia. I pray thee, for the sake of my mother and the glory of thy queen, hold my life precious!"

But Athoss looked coldly upon him and said, "How is it that you seek the refuge of Cadaras now after forsaking it to serve in the hot deserts of Maruda and its king, whom thy mother fought bitterly for four years? The Marudans are no longer our foes, and if you have offended them then it is yourself who must pay the price. If they follow you as you say, then turn away from Cadaras and flee westward, away from here, towards the wilds of Asylia where your brother Baldor reigns in splendor." Athoss said this because he did not want to bring down the wrath of Caeylon upon Cadaras, but also because he mistrusted the sons of Manissa and was not favorably inclined towards Elphas.

Elphas grew angry and said, "Will you not come to the defense of the son of Manissa in the hour of his need? How can you deny me the shelter of Cadaras's white walls when I, your countryman, am in flight from the foreign oppressor? Such treachery has not been heard of since the night Gygas brought Arahaz to Lissus to slay my grandfather!" This angered Athoss and he lashed out at Elphas, saying, "And what problem is it of our queen whether you beheaded the son of some Marudan? Curses upon you for taking up arms with them at first! And are you now surprised that the men of Caeylon are trying to slay you? Ever are the sons of Manissa rash and ill-fated, a bane to their people and blight on their homeland!"

Elphas was infuriated and said, "Choose your words carefully, Athoss, for I have not forgotten the harm that was done to my family in the days of Hadrior, your late lord, and it is no secret that you bear our family ill." Athoss said, "Go your way, Elphas son of Manissa, and perhaps if you are fortunate the angry spears of the Marudans will not find you." But Elphas shook and said, "And perhaps if you are fortunate, my spear will not miss you!" Then he took hold of his spear and cast it at Athoss; the point struck Athoss in the breast, bringing him to the dirt. Then Elphas mocked him upon the ground, saying, "Thy fortune was not so great after all!" But Athoss lifted himself up some ways and said, "Before the end you will pay for your recklessness and go down to death in mourning!" Then Athoss gurgled, collapsed, and gave up his spirit.

Elphas retrieved his spear and fled southwards, the shield of Ioclus slung to his back. He now attempted to bypass Cadaras and make for the city of Engor, where his brother Necho was reigning as lord. He skirted the region of Cadarasia by night and passed southeast into the plains of Díndumon, coming after two days into the vast and vacant flatlands that fall away east of the mountains of Bados. He pressed on hard, though his wound troubled him sorely, till he finally saw Engor rising on the plains on the third day of his flight and sighed with relief when the smoke from his brother's hall was sighted. "Surely, my twin brother will defend me," he said. Yet not long after, Zupha brought his men into Cadarasia and pillaged the villages around there looking for Elphas. When he was not found, Zupha departed and continued south in pursuit.

When Elphas came into Engor, his brother Necho went forth with all the people of the city to greet him, and leading him into the city, they nourished him and dressed his wound. All the people of Engor marveled at Elphas and said, "Behold how he is the very image of his brother!" Save for their dress, Elphas in battle armor and Necho in fine robes, no one could have told one from the other. After they had tended him, Elphas fell into a deep sleep, for he was much wearied by his flight and his wound. Necho said, "I will speak with him when he awakens. In the meantime, the disc of the sun falls to the west behind the mountaintops and prayer beckons me. Perhaps when I return he will tell me from whom he has fled and of what manner of distress he is in." So Necho left the city of Engor and traveled west to the hill of Mimmoth, only a brief distance outside the city, and, ascending the hill of Mimmoth, prayed there until the setting of the sun and the appearance of the first stars, as was his custom.

But Zupha had pursued Elphas all the way from Cadarasia. Though he had a multitude of men with him, he neither stopped to raid villages of the south nor make war on anybody great or small but moved with swiftness, coming into the southern plains only a day behind Elphas. By and by Zupha came into the region of Engor, which sat alone on the plains. He said to his captains, "If Elphas has come this way then there is no other destination he could have gone to save here." One of his captains said, "My lord, see that great hill yonder to the west? Let us ascend it by stealth from the rear and spy out the land and the defenses of the city, whether they are great or lacking." So Zupha took with him twelve men and, waiting until the setting of the sun that day, came to the hill of Mimmoth and ascended it by the rear, hoping to spy out the lay of the land.

Thus it was that Necho was praying upon the hillside when Zupha and the Caeylonics came up. When they beheld Necho they took him to be Elphas by virtue of their great likeness. Zupha mocked him, saying, "Have you put off your armor for the robes of a priest in hopes of appeasing heaven to aid you? I tell you nobody can save you from my hand!" Then Zupha had Necho gagged and bound to a tree, and when he was fastened securely, he took his spear and cast it at Necho. The blade crashed into his chest and pinned him to the trunk, and when he had moaned his last prayers, Necho bowed his head and died.

Yet while Zupha and his men were debating what course of action to take next, they heard the sounds of men ascending the hillside from the east, and so hid themselves in some brush. Then Zupha beheld several servants running up the hill of Mimmoth from Engor, crying, "Lord Necho! Thy brother is awakened and wishes to speak with you urgently, for he says we are in great danger!" But when they came to the summit they beheld Necho slain, still bound, and pinned to the tree by the Marudan spear. Then the servants took the body of Necho and made haste down the hillside, returning unto the city of Engor with great cries of lamentation. When they had departed, Zupha said, "Cursed be my fate, for I have slain the wrong man! Elphas is within the city yet!"

But when Elphas saw the servants bearing the corpse of his brother, bloody and stiff in his priestly robes, he was enraged with a vicious madness, and the rage of the sons of Manissa boiled hot in his blood, like the wrath of Arrax of old. Straightaway he donned his helm, took up his sword, and bearing the shield of Iolcus before him, came forth from Engor, crying for Zupha and swearing oaths terrible and wrathful. Zupha returned to his men and told his captains, "Array yourselves for war, for Elphas has come out of the city and is taken with madness!" So Zupha mustered his thousand men on the plain beside Mimmoth and advanced towards Elphas, whetted spears lowered and ready for battle. But Elphas was like a man beside himself, and as soon as he saw the men of Caeylon advancing over the plain he charged their ranks and crashed into them like Baldor before the walls of Thán. The men encompassed him about, but the sword of Elphas glittered in the starlight and slashed here and there, deflecting every blow aimed against him and slaying every man he came against, shattering shields, breaking sword blades, and cleaving flesh. The Caeylonics cast spears at Elphas but before their very eyes saw their shafts turn aside from him, as if some mischievous sprite sent them astray. Then they were affrighted and said, "Let us flee, for the gods possess this man! What have we to do with the vengeance of Zupha?" So the Caeylonic ranks were cast into confusion and began to be routed by the fury of Elphas.

Zupha and his captains retreated to Anentora and fortified themselves there, fearing the wrath of Elphas. But Elphas sent the swiftest riders of Engor north, and told them, "Go to my brother Baldor in Asylia. Tell him to come at once and avenge the death of our brother, Necho, and overthrow the great city of Anentora where the Caeylonic murderer Zupha has fled." Then he performed the funeral rites for Necho son of Manissa and had him interred in the tomb that Necho had prepared for himself in the midst of the City of Necho, Engor of the plains. Engelé, wife of Necho, wept bitterly, but the older sons of Necho came to Elphas with fire in their eyes and said, "We will go with you to Anentora to slay this Zupha."

Ten days thereafter the riders of Engor came to Baldor in Asylia and told him of Zupha and the death of Necho. Then Baldor trembled with rage and stood up in his hall, his graying locks tumbling down his broad shoulders. He donned his war helm and the great coat of scale armor that he wore when he slew Imbrossé, son of Endumion. Then he took up his mighty war spear and said, "So innocent Necho has been fated to be the first of the sons of Manissa to perish? So be it! But Caeylon shall pay a great price as the instrument of this deed." Then Baldor mustered three thousand riders of Asylia and came south to aid Elphas, and with him was his friend and war chief, Gilgax. Anaxandra, however, would not aid Elphas, because he had murdered Athoss on the road.

Then Baldor came unto Engor, and the young men of that city, about seventy in all, took up arms and mounted their steeds, and riding behind Baldor and Elphas, came unto Anentora. Zupha and the Caeylonics quaked, for they heard Baldor, son of Manissa, was upon them. "This risks turning into open war between Maruda and the Asylians," Zupha lamented. He sent a message to Baldor, saying, "Peace, Baldor of Asylia. I have no grief with you. My grievance is against Elphas, son of Manissa only, for he has done me a great wrong in shedding the blood of my house." Baldor read this message and sent back the following, "Perhaps you have cause against Elphas, and perhaps you do not; this I cannot say know. All I know is that you shed the blood of a son of Manissa, and in this is your doom sealed."

Baldor led the Asylians against Anentora, struck the city, and overthrew it with a great slaughter, burning it with fire and taking much booty. But Elphas was denied his vengeance, for one of the sons of Necho, Aïross by name, a boy of only fourteen, saw Zupha trying to flee the melee and hurled a spear at him. Zupha was struck in the liver and fell howling to the ground. Aïross then fell upon Zupha and struck off his head, and holding it aloft, rallied the Asylians to make a total overthrow of the city. When the city was demolished, the remaining people came and did homage to Baldor and pledged fealty to the Asylians if they would be spared. Baldor said, "Am I king to give or deny clemency to conquered foes, or ruler of Asylia to negotiate terms? Send your envoys to white-armed Anaxandra who reigns from the marbled halls of Cadaras and treat with her." So the people of Anentora submitted themselves to Anaxandra and have paid tribute to the Asylians ever since. But the head of Zupha they brought back to Engor and affixed to a pike that stood over the tomb of Necho.

Anaxandra sent envoys to Elphas with words of peace, saying, "Come, Elphas, son of Manissa and kin of mine. Though you have slain Athoss, an innocent man and one in my grace, you have redeemed your honor by delivering unto me the great city of Anentora, with the aid of Baldor, your brother of great renown. Come, dwell in Cadaras and be my great captain and take the place of Athoss, whom you slew." But Elphas would have none of it, for he wrote to her saying, "Nay great lady, for like thy illustrious grandfather of immortal fame I shall throw away my sword and learn the ways of war no more, for it has brought me nothing but misery and by it have I done much harm." So from that day Elphas lived in peace and dwelt in Engor, the city of his brother, and ruled the people of Engor in wisdom and equity. He took to wife Noria, a relative of Engelé, his brother's widow. By Noria he bore three sons, all of them strong in wisdom and glorious in might. Elphas ruled Engor fifty-six years, and there was peace all his days. The shield of Ioclus he entrusted to his sons, and it remained in the house of Elphas from that time on.

But Elphas lingered into extreme age, outliving both his wife Noria and all of his children, and when everybody he had known as a youth was long dead, he retired from his estate, the lordship passing at that time to Aiareth, grandson of Necho. Then he assumed the rough, woolen robes of a hermit and dwelt atop the hill of Mimmoth, near the spot where his brother had been slain, spending his final days in fasting and prayer. If anyone said, "What do you mean by living this way?" he said, "I am atoning for the men whose deaths I caused in my youth, especially for the deaths of my brother Necho and of Athoss, captain of Anaxadra." Elphas finally expired in his sixth year dwelling on the hill of Mimmoth, being about ninety-eight years of age. The spot where he dwelt became known as *Sinnechan*, which means "Tree of Necho" in the dialect of that region. And he was buried in Engor beside the tombs of his brother Necho, his sons, and his wife Noria, and his tomb can still be seen there to this day.

Secum

꧁꧂ ꧁꧂ ꧁꧂

Not long after Baldor and his kin took the city of Anentora from Caeylon, it came to pass that Queen Anaxandra became sick with fever. Her physicians took it to be light and predicted her recovery with the coming of the spring, but after two weeks, while talking with her ministers in the garden, she became violently ill, vomited up blood, and had to be carried to her sickbed. The following eve she became bitterly cold and could not be warmed, though such a fire was lit in her chambers that all her attendants sweated profusely from the heat. Shortly thereafter her voice failed her, and when it became evident that she was in the throes of death, Hazer was sent for, for he was dwelling not far from Cadaras in An Erras on the hill of the poplars. Some said, "Perhaps if Hazer sings to her, she will be made well." But Hazer refused to come, for he said, "I have sworn an oath to never depart from this hill, Ar Pelaroth." When her ministers heard the reply of Hazer, they cursed him and the house of Manissa, saying, "The one man who has the power to raise her up refuses to come! He does this not because he regards any oath, but because he knows that Anaxandra dies without heir, and he entertains hopes that some of his own kin will come next to the throne!" So they spoke ill of Hazer and the sons of Manissa.* But Anaxandra said, "Leave him be, for such is his oath."

So her ministers gathered about Anaxandra and made oblations and offerings at her bedside. Old men were called in to sing the hymns of Asylia, the lays of Orianna, of Manx, and the dazzling heights of Mount Eriar, where the blue-sky glares eternally upon the radiant snows and the air is ever fresh and life-giving. Then, after lingering for five days, Anaxandra gave up her spirit and expired, being only twenty-nine years of age. She had reigned for seventeen years in Cadarasia. There was wailing throughout the land for Anaxandra, daughter of Erogel and granddaughter of Arrax, for with her passing the house of Arrax was extinct, for she had remained a virgin her whole life through. Anaxandra was mourned in Cadaras, and many of the house of Manissa came to pay her homage. But after ten days she was loaded in a cart pulled by two oxen that had never been yoked and taken to Paros, where she was entombed alongside her mother Analissa and her ancestors, Arrax and Erissa.

When the funeral rites of Anaxandra daughter of Erogel were completed, the lords of all Elabaea gathered in council in Cadarasia. All the lords from Cyrenaica as far south as Engor and Anentora, and as far west as Lugaria and farther Asylia came to Cadaras, whether of the house of Manissa, or of descent from one of the other houses of Asylia, or of the kith and kin of Hadrior (for he had promoted many men to the lordship in his days). When all were gathered together in the great hall at Cadaras, one of the most renowned of all the lords, Gilgax, a companion of Baldor, spoke, saying, "With the passing of Anaxandra of happy memory, the house of Arrax has been spent. Were it not for the treachery of Hadrior, who in the days of our fathers put to death Erogel and the other kin of Arrax, men more worthy and honorable than himself, we would not be in these unhappy straits, our queen dead without an heir and successor! Let us then open this council, invoking the glorious memory of Manissa, thrice blessed, and be now resolved not to leave these hallowed halls until we have settled upon a successor to the throne from among our number."

At once Elphas, son of Manissa, stood up and said, "My brethren and fellow lords, while we peoples of Asylia and Cadarasia have been blessed in recent times with peace in our realms following the glorious victories of Anaxandra in the south over the people of Illyrana, it seems to me that since the days of Hadrior unto this day a very grave injustice has been done to the house of Manissa, my house, of which I dare any man here to speak against: that though it was through the valor and splendor of my mother that we were delivered from the thralldom of the Marudans, and though she governed happily for nigh unto twenty years, nevertheless since the day of her departure the throne has not been held by one of her sons, despite that there are still five living, Necho my twin having been recently slain by Zupha the Caeylonic. This is an outrage against my house and the memory of my mother, over whose sons ye have preferred Hadrior, brother-in-law to Manissa, a treacherous murderer and coveter of an illicit, incestuous union with my sister, Mariammné. Then, by way of atoning for the murder of Erogel son of Arrax by your king, after his death you retrieved Anaxandra, daughter of Erogel, and set a granddaughter of Manissa's uncle upon the throne, a female second cousin ruling while Manissa's sons live, disinherited! Let this travesty proceed no further! Return the throne of Elabaea to the house of Manissa and give the regal authority to none other than Baldor, lord of Asylia and son of Manissa, first among her sons, first in battle, and a ruler of proven justice and nobility, who this past thirty years has ruled old Asylia in peace and prosperity." Many of the lords there assembled crashed their spears to their shields and assented to everything spoken by Elphas, son of Manissa. But some dissented.

Then Gilgax stood up again, and the entire hall fell silent. Now this Gilgax was one of the lords of western Asylia, a close ally of Baldor who had been with him on the campaign in Cyrenaica when he was a youth. Baldor valued his friendship in peace and arms so greatly that he gave unto him the hand of his daughter, Calanthé, though she was his junior by seventeen years. Gilgax held his spear aloft and said gravely, "I am not of the house of Manissa, save by marriage to the daughter of Baldor, golden-locked Calanthé, jewel of the west. But I concur with Elphas, for I have fought with my own spear that I now bear aloft beside Baldor, son of Manissa, in many campaigns. I testify now before Manissa and all the gods and spirits of heaven and earth that there is no man who has more right by blood, by valor, or by virtue than Baldor. Let Baldor be made king!"

But then stood up Egol, grandson of Eridax, whose house had held sway in Cadaras since the days of Manissa. The lordship of that city had passed from the house of Garba to the house of Eridax following the death of Aenon, son-in-law of Garba, at Ehuiel during the war with Maruda. This Egol was a wiry fellow, lean with a sour demeanor and hair of black. Grim Egol said, "Let no man doubt or deny the valor of Baldor, son of Manissa, or of the great deeds which our lady's house has done and continues to do unto this day, for who is not acquainted with the wonders they work on the earth? But nevertheless, it is the rule of custom which must prevail in our land, and we have a custom that our ruler is to be chosen by the assembled lords of Elabaea. This you all know, for thus have you come to gather here in this hall today. Yet now Gilgax, son-in-law of Baldor and Elphas, son of Manissa, would have us believe that the kingship passes always from generation to generation in the same house, and that one may lay claim to the kingship by virtue of blood apart from merit. This may have been true of the kingship of Asylia, which is held by Baldor, but it has not been so for the lordship of All Elabaea, which is not Asylia alone, but Asylia united with Cadaras. Only recently established in the hands of Manissa, the inheritance of which has not been assigned to one house by any law. For though Baldor or Elphas be virtuous, what shall become of us when their sons or grandsons arise up, who may not be so virtuous, and demand the throne by right of birth alone? Therefore, let there be a vote taken among all those who have lordship in Elabaea, and let whomever the lords choose become our king." Many of the lords shouted their assent to the words of Egol, especially those who were not of the house of Manissa.*

Then Secum, wisest of the sons of Manissa stood up and said, "Egol does not speak rightly, my lords. For those old enough to recall, let it be known that while it is custom for the lords of Asylia to select their lord by acclamation, nevertheless until the time of Manissa the lordship of Elabaea passed unbroken from father to son: we know that Laban came into the west and was wed to Uta, and from their union came Machor, who became a mighty lord and father of Anrothan. Anrothan begot Eamon, father of the splendid Orianna who was taken to wife by none other than Manx, highest lord of Eriar. By Manx she begot noble and divine Orix, who was the first to be called king in Asylia. Orix was succeeded to the kingship by his son Andor, who was made king by right before any assent of the lords. Andor in turn passed the kingship on to his son Ancyrus, who likewise claimed his right by blood, and so on to his son Ioclus. The only purpose for the choice of Manissa by vote of the lords was because Ioclus's sons had all perished on Lissus. Had they not, the kingship would have assuredly passed to them. Therefore, since the sons of Manissa are still living, it is more in keeping with our custom for the kingship to devolve upon Baldor. Though Asylia has only recently been united to Cadaras, it was nonetheless done in the person of Manissa, whose descendants ought to have primary claim." Many of the lords nodded at this, but grim Egol scowled.

Then a bitter dispute broke out, some putting forth Baldor as rightful king, and others supporting Egol, for he was of a noble house that had a claim to the lordship of Cadaras and alone among the other lords possessed the guile and will to oppose the sons of Manissa. The hall was filled with yelling, and a furor arose so that some men began to take up spears. But when Baldor, who had previously been sitting silently listening to the arguments, saw men taking up spears he stood up and cried out with a loud voice, and the hall fell still. Then he said, "My brethren, I am advanced in years. Though not elderly by any means, I am past the prowess of my youth. These last twenty years have I resided in peace in Asylia, reclining on my great oaken throne, drinking ale in leisure, and making merry with my kin, being disturbed only occasionally to go out to war, a thing which, though I excel at, I have no love for. Now I see men of different minds, men whom I respect, about to come to blows over the opinions of my brother Elphas and my kinsman Gilgax, both of whom would entrust the throne of Cadarasia and all Elabaea to me. Yet what is Cadaras to me? Are not the tombs of my grandfather and ancestors in fair Asylia? Is the tomb of my mother among the Cadarasians?* Are my kin in Cadarasia? Nay, everything I know and venerate lies to the far west, in the ever-green hillocks of Asylia beyond the Erriad, not least of all my lovely wife, Oxanna. I shall therefore withdraw my name from any consideration of the kingship and accept no nomination, for I have no desire to rule any more than has been entrusted to me and I wish not for anyone to come to blows on my account. The unity of Elabaeans is of greater value to me than my own advancement."

Then Elphas and Gilgax were crestfallen, for both had argued vehemently for Baldor. But Baldor continued, saying, "Nevertheless, I cannot endorse Egol for the kingship either, for he has no experience of war, is full of guile and cunning, and comes from a house that has never had anything to do with the west, for they ever look towards Cadaras and the east. How can he govern so vast a realm as greater Asylia and all Elabaea? Therefore, I put forth as my choice none other than my son-in-law and trusted companion, Gilgax. He is well respected in the west but has fought many battles in the east and knows it well; he is related to the house of Manissa by marriage to my daughter, golden-locked Calanthé, but is of no blood relation to our house. He is in all things capable, virtuous, trustworthy, and deadly in battle with spear or sword."

Then a great din erupted in the hall, for many supported the proposition of Baldor and began chanting for Gilgax, but some still supported Egol. Egol said, "Secum, wisest of all Asylians, how shall this be resolved?" Secum said, "Let a vote be cast, but not here; let us proceed to the Hill of Cruachan, wherever and anon such matters have been settled by the lords of Asylia." But the council scoffed at this, for no meeting had been convened on the Hill of Cruachan for fifty years, since Manissa was made queen, and the hill was very remote from many of the eastern lord. So they cried, "Not at Cruachan, but here and now!" Therefore Gilgax and Egol sat on opposing ends of the hall, and each lord was called forth by name. Upon stepping forward, each laid his spear at either the foot of Gilgax or Egol. After all the lords had been called and the spears tallied, it was discovered that Gilgax and Egol had the exact same number of spears at their feet. Baldor said, "This is a dilemma such as never been heard of before. Brother Secum, wisest of all men, what shall be done?"

Secum said, "This is a curse that comes upon us because of our indecision. Since we cannot resolve whether we shall follow custom by devolving the kingship upon the sons of Manissa and proclaiming it at Cruachan as is tradition, we are punished by being unable to resolve who should reign; Fate taunts us cruelly. We have done ill this day in forsaking Cruachan and the sons of Manissa for these two men who have little claim to royalty. Therefore, let the lords have as they have chosen; I say Gilgax and Egol shall rule together, Gilgax having authority over the west and Egol over the east, each supreme in his realm. Six months shall they sit enthroned in the fair marbled halls of Cadaras, side by side dispensing justice and wisdom for the people of Cadarasia, and six months shall they sit enthroned in the oaken halls of Baldor in Asylia, doing likewise there. Each man shall acknowledge each as his lord, and neither king shall contradict the other, for they are equals in dignity and power." Then all the lords assented to this, and it seemed good to Egol as well, and so Gilgax, son-in-law of Baldor, and Egol, grandson of Eridax, were proclaimed Kings of Elabaea.

But Baldor took Secum aside and said, "Brother, what ill counsel is this you have given us? In proposing this arrangement, you almost certainly provide for warfare between the two!" But Secum said, "If thou art concerned with unity, brother, then you should have stepped forward to take your appointed place instead of preferring the comforts of your hall. If the Asylians cannot decide on a single ruler, then Fate will decide for us." So the council was dismissed, and the two kings were proclaimed throughout the land with fanfare and much feasting, though the hearts of Baldor and Secum were filled with foreboding.

Now Secum was the fifth son of Manissa, and youngest child save for Perior, his brother, who dwelt in the far west. Like Hazer, Secum was a gentle man and never was known to wield a spear or sword. But from his earliest youth he uttered words of great wisdom, so much so that his mother, when he was but a youth, sent scribes to copy down his words. His counsel was always prudent and his speech moderate, and seldom did he lay forth a plan which did not come to fruition exactly as he said, and for this reason his counsel was earnestly desired by many of the rulers of the lands roundabout. In his youth he had counseled Baldor in his dispute with Belar his son over the war in Lugaria, and later was taken as a counselor to Anaxandra and stood beside her throne speaking pure words of righteousness into her ears. At times he had been summoned from as far away as the court of Cygnus by his sister Mariammné to speak before the king there; on one occasion he was called for by none other than King Juna of Epidymia, who sought his counsel on a difficult matter relating to the governance of that kingdom. Of him, Juna marveled and said, "I would gladly give away half of my lands for a counselor in whom is such a spirit of wisdom and excellence." Thus was Secum's wisdom renowned throughout the west. Yet despite all this he was not puffed up with pride, for he was also a very meek man and always kept his own opinions in his heart.

Gilgax and Egol reigned together from Cadaras, and Baldor and the other lords returned to their cities. Secum, too, would have departed, for he intended to dwell with his sister Mariammné in the west, but Egol constrained him, saying, "Great Secum, your knowledge is renowned throughout the world, and only by your word could the kingship have been established in the hands of Gilgax and myself. Therefore, do not go west, but remain here in Cadarasia and be a counselor to our throne, that our kingdom may be happy and prosperous." This seemed good to Secum, and so he remained behind in the court of Gilgax and Egol and advised them. A second throne was constructed of marble and brought in to stand beside the other, so that Gilgax and Egol would don their regal vestments and sit beside one another reigning and making judgments.

It came to pass during the six months at Cadaras that Secum ministered to both Gilgax and Egol and was held in high esteem by both. The lords of Cadarasia and Asylia went in and out before him and treated Secum with great respect. In such esteem did they hold him that they sometimes came not to confer with the kings but with Secum, and if Egol came forth, they said, "My king, we have come to seek the advice of Secum son of Manissa; may we have audience with him?" Gilgax rejoiced that the brother of his lord Baldor was honored such, but Egol grew envious.

Yet Secum, though wise, became corrupted by the taste of power. He who had always been cautious grew imprudent, puffed up with pride by reason of his new importance. He began to give his advice from impure motives, so that the spirit of wisdom left him and was replaced by a spirit of pride and folly.* In his arrogance he began to act regally and with too much familiarity before Gilgax and Egol, so much so that Gilgax began to neglect his kingly duties, preferring to entrust them to Secum and spend his time on the hunt. Egol perceived the dereliction of Gilgax and the haughtiness of Secum and began to brood on evil thoughts.

One day, while Gilgax was away on progress, the servants of Egol spied Secum using the seal of the king to promulgate decrees in the name of Gilgax which Gilgax had not decreed, and they ran back to their lord King Egol and told him this. So Egol pondered this and held it in his heart for the duration of the six months in Cadaras.

But when six months were completed and it came time to remove the court to the west, to Asylia as had been agreed, Egol became troubled. Secum perceived that he was downcast. So Secum took Egol aside under the great pillared portico in the Citadel and said, "What troubles you, my lord Egol?" Egol said, "My lord Secum, wisest of men, though I swore to remove myself and my throne to the west at the end of the duration of six months, to reign in old Asylia beside noble Gilgax in the hall of Baldor, I am now fearful and full of trepidation. For when the kingship was not yet claimed, many of the partisans of Baldor raised spears against me in the council hall and we scarcely avoided coming to blood over it. I fear that if I remove myself to the west, I will be in the company of bloodthirsty men who will seek my death."

Secum said, "Oppose thee as they might have when you were but Lord of Cadaras, the men of the west are loyal and will not do so now that you reign as king beside their own Gilgax. Fear not, but go into the west, as you swore." But Egol said, "Nay, Secum, it is not my intent to remove myself into the west. I will establish my throne here in perpetuity and claim the kingship of all Elabaea alone, barring whatever Gilgax may say about it." Then Secum trembled with anger and said, "How can you be so vile? Six months have not yet elapsed, and you are already violating your oath!? If you do not fear the gods, whom you blaspheme, do you yet fear the sons of Manissa? For how do you imagine this will come to pass after telling me, the brother of Baldor and kin by marriage to Gilgax? Do you vainly imagine I will keep silent about this to Baldor and Gilgax? Assuredly not!"

Egol said, "You will surely keep silent, fool among the wise! I know your pride and arrogance and have seen your treachery, for in the absence of your lord, King Gilgax, you dared to issue decrees and judgments in his name using the royal seal, something that merits death according to the traditions of our people. Do you not recall the days of Ancyrus, father of noble Ioclus, and the affair of Mannoth son of Irox? The tales say that Ancyrus was laid low with fever, and thinking to do his lord a service, Mannoth, his companion, took up the royal seal and issued judgments in the king's name. Yet when Ancyrus recovered and learned what Mannoth had done, he was wroth and had him put to death. Is it not written in the histories?" Secum said, "It is so."

Then Egol was emboldened and said, "Yet the sons of Manissa act with impunity against king and country! Any other man, be he ever so exalted in the sight of the king, would have been slain for such presumption as you have exhibited in issuing decrees in the name of Gilgax." Secum stood dumbly before him, for everything Egol said was true. Then Egol said, "If you wish to maintain your dignity and your ill-gotten distinction of wisdom, then you will go unto Gilgax and coax him with gentle and graceful words to remain behind in Cadaras and by no means seek to go west to Asylia. If you do this, you will do well; but if not, I will expose you to Gilgax and before all the people and will see that justice is done upon you. By my authority as king, I will have you put to death, for it is my prerogative to see to it that those guilty of treason are thus punished, and what you have done is treason indeed."

Then Secum tore his garments and took the regal rod which he bore about, and breaking it over his knee, said, "Thus is the unity of Cadarasia and Asylia broken; my bones will be dust before it is renewed." Egol said, "Speak plainly, philosopher! Will you compel Gilgax to remain in Cadaras or shall I expose you?" But Secum turned and fled from Egol, leaving the Citadel, and vanished into the city. Egol sent his guardsmen to find him, but after scouring the city for a day they were unable to produce him. Then Egol began to panic, for he feared that Secum might seek out Gilgax and make the whole affair known to him, pleading forgiveness by virtue of the close relation between the two, and, thus securing his forgiveness, turn him against Egol. Therefore, he gathered ten of his most loyal lords and several guards and said, "Come, let us go forth and seek Gilgax."

Secum had fled Cadaras, seeking not Gilgax, but the court of Baldor, which was many days journey away. But Gilgax was at that time returning from Molossía where he had been in counsel with the lords of that region. King Egol and his party saw him coming up the road from Molossía and went forth to meet him. The two parties met on the highway in the wooded region near Avlos. Then Gilgax said, "Hail, lord Egol! Is it well with you?" Egol said, "My lord King Gilgax, something dreadful has befallen us! We are in urgent need of your counsel!" So Gilgax dismounted from his horse and came unto Egol, but when he approached, Egol gave a sign, and those who were with him hurled their spears at Gilgax and slew him upon the road. Those who were with Gilgax were also slain. Then rash Egol cried, "There is no return now, my lords! Let us see this through to its completion!"

Egol returned to Cadaras and summoned all the lords of the east before him. Then, donned in regal robes and bearing his scepter, he accused Gilgax and Secum as traitors and passed sentence on them. When some of the lords protested that Secum was loyal, Egol said, "Has he not fled the city since yesterday? For he knows his treachery has been discovered and he seeks to flee before we lay hands on him." Then many of the lords who had formerly been loyal to Gilgax and the house of Manissa were turned by the words of Egol. Yet some of the lords sensed deceit in Egol's words and sought to flee, but Egol captured them, and taking them into the courtyard of the Citadel, had their heads struck off. Then the lords cried, "Hail King Egol! Hail mighty lord of the house of Eridax! May his reign be blessed forever!" So Egol became King of All Elabaea. As Secum could not be found, the king issued a decree banishing him from Cadaras and Asylia on pain of death and caused this proclamation to be sent far and wide throughout the kingdom, posted in every village and at every crossroad.

Secum meanwhile was fleeing west through the wilderness, making his way towards the Erriad by the southerly route, when on the fourth day he came to the crossroads of Limnor and saw the sentence of banishment posted on the pillar at the crossroads. Then he said, "I will not be able to come into Asylia, which is still a fortnight's journey away on foot. I must flee into the uttermost wilderness, as my mother did when fleeing from Arahaz." So he waited by the reeds at Limnor until nightfall and then made his way north, and instead of crossing over the Erriad, skirted its easternmost banks till passing into the kingdom of Epidymia. He came into the regions on the eastern banks of the Gihon, going up towards the Plains of Anorel. There he put off his Asylian raiment and took up the garb of a traveler.

Secum went on east from the Gihon and came unto
Anaroth, by the sloping grasslands that go up towards Anorel.
As he came to Anaroth, he was wearied with the rigors of his
flight and collapsed by a shallow brook that ran near the city.
There he was found by a young maiden called Cilla who took
him up and brought him into the village. Cilla was black
haired and of pale complexion, very beautiful to behold and of
a kindly disposition, as was her whole house. The family of
Cilla bandaged the bloody feet of Secum, kept vigil by his side,
and in all things showed great concern for his well-being,
refusing to leave his bed until he should awake.

Sometime later Secum came to his senses, and seeing
himself surrounded by unfamiliar persons, was unsure what
had befallen him. Black-haired Cilla said, "Fear not, fortunate
stranger, for you have come to the fair town of Anaroth-upon-
Anorel, whose fertile fields and rush-laden streams are the
heart of the Kingdom of Epidymia." When Secum heard that
he was in Epidymia and that he was not recognized by any, he
said, "Many thanks, glorious maid, for thy care of a weary
traveler. Long days and nights have I been cast upon the road,
and yours is the first friendly face I have seen in as long."

So the house of Cilla took Secum in, though they knew
neither from whence he came nor of his lineage but supposed
him to be some vagabond or pilgrim. Nor did Secum dissuade
them from this opinion but allowed them to believe what they
would of him. Then the father of Cilla, who owned a modest
estate in the region, took Secum as one of his fieldhands and
put him to work in the vineyards.

Now the vineyards of west Anorel are very great,
covering the hillsides in all directions for many leagues. So
Secum labored daily from cockcrow until sundown in the
vineyards outside Anaroth, working by the sweat of his brow
until his noble face became cracked and weather beaten by the
sun, and his fair hands became calloused and hard. In all things
Secum became like a simple laborer, and the knowledge and

wise sayings that he spoke in his youth continued to elude him. He remained humble and quiet, earning his keep by the work of his hands. In this manner he labored in the vineyards for five years.

Then the father of Cilla gave her unto Secum in marriage in payment for the years of service that Secum had rendered him. So Secum built for himself a home near the vineyards and was made captain over the other laborers. There black-haired Cilla bore to him Orius, their only son. Then Secum said to himself, "Perhaps this exile has been providential, for though I have lost the honors I once enjoyed at Cadaras, I have found true joy in fruit of the vine, the tilling of the earth, the sun upon my face and the embrace of kith and kin at the closing of the day. In comparison to these, worldly wealth and privilege are as dung." When he had said these words, immediately his eyes were opened and the wisdom that had fled from him came flooding back and filled his mind with light.

Then Secum opened his mouth in the vineyards and began to speak in proverbs, saying:*

What can be compared to life of man? It is like a passing shadow or a mist upon the river at the rising of the sun; but a man will give all he possesses to cling to it for but one hour more.

The good and the evil alike come to a common end, and all go down to death; but the memory of the wicked is a curse while the name of the just is pleasant to the ears.

A wise man puffed up with pride is as good as a fool; but silence is the way to true wisdom, industriousness with the hands makes one humble, things the wise will not scorn.

To what can be likened the vice of pride? It is like poison thrown into a well or mold upon the loaf.

Thus did Secum say many such things at Anaroth, so that the laborers came to Cilla and said, "Mistress Cilla, behold, thy husband has turned philosopher!" Black-haired Cilla came out to the fields and beheld Secum uttering proverbs to whomever passed by, whether laborer or freeman. Cilla was greatly amazed by this, for since his coming to Anaroth Secum had been a man of few words.

Word spread that there was a sage of great wisdom in Anaroth, so people came from all over Anorel and the regions by the Gihon to hear Secum teach. At that time King Juna was ruling over Epidymia. He was told, "Behold, great king, there is a man in Anorel who is reputed to be wise and possess the knowledge of the ancients. Let him be brought to thy court that his wisdom be proven." Juna said, "By what name is he called?" and he was told, "He is called Secum of Anaroth." Then Juna marveled and said, "Can this be the same Secum, the son of Manissa, who was exiled from Cadarasia when Egol seized the throne from Gilgax?" So King Juna sent his servants to find Secum and bring him at once to Epidyne, the capital of Epidymia. When the men of Juna came to Anaroth to seize Secum and take him before the king, Secum wept and heaped ashes upon his head, for he knew that Juna would recognize him and would no longer leave him in peace.

When Secum was brought before Juna, the king recognized him at once, for Secum had journeyed to the court of Epidymia in his youth and had once counseled Juna in an important matter. Therefore Juna ordered Secum clothed in royal garments and at once made him one of his ministers. Cilla and Orius, the son of Secum, were sent for and brought to the royal palace at Epidyne to dwell there with Secum. Only then did Cilla come to understand from whence Secum came, and that he was of the house of Manissa. Therefore Juna established Secum in his court, heaped honors upon him, and exalted him above all his other counselors. Secum counseled him, and inasmuch as Juna heeded the words of Secum, hi rule was blessed. So Secum rejoiced again in his good fortune.

But not long after this, word was brought to the court of King Juna that King Egol, Lord of Elabaea, had become a tyrant and was detested by those who had elevated him to the kingship. He was told how the lords of Elabaea had risen up and deposed him, slaying him in the streets of Cadaras. The lords of Asylia had convened at Cadaras and, upon hearing that Secum had been found alive in Epidyne, entreated King Juna to return unto them Secum, who had been abused and wrongfully exiled by Egol. Juna, therefore, reluctantly gave Secum leave to return to Cadaras. Secum arose and took with him Cilla his wife and his only son, Orius, and returned south to Cadaras in hopefulness but with much trepidation.

When Secum arrived in Cadaras, the lords and peoples of that city bowed the knee before him and did him homage. With many gifts and words of kindness they expressed their repentance at the evil which Egol had done to him in the past and entreated his forgiveness. Secum forgave them and blessed them in the name of his mother, and was ushered into the Citadel, where the lords were convened in council to select a new king of Elabaea. But though Secum earnestly looked for his brother Baldor, he was not among them, for Baldor was ill and had not made the journey east from Asylia. Nor was Elphas, lord of Engor present. The absence of his brothers sat ill with him, for he had not seen them in many years.

Two lords were put forth for the kingship, Pirox of Cadaras, son of Lothaross, who had been established in his lordship by Hadrior, and Irodel of Anentora, a lord of that city and an ally of Elphas, brother of Secum. When many arguments had been put forward for each man, the assembly turned to Secum and said, "Wise Secum, let us atone for the evil which was done unto you in the days when we heeded the wicked counsel of Egol, of accursed memory. Please, choose for us one of these two men to be king, and whomsoever you shall choose we shall acknowledge as rightful successor to the throne of Manissa."

But Secum wept, for he foresaw that their hearts were yet far from their words. He said, "You entrust this to me after the affair with Gilgax? Though you rightly value wisdom, you have yet to learn what I have seen by much suffering: that wisdom alone is not enough, for it can succumb to pride and become imprudence, or give way to fear and act out of cowardice. Truly is it said that with much wisdom comes much sorrow, and he who increases in learning increases in tears. You may seek my wisdom to secure the common good, but Fate may arrange things as she pleases. I fear Fate has brought me back into my land only to taunt me with destruction a second time."

But they pressed him, and said, "No, but we will heed you. Give us a king." When he saw that they would not be moved, Secum acceded to their demands and ordered Pirox and Irodel brought before him. Then he said to Pirox and Irodel, "Do you solemnly swear before the gods in the heavens and before Manissa, she who broods behind the clouds and hurls down judgment like a blazing spear, that whatsoever I judge shall be acceptable to you, and that the man I choose will not persecute or slay the man who is not chosen, and that the man who is not chosen will not burn in envy at the appointed ruler, but will serve him with humility?" Then they both said, "We do so swear it."

Then Secum said to all assembled, "Leave me," and when they all left him, he entered the sanctuary of the Temple of Mironna and worshipped alone. Then emerging sometime later, he said, "Bring the men before me," and Pirox and Irodel came before him and knelt. Then Secum took the crown of Manissa and placed it on the head of Irodel, saying, "Hail Irodel, King of all Elabaea! May his reign be blessed and his days long!" But the party of Pirox immediately grumbled and said, "This son of Manissa has passed over our lord Pirox and selected Irodel only by virtue of the latter's friendship with Elphas, his kinsman."

Irodel was indignant and cried out, "My brethren, have you so quickly forgotten your sacred oath?" But the party of Pirox grew angry, and seizing their spears, fell upon Irodel and his men. Then there was fighting throughout the Citadel, Asylian slaying Asylian, and Cadarasian killing Cadarasian, and each killing the other. Then Pirox took up his heavy ashen spear and hurled it at Irodel; the blade pierced his flesh below the heart and brought him crashing to the pavement, blood and life draining from him as his eyes darkened. It so happened that in the fray Secum was struck forcefully with a spear in the back, so that the spearhead came pushing through the front of him. He collapsed to the floor, and when he who had cast the spear drew it forth there was a great wound which could not be staunched. And so Secum son of Manissa gasped and fell dead on the pavement. When the partisans of Pirox had killed or routed all the party of Irodel, Pirox seized the crown of Manissa from the cold body of Irodel and with his bloodied hands placed it upon his own head. Then all raised their gore-soaked blades and cried, "Long live King Pirox! May his reign be blessed!"

The friends and kin of Irodel who escaped the slaughter brought word to black-haired Cilla, who was nursing Orius and awaiting the return of Secum her husband. She wept bitterly at the news, and taking up her son Orius, fled into the west to dwell in the court of Baldor until her days should be completed. But the kinsmen of Irodel gathered outside Cadaras and said, "Shall the death of Irodel go unavenged?" Then they laid siege to Cadaras and stormed the gates, and there was open warfare in the streets for two days. Pirox came forth in battle array to defend his kingship, and the kin of Irodel made fierce war upon him, so that the partisans of Pirox were forced to flee back to the Citadel. Pirox took with him two hundred of his most loyal men and barricaded himself within the Citadel, saying, "They shall not breach the great walls of the Citadel or lay hands on me so long as I remain hidden behind its mighty gates." But the people of Cadaras rose up and joined the kinsmen of Irodel, so when the men of Pirox saw that they were greatly outnumbered, they said among themselves, "What inheritance have we in Pirox son of Lothaross?" Then they seized Pirox and struck off his head, and hurling it over the walls of the Citadel to the mob, secured their lives.

But Secum, son of Manissa, was grieved over by the people with much lamentation and was entombed in the courtyard of the Temple of Mironna in Cadaras, near the spot where he was killed at the foot of the stairs, by the place where the morning hymns were sung.

The Council of Lords and the Great Census

ꙮ꙯ ꙮ꙯ ꙮ꙯

Following the deaths of Anaxandra, Egol, grandson of Eridax, and Gilgax, the son-in-law of Baldor, were elevated to the kingship. Yet not long after this Egol slew Gilgax and seized the fullness of the kingship for himself, reigning as a tyrant for five years. This Egol, when he had dispatched Gilgax and exiled Secum, son of Manissa, slew many valiant men of Cadarasia, even daring to strike one of the sons of Elphas. He also pillaged the treasury of the Citadel and robbed many of the lords of both their wealth and their daughters, so that he grew hateful in their sight and became like a stench in their nostrils. Finally, when the lords had their fill of Egol's thievery, they laid hands on him and cast him down the steps of the Citadel, into the streets of Cadaras, and there fell upon him and beat him to death with clubs, leaving his body for the dogs and the carrion.

Then was Secum recalled from Epidymia, and Irodel, a companion of Elphas, was put forth and chosen for the kingship. But those supporting his contender, Pirox, prevailed, for Baldor was not present at the assembly, being too old to make the journey east, and Elphas was laid low in Engor with a fever. The partisans of Pirox, therefore, overcame Irodel and slew him, and with him Secum, son of Manissa. But the people of Cadaras were repulsed by the arrogance of Pirox and besieged him in the Citadel. So fierce was their opposition to him that Pirox's own men mutinied and beheaded him, casting his head to the kin of Irodel in exchange for their lives. Then there was no king in Cadaras, for no lord was strong enough to take upon himself the kingship. The lords, too, were weary of intrigue, for in five and a half years the kingdom of the Manissans was ruled by four kings who had each gone down to death in blood.

The lords therefore assembled themselves together in Cadaras after the burial rites of Secum were completed and said, "Let us be done with kings!* For in the days of our fathers' fathers, before the coming of Manissa, it was custom that each city was ruled by its own liege-lord, whose dignity was only as great as the city he ruled. Search the records of the deeds of our fathers and you will see that Ioclus and Garba had no regal authority over other cities save a primacy of honor, and that it was only by the victories of Manissa and the expansion of her house that all Elabaea was united under a single crown. Therefore, let Cyrenaica see to Cyrenaica, Asylia to Asylia, Cadaras to Cadarasia, Anentora to the Anentorans and every city and village unto itself."

All of the lords agreed to this, for it increased their own power and removed from them any king or ruler to whom they would have to answer. But some said, "Let us still gather together here for the discussing of matters that pertain to the whole realm, as it was wont to be done in the days of our grandfathers." So from that day forward there was no king in the land, but a council of lords gathered in Cadaras to decide what each region would do. The first act decreed by this Council of Lords was a census of every important city in the realm and to whom it was subject.*

Who can tell of all the mighty men of renown who were counted in the census? And since when have so many great ones lived at the same time, in the shadows of each other? For from the south there was Elphas, son of Manissa and Lord of the South, who ruled in Engor, the city of Necho, and with him the three elder sons of Necho: Necastor, Aïross and Pilux, the youngest of whom was but ten years of age and who later grew to be a mighty lord in Corbalund. Elphas also had his own sons who became mighty men of renown, two in number: Nelus and Ereth; the third, Assio, having been slain by Egol. Also present from the south was Numo, a warrior of Engor and companion of Elphas who was created Lord of Anentora upon the taking of the city by Baldor and Elphas. Besides Numo and Elphas were many other lords from the south, all rulers of great houses: Indaross, Aigos, Emmurax, Giathor and Aranoss. So all the lords from Anentora and the southlands were twelve, and they ruled over Engor, Anentora, and their environs, forty thousand souls.

And what of the hill country going into the mountains of Bados, and going northwest by the Nimru Pass and the desolate region of the Dindumon? The lord of this realm was Calcax of Avlos, who built the fortress Temoras in the Dindumon and made war on the hill people of the Bados from there. Thus Calcax was lord of all that land, seven thousand souls.

Cadaras, the City on the Plain, was given over to the house of Eridax, according to the will of Manissa, yet not of the line of Egol, who had profaned the kingship and done wickedly. Rather, it was given unto the son of the brother of Egol, Rammol, who was made Lord of Cadaras by the Council of Lords. Rammol in turn set Iös over the regions of Molossía, Elos, and Avlos, and Indrior over the regions east of the Cadar, going towards Caeylon; but the northernmost marches of Cadarasia, those that border Epidymia and mingle their waters with the Gihon and the Sehu, were ruled by Mammux. Many other lords and men of renown dwelt in the east: Thrasos, Narox, and Panastor. So all of the lords of Cadarasia and the east were eight, and they ruled all the lands of that region, one hundred thirty thousand souls.

In the lands bordering the Erriad to the east and to the west, the region called Nearer Asylia or Asylia-by-Erriad, Irux held the lordship. This Irux had held sway there for many years since the death of Arummnax of Orioön and his house and was friendly to both Anaxandra and to the Hazerites, the latter of whom were still dwelling in An Erras. Irux gave the lordship of An Erras to Milco, a companion of Hazer, and entrusted the northernmost parts of Nearer Asylia—those reaching into the wilds that border on Ituria—to a kinsman of his, Ninus by name. Ninus also ruled over Gela, the family of Gygas the Accursed having been displaced in the time of Anaxandra. Thus the lords of that region were three, and they ruled over An Erras, the lands skirting the Erriad, and the frontiers going up as far as Ituria, twenty thousand souls.

Cyrenaica was forfeited by the house of Toranoss after the defeat of Hadrior at Enna, but it passed to some distant kin of Hadrior, the Temenids, from Temenus, first lord to rule that land after the death of Toranoss and his house. In the days of Anaxandra it passed unto Peredoss son of Temenus, who held it at the time of the census. Peredoss ruled Cyrenaica as a king and appointed no other lords, so that land was subject to one lord alone, governing seventy thousand souls.*

Farther Asylia, also called Western Asylia or old Asylia, was still in the keep of Baldor, son of Manissa, who was fifty-two years of age by the time of the census and in poor health. Though Asylia was the seat of Baldor's power, he had also five lords who ruled with him: Nico of Kerion, Manlius of Paros and Teleth of Argenna, in addition to Maxos (who held the regions of Enna and the frontiers with Lugaria), and Ossarion, a half-Marudan of the Manruthim who kept watch over the Cyrian Highlands and served as an envoy from the court of Baldor to the Manruthim. Thus all the lords of Farther Asylia were six, and they ruled over Asylia, the Cyrian Highlands, the regions of Kerion, Paros and their environs, with Enna, some ninety thousand souls.

Thus all the Manissan peoples, those who were of the Asylians or Cadarasians or pledged loyalty to the lordship at Cadaras and followed Manissa, were three hundred and forty-seven thousand persons, not counting women and children.* This census was delivered to the Council of Lords who sat enthroned in white-walled Cadaras in the Citadel on the first day of the sixth month in the second year of the sitting of the Council, being the fifty-seventh year since the Asylians first took up arms against the Marudans and the thirty-ninth year since the passing of Manissa from the world. So the land roundabout had peace under the administration of the Council of Lords, who nevertheless excluded the sons of Manissa from a share in the rulership of the realm, for which they were to be justly punished thereafter.*

Perior

⬥⬥⬥

he last child born of Blessed Manissa was Perior, who came into the world the same year Manissa departed it and had no memory of his mother. For some time he was a ward of Hadrior, but after the fall of Cyrenaica he went west with his brother Baldor and was raised in his court at Asylia. At the court of Baldor he was given into the care of an old nursemaid named Lana. This Lana had been a servant of Ioclus in her youth, had ministered at Manissa's table for many years, and was devoted to the house of Ioclus. She reared Perior like he was her own. In all respects Perior was like other children, handsome and of average intelligence, with curly black locks that caused the older men of Asylia to say that he bore the image of Arrax of old.

But when Perior was about seven years of age he manifested his great strength for the first time. He was assisting his nursemaid Lana and some of the other servants in the stables of Baldor when one of the horses tripped in a rut and fell on top of a stable hand, crushing him grievously. Immediately Perior rushed upon the horse, and heaving it up, flung it off with little effort, thus saving the servant and stunning those who stood by. Lana then took the boy into the rocky wilds west of Asylia, in the region of the Manruthim, and ordered him to cast stones, each time picking up a larger stone until he found a one so large he could not hurl it. The boy Perior obeyed Lana but found that they ran out of stones to throw before they came across one so large that Perior could not lift it.*

Lana brought the boy before Baldor, his brother, and told him of his extraordinary strength. Baldor put Perior to similar trials and marveled at his great power, for unlike the might of Baldor, which came and went with his rage in battle, the strength of Perior abided with him at all times. Therefore, Baldor took Perior from the care of Lana and entrusted him to Gilgax, his friend and fellow war-captain, to be trained in the art of war. When Perior had finished training with Gilgax each day, he was sent to Indor Aíroth, that is Indor the Star-Gazer, servant of Baldor, to be taught poetry and writing. As the boy Perior grew, all the court of Asylia marveled at his power and the feats of strength he continually performed there. When he was fourteen years old, he pulled up the two great posts of the Hall of Orix (all that remained of the ancient Hall, the rest having been burned by the Marudans in the time of Manissa) and carried them on his shoulders to the Hall of Baldor, where they were set up about the throne of Baldor and remain unto this day.*

But though Perior excelled at the craft of war taught to him by Gilgax, he disdained the poetry and the writing which Indor attempted to impart to him. In Perior's eighteenth year, Baldor and the armies of Asylia went forth to make war on the Illyrs in accordance with the will of Queen Anaxandra. Though Perior earnestly entreated Baldor that he might be permitted to go also to war, Baldor refused, for he remembered the death of his own son Belar in the war with the Lugars and feared that his brother might similarly perish. Therefore he left Perior in the care of Indor and went forth to the south. But Perior was very wroth about this and treated Indor poorly, speaking rudely to him and refusing to present himself when it was time for his lessons.

One afternoon Indor went hunting for Perior and found him some distance from Asylia at the Brook of Elor, for the boy was reclining and attempting to catch fish with his bare hands. Indor rebuked the lad for his truancy and ordered him to return to the city, but Perior refused. Indor insisted that Perior return at once, but Perior only laughed and remained obstinate. Then Indor became angered and threatened Perior, saying "I will give your brother Baldor an ill report and he will chasten you with lashes!" Then Perior took up a branch that had fallen from a nearby tree and struck Indor in the head, hoping to knock him senseless so that he could flee and hide somewhere for the remainder of the day. But when the blow landed it shattered the skull of Indor, so that his brains were dashed out and splattered about the place. When Perior realized that he had unwittingly killed Indor, he wept vehemently and fled into the wilderness. Thus perished Indor Aíroth, he who had first spied Laoön in the heavens.

It was many days until Baldor returned from the war and was told about the killing of Indor. Baldor was deeply grieved for the loss of his friend, but also concerned about the whereabouts of Perior. He immediately sent his scouts out to find the lad and bring him back to Asylia. But search as they may, they could find no trace of him.

Perior fled into the west and dwelt in the wilderness of Enna for some time, living off harts that he snared and fish that he was able to catch. It was in the wilderness that Perior grew to manhood. He became exceedingly hairy, so that his front and back were covered with thick hair and his face covered by a great beard. The hair of his head grew long and wild and his clothes deteriorated, so that he was forced to wear the skins of the deer he killed for his food. By and by he came to the Kingdom of Lugaria and the pillared city of Karanak, where his sister Mariammné was reigning gloriously as wife of King Cygnus. When he was shown into the presence of Cygnus and Mariammné, his sister did not recognize him at first. He said, "Do you not know me, sister? I do not marvel at this, for I have but seen thee only three times in my life, for since I was young you have dwelt here as Queen of Lugaria. Know with certainty that I am no common rogue wanderer, but am Perior, son of Manissa and youngest of your brothers."

When Mariammné heard this she rejoiced to see her brother but wondered at his appearance. They spoke together at great length and talked of many things, and Perior said to his sister, "Gracious sister, your kingdom is pleasant, and your realm blessed. Therefore, grant that I may abide here with you. Petition your husband, lordly Cygnus, to grant me some position or office in his court that I may abide here in your presence." Mariammné brought this petition to Cygnus, but Cygnus had heard from Baldor of all that had occurred in Asylia and of the killing of Indor. He said to his wife Mariammné, "Dearest wife, though the affection you show towards your brother moves my heart, I fear to have him too close about, for his strength is very great and he knows not his own power. Have you not heard how he slew the favorite servant of your brother by sheer accident? I fear that if we retain him here in Karanak, sooner or later some disaster will befall us, for I have an ill feeling concerning him. Therefore, grant him land in the far west, on the borders of our country near the wilderness, far from Karanak and Asylia."

This advice seemed good to Mariammné, and so she said to Perior, "Brother, take the lands my husband lord Cygnus has given you and dwell in the west, to be lord of the western marches." So Perior withdrew to the west with joy, for he said, "I will be a great lord among the Lugars." But when he reached the lands allotted to him, eleven days from Karanak going west, he saw that they were bereft of people and desolate, for the trees fell away and the land was rugged and empty, covered only by short heather and bracken, and buffeted by fierce winds and storms from the southern sea. He was offended by the trickery of his sister and wandered further west, departing Lugaria and coming into the westernmost wilderness that borders the sea. This land had once been inhabited by the sons of Samnor, but it was now a rugged place that had for some time been the abode of a cruel race of hill giants who were accustomed to devour any man who attempted to pass by this route.*

When Perior came into this land, he was accosted by a certain giant named Goar, who fastened his belt a cubit above the head of an average man. When he saw Perior coming, he came down from his abode on the hilltop and brought with him his kin. They surrounded Perior, mocked his rugged appearance, and said, "Does a man now wish to dwell among the giants?" But Perior said, "If you are going to slay me then make your move, for this coarse jesting wearies me." Goar was incensed and said, "Impudent wretch! We will show you how we deal with your kind. I shall pull your limbs off and feast on your flesh!" Then Goar attempted to grasp Perior, but Perior was stronger than he had reckoned, and the two wrestled about on the hard earth. By and by Perior prevailed and caught the head of Goar beneath his arm. Goar begged to be released, but Perior cried to those kin of Goar who were gathered nearby, saying, "Mark this well you bastard sons of earth! Here is what becomes of those who trade blows with Perior son of Manissa!" Then he squeezed the head of Goar within his iron arms until he heard the bones of the giant's neck crush. Goar went limp, and Perior cast his lifeless hulk upon the heather before the other giants, who stood dumbfounded and then fled. For four years Perior roamed that wasteland, and whenever he encountered the hill giants he wrestled them to the death or otherwise slew them, until the land was free of them, and men could again pass freely from east to west.

When the land was cleared of giants Perior again set out, and wandering north, he came to the southern edges of the great Arcorian Wood, which the Lugarians called Adarwood, for it was here that the Caeylonic general Adaran was defeated and routed by Manissa in days gone by. Perior came to the Arcorian and dwelt in its shadow, building himself a cottage in its breezy shade. Then he went forth into the wood several days until he came to a place thick with a multitude of elms that came rolling down to a riverbed. There a delicate crystal stream tumbled over the rocky bed and passed on towards the southern sea. The bank of the stream was dotted with rowan trees, ripe with their bright red clusters of berries. Perior began to descend the hill to cross over the stream and feed on the rowan berries, but lo, he heard footfalls in the wood and hid himself behind the trunk of a mighty elm. Looking out he saw a train of nymphs approaching, glorious and beautiful in the dappled sunlight. Nine of them there were, arrayed in delicate gowns of finest linens colored with viridian and aquamarine and every shade of green, their hair worn up in intricate loops and braids adorned with flowers of various kinds. They processed down to the bank, laughing gaily and moving lightly over the mossy earth. Music and joy were in their laughter and their every movement was full of grace and beauty, so much so that Perior was stricken with love. They came unto the rowan trees and began picking the berry clusters, talking merrily and eating the sweet berries that they picked with their flawless hands.*

When Perior could no longer restrain himself he lunged forth from his place of concealment. He was a frightful sight to the nymphs and caused them to shriek and vanish away into the wood. Yet, before they could all flee, he grasped the arm of the maiden nearest to him. She struggled and pleaded but try as she might she could not free herself from the grasp of Perior. She turned herself into a great swan, but Perior held her fast about the neck and would not be parted from her. Then she turned herself into a doe and attempted to dash away, but iron armed Perior held her fast and refused to let her go. Finally, she changed her form to that of a great snake, a form nymphs are usually loath to take, and by this tried to wrest herself out of Perior's grip. But Perior held fast, and she could by no means extricate herself from his grasp. Finally, she revealed her true form to him and said, "No mortal can hold me as fast as you have done so this day. What must I do to get you to release me?" Perior said, "I will release you only if you swear to give yourself to me in marriage." The nymph said, "Surely you must know that if a nymph gives herself to a mortal that she will lose her immortality? True, my beauty and powers will remain for some time, perhaps even longer than the life of one of your women, but in the end they will fade away and I will dissolve into nothingness." Perior said, "Even so, I will have thee to be my wife. Swear it by all you hold sacred, and I will release thee." Then she said, "I do so swear it shall be so, by holy Agenor, by this hallowed wood, and by all the gods invoked by thy people." So Perior released her, and the nymph returned with him to his home in the shade of the southern woods; there the two became husband and wife. The nymph's name was Ciphoné, and from that day forward she lived as a mortal, though she sometimes heard the whisperings of the trees on the breeze of the evening.

Ciphoné and Perior dwelt together on the border of the Arcorian for many years. Ciphoné came to love Perior and was devoted to him, and he to her. She bore to Perior ten sons. The first were twins, Erytas and Marax, both mighty men of valor. Then followed Echol, Semnos, Antyas, Aïos, Crastor and Arrax, who was called Arrax the Younger. Then some years passed, and Ciphoné conceived and brought forth Cassos and then the youngest son, whom they called Cerdos, which means "return." Each of the sons of Perior was marvelous and beautiful like their mother but excelled in strength like their father, so in all the west there was no one as glorious as they. When they went down to trade with the villages of Lugaria, the people there fled from them and called them the *Tythodii*, which means "gods of the west," for their countenance was radiant, their voices commanding and sure, and their strength matchless.

But in the fifteenth year of the marriage of Ciphoné and Perior, word made its way west that in far off Cadaras two rival factions, one led by Pirox, another by Irodel, strove for the kingship. Perior heard that these two lords had both been killed in an insurrection in the city, in which his brother Secum had also been slain. He learned that the great men of the kingdom had sworn off any kingship, choosing instead to be governed by a Council of Lords.

When Perior heard this he wept, not only for the death of Secum, but for the ill fortune of the house of Manissa, which was thrust out of power everywhere in the west save for the court of Baldor in Asylia. Therefore, he burned with anger and told Ciphoné, "I must return to the court of my brother Baldor, whom I have not laid eyes on in nearly twenty years. I must make amends with him while he still lives and see if I can regain the fortunes of our house." But she said to him, "Nay, let it not be so, my lord, for you will leave me behind here alone when our children are but young and some are not yet weaned. Put this deed off until the youngest can stand with his brothers and the oldest have hair on their faces." So Perior heeded the words of his wife and brooded.

Thus Perior remained in the west for eight more years with his wife, the nymph Ciphoné, while his sons grew in stature and power. When eight years had been completed, he said to his wife, "Let me depart, my wife, for our youngest son, Cerdos, is now ten years of age and able to walk with his brothers and carry the burdens of manhood. Our eldest, Erytas and Marax, are two and twenty and in all things able to care for you in my absence. Therefore, give me your blessing, gracious lady, that I may depart east to see my brother Baldor and restore the fortunes of my house." Ciphoné said, "Go, my beloved, and may Fate be kind unto thee." So Perior bid Ciphoné and his sons farewell and departed for the east.

When he came to the court of Baldor he was welcomed by his brother. Baldor now old and advanced in years, with a gnarled grey beard and locks of silver upon his hoary head. When Perior saw Baldor, he embraced him and begged forgiveness for the killing of Indor. Baldor absolved him of this crime in the sight of all the court; Perior paid five bars of gold to the kin of Indor Aíroth as blood money. So all rejoiced for the return of mighty Perior. There was feasting and excitement in Asylia, for also at the court of Baldor at that time were also Calanthé, daughter of Baldor and widow to Giglax; Cilla, the widow of Secum with her young son Orius, and Mariammné, who had come east to dwell with her brother after the death of her husband, King Cygnus. There was merriment and joy at the reunion the three children of Manissa and their kin.

But when the days of feasting were over, Perior urged Baldor, saying, "Brother, the time is come for us to reclaim our inheritance which was stolen in the days of Hadrior. Let us ride together to Cadaras! You and our brother Elphas are mighty men of war, and my power is unmatched anywhere in Elabaea. Let us storm the gates of Cadaras and hurl these robber-lords from their thrones, that once again the land our mother struggled for may be ruled by her house as is fitting."

Baldor scoffed and said, "I am old and wretched, brother. All whom I cared for have been taken from me, save Calanthé, my daughter. In the days of my youth, Erogel, son of Arrax, our kinsman and my companion, was killed by Hadrior. Not long after I was bereaved of my firstborn son, Belar, who went to fight in Lugaria and was slain before he yet had a hair upon his chin. Alas! Then some years later, by your own hand was taken from me Indor, dearest of all my servants, he who first sighted the sign of the spear, Laoön, north in the Rua Calidé in the days of my glory. Now I have only recently ended the days of mourning for my kin in arms and son-in-law, brave Gilgax, who was treacherously murdered by the tyrant Egol when he came in peace. I have no desire that any

124

more men should perish or that more I care for should be taken from me. Therefore, do what you will, but do not presume upon my aid."

Hearing this, Perior grew angry and said, "Do not bring up your sorrows to me, you son of sloth and lord of laziness! Shall I tell you why your woes have befallen you and our house? Behold, I shall tell you what no other will say to thy face, for I will recount the sins of Baldor. First, that when Hadrior betrayed and murdered our cousin Erogel, son of Arrax, you would not avenge his death but instead swore an oath of kinship and faithfulness to Hadrior when you ought to have thrust a spear through his belly. Furthermore, though you were entrusted with the most precious heirloom of Asylia, the great spear of Ioclus our grandsire, you recklessly gambled it away; then, after reclaiming it by murdering three men, you again lost it by hurling it into the sea after you foolishly challenged the army of Hadrior to fight to the death for it. Thus you lost the last relic of our mother and the symbol of our authority. In the third place, when the house of Arrax was extinct upon the passing of Anaxandra, and many of the lords were clamoring for you to take your rightful place upon the throne of Cadaras, you instead withdrew your name, for you had grown fat and complacent, and rather than reaching forth and grasping what is rightfully ours, you put forth your comrade Gilgax, one who had no part of the house of Manissa save by marriage to your daughter. For these three sins have you been bereaved three times, and by your foolishness we have been disinherited all throughout Elabaea."

When Perior finished saying these things Baldor was speechless. His companions cried out, "My lord, will you give no answer to these insults?" But Baldor said, "Though a man in this life weighs his decisions carefully, taking no action without first considering all its consequences, yet even the smallest of choices is carved in stone, for no man can go back and undo even the littlest of all his deeds. What my brother

Perior says is true, for I have preferred the comfort and fellowship of my hall to the struggles that would have surely awaited me had I asserted myself and our house. Yet even so, I remain firm in my judgment. Though men once trembled before my gore-soaked spear as I made war on Cyrenaica and Illyrana, it shall be so no more, for my hairs are grey and my arm has fallen weak, nevermore to cast a spear in anger. Go thy way, Perior my brother, and may your actions be guided by prudence and courage."

So Baldor sent Perior to Nico, lord of Kerion, who fitted Perior in royal garments and a suit of armor of finely beaten bronze overlaid with scales wrought by Belar. Then Baldor gave Perior his own sword which he had fought with at Anentora, that which had been forged by Belar in the flower of his youth. And Baldor blessed him and went with him as far as the crossroads at Croas, there embracing him once more, and afterward returned to Asylia.

Perior went east into the domain of Asylia-by-Erriad, where Milco, a companion of Hazer, was holding dominion under Irux. Here he turned aside and came into An Erras, where his brother Hazer dwelt on the poplar covered hill of Ar Pelaroth. When Perior came to An Erras it was night, but he ascended the hill of Ar Pelaroth and demanded to see Hazer his brother. Hazer, not knowing it was his brother Perior, replied that it was too late to receive guests and that he should return in the morning. But Perior said, "It is I, your younger brother Perior, who has come from the remote west." When he heard this, Hazer arose and received him rejoicing. Perior wasted no time, but said to him, "Brother, since the time of your youth the power of life and death, of blessing and cursing, has been in your tongue. Therefore, come forth and sing towards Cadaras, the City on the Plain; sing of victory and triumph of the house of Manissa and of woe for those who oppose her sons."

Hazer said, "The stars are still high in the firmament, and it has not been my custom to sing during the night. Let this matter be put off until morning; for now, let us talk together and feast." But Perior did not want to be detained and pressed him vehemently, so that finally Hazer went forth groggily and stood upon the stone which he was accustomed, and looking eastward toward Cadaras, began to sing. But because of the lateness of the hour and the heaviness of his eyes, he erred in singing the words Perior had given him, and instead of blessing, pronounced woe upon the sons of Manissa and blessing upon their foes.

When Perior realized this, he beat his fists to the ground in anger and said, "What have you done, you fool? You have cursed me and blessed my enemies! Therefore, take it back and sing as I have said." But Hazer said, "Did I not tell you it was night? What I have sung, I have sung. Yet shall the sons of Manissa be blessed in the end (for this has been revealed to me), but it shall come many years off, and not before our enemies trample our house underfoot." Perior marveled at the words of Hazer, saying, "I have come to you seeking blessing and instead find our house cursed! Cursed be the day my eyes see you again, brother!" Then Hazer said, "You have said it." Then Perior left Hazer and descended Ar Pelaroth, and crossing over the Erriad, came into the region of Cadarasia, which was being ruled by Rammol of the house of Eridax, all Elabaea being at that time governed by the Council of Lords.

When Perior came into Cadarasia he was accosted by the lord Indrior and a party of his warriors on his way east. This Indrior was a friend of Rammol and a lord in that region. Indrior said to him, "Who are you who walk with such boldness and power in your strides? Are you of the house of Manissa, perhaps some son of Baldor?" Perior said, "I am Perior, son of Manissa, my lord." When Indrior heard this he trembled, for the strength of Perior was known throughout the west. Indrior said, "What business have you here, Perior son of

Manissa? Is not your dwelling in the far west with the giants and nymphs, in lands of bracken and wind?" Perior did not conceal his intentions, but said plainly, "I am come east to claim the throne of Cadaras, which rightfully belongs to the house of Manissa, for since the days of Hadrior we have been disinherited from the kingship our mother won. Furthermore, the land has been without a king these eight years since the Council of Lords set up their thrones in the Citadel."

Then Indrior drew his sword and said, "Know you not to whom you speak? I am Indrior, one of the lords of Elabaea of this very Council, which you would seek to overthrow. Turn back, son of Manissa, for no good can come of your plan." Then Perior laughed, and his laugh shook the trees and caused the horses of Indrior and his men to tremble. He said, "It is you, my lord Indrior, who do not know to whom you speak. I have crushed the heads of giants within these hands of mine and thrown others to the ground in submission; I have grasped the nymphs of Arcoria so tightly that they could by no means escape my hold. I have pulled the very beams of Orix from the earth, which Orix, son of Manx, planted in days gone by. Will you now threaten me with your sword of beaten bronze?"

Then Indrior lunged at Perior and swung his glittering blade at him, but Perior dodged the blow, and grabbing the horse of Indrior by the legs, swung the steed through the air and flung Indrior off. Indrior crashed into a bramble bush in stunned amazement. The warriors with Indrior, seven men in all, cast their spears at Perior. No cast hit its mark, for they all fell short or sailed past him harmlessly. Then Perior picked up a boulder and cast it at the seven men, crushing all but two beneath it. Indrior cried out, and, coming forth from the brambles, again attacked Perior with his blade. Mighty Perior wrenched the blade from Indrior's hands and broke it over his knee, laughing in scorn. At this Indrior wept and fell to his knees and said, "Woe to me that I fell in with thee. I pray, hold my life precious in your sight!" Perior said, "Return, you and your men, to Cadaras. Tell the lords who hold title to this land that I have come to claim the throne of Manissa." So Indrior and the remaining warriors fled back to Cadaras and told Rammol and the Council of Lords all that Perior had done and spoke. Then a great fear fell upon the lords and all the people of Cadaras.

It was not long after this that Perior came up to Cadaras and was sighted approaching the city. The Council of Lords had been seated in the Citadel, debating what to do regarding Perior. When they were told that he was approaching, they cried, "Bar the gates!" So the gates were locked, and the city made secure. Within the city were the eight lords of Cadarasia and the east: Rammol, Iös, Indrior, Mammux, Thrasos, Narox, and Panastor, as well as Calcax of Avlos, who reigned in the south going towards the lands of Bados. When Perior came to the gates of Cadaras and found them sealed fast against him, he cried out, "A curse upon those who would seal the gates of this city against me, whose own house has delivered it from the tyranny of the Marudans in the days of my mother and her kin!* Will you now cede the kingship unto me, rightful heir to the throne of Asylia and all Elabaea?" But the lords sent word to Perior saying, "We will not cede the city, nor will we serve any of the sons of Manissa."

Perior, full of anger, grasped the northern guard tower, which stood beside the west gate of Cadaras. With a terrible roar he ripped the stones from the foundation so that the tower came toppling down, crushing all those men stationed upon it. A frightful cry went up from the warriors manning the walls, and with one accord they began to hurl javelins and fire arrows at Perior. But Perior swatted them away with his arm like so many gnats, and making his way to the south tower, wrapped his iron arms about the base of it and pulled apart its foundations, so that it collapsed and became a heap of ruins, killing all the men who were upon it. The height of the towers was twenty cubits each, and their width such that seven men locking hands could not encompass them.

Then Perior went up straightaway and smashed the gates of the city, destroying them utterly. All the people fled before him, as before a god in the day of his wrath. The Council locked themselves in the Citadel and gave orders that the entire garrison of the city be dispatched against Perior. So Indrior and Rammol took charge of four thousand men bearing spears of whetted bronze and led them up the main thoroughfare of the city to block Perior's approach. Perior drew the sword which his brother Baldor had given him and roared like a lion about to pounce. Then he cried "Cruacha!" and raged into the legions brought against him, striking with ferocious power every which way, severing limbs, and cleaving men in two down to the navel.

Who were among those he slew in his rage? Two arrogant young brothers, Iulos and Ennos, sought to win glory and thought to bring down Perior son of Manissa. Fools! They took their aim, they cast their spears, but the blades crumpled against the armor of Belar that Perior wore. Perior said, "Let me show you how it is done!" Then he picked up a spear from one of his slain foes and cast it at the brothers. It struck Iulos with great force, driving through his belly and out his back and sunk also into the gut of Ennos who was behind him. The brothers groaned and thrashed like boars stuck on a spit. Both collapsed upon the pavement, their blood mingling together in death.

Another fool sought to cross blades with Perior, one Beryx, a young companion of Rammol. He thought to come upon Perior from the rear by stealth, but Perior turned and hacked off his arm at the shoulder. Perior gnashed his teeth and struck again at Beryx with such force that he halved that wretch in two, and his torso was separated from him at his hips. A kinsman of Beryx, Goras, came to drag away the body of his friend, but Perior caught him in his eye and thrust his blade at him. It sunk into the soft flesh of his throat and Goras collapsed beside the trunk of his companion, blood and life draining from his open wound.

When the warriors of Cadaras saw how Perior raged and how all who came near him fell, they cried in fright and retreated. Rammol and Indrior sought to rally them, but the guards of the city fled as men doomed, like the gazelles of the plains flee before a lion. Rammol said to Indrior, "I will not be deprived of my rule so easily. Is not the blood of Eridax the bold in my veins? Perhaps Perior will not dispatch me so easily!" Indrior said, "Your blood is upon your own head if you cross him." So Rammol took up his spear and cast it at Perior, but it missed its mark. Perior growled in rage, and when he turned and saw Rammol his blood became hot. Rammol drew his sword and closed with Perior, but when they locked blades, Rammol saw that Perior fought unlike any other man, and that compared to Perior he was like a child in strength and stature. He turned and sought to flee, but Perior grasped him about the belt and heaved him up over his head, bearing him aloft in the sight of all. Rammol wailed helplessly, but Perior laughed and said, "Behold what becomes of those who war against the house of Manissa!" Then, seeing a troupe of spearman nearby watching in terror, Perior hurled him upon them so that the body of Rammol was impaled upon the upright spears of his own warriors which they bore aloft.

Then came Indrior, sword drawn. Perior said, "You are guilty of your own death, Indrior, for I turned you loose when I had you in my grasp, but I shall not spare you from death a second time." But Indrior said, "I may not match you in strength or skill with the blade but let no one say I was not your equal in bravery. Let us lock blades, come what may." Perior replied, "Well said, brave and noble Indrior. I wish Fate had arranged our allegiance otherwise. But let us be done with it." Then Indrior closed with Perior, and the ringing of swords pierced the air. But Indrior was no match for the son of

Manissa; Perior struck him but once and knocked his head off his body, leaving the lifeless trunk of Indrior crumpled upon the flagstones of the street.

Perior leapt into the fray and struck this way and that, bringing death all about him. All the men sent against him were in rout; the streets of Cadaras were littered with the bodies of the slain. Perior came unto the great gates of the Citadel, which were sealed fast against him. The lords therein went to the battlements and saw him standing there, mired in dirt and gore, breathing threats against them, and they feared for their lives. Perior called out, "It is to your benefit that it is now the closing of the day. I will give you the night to surrender the Citadel to me while I take my rest. If you have not handed it over by sunrise and exiled yourselves from Elabaea, I will demolish this fortress, ancient though it be, and bring you down to the pit in death. Nor will I withdraw my hand from the slaughter till every one of you is slain." Then he reclined in the courtyard outside the Citadel and napped against an elm tree there. He slumbered in peace, for no man dared approach him.

Then the lords said to one another, "Both Rammol and Indrior are slain. We cannot hope to prevail against him by force of arms. We need some stratagem to deceive him, or some means of trickery by which he can be ensnared." Then Thrasos, one of the lords of the east and a companion of Indrior, said, "I have in my keeping a certain poison that I have obtained from the Caeylonic merchants who come from Ganas. Let us find some woman to mingle it with some wine and bring it to him." This seemed good to the lords, and so they fetched a certain prostitute and bid her mingle the poison with some wine and take it to Perior, promising her one thousand gold coins if she would accomplish this task. So she did as she was instructed, and approaching Perior in the courtyard said, "My lord?" He leapt up with a start, sword in hand, but upon seeing it was only a woman, sheathed his blade and said, "Why do you wake me, woman?"

She knelt before him, saying, "My lord Perior, have mercy on your people! Let it be known that we of Cadaras have no love for these arrogant men who claim to rule what rightfully belongs to thee. We earnestly pray for thy success on the morrow when you drive them out of this place and claim the throne that is rightly thine!" Perior softened his demeanor to her and said, "Well spoken, woman. May it be as you have said. But what do you bring me?" She gave him the flagon of wine and said, "Fine wine to quench your thirst and lighten your heart." Perior took the poisoned flagon gladly and drank it to the dregs, then resumed his slumber under the elm. The woman returned to the lords and said, "It is done." So each of them gave her a sum of money amounting to one thousand gold coins, and she departed to go to her own place.

At sunrise Perior stood up boldly, intending to destroy the gates of the Citadel and slay the Council of Lords. But when he arose and saw the light of the sun in his eyes, his stomach turned, and his head was wracked with pain. He tried to walk but his steps were unsure; faltering, he leaned upon the elm tree for support. The world swirled before him, and in that moment he knew he had been poisoned. The lords upon the battlements saw him stumble and said, "Perior has succumbed to the poison! Every man to their spears! Let us take him!" When Perior heard this cry and saw that the men were losing their terror of him, he turned and fled. The lords came forth from the Citadel and pursued him with a hastily assembled legion of two thousand men.

Finding a steed, Perior mounted it and rode swiftly out of the city, weakening with sickness at each passing moment. He crossed the Erriad by nightfall and came into the region of An Erras, near the place where Hazer his brother was dwelling, and managed to bring himself to the hill of Ar Pelaroth. No sooner did he arrive at Ar Pelaroth that his strength failed him, and he collapsed at the foot of the hill. Hazer came forth, and, seeing his brother ill, carried him up into his dwelling. Iyla, wife of Hazer, was also there, for it was the time of the month when she dwelt with him. Hazer and Iyla ministered to Perior and tended him through the night while Perior thrashed with a severe fever. Iyla said, "My husband, your words have the power to bring life to the dying. Sing unto thy brother and restore him to life." So Hazer knelt before the bedside of Perior and sung a song of blessing, invoking the aid of his immortal mother and telling of many glorious things. Even so Perior did not improve, but rather seemed to grow more ill. Hazer's wife Iyla said, "How is it that your song cannot heal him?" Hazer said, "My wife, the sons of Manissa have diverse powers and gifts. In my voice is the power of life or death, blessing or cursing. But in Perior is the gift of strength surpassing all other strength of men, and he, too, is a son of Manissa. Therefore, his power is greater than mine, inasmuch as he is mightier than I. My words now seem to fall impotent before him, even as he lies impotent." Iyla wept and said, "Must he die then?" Hazer said, "I have sung the song of Manissa. Let it be as she wills." So they remained with Perior through that night.

In the morning Perior awoke and was chilled through and through. "Brother!" he cried to Hazer. "Come to me, for I have had a dream that has stolen the life from my veins." Hazer said, "Tell me." So Perior said, "Behold, all was darkness, but then, in the midst of the darkness, I saw a fire, like the watchfires that men of war set at night in the camp when they are on the march far from home. The fire burned fierce and bright for a time, but then the flame dwindled, becoming a bed of glowing coals. Then I saw a woman, beautiful and glorious, come upon the dying fire, and I said, 'Who are you my lady?' She said nothing but brought forth a great spear and thrust it in the midst of the coals. Then she stirred the coals with her spear violently, so that the coals were disturbed, and thrown upon the earth, some closer and some farther from the fire, so that the coals of the fire were scattered all about. Yet they still glowed red, and behold, as I gazed upon them they were transformed into stars shining in the dark firmament of the heavens."

Hazer said, "I know the meaning of your dream, for it has been given to me to understand such things. The darkness is the land of Elabaea, and the fire is the house of Manissa, which was strong and glorious for a time; this is what is meant by the fire burning brightly. But by and by the house of Manissa has become weakened, which is signified by the dying fire. The woman is Manissa, our mother, whom thou hast not known in her life but have now seen this singular time in a vision. The spear is a spear of judgment, and the coals are the children of the house of Manissa, who henceforth shall not be united but scattered about the land." Perior said, "But what of the coals changing their forms to become stars? What can this mean?" Hazer said, "That part of the vision is sealed from me."*

Then the poison worked upon Perior; his eyesight began to fail him, and he convulsed in great pain. But while Hazer and Iyla were ministering to him, several thousand men of Cadarasia came out to the hill of Ar Pelaroth, led by Calcax of Avlos, Thrasos, Narox, and Panastor, all powerful war captains and foes of the house of Manissa. They cried out, "Send forth Perior, that he may be punished for the crimes he committed in slaying the lords Rammol and Indrior." Hazer was not willing to give up his brother but prepared rather to come out and make some stand against the men of Cadaras. Struggling, Perior rose and said, "It is not for you to suffer for my sake, brother. Did I not say the next time we met would be cursed? Let me find my end here, but an end which no man who walks the earth hereafter shall ever forget until the very ending of the ages." So he departed the dwelling of Hazer and Iyla and stood forth upon the poplar studded hillside of Ar

Pelaroth, bearing the great sword of Baldor, that which was forged by Belar and had once caused all the lords of Asylia to bow at its splendor.

The men of Cadarasia trembled and stood back, but Calcax said, "Fear not, for he is greatly weakened by the poison which is even now coursing through his veins." So the lords rallied their men, and they charged the hill of Ar Pelaroth. Perior stumbled and held his sword clumsily, but when he heard the cry of battle and the din of men roaring and clashing spear to shield, fire flared up in his bosom one last time and his hand steadied upon his blade. Then he rushed down the hill to meet the attack, his sword a blaze of light in the morning sun, slashing men and casting them this way and that as a mountain lion thrashes prey caught in its jaws. But his arm was slower than before, and his knees unsteady; Panastor cast a spear which struck Perior in the thigh. He howled in agony, for he had never before felt the cut of a brazen spearhead, nor had his flesh been pierced by any blade. The men of Cadaras closed upon him, but he pulled the spear from his leg and hurled it mightily back at his attackers. It struck one Dinoös, a Cadarasian captain, hitting him in the breast and sending him tumbling down the hill in death.

Thus Perior fought on and slew many more men. But by and by he began to be faint, and his vision so blurred that his strokes began to miss. Then Calcax of Avlos closed with him and crossed blades; Perior and Calcax struggled bitterly in the throes of combat, neither able to overcome the other. But while they were thus engaged, Thrasos, a bold but worthless fellow, the one who had procured the poison with which Perior was afflicted, came upon Perior from the rear and thrust a dagger into his side, piercing his liver. Perior cried out and collapsed to his knees. But when he saw Thrasos upon him with the bloodied dagger in hand, he roared and called upon his great strength for one last feat. Quick as a leopard he lunged forth and grasped Thrasos by the hair, and holding him firmly in his grip, placed his hands upon the sides of his head. He pressed them until the skull of Thrasos collapsed like a rotten melon; his head was crushed within the unforgiving hands of Perior, so that bits of skull and brain splattered upon Perior's face and arms.

But then the foes of Perior fell upon him savagely, and a spear was plunged into his back. Perior groaned and fell, surrounded by a host of men who thrust him through with spears again and again until he had poured all his blood out upon the matted grass. Then they stripped him and brought his body to the Erriad, and after cutting his head off, threw the corpse into the stream.

When Hazer looked from his hilltop and beheld what the men of Cadaras had done to Perior, he wept bitterly and came down to lament his brother's death and to retrieve his body if possible. But Calcax and the lords of Cadaras said, "Here comes Hazer, brother of Perior, who can slay men with his song. Make haste and silence him before his weeping lays us all low!" So one of the men of Calcax took aim at Hazer with his bow and fired at him. The arrow struck Hazer in the throat above the collarbone, dropping him upon the hillside gurgling blood and thrashing. Iyla, his wife of many years, came forth and removed the arrow from his throat, bandaged his wound, and ministered to him. Hazer survived, but he could no longer sing or even speak. Thus the song of Hazer and the strength of Perior failed on the same day.

When Baldor heard of the death of his brother Perior and the silencing of Hazer, he fell sick with grief and took to his bed. Mariammné his sister ministered unto him, but his strength waned. Shortly after the turning of the new year he perished, being sixty-two years of age. Mariammné lingered for some time after the death of Baldor, but she, too, fell ill and died in the thirteenth month after her brother's passing. Her body was returned to the land of Lugaria to be buried beside the tomb of Cygnus, her husband.

Hazer continued to dwell on the hill of Ar Pelaroth, cared for by Iyla, his wife of many years. As his voice was now silenced, Iyla dwelt with him continually, loving him in his duress. Their sons Erras, Pelarus, and Asaph, as well as their sons' sons, also dwelt in An Erras. But without his voice, Hazer's strength and vigor faded, and by and by his eyesight left him, so that he could neither speak nor see. Finally he lay down upon the floor of his abode and fell asleep in death, being sixty-five years of age. Then his wife and the sons of Hazer wept and entombed him in the hill of Ar Pelaroth in the land of An Erras. He was buried within the shrine to Manissa that Iyla, wife of Hazer, erected there in days gone by. His body remains there even now, though the shrine has long since vanished.*

This is how all the children of Manissa passed from the world, some at the midday of their lives, such as Secum and Necho who were slain wrongly, and Perior, who fell amidst a score of bodies on the hill of Ar Pelaroth; some fell later, such as Baldor, Mariammné, and Hazer. All fell in sadness. Only Elphas endured, he who dwelt on the hill of Mimmoth in the far southern reaches of Elabaea west of Engor, the city his brother Necho founded. And the lords and great men of the west returned to Cadaras in security, knowing that the power of Perior, son of Manissa, had been broken.

The Sons of Perior

☙ ☙ ☙

n the days when Perior, son of Manissa, fell in bitter combat on the hill of Ar Pelaroth against the men of Cadaras, news spread to the western realms that the youngest and most powerful of all the sons of Manissa had been slain. Finally, the word reached the westernmost reaches of Lugaria, near Arcoria, where Ciphoné, wife of Perior, was dwelling with their ten sons. When they heard of the wondrous deeds their father had accomplished at Cadaras and of his poisoning and death in An Erras, they were filled with fury and vengeance boiled in their blood. Erytas and Marax, the eldest and in the prime of their strength, grasped their spears, fine shafts of hard Lugarian ash, and said, "What do we do here in the wilderness? Let us make haste and fly east, to the city of Cadaras, to avenge the death of our father and accomplish all he set out to do." But their mother Ciphoné said, "Shall I lose my husband and my sons under the same moon? I beg thee, do not go east." But they would not be persuaded, saying, "No, but we will avenge our father." Therefore, the sons of Perior made ready to venture into the east to execute judgment on the lords of Elabaea and the people of Cadaras. But Cerdos, the youngest of the sons of Perior, remained behind with his mother and comforted her.

Now the sons of Perior were mighty, and each one was full of power and strength like their father and shone with grace and glory like their mother, who was of the nymphs of Arcoria. Thus were they called the *Tythodii*, which means "gods of the west" in the tongue of the Lugars; but the people of Asylia called them the Periorids, after their father Perior.

So the Periorids came east, passing through the pleasant lowland fields of Lugaria until they came to the rugged moors and wilds of Enna, bordering on Asylia. From there they ventured east by a southerly route, coming after many days into the hill country by the Nimru Pass and the domains of Calcax. Calcax was then dwelling at Temoras, for after the killing of Perior the lords said, "Now we can rest in ease, for the one who sought our lives is dead," and thus Calcax had returned to his hall. But the Periorids fell upon Temoras by night, set fire to fortress, and slew Calcax of Avlos. Then they struck the surrounding village with the edge of the sword and slew about a hundred men of that place before moving on.

From there they went north, to the region of the Erriad and Asylia-by-Erriad (also called Nearer Asylia) bordering on An Erras. Then they found Pelarus, son of Hazer, who brought them unto the spot where their father fell fighting. After visiting Hazer, their uncle, and doing him homage, they traveled south along the Erriad and found the body of their father, though they did not recover his head, which had been severed and brought to Cadaras as a trophy. Then a dispute arose over where to bury him, for they said, "Inasmuch as he was rightful King of Asylia and Elabaea, he ought to be entombed in Cadaras." Some wanted to bury him in Asylia in the ancestral burying ground of the house of Ioclus, but in the end they traveled west, bearing the body of Perior three and half days into the wilderness, until they came upon the Hill of Cruachan. No one of the house and lineage of Ioclus and Manissa had set foot upon the Hill of Cruachan since the day Manissa was proclaimed queen upon it. They ascended the great Hill of Cruachan and buried Perior atop it in the shadow of the stone where their grandmother Manissa was acclaimed. Then they swore an oath, that on the day the throne was rightfully returned to the house of Manissa would they return thither and bear the body of Perior away to the east to be entombed in Cadaras, near the tomb of Secum in the great Citadel.

From there they went east for many days, and crossing over the Erriad again, came into the regions that border Epidymia and Cadarasia. Then, around midsummer, they came south into Cadarasia and began to plunder and burn the villages there, sending many in flight to Cadaras. Then it was told to the lords, "The Periorids are in the land and are filled with great wrath." So all of the chiefs of Elabaea were summoned to the Council of Lords (but Milco, Irux and Ninus, lords of Nearer Asylia refused to come, by reason of their friendship with Hazer, nor came any of the lords under Baldor). When it had been told that the Periorids were ravaging the east and had murdered Calcax of Avlos, they trembled in fear. They recalled the havoc that Perior had wrought upon the city, which was still not yet repaired, for it had not yet been two years since Perior tore down the watchtowers and destroyed the gates with only his hands. Therefore they resolved that the Periorids must be destroyed before they came to the City on the Plain.

But before the lords could muster their power, the Periorids appeared before the gates of the city. The lords said, "To arms! Secure the gates!" But it was to no avail, for the gates were not yet repaired. The nine sons of Perior overcame the men sent to stop them and rushed headlong into the city. Then there was a terrible slaughter, for the sight of Cadaras filled them with anger and bloodlust. They struck down every man who came into their sight, be he armed or not. They rushed to the Citadel and tore up its gates by the foundations, gates which had stood firm for three hundred years and had not even fallen when Arahaz burnt the city in the days of the Marudan war. Then the Periorids seized the lords of Elabaea, who had taken refuge in the sanctuary of the temple, and with them all of their captains and their aids. These they bound and dragged out into the courtyard of the Citadel and struck off their heads one by one, about fifty men in all.

When they had done thus, they went out and set fire to Cadaras, and taking up positions outside the city, they laid in wait and slew many of those who fled from the conflagration, shooting them with arrows or hurling spears at them, saying, "Thus was it done to Perior, son of Manissa." They did not weary of their slaughter until the setting of the sun.

When they looked, they saw the smoke of Cadaras ascending before the red sky of the dusk and heard the lamentation of women weeping for their dead. Then Crastor, one of the Periorids, said, "Brothers, what have we done? In avenging our father, we have destroyed the City on the Plain with a destruction so great that the likes of it has not been seen since the days of the war with Maruda. How shall we rule now when we have slain so many? Shall not the boys weeping today rise as men tomorrow, seeking to avenge their father as we did ours? How will these people ever accept us?"

Then Arrax the Younger said, "Furthermore, all of the lords we slew have other kin, men who will hunt us down and attempt to slay us in retribution for what we have done here today. We shall be hunted for the remainder of our days, for we have slain so many that there will always be some bereaved son or brother seeking to kill us."

So Erytas said, "To the wilds, sons of Perior! Let us gather at the Stone of Cruachan and the tomb of our father in a fortnight to lay our plans. In the meantime, let each take his own path and scatter one from another to better elude our enemies." So they all agreed to meet again in a fortnight at the Stone of Cruachan and thus parted ways.

But this was not to be, for it was as Arrax the Younger said. The kin of the fallen lords rose and pursued the Periorids, so that they became hunted men; not one of the nine were able to come unto the Stone of Cruachan. The slain lords were replaced in their offices by new ones, and there was war between the Periorids and the lords of Elabaea for many years thereafter. And the tales of the great battles of Erytas, Marax, and all the other Periorids and their struggle against the lords of Cadaras, are they not sung of in the lays of the sons of Perior?*

But when Cerdos and Ciphoné, who were dwelling together in Arcoria, heard what the Periorids had done to Cadaras and how they had fled, Ciphoné said to Cerdos, "Come, my son, for we shall no longer have peace among the sons of men." So Ciphoné and Cerdos, youngest son of Perior, arose and went north, into the Arcorian Wood, and dwelt among the nymphs of that place. How they finished their days and when is unknown, for they never returned to the world of men, and no other tale sings of their end.

Here ends the deeds of the sons of Manissa.

Anridion

(Paladologies)

Major Paladologies
(*Anridion Aior*)

Belar

🙞🙜 🙞🙜

In the glorious days of old, when Baldor and the Asylian armies were returning in triumph from the conquest of Cyrenaica, it came to pass that a train of the most elegant and beautiful maidens came forth from the city of Asylia to greet Baldor and his men as they returned from the campaign. As Baldor came over the plains at the head of his warriors and first sighted fair Asylia, sitting like a jewel beneath the shadow of the highlands, there were maidens within and without the city walls strewing flowers upon the road, chanting songs of victory. And as Baldor returned to the city, and the train of maidens with him, his eye was caught by lovely Oxanna, a maiden of excellent beauty and virtue. Her form was lithe and movements full of grace, and her eyes like chestnuts. In years later many songs were sung about the first meeting of Baldor and Oxanna:

Behold she comes like the glorious dawn
Her braids decked with the wildflowers of Enna,
like the boughs of Eidyllion

She came with the maidens leaping and dancing over the hillocks
To greet the son of Manissa, singing songs of triumph

Behold his glorious frame, arms like oaken trunks
Eyes bright with flame of life

Fearless Baldor who never from challenge nor battle shrunk
Gazing upon fair Oxanna, his mighty heart was turned
And lifting her upon his horse took her to the bridal chamber

Baldor saw Oxanna and loved her. He halted the victory procession and came down from his steed, and standing before the fair maid Oxanna, said, "Tell me your name, most beautiful of all maidens." Casting her eyes down in modesty, she said, "My lord, I am called Oxanna, daughter of Lord Nelus, who hath ridden with thy mother in Arcoria." So Baldor took the maid Oxanna in his arms and set her upon his own horse, then led the beast on foot back to Asylia, whereupon he took her to wife. Then began the long reign of Baldor and Oxanna in the city of old Asylia, and all the land rejoiced in their wise rule.

Soon after Baldor was joined to Oxanna, she conceived and brought forth her firstborn son, Belar. From the time Belar was young he displayed great skill in metalwork, for he used to spend hours in the smithy of his father's servants observing the working of metal, its properties, and the manner of fashioning it. So it came to pass that though he stood barely to his father's waist he was permitted to work alongside the Asylian smiths learning the art of metalcraft. After working with metal for some time, the master smithy came to Baldor and said, "My lord, in the time your son has been with us he has already exceeded even I in skill." Baldor came down to the smithy and saw his young son Belar working diligently at the forge and fashioning many objects, both great objects, such as axe blades and chariot wheels, as well as intricate objects, such as fine bracelets of bronze and silver, as well as many other articles of jewelry. And Baldor marveled at Belar's skill, for other boys his age could scarcely hold the blacksmith's hammer let alone work with the excellence which his son displayed.

Baldor therefore decided to put his son to the test. He commanded Belar to fashion for him a sword excelling all other swords of the kingdom in both firmness and beauty. "Let it be a sword fit for the son of Manissa," said Baldor, "and a suitable weapon to stand in the place of the spear of Ioclus, which I cast into the depths of the sea." So Belar, son of Baldor, worked feverishly for six days, and on the seventh came before his father in his hall and presented the sword to him. When Baldor beheld the sword he rose from his seat in the hall and bowed before his son, and all his lords did likewise, for the sword was truly the most marvelously crafted blade ever seen in all Elabaea. Its blade was slender but firm, finely tempered and sharp enough to sever flesh and bone with little effort. The hilt was wrapped in leather dyed red, capped by a pommel of pure gold fashioned in the likeness of an eagle. Upon one side of the blade was engraved, in the script of old Asylia, the names and deeds of the ancestors of the house of Ioclus back to Laban, while upon the other was the account of his father's exploits in Cyrenaica. It was a blade elegant and strong, fearsome and beautiful. Baldor held the sword as a sacred possession, bearing it only once, when in years later he went into battle in the south to avenge the death of his brother, Necho. Belar was about seven years of age when he forged the sword for his father.

Immediately after those days he became the master smith of Asylia and crafted many excellent suits of armor and weapons of various kinds. So marvelous was his work that great men came from as far away as Epidymia, Elam, and even Lyson to have armor and other articles crafted from the hands of Belar. Even Hadrior came once to see Belar's craftsmanship, returning to Cadaras with many suits of armor fashioned by him. Hadrior praised Belar's work and heaped praise upon the boy. Thus Belar bore affection for Hadrior, and all Asylia marveled at his skill— for whether he crafted suits of mail or delicately wrought rings and brooches, everything he set his hand to became exceptionally beautiful. So Baldor loved his son Belar and took deep delight in the works of his hands.

In those days, Secum, son of Manissa was renowned as the wisest man then living. He came for a time to dwell with Baldor his brother in the court of Asylia, for Hadrior had purposed to go to war against the Lugars over Mariammné, daughter of Manissa, whom he wished to wed, though many said such a union would be incestuous. Secum had fled west, for he feared that Hadrior would seek to harm him on account of his sister, Mariammné. Though younger than Baldor, Secum was accounted as a trustworthy counselor, and Baldor said to him, "Brother, it is good that you have come at this dire time, for I am in desperate straits. Though the deeds of Hadrior are detestable to me, and though I would in normal course rise and defend the honor of my sister to the death, I have bound myself by an oath which constrains me. In the days after the killing of Erogel, I swore a covenant of kinship with Hadrior to never raise a sword against him or hinder him in his deeds as king. Now that he proposes to take to marriage Mariammné, who is his niece by virtue of his late marriage to Saraeth, my aunt and sister of our blessed mother, I find myself unable to oppose him in such a vile act! What shall I do?"

Secum said, "My brother, it is true that you cannot raise sword against him nor lead others in doing so, by reason of your oath. What is left then? To join and aid him in apprehending our sister? By no means! Since thou can neither oppose nor aid him, then you must resolve to remain here at Asylia in thy hall and do nothing." Baldor said, "Shall I truly do nothing?" Secum said, "Had you not sworn rashly I should say otherwise. But sworn you have, and now you must leave the course of things to Fate to arrange how she wills." So Baldor was content with this advice.

But Belar his son opposed him to his face, saying, "My father, does not Hadrior occupy the throne of Manissa our mother? And do we not owe allegiance to him as King of All

Elabaea?* How can we then justify ourselves in disobeying his summons for all his lords to come with him to Lugaria to fetch your sister, Mariammné? Is it not she who proves disobedient? Furthermore, she is no relation of his by blood, for she is only his niece by marriage. If Hadrior be not wed to her for the raising of offspring, who shall inherit the kingdom in his passing?" Thus Belar argued in favor of Hadrior, for he had from youth heard the tale of Hadrior's battle in the pit of Ochu and admired the man. Furthermore, Hadrior had greatly praised his work and had puffed Belar up so that he thought his father's words were folly. Belar disputed with his father in his hall for many days, until one day he said to his father, "Is it right that Asylia should lend its support and sympathy to a foreign king rather than to a full-blooded Asylian who has ridden in battle with Manissa, thy mother?" He said this because he was youthful and rash. Baldor looked at his son, and loving him, said, "My son, I have sworn an oath regarding myself only, but I bind no other man. Let every man do what seems best to him." So Belar said, "I will go forth with Hadrior to make war on Cygnus."

Secum tried to prevail with Belar to remain behind, but Belar said, "Thou counselor of foolishness! May your own ill advice return to curse thee!" Then he donned a splendid coat of mail which he had fashioned for himself, and after saddling his horse, departed south to join the army of Hadrior which was then encamped east of Enna. When Belar came and joined himself to Hadrior, the king rejoiced and said to himself, "After my victory over Cygnus, I will retain Belar in my service in Cadarasia and he will make many marvelous things for me as he has done for Asylia."

But in the company of Hadrior was Arummnax of Orioön, whose brothers had been slain by Baldor many years earlier over the spear of Ioclus. Arummnax called his son Eburax to his side and said, "My son, Fate has given us an opportunity to avenge ourselves upon Baldor for the slaying of my three brothers, thy uncles, whom Baldor killed outside of Thán over the matter of the spear of Ioclus." Eburax said, "How shall we avenge ourselves upon him, father, for he has not come out to fight, either for us or for Cygnus?" Arummnax said, "Have you not seen that Belar, the young son of Baldor, is now among the men of the camp? Behold, Baldor deprived me of my three brothers in a single day, and so shall we deprive him of his son." But Eburax was troubled and said, "Has not young Belar come out to fight with us against his own aunt Mariammné in the service of the king? How then shall we oppose him?"

Arummnax spit and said, "Hadrior be damned! Did he not put my sons, thy brothers, to death upon little pretext? By Manx I would have cast my spear at his bloated belly had I not feared for thy safety as well! Think not of Hadrior, for we shall be avenged upon him soon enough. But blood for blood and kin for kin first of all! We shall watch for the opportune time and then shall smite Belar, so that his fine workmanship shall be seen no more among men." So Eburax and Arummnax his father bided their time.

Is it not told in the deeds of the sons of Manissa, how Hadrior traversed the wilderness of Enna attempting to march his army into Lugaria? And how Cygnus came and gave him battle on the plains west of that place? Now when the battle began to go badly for the Asylians, Hadrior turned to retreat with his army back through the wilderness, but they were hotly pursued by the Lugarians. The Lugars knew the region well and moved swiftly over it, so that many of the Asylians were cut off from each other and perished at their hands. Much of Hadrior's army fell, and many of his captains. It was in the midst of the retreat that Arummnax called to his son Eburax and said, "My son, the king's cause is lost, and we are vanquished. If we are to go down in death, let us bring Belar to the darkness with us." So they found Belar son of Baldor, who was someway off alone from the main column, and drawing him into a gully, fell upon him. Belar tried to fight them off, but despite his skill in forging weapons, he found he had little skill in wielding them.

As Belar was assaulted in the gully, King Cygnus of Lugaria came by in pursuit of Hadrior, and with him was Indor, servant of Baldor. Indor said, "My lord, down there in the gully by the hillside! That is Belar son of Baldor, thy brother-in-law, and he is in great duress!" Cygnus looked and saw Arummnax and Eburax fighting with Belar. He cried out and rode towards them, for Belar was greatly beloved by Cygnus and his wife Mariammné. But before he could deliver him, Arummnax cast a spear at Belar and struck him in the gut, piercing armor and flesh. As Belar fell wounded, Eburax approached him and said, "Now you shall pay for your father's crimes!" Then he thrust his blade into the throat of Belar and killed him there in the gully among the hillocks and ditches of Enna.

No sooner did Belar fall than Cygnus rode upon Arummnax and his son Eburax. Eburax rose to defend his father, but Cyngus overpowered him and struck him at the nape of the neck, killing him. Arummnax wept and fell upon the body of Eburax his son, but Cygnus, looking down from his horse said, "In the same hour you have treacherously taken the life of the son of Baldor you have justly been bereaved of your own. Now join him!" Then Cygnus swung his blade and cut off the head of Arummnax of Orioön; it toppled down and fell beside the body of Belar.

Thus perished Belar, son of Baldor and the greatest craftsman of Asylia, being about age thirteen when he was slain. King Cygnus wept bitterly when he beheld the body of Belar. He ordered it washed, anointed, and dressed in new robes of linen. So Cygnus returned to Karanak and summoned Mariammné and Indor, servant of Baldor, and told them of the victory and of Belar's death. And Mariammné wept. Then Cygnus sent Indor back to the court of Baldor bearing the body of the king's son, and this reconciled Indor with his lord for fleeing Asylia. Baldor wept bitterly for Belar, his firstborn son, and his lords marveled at how he grieved. Baldor said to them, "I foresaw it would come to no good end." Then the customary rites were performed for Belar, son of Baldor, and he was buried in the tombs of his fathers in Asylia.

Elifanora

At the time of Queen Anaxandra's accession, it came to pass that the fair and beautiful maiden Elifanora came to reside in the court of Cadaras. This Elifanora was especially renowned among all the peoples of Asylia and Cadarasia, for she was the sole heir of the house of Naross, the brother of Ioclus and uncle to Manissa. She had fled Elabaea when Hadrior massacred the descendants of Arrax and dwelt in Epidymia until word came that Hadrior was dead and that Anaxandra, daughter of Erogel of the house of Arrax, was ruling at Cadarasia. So Elifanora returned to the land of her fathers and abode in the court of Anaxandra. In old Asylian, Elifanora means "might through virtue," but some say that it means "the mighty will prevail." She was exceedingly beautiful, for her figure was slender but strong, and her hair of flaxen yellow that curled and fell gracefully about her shoulders. Her eyes were of deep blue, her laughter light and joyous, and her face well-proportioned and delicate. She was the envy of every woman of Cadaras and beloved by all the young lords of the city.

For two years she abode in the court of Queen Anaxandra and was the queen's constant companion, along with Annete, one of Anaxandra's ladies-in-waiting, becoming fast friends with them. Together the three maidens meandered by the banks of the Cadar when the *trianta* roses blossomed in the spring or paced the colonnaded courtyard of the Temple of Mironna in the cool of the day, arm in arm, laughing and jesting as young women do. Their footfalls were light upon the flagstones of the Citadel, for joy was in their hearts and all Elabaea rejoiced in their good fortune at being ruled by such a gracious and prudent queen as Anaxandra. And Anaxandra rejoiced in the companionship of Annete and especially of flaxen-haired Elifanora, whose radiant beauty only magnified the splendor of the queen even more. The cheer and mirth of Elifanora soothed the heart of Anaxandra.

In the second year of Anaxandra's reign, the southern kingdoms of Illyrana and Emeric waged war on all the peoples of the plains, raiding north as far as two leagues from Cadaras.* Having come so far north, they sent envoys to Anaxandra demanding the submission of Cadaras and Asylia to the King of Emeric. Anaxandra was irate with the envoys' arrogance and had them whipped before sending them on their way. This angered the lords of the Illyrs and the King of Emeric, and in retaliation they raided the regions around Elos and Avlos, slaying a great many of the people there. Some they took as hostages back to Illyrana and offered them up as sacrifices to the detestable gods of the southlands, burning them in the smoldering ovens atop their abominable temples which ever belched forth vile, black smoke day and night.

Anaxandra summoned all the great men of her realm: Baldor, son of Manissa and his companion Gilgax; the brothers Necho and Elphas, sons of Manissa, both young and unproven in war but eager for glory; also summoned was Athoss, an old and experienced captain who had served under Hadrior but pledged fealty to Anaxandra. Anaxandra said, "My lords, the Illyrs have been sighted raiding only two days south of this very city. They have pillaged the towns subject to Cadaras and have even taken persons under our care and brought them back to Illyrana to be offered to their detestable idols. How shall we respond to their aggression?" With one voice the assembled lords clashed their spears to their shields, saying, "Let blood be met with blood! Call forth the peoples of Asylia and Cadarasia and let us make an end of our foes!"

But Anaxandra was uncertain in her judgment, for she was very young and had not been long on the throne. She said, "You know that the Illyrs are the greatest kingdom of the south; their warriors are fearless in battle and merciless in victory. Furthermore, our kingdom has not long ago suffered a shameful and crushing defeat against King Cygnus of Lugaria over the matter of Mariammné. We cannot yet risk another such defeat at the hands of the Illyrs. If there remains a chance to make peace it ought to be pursued." Baldor and the sons of Manissa balked at this, but Athoss, being older and not as eager for blood, said, "My lady, let us send emissaries to the court of the King of Emeric, who is the leader of the southern peoples, and come to terms with him regarding our southern frontiers. Perhaps we can enter into treaty or covenant with him and yet preserve the peace."

Baldor scoffed and said, "Shall you enter into covenant with one who has shed the blood of your own people? Is this not cowardice? Heaven forbid my blessed mother, Manissa of happy memory, should have taken such a stand with Belthazre." But Athoss replied, "You mock me for suggesting we make a treaty with a foreign king who has slain some of our own, yet you yourself entered into a covenant with that scoundrel Hadrior. This you did even though he had murdered your own flesh and blood, Erogel the son of Arrax, the father of our beloved queen. Through the foolishness of this oath, you allowed Hadrior to march unopposed into Lugaria where your own dearest son, Belar, was also slain. Is this the counsel we shall listen to? You have no standing in this matter, son of Manissa." Then Baldor was shamed into silence, for he knew Athoss spoke the truth regarding these things.

Anaxandra weighed the words of her lords, and after pondering for some time said, "We shall send emissaries unto the King of Emeric and the lords of Illyrana, that perhaps peace shall be preserved." All present bowed, and said, "So shall it be, my lady." Athoss said, "Whom will you send?" Then Anaxandra said, "You shall go, lord Athoss, as well as the lady Elifanora, granddaughter of hoary headed Naross the Wise, for perhaps if the stern words of Athoss do not restrain the King of Emeric it may happen that the humility and grace of Elifanora will." So gnarled Athoss and flaxen-haired Elifanora made ready to depart for Illyrana and the court of the King of Emeric. Athoss brought with him servants and a dozen stout Asylian spearmen, but Elifanora brought only her handmaiden Oria. Thus they departed fair Cadarasia for the harsh southern plains and the dominions of Emeric and the Illyrs.

The Illyrs were a very ancient people who inhabited the southernmost lands of the west and were not reckoned among the peoples of Elabaea. While the Elabaeans counted themselves as descendants of Laban (from whence comes the name Elabaea), the Illyrs and the peoples of Emeric were more akin to the people of Caeylon. According to their own histories, the Illyrs had once dwelt in the arid lands bordering upon southwestern Caeylon, where they were vassals of the Zhinkanthans. Of old Zhinkanthas was a foe to Caeylon and Maruda, and at one time the Zhinkanthans had oppressed the Marudans and made them slaves.* But later the Marudans waxed strong and utterly destroyed the Zhinkanthans, rooting them up from the land. Thus many of the Zhinkanthans fled west and took up habitation in the lands of the Illyrs. It was from these Zhinkanthans that the Illyrs learned the art of building great cities and of constructing the massive temples where their abominable acts were carried out. It was also from the Zhinkanthans that the Illyrs and the people of Emeric learned the worship of their detestable gods, for the Zhinkanthans had paid homage to three gods, the greatest of which was Urilla, which means "The Worm." And so the Illyrs appropriated all the knowledge of the Zhinkanthans but also took up their vices, becoming corrupted and perverted in their thoughts. They had been strong for many generations and did not know of the Asylians or the house of Manissa until the time when the Asylians began to settle south of Cadarasia in the latter days of Hadrior's reign.

The envoys of Anaxandra came unto the court of the King of Emeric, who received them coldly at first, until he beheld the beauty of flaxen-haired Elifanora and was told that she was of noble lineage.* Thereafter he treated the emissaries well and feasted with them many days in the great hall of Emeric. Grand tables were laid out and made ready, at which the King of Emeric and all the highest lords of the kingdom dined in the company of Athoss, Elifanora, and the Asylian envoys. The king spoke familiarly with Elifanora and went to great lengths to receive a smile or glance from her, being sorely smitten by her beauty and gentleness. But whenever Athoss attempted to speak with the king about the matter of peace he was irritated and turned his speech to other matters. Yet he was enthralled with Elifanora and determined that she should not return to Cadaras but should abide there with him. Gentle Elifanora delighted in the sumptuous banquets and the attention of the king and lords, but Athoss had no patience for such things, for he was grey headed with a grizzled beard and many scars from various wars and inclined to brevity. Yet he bided his time and continued attending the feasts with Elifanora.

After a fortnight of feasting that hardy Athoss turned to the King of Emeric and said, "My lord, while we do not begrudge the hospitality you have shown us these past many days, the time has come for us to receive an answer from your lordship. Will you yet make peace with Cadaras and drop your demands of tribute from my Queen Anaxandra? Whatever your answer be, let it be made swiftly so that we may depart for our homeland and bear your message to our queen, who is eagerly awaiting news from us." The King of Emeric was insulted by the words of Athoss and said, "You presume to force the hand of the king? Are all Asylians as foolhardy as yourself?" Athoss replied, "Even more so, sir." The King of Emeric scoffed, saying, "Depart from me and return to my hall at the rising of the sun, for I shall confer with my counselors this evening and have an answer for you on the morrow." So Athoss bowed, and he and the Asylian envoys, with Elifanora, departed. Then the king summoned his counselors and pondered what answer to give Athoss.

At first light, Athoss and the entire Asylian company presented themselves before the King of Emeric as he had requested. The king sat enthroned, arrayed in marvelous silken robes of various colors surrounded by his ministers. Then he said, "Hear what I have to say, lord Athoss and lady Elifanora, envoys of Anaxandra. This I have determined: there shall be peace between Illyrana and Cadaras, upon the condition that forthwith and without delay the lady Elifanora is betrothed unto me and remains behind in the city of Emeric as a pledge of her faithfulness. Thereupon the people of the north and the people of the south shall be joined together as one. If she refuses to be joined to me, then I shall press my claim to the lands south of Cadaras and will exact a heavy tribute from your queen."

Athoss and Elifanora recoiled at the king's words, for the Illyrs were detestable to the people of Elabaea by reason of their abominable gods and were accounted heathens. The king saw their countenance fall, and frowning, said, "Is my offer not generous? Behold, I am a king of a great people, and at my word all the peoples of Illyrana and Emeric make war or enjoy peace. But what of flaxen-haired Elifanora? Is she anything other than the granddaughter of the uncle of the foundress of your dynasty? Such a tenuous connection to the ruling house is considered as nothing in Illyrana. What future can fair Elifanora have in the courts of Cadaras? Here she will be a great queen and mother of a glorious house."

Athoss said, "My lord, even were we to accede to your offer, Elifanora is a ward of Anaxandra and a relation of our fair queen. She could not give her consent to be betrothed to you without leave of Queen Anaxandra." But Elifanora stepped forward and spoke, saying, "Even were Anaxandra to give me leave to join myself to you, my lord, I would be loath to do so, for your customs are horrible in my sight and I detest the sacrifices of men and women which your people daily make atop your grotesque temples; indeed, I shudder to think that already some of our own countrymen have perished thus at your hands! I can never consent to become your bride nor will I so long as strength remains in me!"

The King of Emeric attempted to persuade Elifanora with many promises and gifts to remain behind, even offering her a room full of gold bars, but these offers only strengthened her resolve. At last Athoss said, "All that has been done is done. We take our leave. If it is to be war, then let it be war." Then they left the palace of the King of Emeric and made for Cadaras along the northern road.

But the King of Emeric could not shake the thought of Elifanora from his mind. He went to the walls of his palace from where he beheld Elifanora and her countrymen leaving the city. When he saw her delicate yellow hair falling gently upon her back, her golden skin and graceful form, his heart beat heavily with passion and he was beside himself. He attempted to take his rest in the cool of the day, but he only tossed and turned, and groaned in his lust upon his bed, his mind tormented by the beauty of fair Elifanora. Finally he summoned the captain of his guard to his chambers and said, "Take a troop of riders and go up the northern road until you come across the caravan of Asylians that departed this morning. Bring back to me the fair maiden, Elifanora." The captain said, "It shall be done, my lord."

The captain gathered his men, and mounting their steeds, they sallied forth from the mighty fortress of Emeric along the northern road. The sun was setting below the western mountains when they came upon the company of Athoss and Elifanora. At first Athoss hailed the captain, for he thought he was bearing a message from the King of Emeric. But when he saw their swords drawn and their eyes dark for battle, he cried out to his servants, "Every man to his spear! Defend the lady Elifanora!" Then he took his spear in hand and charged at the guards from Emeric. "My lady, flee!" he cried to Elifanora. But Elifanora said, "Shall I flee from harm when my Lady, fairest Manissa, has done such marvelous deeds in war?" Then she brought forth a sword which she had on her person and cried, "Cruacha!"

The men of Asylia and the guards of Emeric crashed into each other, men falling to the dirt and spears shattering upon shields. The Asylian servants of Athoss fought well, but the men of Emeric overcame them, for they wore thicker armor, were better equipped, and came in greater numbers. One by one they were slain, until only Athoss and Elifanora remained. Athoss roared and cast his ashen spear at the captain of the guard, but it missed its mark and sank instead into the flesh of the captain's horse behind the shoulder, causing it to rear up and hurl the captain violently to the ground. When the captain's guards saw this, they fell upon Athoss with one accord and dragged him from his horse. The captain cried out, "Do not slay him! Bind his arms!" So they bound the arms of Athoss.

But Elifanora charged at them, her sword gleaming red in the light of the dying sun. She swung her sword wildly at the men, keeping them at bay. A certain guard tried to pull her from her horse, but she struck him with her blade and cleaved off his nose. Then the guards of Emeric stood off, fearful to approach her. Seeing this, the captain picked up his lance and said, "This witch will not undue me," and having said this, struck her fiercely upon the head with the butt of the spear. Elifanora tumbled from her charger and struck the ground violently, her golden hair matted in dirt and blood. The guards fell upon her and bound her tightly with cords so that her arms became bruised. But the nursemaid of Elifanora, Oria, had been hiding in the bushes nearby. She came to the aid of her mistress and tried desperately to loosen her bonds. The soldiers tried to send her away, but she wept and would not be parted from her mistress. When the guards saw that Oria would by no means depart, they permitted her to accompany them and minister to Elifanora in her captivity.

The captain said, "Return this woman unto our lord the king, but string up lord Athoss from yonder tree that I may chastise him for slaying my steed." So flaxen-haired Elifanora was brought hastily back to the King of Emeric, bound and weeping, while Athoss was stripped and bound hanging from a great tree branch off the side of the road. Then the captain, removing his cloak, took a thong of cords and flogged Athoss violently until late into the night. When he grew weary from flogging Athoss and had drawn much blood, the men unbound Athoss and shaved off half of his beard. But Athoss growled and said, "Fate is a strange thing, my good captain, and she will requite you for the evil you have done this day!" The captain only laughed at this and had Athoss bound again and set upon his horse backwards, and in this manner sent him off north. Then the captain and his men turned south to rejoin their other companions who bore Elifanora.

The King of Emeric was pacing his chambers anxiously when word was brought that Elifanora had been captured. He rushed to his hall to view her, eagerly desiring to look upon her beauty again. But when he beheld her he saw her hair matted with dirt and blood, her face smeared with grime, shoulders bruised and her clothes sullied and disheveled, he became very wrathful. "Captain," he said, "I ordered you to retrieve the lady Elifanora so that I could again gaze upon her graceful form, not mar her beauty with your rough treatment!" The captain protested and said, "My lord, this woman by her own hand sliced off the nose of one of my guards, and you marvel that her clothes are defiled with dirt?" This infuriated the king and he said, "In taking such an arrogant tone with me you have lost your life!" Then he ordered his guards to lay hold of the captain, and they dragged him to the top of one of the temples of the city and offered him as a burnt offering to their vicious gods.

The King of Emeric sent Elifanora to be washed, anointed, and donned in the finest robes, for he was full of lust and thought to take her to himself that very evening. So Elifanora was bathed and ministered to, and her wounds were treated. She wept violently, but the bitterness of her captivity was ameliorated somewhat by the presence of her maid Oria who comforted her. When she had been fully bathed, clothed, and anointed with precious oils, she was sent into the chambers of the King of Emeric. She entered trembling and beheld the king reclining on his couch, and upon seeing him, collapsed at his feet, saying, "Mercy king, have mercy on me, a frightened and forlorn girl!" The king laughed and said, "Have no fear, Elifanora. Are you not beautiful? Come and sit beside me. I will teach you to love me." But Elifanora thrust him away from her and fled to the balcony.

The King of Emeric laughed and said, "Do you yet dream of escape? Resign yourself to your fate! Why do you yet resist? Give yourself to me willingly. It will be more tolerable for you." But noble Elifanora cried, "Come no closer! True, I am unarmed and cannot do unto you as I did to your men who tried to lay hands on me, but I swear by the grace of Manissa and all that is holy that if you persist in this evil you will pay for it dearly!" But the King of Emeric was full of lust and wine and came near, reaching out his arms to lay hands on her. Then she cast her eyes to the night sky and seeing the sign of the spear in the north, Laoön, she murmured a prayer and leapt from the balcony. Her body broke upon the stones of the courtyard. The king's servants came running forth into the courtyard to see what had happened, and Oria was among them. When she saw her mistress smashed upon the pavement she wept and tore her hair, uttering curses against the King of Emeric and the people of Illyrana. The King of Emeric was greatly distraught and knew not what to do, so he ordered Oria thrown out of the palace. Then he went to bed drunk and downcast that he had lost fair Elifanora.

Not long after, Athoss was found on the road to Avlos, still bound and in a swoon from the flogging. After he was ministered to and able to stand before the queen, he presented himself to Anaxandra and recounted in detail all that had occurred from the time he departed for Emeric to the time he was flogged and sent home. Then Elphas and Necho, brothers in arms and sons of Manissa, were enraged and said, "Allow us to lead out the forces of Asylia and Cadarasia against this pagan! By Manx, does he think he can lay hands on the heir of the house of Naross with impunity? Does he think to pollute the bloodline of Naross with his heathen seed?" Just as they were speaking, word was brough to Anaxandra that Oria had returned from Emeric. The weeping maidservant came before the queen trembling and told Anaxandra and the lords everything that occurred from the time Elifanora was apprehended to the moment she flung herself from the palace balcony in despair.

When Anaxandra heard this, she trembled with rage and the fire of Arrax her grandsire burned in her heart. She stood up in the marble hall of the Citadel and cried, "Where are the lords of Asylia?" All her lords clashed their spears to their shields and said, "Here, my lady!" She said, "To the winds with caution! By the gods, the King of Emeric has brought doom upon himself by this foul deed! We shall yet go to war, and such a war it shall be that by the end Illyrana and Emeric shall be nothing but smoking ruins upon the dusty plain." Then all her lords cried, "Yea! Cru Cadara!" So all the armies of Cadaras were mustered with great fervor to strike the people of the south, for Elifanora had been beloved by her countrymen. Anaxandra sent a message to Baldor, son of Manissa, who was then reigning in splendor in fair Asylia, saying, "Will you come out to war with me to avenge the treachery done to flaxen-haired Elifanora of the house of Naross?" When Baldor heard what befell Elifanora, he shook violently and cried for his sword, the blade crafted by Belar his son. Then Baldor, Gilgax, and all the lords of the west mounted their steeds and thundered across the plains until they crossed the Erriad, joining up with Elifanora's army in the sloping valley south of Cadaras by the ruins of Danath Hered. There was mirth at Baldor's arrival; he was promptly made commander over all the armies of Asylia and Cadaras. Athoss went out to war with him as well, seeking vengeance for his stripes.

The war was bitter and long, enduring for three and a half years. If the Illyrs or the people of Emeric prevailed in battle over the Asylians, they dragged the prisoners and the wounded back to Illyrana and offered them up to their vile gods as sacrifices. When it became known among the Asylians that the Illyrs were sacrificing their comrades, the Asylians likewise beheaded any Illyr prisoners that fell into their hands. Thus the battles became very desperate, and men fought to the uttermost end of their strength, for they knew there would be no quarter if they faltered.

As the war entered its fourth year, the armies of Baldor laid siege to the city of Emeric. The city was constructed upon a great mound, so that its walls could be breached only by scaling a large hill first. Scores of Asylians fell dead upon the dust as Baldor led them up the ascent to the walls of the city. The people of Emeric fought bitterly and fired many arrows and javelins at the Asylians, but Baldor prevailed and became enraged, as he did before the walls of Thán. A fury entered his heart; he cried with a bestial yell, rattling the ears of the garrison of Emeric and sending them fleeing. Any man who crossed swords with Baldor fell, and every man on whom he fixed his eye perished by his deadly strokes. The wall was breached, and the Asylians poured into the city pillaging and burning. It was summer and exceedingly dry, so that once the city was torched it burned without respite for four long days.

The King of Emeric withdrew to the main fortress in the royal quarter of the city, which had not caught fire because it was cut off from the rest of the city by a great wall. When the fire began to falter on the fourth day, the King of Emeric sallied forth from the royal quarter and engaged Baldor and the Asylians. Baldor slew a great many men and covered his sword in gore, but it was Elphas who won glory that day, for he saw the King of Emeric some ways off and dashed to engage him. The King of Emeric was surrounded by a bodyguard of ten mercenaries from Maruda, each tall and bearing a spear of bronze. Yet so quick was Elphas and so sure his strokes that he laid all ten of them low, one after another, until the King of Emeric was left alone. Though he was armed, the king was an effeminate man and feared combat, and so tried to pacify Elphas by offering him a large sum of gold in exchange for his life. But Elphas said, "And with similar promises did you attempt to win the heart of Elifanora, jewel of Cadaras? You should have known that Asylians cannot be bribed with such trifles. But since you did not learn it from her, you shall have to learn it from me!" Then he slashed the King of Emeric with his blade and opened his belly, so that the king struggled to hold his entrails within him. The King of Emeric stumbled, fell to his face upon the pavement, and darkness overtook him. Thus was Elifanora avenged.

After this victory the Asylians began to prevail over the Illyrs. They laid siege to Illyrana, the other principal city of the Illyrs, and after some time took it by storm. The Illyrs fought savagely from house to house, yielding ground only very slowly. Their resistance compelled the Asylians to torch Illyrana as they had torched Emeric, so that it was destroyed utterly. Any Illyrs that fell into the hands of Baldor or the Asylians were slain, so that by the third day there remained none living in Illyrana. As they fought, the Asylians cried, "Elifanoré! Elifanoré!" They continued their butchery for a long while, until Elphas told Baldor, "There is no one left to kill." Later, when the Illyrs and the people of Emeric had been completely destroyed from the face of the land, Anaxandra renamed the city of Illyrana, calling it Annete after her companion; but the city of Emeric, where Elifanora had perished, was called *Mironniur*, which means "Fate is just."

Then the armies of Baldor scoured the land and overthrew the foul idols of the Illyrs. The smoke of the sacrifices ceased, and the bloody offerings were cut off. The great temples were thrown down, and shrines of Manissa erected in their place. Thus was the abomination of Illyrana stomped out of the land forever. But the praises of the beauty, virtue, and valor of Elifanora are ever sung in all the halls of Asylia and Cadarasia even to this day. A commemoration to her memory is held every spring in Cadarasia, where the maidens wear woven wreaths of flowers upon their heads called *Elifa* crowns.

Asaph and Elora

※ ※ ※

Hazer, second son of Manissa, was wed to the Cadarasian maiden Iyla. By her he begat three sons: Erras and Pelarus in the days when Iyla was taken away from him and detained with Andross in Cadaras, and then after the return of Iyla and the death of Andross she gave birth to Asaph, in whom the power of Hazer lived on.*

After the deaths of Hazer and Iyla, the sons of Hazer abode in An Erras and were known as the Hazerites. Erras dwelt some ways north of Ar Pelaroth going towards Epidymia, but Pelarus dwelt south, in the shadow of Ar Pelaroth where his father had lived. There he tended to the shrine of Manissa and the pilgrims that came to venerate the bones of Hazer and Iyla. Erras and Pelarus took wives from the women of Nearer Asylia and established their houses there. But Asaph, who was some years younger than his brothers, dwelt east of the Erriad near the Cadarasian frontier.

It came to pass that the Council of Lords took power in Cadaras following the war between Irodel and Pirox. The Council hated the sons of Manissa and excluded them from influence in Cadaras, by reason of which Perior came east in the latter days and assaulted the lords with a great slaughter, as is told elsewhere. After Cadaras was overthrown by the Periorids, the next of kin of those lords who had been slain came together and swore vengeance on the house of Perior. Therefore Asaph and the Hazerites were fearful, for they said to themselves, "Perhaps they will lay hands on us because we are of the kin of Perior." The houses of Erras and Pelarus resolved to remain in their ancestral home of An Erras, for they were firmly established therein, and each had many children. Asaph however was yet unattached and decided to flee into Epidymia until the anger of the lords had cooled against the sons of Perior.

While going up into Epidymia, Asaph pitched his tent by the northern banks of the Erriad, not far from the Epidymian city of Koharth. While resting under the stars among the reeds that he saw a vision. Behold! He arose from his slumber, and before him he saw the course of the Erriad flowing southwest into Asylia and the plains. But the river did not end there, and as he watched he seemed to be lifted up, so that the whole earth was before his eyes. The Erriad tumbled down the grassy lowlands of Nearer Asylia and branched out into seven courses.* Three of the courses grew and became great rivers in their own right, providing water for many people before finally draining into the ocean after many leagues. But four of the courses ran down into dry lands, into arid, deserted regions and dried up. The men of those regions came forth seeking water, but only found dry riverbeds full of stones and brambles.

Then Asaph looked up and saw a great range of heather-clad hills; upon them leapt what appeared to be a great stag, marvelous in size and splendor. The stag bounded over the hilltops with mighty strides, and coming before Asaph, spoke to him, saying, "Asaph, son of Hazer, cast your eyes east and tell me what you see." So Asaph looked east and beheld what seemed to be a great army falling slain upon the desert sands. So he said, "Master, I see what appears to be a multitude of soldiers falling slain upon the desert, both the small and the great. What is the meaning of this?" But the stag said, "Look to the north."

Then Asaph looked north and beheld a pleasant garden, and therein growing many delicious fruits and fragrant flowers. In the midst of the garden was a magnificent tree, more beautiful and desirous than all the others. It bore a fruit that was lovely to look at and sweet to the taste. Yet it was enclosed by a large stone wall. The stag said, "What will you do, son of Hazer?" Asaph looked at the tree and said, "A most beautiful tree! I will go and eat of its fruit." Then he leapt over the stone wall, and plucking some of the fruit from the tree, ate it and found it sweet to the taste. But after he had tasted of it for but a moment, it became ashes in his mouth and caused him to gag and struggle for breath.

Then the stag said, "Son of Hazer, look south," so Asaph cast his eyes south and saw a crystal fountain bubbling up amidst lichen covered rocks and sweet-smelling ferns. The stag said, "Asaph, son of Hazer, wash your eyes in this fountain." So Asaph knelt down and washed his eyes with the pure water flowing up from the fountain. Then the stag said, "Henceforth you shall see marvels." But Asaph said, "And what of the west?" The stag said, "Come and see." It led him to a high point where Asaph stood and beheld the west. There he saw all the western plains stretching before him, all the great wilds west of Epidymia into Ituria for many miles, terminating in a great darkness. Then Asaph seemed translated from his place and thrust into the darkness and was in great fear and terror. Then the visions fled from him.

Asaph awoke and found the sun at noontide, the day being already far spent. Therefore he took up his tent and continued northeast to the Fords of Esmer, and there crossed into Epidymia. He pondered the things he saw, and from that day forward began to see many things in visions and dreams.

The reputation of Asaph spread, for everywhere he went he had visions and demonstrated skill at interpreting dreams, so that there was always a mass of people seeking him for the interpretation of some dream or omen. It was not long before a certain Epidymian nobleman, Zinzarel, heard about Asaph's power and came before him seeking aid. This Zinzarel was a distant kinsman of King Belabret of Epidymia and was an important court official. He came to Asaph while he was dwelling east of the Sehu between Epidyne and Emerias. Zinzarel fell down before Asaph, saying, "Asaph, son of Hazer, word has come to me that you have the gift of second sight. I unwittingly find myself in a precarious place regarding my lord, the King Belabret, and plead humbly for your assistance." Hazer said, "Tell me your trouble and I will assist you however I can."

Zinzarel told him, "Some time ago, King Belabret gave unto me a golden horn of great value as a gift and token of his esteem. This horn had always been kept among the treasures of my house for many years. But the king has of late decided to go forth to war and requested that I return the golden horn in exchange for its price in silver. My lord King Belabret desires to bear it into war as part of his battle dress. I told him it would be done, and I went to fetch the horn. But when I came into my chambers, I found the horn to be missing. My servants all plead ignorance, and though I threaten them with fire and the wrack they maintain their innocence. O' son of Hazer, if I cannot produce the horn for my lord the king, he will think me ungrateful of his gifts and will despise me ever after."

Asaph said, "Return to me on the morrow and I shall tell you where your horn is to be sought." So Zinzarel departed. That night, Asaph stood upon the Plains of Anorel and gazed up at the night sky, as he was accustomed to do when discerning such matters. He stood there upon the plain the whole night through gazing at the constellations of the dark north. In the morning, Zinzarel returned, and Asaph told him, "There is a certain merchant who comes regularly to your estate on business. Not more than a fortnight past he was at your home. Upon seeing a moment when your servants were disposed outdoors, he seized the opportunity and took the horn from your chambers. He dwells in Emerias, and if you seek him out there, you will find the golden horn concealed in a small chest in his chambers." Upon describing the merchant, Zinzarel knew at once of whom Asaph spoke, and taking his words to heart, sought the man out in Emerias. Just as Asaph had spoken it, so did it come to pass, for the horn was found in the chambers of the merchant. Thus Zinzarel reclaimed his horn, but the merchant he had hanged. Zinzarel returned to Asaph, gave him a great sum of gold in reward, and then departed to the court of King Belabret in Epidyne. And Asaph did many such wonders in Epidymia, so many that they could not all be recounted.

Not long after the affair with Zinzarel, it came to pass that the King of Epidymia, Belabret, raised an army to make war on Caeylon. Remembering Asaph, the nobleman Zinzarel came to King Belabret and said to him, "My lord, there is man of Asylian descent of the house of Manissa, Asaph by name, who dwells near Emerias in the south. He is gifted with the power of second sight and once used this power to work a great miracle for me. Such a man would be valuable, for he is able to tell what will be before it occurs and can see things veiled to other mortals." So Belabret sent and had Asaph brought to his court at Epidyne to be one of his counselors in the war.

Belabret said, "Zinzarel, while I hold thy word as truth itself, I must put this Asaph to the test before I can take his counsel to heart." Therefore he called Asaph to him, and Asaph said, "Here I am, my lord." The king told him, "Asaph, my scouts tell me there is a company of Caeylonic cavalry raiding east of the Gihon. Can you tell me where they will next strike?" Asaph thought within himself and was silent for a great time, so long that the king began to think he had fallen swoon. Then he spoke and said, "The Marudans will strike Rehobat." King Belabret sent his armies at once to the region of Rehobat, and within seven days the Caeylonic cavalry appeared as Asaph had foretold, attempting to raid the city. But the forces of Belabret and Epidymia came forth from a nearby wood where they had been encamped and put the Marudans to rout. When the Epidymians returned to the court of Belabret, they told him excitedly, "Everything came to pass just as the Asylian said!"

After this Asaph was exalted in the sight of Belabret and the court of Epidymia. He was consulted before every campaign that the king made and counseled the king in his judgments. King Belabret began to prevail over the Marudans in every engagement, as the men of Caeylon could in no wise outmaneuver him, for Belabret knew their movements before they were even made. But in the midst of the war Asaph came to lay eyes upon the wife of King Belabret, Inaya. Furthermore, because of the prolonged absence of the king on campaign, Inaya began to spend much time with Asaph in the court, so much so that it became a scandal among all the nobles of Epidymia. Asaph heard the grumblings of the court and intended to not see Inaya anymore, but he was nevertheless drawn and allured by her great beauty, for she was tall and voluptuous, with hair of chestnut that was exceedingly long. Her eyes were dark and her skin olive, for she was of the people of Elam, a remote and wild country to the north of Epidymia. Therefore Asaph's wisdom became perverted, and he indulged his desire. He took Inaya unto his chambers and lay with her there. This he did often, drinking deeply from the fountain of adultery while the king was on campaign.

Sometime later, King Belabret returned from the war in great cheer, for he had won many notable victories against Caeylon. He said, "With one more such grand campaign as we have won of late, the war shall be concluded next spring and Caeylon will be compelled to come to peace." So there was rejoicing and merriment all that winter at the victories of Belabret and the good fortune of Epidymia. But in the dead of winter, Inaya crept away from her husband and came to Asaph, saying, "My lord Asaph, we are in great peril, for I see that I am with child by thee." Asaph was greatly afraid of what Belabret would do when he found his wife was with child, for reckoning from the time he had returned from campaign he would easily deduce that she conceived while he was away. Asaph was thus in turmoil about what was to be done.

Not long after this, Belabret came unto Asaph and said, "Asaph, I have resolved to again assemble my armies and make a foray into Caeylon before the coming of spring. In this manner I will be able to penetrate far into their interior and perhaps lay siege to the city of Caeylon itself, for they will yet be weary from last year's campaign and will not be at their full strength. Tell me therefore whether such a venture will succeed." So Asaph said, "I will give my lord an answer on the morrow."

Asaph retired to his chambers and went forth upon his balcony, gazing up at the northern stars and the sign of the spear blazing in the dark blue heavens. Then he fell into a trance and a vision seemed to come before his eyes, like the vision he saw when he was encamped by the River Sehu. Behold, a great army was setting forth across the desert going east, and Asaph recognized them by their arms as men of Epidymia. Then there was a great commotion in the desert; the column of men was encompassed all about by warriors in black, so that they could neither advance nor flee. Then the great army was destroyed, and its king taken into servitude. When Asaph awoke from the vision he perceived its meaning immediately, for by it he understood that if Belabret went ahead with his strategy then the Epidymians would be defeated.

The following morning Asaph presented himself before King Belabret. The king was eager to see Asaph and said, "My good lord Asaph, has it been revealed unto thee what Fate decrees of my plan?" Then Asaph reasoned within himself, "If the king goes forth to war, he will surely fall, and the matter between Inaya and myself will be unknown to him." Therefore he said, "My good king, Fate has looked kindly upon your plans concerning the war, for I have seen a great victory for Epidymia and much glory for your majesty, only provided you assemble the armies and set out with utmost haste." This word pleased Belabret greatly and he hastily assembled his army for war. Very great was that army, for the king anticipated that he would lay siege to the city of Caeylon itself. Within a fortnight Belabret led his army off east with great excitement to a fanfare of trumpets and cheering crowds. Inaya came to Asaph and said, "What will be done? When the king returns from his great victory he will see clearly that I am with child!" But Asaph said, "He shall never return to behold fair Epidyne again." Then Inaya went off and wept.

It came to pass as Asaph had foreseen, for Belabret, believing the Caeylonics to be ill equipped and unprepared for an early campaign, marched east with great arrogance and bothered neither to send out scouts nor secure his rear. The men of Maruda knew of his movements and mustered their troops by their hundreds and by their thousands and came upon Belabret within a fortnight after he entered Caeylonic lands. Belabret acted foolishly in the battle and allowed his column to be outflanked, so that the Marudans pressed them from the left and the right. It was not until the setting of the sun that Belabret knew that his army was in disarray, and he tried zealously to rally them. But the Caeylonic cavalry kept them hemmed in, and firing upon them relentless volleys of arrows, slew many of them. The army of Epidymia fell in the desert; but Belabret was captured alive and taken to Caeylon to be held for ransom. That day fell sixteen thousand Epidymian spearmen, five thousand cavalry, eight hundred charioteers, and twelve hundred picked men who served alongside King Belabret.

When Belabret's defeat and capture was heard of in Epidymia, there was great mourning and weeping. The lords of the court declared forty days of fasting and mourning for the return of the king, and there was deep sadness throughout the land. But after the forty days were over, men both great and small began to murmur against Asaph for the false prophecy which he had given the king. When it became evident to all that Inaya was with child and she could no longer conceal it, the hatred of the people of Epidymia against Asaph was aroused all the more, for it was common knowledge that the queen had been his mistress. Not long after this the queen refused to see Asaph anymore, and he began to be in fear for his life. He said, "I will search within myself for what shall be and act accordingly." Yet try as he might, he found that his vision had died, and the gift of prophecy abided with him no longer. When the time drew near for Inaya to be delivered of her child, the lords of Epidyne began to grumble and said, "Shall the bastard son of Asaph have a place in the court of Epidymia?" And they began to openly talk of killing Asaph and expelling Inaya.

Meanwhile the Caeylonics treated King Belabret very poorly, keeping him in a dungeon beneath the royal palace in Caeylon for four months. Of the lords of Epidymia they asked a ransom of ten thousand gold bars. When the lords of Epidymia heard this, they balked and said, "Such an amount does not exist in our entire kingdom or the kingdom of the Asylians!" So the ransom money was not paid, and the lords elected one of their own, a war chief named Azael, to be king, for they gave up on Belabret as one lost. Word was brought to Belabret that he was not to be ransomed and that his kinsmen had elected Azael to reign in his stead. When the Marudans realized they would receive no ransom for the king, they took Belabret and strangled him, then cut his head off.

But once Azael was king, he determined to blot out
Belabret's house so as to have no contest to his authority. He
sought to lay hands on Inaya and put her to death before she
was able to bring forth her child. Inaya, however, arose and
fled to Leman, thus eluding Azael's thirst for blood. When
Asaph heard of Azael's accession to the throne and the flight
of Inaya, he said, "My time here is over. I must return unto the
land of my ancestors, for with the death of Belabret comes the
extinction of the house of Dyans and the fall of all Epidymia.
The kingdom is lost." So he stole out of Epidyne by night and
fled west on a mule, hoping to pass over the Sehu into
Cadarasia by the breaking of the dawn.

As soon as Inaya was settled in Leman, she sent her
servants to retrieve Asaph from Epidyne, for she thought,
"Though we are in exile, at least we shall live in peace and
dwell together as man and wife now that Belabret is dead." But
it was told to her that Asaph had fled and was making for
Cadarasia. Then her rage was enkindled; she bitterly regretted
her actions with him and wept for the death of her husband. In
her fury she summoned one of her most trusted servants, a
eunuch called Cerigo, and said, "Take the swiftest horse you
can find and go westward along the road that leads to the
Fords of Esmer. There waylay Asaph and strike him down."
Cerigo, who was a brutal and powerful man, said, "I swear it
shall be so, my queen."

So Cerigo pursued Asaph and came upon his trail going
west. Though he could not catch him at the fords, he followed
over the Sehu by Koharth. He came upon Asaph sleeping
fitfully beneath an apple tree in the glade of an orchard not far
from the main road. Seeing him thus at rest, Cerigo crept up
upon him and thrust his dagger into his heart. Asaph gasped
and thrashed about beneath the tree for a moment until
darkness overtook him. Then Cerigo sliced off his head, stuffed
it in a sack, and returned with haste to Leman. When he came
to Leman and presented himself before Inaya, he said, "My

lady, I have done what you have desired and slew the Asylian Asaph." Then he brought forth the severed head of Asaph and showed it unto Inaya.

When she saw the head of Asaph, she repented of her rash orders to Cerigo and began to weep, saying, "Now am I utterly alone!" So vehemently did she weep and tremble that she began to be in labor and delivered the child of Asaph at that very moment. After she had delivered the child, her maidservants told her, "It is a girl, my lady," and Inaya said, "Let her be named Elora." Then Elora was laid upon the breast of Inaya. But Inaya was faint and felt the vigor of life draining from her. She summoned Cerigo and said, "Cerigo, I heartily repent of the evil I commanded you to do to Asaph, father of this child Elora. Therefore, when I am gone, take this child and return her unto the people of her father. Bring her back to fair Asylia, where the fields are ever lush and the Erriad tumbles down watering the plains of that happy land. The future of Asylia is brighter than that of Epidymia." So Cerigo said, "As you command, my lady." Then Inaya breather her last and expired while the infant Elora slept upon her breast.

Cerigo delivered Elora to the maidservants of Inaya, that she should be suckled by a wetnurse. When the child was weaned, Cerigo took her up and brought her west over the Sehu into the land of Asylia. He knew naught of the kin of Asaph nor of the house of Manissa, and thus entrusted Elora to an honest shepherd and his wife who were old and childless. They received the girl with joy and raised her in the wild moorlands that border Ituria on the southeast. The girl was perfect in every way, for she was beautiful and rugged, as are the women of that region—but also virtuous and humble, and in all things was a blessing to the shepherd. The shepherd and his wife knew not that she was the daughter of Asaph, nor that she was the great-granddaughter of Manissa, until the day when the girl was thirteen. On that day Manissa appeared to the shepherd in a dream and said, "See to it that no harm comes to Elora, for she is the daughter of Asaph, son of Hazer of the royal house of Asylia. Take the girl to the Temple of Mironna in Cadaras and present her to the old priest Inorax." So the shepherd and his wife were in great fear of the dream and made all this known to Elora.

Thus the shepherd brought Elora to the priest Inorax at the Temple of Mironna in Cadaras and told him of the dream and of the command to bring Elora thither. But Inorax said, "And what shall I do with the girl? The priesthood is reserved to males alone, and we accept no wards."* But the shepherd insisted, saying, "Our Lady herself has demanded that it be so!" Inorax scoffed, saying, "She shall have to demand it of me as well!" That very night Inorax was visited in a dream by Manissa who showed him many wonderful things and verified the truth of all the shepherd had told him. The following day, Inorax arose and sought out Elora, and finding her, said, "Manissa has made known to me what is to become of you. Inasmuch as Asaph, thy father, committed a great evil by his impurity with the Queen of Epidymia, so shall you atone for the sins of your family by your great purity. Therefore you shall be consecrated as a virgin from this day forward and shall minister in this temple, not as a priest to offer sacrifice, but as a servant and holy virgin to offer prayers and petitions for our blessing and good fortune."

When the shepherd heard this, he was saddened, for Elora was very beautiful and he had hoped to wed her to a man of good means. But Elora said, "My father, the words of Inorax bring to me a great peace and quench all my fears. This is what has been willed for me and my house, and I shall not flee from it. If the ill done by my true father must needs be atoned for in this manner, so be it." Thus the shepherd bid her farewell and entrusted her to the care of Inorax.

Thereafter the maiden Elora became a virgin at the Temple of Mironna. Inorax had a special chamber built for her off the anteroom of the outer sanctuary where she could dwell and abide perpetually inside the confines of the Citadel. She came forth frequently to offer prayers for the forgiveness of the sins of Asaph and of the kingdom, and prayed frequently at the tomb of Secum, which was within the Citadel. She grew in virtue and purity, and as time passed she became silent and thoughtful, in all things modeling exceptional humility. Many of the priests of Mironna and important lords of Cadaras and Asylia came to converse with her about various things, so that word of her grace and goodness spread abroad.

It was in the tenth year of her residence at the Citadel that other young women of the land came to devote themselves to the same mode of life and discipline as Elora. At first Elora sent them away, for she said, "This task has been appointed to me by the glorious Manissa herself; how shall anyone else take up this discipline which has been entrusted to me alone?" But the women would not relent in their requests to join her, and so Inorax granted Elora permission to allow other virgins to join in her prayers and had constructed for them a wing on the southwest edge of the temple complex. This was how the House of Virgins came to be, which endures in Cadaras to this day.

Elora passed her years there in peace and solitude. Many women flocked to the Citadel to become her followers, so that the temple in the latter days had more virgins than priests attached to it. But it came to pass that Elora's eyes grew dim and her body became bent with age. Her dark hair silvered and then turned to white, and she moved about only with great difficulty. Finally, one year when the hot Cadarasian summer passed and the chill of winter was upon the land, Elora took ill with fever and was stretched out upon her bed in great pain. The priests and virgins of the Citadel came to minister to her, but she said, "Get away from me. I wish to depart unseen by the eyes of men." So all her attendants left her alone to writhe and shake on her sickbed.

It came to pass that in her extremity she had a great vision.* Behold, she was taken up to the Hill of Cruachan and saw that the place was overgrown with weeds and in a state of neglect, for even the Stone of Cruachan itself where Blessed Manissa had stood barefoot before the lords of Asylia was covered with moss and thorny brambles. She tried to clear the weeds and thorns from the place, but in doing so she pricked her fingers until they were covered in bloody wounds.

Then she looked down upon the plain and saw a great herd of deer running wild across the land. Some were pressing hard towards the south, but others stopped to graze or lap the waters of the rills and pools that dotted the fields of Asylia. Then came the sound of thundering from the east, and a troupe of riders came upon the deer. They were fiercely attired, all donning the blackest of cloaks with heads covered by helms of bronze. They wore upon their breasts glistening new mail and bore deadly spears of exceeding length. With great ferocity they came upon the deer and cast their spears at them, felling many as they drank at the rills or grazed. When the deer perceived they were under attack they fled, but some of the bucks turned and tried to gore the black-cloaked men, though to little avail, for no matter where they turned there was a whetted spearhead waiting to pierce them and bring them down to death. Yet the riders were not able to make a total end of the deer, for a single doe fled to the uttermost west, while a solitary buck fled to the remote south and was unreachable. But the fiercest of all the bucks leapt and thrashed wildly about the plains. So vigorous was he that the riders could not bring him down, neither with spear nor net, so that they retired exhausted, and the wild buck pranced off into the wilderness. But the plain was littered with the bodies of the fallen deer.

Then Elora looked and beheld another vision, and it seemed that the Erriad was polluted with a vile black sludge that bubbled up from the ground, making the whole land round about stink. Then out of the putrid water came forth a multitude of hideous and deformed frogs, swollen with skin of darkest black. They spread out over the land, befouling every spring and trampling down the wildflowers that flourish in the warmth of the Asylian summers. They came into the villages and towns of Asylia and defiled all the shrines and sacred groves, so that every holy place was polluted with stinking muck. Then many of the people of Asylia began to go out after the frogs to ally with them and serve them, so that men and women aided the frogs in fouling up the land, until from the depths of Arcoria unto the eastern marches of Cadaras the entire land round about was a putrid waste.

But suddenly a whirlwind came out of the west, and from the whirlwind came forth twelve gloriously armored warriors, so lordly and powerful that Elora trembled when she saw them. Their helms glistened in the rays of the morning sun, their arms and legs were thick like tree trunks, like the cedars of En Gihor. Their shields were large and of hard ash, covered with four layers of hide and rimmed in glittering silver. Each bore a spear, massive in length and in sharpness of blade, and not unlike the spear of Ioclus in appearance. Each was mounted upon a white stallion of mighty stature and was robed in a woolen cloak of green. The glorious riders cried, "Cruacha!" and thundered across the land, and wheresoever they went they slew the vile frogs that were polluting the countryside. Some of the men and women who were in the power of the creatures rose to defend them, but the warriors rode them down and speared them to death along, with their detestable masters. The riders traversed the entire land, as far west as the white beaches that terminate at the shining blue sea, and as far east as the arid and hard lands of Elam; as far north as the white walls of Thán in Cyrenaica, and south to the endless grasslands of Corbalund and the pleasant regions that border the dominion of the Enlilim. Everywhere the land was filled with warfare and destruction, the twelve riders warring against the frog creatures and their servants. It seemed to Elora to go on for a long while, so that whole cycles of the moon and seasons of the harvest elapsed; yet it passed by her at once as a breeze.

At last the riders made an end of the foul creatures from one end of the land to the other. Then they mounted their horses and began to ride towards the uttermost north. Elora cried out and said, "My good masters, where goest thou?" One turned to her and said, "Come and see." Then she was taken to the summit of a tall mountain, and the twelve men were there. One of them pointed to a cave near the summit and said, "Look in the cave." Elora stooped and entered the cave and saw an infant resting upon a bed of straw, slumbering peacefully and oblivious to the presence of either Elora or the men. Elora said, "What can this mean?" One of the men said, "This is he who has been hidden away for the appointed hour." Then, behold! A glorious light appeared on the mountaintop, so bright that the twelve men shielded their faces with their cloaks. Elora looked and beheld Manissa descending upon a cloud until her feet rested upon the summit of the mountain. She took up the child from the cave and kissed him upon the brow. Then she said to him, "Go and make things right with my people," and having said this, hurled him to the earth with great fury like a thunderbolt from heaven.

The child struck the earth with great force so that all the mountains and the trees were shaken. Then it seemed to Elora that though an infant, he stood up erect and in the breadth of a moment became before her eyes a tall and glorious lord, fierce in war and prudent in rulership. Then Manissa called forth from the clouds and said, "Henceforth I will be ever with my people." Then the child who had become a man ruled with great might and wisdom for many years, so that the pollution of the former days was cleansed, and the land again prospered.

Elora awoke from her vision and again found herself on her sickbed, wasted away and exhausted, for she told her attendants, "I feel as though I have traveled all night long and been in intense labor." Then she called for a temple scribe and had her vision committed to writing, and having done so, she fell swoon and expired, being about eighty-five years of age. Thus passed Elora, daughter of Asaph; she was entombed in the Citadel at Cadaras beside Secum her kinsman. But across Asylia and Cadarasia young women gathered together on her example and pledged themselves to virginity and prayer for the kingdom and the house of Manissa, so that when she died there were orders of virgins throughout the entire realm.

Apollus and Sammas

꧁ ꧁ ꧁

In the days when Elora dwelt and prophesied at Cadaras and the Council of Lords ruled the realm, a great war erupted between the Manissans of Cadarasia and the kingdom of Epidymia. Every spring, when the days began to wax long and the trianta roses blossomed along the banks of the Cadar, the rugged shepherds and farmers of Asylia and Cadarasia left their lands under the lords of Elabaea and ventured to the northern frontiers.* There they waged war all throughout the summer months until the time of the harvest, returning then to their homes and kin. But though the war was hotly contested and renewed year after year, neither kingdom was able to prevail, for the Epidymians were too mighty to be utterly overthrown, but not yet mighty enough to decisively defeat the Manissans.

One of the lords who went forth to battle in the well-watered valley of the Gihon was Issos, a powerful and noble man from the region of An Hered. This Issos had fought in many campaigns in Epidymia and was renowned among all the Manissans, both in Asylia and Cadarasia. He took to wife a Caeylonic woman called Nimrah whose people were from Caina in the east. By Nimrah he bore a single son, whom he named Anthalus. This Anthalus was not yet weaned when Issos again donned his shield and spear and went forth to make war on the Epidymians and was slain. So the servants of

Issos brought his body on a bier back to An Hered and the house of Nimrah, where he was buried with all the customary rites of his people. But when the days for the mourning of Issos were over, the men of An Hered and Cadaras began to speak of the boy and say he was unlucky, for it soon became apparent that Anthalus was left-handed, something the Cadarasians hold to be an ill omen, and this even more so since his father Issos had so recently been slain.* The wagging tongues of the Cadarasians of An Hered unnerved the child and his mother, and so not long after Nimrah, the widow of Issos, arose, gathered her property and her servants, and returned east to her kin in Caeylon, bearing Anthalus her son away with her. Thus Anthalus was raised upon the scorching deserts of Caeylon and educated alongside the sons of Caeylonic noblemen from Maruda and Lyson. His fair skin became brazened by the relentless sun of the east, and he gradually became accustomed to walking the desolate wastes of western Caeylon where his mother resided.

Though he never forgot the Elabaean tongue which he had spoken in the days of his youth, Anthalus gradually learned the tongues of Maruda. The lad was sent to the city of Caeylon to study under the scribes of the Temple of En'Thoth. He dwelt in the shadow of En'Thoth in the heart of Maruda for six years, and in that time forgot the traditions and stories of wild Elabaea, instead attaching himself to the gods of Maruda. He offered sacrifices to Mardu, the mightiest of the gods of Caeylon, and was initiated into the mysteries of the Nergalim. He studied the courses of the stars, learning the art of astrology from the priests of Adar, and the magical rites of the storms from the wizened old priests of Burzi. He frequented the sanctuaries of Innana and committed vile acts there under the moon, bloodying his hands in sacrifices to Neb, the bronze-headed god of war. Most of all he was taught to adore the sacred sun, Shamash, and was an ardent patron of the cult of Shamash in Caeylon. Thus did he abandon his Elabaean name

Anthalus and was given instead the Marudan name Sammas in honor of the sun god. So his mind and heart were darkened by the bloody and immoral rites of the Marudans, and his will became enslaved to their gods and their priests.

After this Sammas-Anthalus was sent away to be trained in the art of Marudan warfare, and because he was left-handed he excelled at this, for men could only match him in battle with great difficulty. So Sammas-Anthalus mastered the spear and the scimitar and became a great marksman with the bow. When he was thus trained in both the lore and warfare of the Marudans, he was sent to minister to the king of all Caeylon, mighty King Bakku, who sat enthroned in the great city of Caeylon. Sammas ministered in the presence of the king and became a valued counselor in the court of Bakku.

But when Sammas-Anthalus reached his twenty-ninth year, word came that the fighting between the Manissans and the Epidymians had grown especially hot. The Manissans launched a great campaign to press into the Gihon Valley through the Plains of Anorel and split the Kingdom of Epidymia in two, but the Epidymians had mustered a great resistance and drenched Anorel in blood through the first months of spring. Thus the campaign went very poorly for the Manissans, and King Azael of Epidymia began to talk of pressing south and taking Cadaras. The Council of Lords were in disarray, for some advocated making peace with Azael while others were for prosecuting the war further. Not a few of the lords had been slain upon Anorel's fertile soil and rested their bones far from their homeland. While the lords argued bitterly, King Azael of Epidymia brought forth a great army from the north and assaulted the Manissan lines on the Plains of Anorel, slaying a multitude of them and driving the Manissans south to the borders of Cadarasia. There was great panic throughout the city of Cadaras, for the armies of Azael were but three days from the borders of their land and the armies of the Manissans were routed. Therefore the Council of

Lords issued a decree that any man who would muster the armies and lead the Manissans to victory in Epidymia should be granted the office of the kingship, for the Asylians had no king for over a generation.

It was Nimrah, mother of Sammas, who came to him in Caeylon and said, "Have you not heard the desperate straits the people of Manissa find themselves in? They are routed and destroyed before the Epidymians and freely offer the throne to whichever lord among them who shall lead them victoriously into battle against Azael!" Sammas scoffed and said, "Indeed! You would have me make this attempt? Am I not a Marudan and minister of the King of Caeylon?" His mother said, "But you are half-Asylian, which you know well, for your father Issos was accounted a great war-chief among the men of Cadaras.* You are within your right to lead Asylians into battle and to lay claim to the kingship, at least as much so as any other man." Sammas jested about the remarks of his mother and sent her away, but her words gnawed away at his mind like a relentless worm.

It soon came to pass that Sammas was moved by the words of Nimrah and obtained leave from King Bakku of Caeylon to journey west to his homeland, there to secure the defeat the Epidymians and obtain the throne. This was acceptable to Bakku because Caeylon at that time was also engaged in a struggle with Epidymia, thus accounting it all profit that the Manissans should exhaust themselves fighting Azael. Before Sammas departed, King Bakku summoned him to come and stand in his presence. Sammas appeared before the king and said, "Here I am, my lord." King Bakku said, "My dear Sammas, may the gods bless your endeavor. Come, make sacrifice at the Temple of Shamash with me for your victory." So King Bakku took Sammas and went out through the south gate of the palace, which leads along the main thoroughfare of Caeylon. They came to the Temple of Shamash, which was constructed atop a mighty terraced complex of seven stories, so that Sammas and King Bakku had to many steps to ascend to reach the Temple.

After they had sacrificed to the undying sun, Bakku said, "Sammas, if you should drive the Epidymians from the land and inherit the throne of Elabaea, remember that the Asylians are an arrogant and rustic people and that they treat their kings with contempt." Sammas said, "How so, my king?" Bakku replied, "They feign obeisance to their kings, but in fact they hold them in their power, for their custom is that a king cannot assume his authority until he is acclaimed and ratified by the lords of that land. Even so, once he is acclaimed, it is custom for the lords to put his decrees to a vote, so as the king is seen as the first among the lords rather than as the lord of lords. Some lords, such as those of western Elabaea, openly hold the throne of Cadaras in contempt and refuse to obey their king, as in days past Baldor refused to hand over his sister Mariammné to satisfy the lust of Hadrior." Sammas said, "Such affrontery would never be tolerated in thy court, your majesty!" Bakku said, "Indeed not. Furthermore, they do not accord their kings divine honors, as is custom in Caeylon, for they hold them to be but mere men; many lords even speak familiarly with their kings and treat them as comrades rather than as the offspring of gods." Sammas said, "I see their customs are far inferior to our own in these matters, but supposing I attain the kingship, what shall I do regarding these things?" Bakku said, "Let them not treat you with contempt as they treated their last king, against whom they revolted and slew in the very confines of the Citadel. Rather, make your authority felt among them." Sammas kept the king's words in his heart. And after offering sacrifices at all the temples of the gods for his success, departed the city.

So Sammas journeyed far north and west, to the boundaries of Caeylon, until he came to the place where the desert sands drift away into sturdy dirt hillocks covered in hardy field grass, and the rivers flow down from the Gihon to water the land round about. After many days he finally passed into easternmost Cadarasia. When he returned to An Hered to claim the holdings of his father, the Council of Lords was suspicious of him and said, "It is not our custom that a son who has for so long been abroad in a foreign kingdom should come suddenly to claim his father's lands. Yet we are in dire straits and will recognize your claim if you will lead men into battle against Epidymia." Sammas said, "For this very reason did I come forth to Cadaras from Maruda." So the lords entrusted four thousand men to Sammas with which to make war on Azael and prove himself worthy of the lordship.

Sammas put off his Marudan garments and took up the coarse wool of Elabaea. Then he donned a glittering coat of bronze mail and took a spear of hard Cadarasian ash into his left hand, bearing up his great shield with his right. When all the men were mustered, he mounted a steed of ebony and rode forth with the spearmen of Cadaras to drive Azael from their frontiers. Sammas was only two days north of Cadaras when he encountered the Epidymian army scattered in southern Anorel, making a determined but disordered march towards Cadaras. Sammas let forth a great roar and led the Cadarasians against the Epidymian lines, smashing them with fury. The Epidymians endeavored to bring down Sammas, but every man that engaged him was brought low, for Sammas fought skillfully and with his left hand, and the Epidymians could bring forward no left-handed champions to match him. By and by the Epidymians fell back until their retreat became an utter rout. Sammas cried, "Forward! Press them hard!" The men of Cadaras harried them north all that day and into the evening. The Epidymians were pushed off Anorel and into the verdant farmlands that lay round the environs of Epidyne by the northern course of the Sehu River. When the battle was over, Sammas had the fields of Anorel scouted and found that they had slain ten thousand men of Epidymia, with many nobles and lords among them.

Then was there great rejoicing among the Cadarasians, for such a victory against the Epidymians had not been had in many years. They immediately elevated Sammas upon their shields, crying, "Hail, King Sammas! May his days be blessed!" for they knew the decree of the Council, that whatever lord should step forward and drive the Epidymians from the frontiers should be made king. So the army escorted Sammas back to Cadaras proclaiming his kingship the entire course, so that all the way many farmers and herdsmen came out to pay homage to Sammas and swear fealty to him. But when the throng arrived at the walls of Cadaras the lords were unnerved, for they said, "We know nothing of this Sammas who has for his whole life dwelt among the Marudans. Though he is the son of Issos, he is in all other things a foreigner. Shall a foreigner rule over us?" Nevertheless, because of their decree, and because of the throngs of soldiers and common people who followed in the train of Sammas, they relented and opened the gates of the city unto him.

But when Sammas had come into the city, he said, "I shall not take the crown here, for in ages past it was custom for the kings of the Asylians to take the kingship at the Hill of Cruachan. From thence shall our kingship be inaugurated." The people marveled at this, for no king or lord of Cadaras or Asylia had been crowned at Cruachan since the days of Manissa. So Sammas proceeded with a great throng several days journey northwest, into the wilds of Asylia, and there came upon the Hill of Cruachan. When the procession came upon Cruachan and beheld it standing looming and solitary upon the verdant plains, they all cried with joy, and some said, "The glory of the days of Manissa are come upon us again!" And everyone was carried away with rejoicing and merriment and blessed the name of Sammas. Yet when they approached the hill they found it very wild and overgrown with many thorns and brambles, so that it took the people some time to clear them away.* But by and by the Hill of Cruachan was cleared of the brambles, and Sammas and the lords proceeded to the Stone of Cruachan atop the hill.

Sammas was borne upon shields to the stone and there stood upon it, receiving the kingship from the Council of Lords. He was robed in regal robes of whitened linen and stood barefoot upon the rock, and there accepted the crown of the kingdom. Then the people cried and wailed for joy, for it had been over one hundred years since Manissa stood upon the stone and vowed to free Asylia from the Marudans. They all cried out, "Fate has graced us with a wise and valiant king who will rule in the spirit and power of Manissa." So Sammas accepted the kingship and with many vows swore to defend the people of Elabaea and to uphold their traditions. But some said, "He is left-handed and ought not to take the oaths with his right hand." So Sammas took the oaths a second time, swearing with his left hand and clutching his sword in the right. Thus Elabaea again had a king after fifty years of being ruled by the Council of Lords.

Yet not all the lords were of one mind with regards to Sammas; many mistrusted him because of his upbringing in Caeylon and his sudden rise to notoriety. Some treated him with contempt and refused to address him with the title of king, considering him a usurper. Sammas was thus in fear for his life, and so sent word to Caeylon, summoning twelve captains of the Marudans that he had known during his youth and bidding them come serve him in Cadaras. The Marudans were ushered into the Citadel at night by stealth, so that when the Council of Lords was summoned before the presence of Sammas on the following day they were astonished to see King Sammas flanked by the Marudan captains. Each captain was tall and dexterous, bearing a blade of cruel Caeylonic bronze and draped in a black cloak. From that day forward Sammas kept them as a perpetual bodyguard about him, and

though no lord made a move against his person, many of them grumbled against this, for Sammas lorded his authority over them and treated them as inferiors. Finally Sammas gave the order to seize the lords who were chief among the grumblers, and the Marudan captains seized them and imprisoned them in the Citadel. Sammas did not have them put to death, but rather compelled them to abdicate their titles and their lands. And as many as did so were turned free, but their lands were bestowed upon the captains and friends of Sammas. After this he increased his bodyguard from twelve men to fifty and began to rule with a heavy hand in Cadaras.

Then Sammas began to eject the priests of Mironna from the temple and the Citadel and replaced them with priests of the various cults of Caeylon, such as he had known in his youth. The yearly offering of incense was halted and the vile ceremonies of the Nergalim were carried out in the sacred temple.* The walls and the towers of the Citadel were given over to the priests of Adar and the gardens of Anaxandra bloodied with sacrifices to Neb. He also caused to be erected a great bronze statue of Mardu in the temple precinct, so that all who passed in or out of the Citadel were compelled to walk in its shadow. The statue was twelve cubits high and made of two thousand pounds of melted bronze. He also caused all who passed by the image to bow in its presence, and if any man failed to bow or showed disrespect to the image he was taken and beaten.

But this was not all the evil that Sammas did, for he also summoned the remnant of Illyrana, sages knowledgeable in the lore of the Illyrs and the Zhinkanthans, to come into the land and erect shrines to the detestable gods of the south in the fair vales of Cadarasia and the pasturelands east of the Erriad. So the vile practices of the Illyrs gradually spread throughout the land like a plague, and the hearts of the Asylians and Cadarasians living in those regions became cast down with despair, for in a very brief time their customs and practices had been displaced and their land taken over by foreigners. There were even some remote regions of the east, where under the shadows of dense groves or within barren rocky gorges, the Illyr sages offered sacrifices of men and infants by the black of night. So all of Cadarasia was polluted with blood and the filth of the east. Many Cadarasians and those of Nearer Asylia who knew no better began to frequent the shrines of the Marudan gods and adopt the despicable practices of the Illyrs.

But Sammas was not content, for when he was crowned at Cruachan he was not given the title "King of Elabaea" but rather "King of the Manissans," for after the establishment of the Council, the unity of Elabaea had been broken. The western regions of Elabaea in Asylia and Cyrenaica had fallen away from the dominion of the lords at Cadaras; these realms remained under the dominion of the house of Baldor and the Periorids, though no man of those houses took the title of king. Therefore, after Sammas had been installed at Cadaras and had reigned for some time, he resolved to summon the lords of the west to swear fealty to him before the throne at Cadaras, that all Elabaea might be united as in days of old, both east and west of the Erriad. This decree went forth in the sixth month of the fifth year of his reign.

Now around the time that Sammas was being enthroned in the east, there was ruling in old Asylia the lord Apollus, eldest of the house of Baldor, for he was the firstborn of Baldor's grandson, Scylax.* Apollus had sat enthroned in Asylia for some years and was in the prime of his days, being about thirty years of age. He was of great strength, with thighs as round as logs and a breast of iron, but also short and broad, like all the sons of the house of Baldor. The eyes of Apollus shone brightest blue and his hair was dark, though his complexion was fair. All Asylia had peace in his days, for the land of the far west was sundered from the control of the Council of Lords and was not caught up in the bloody wars against Epidymia. Thus the western Asylians prospered, every man secure on his land and the flocks and produce of the realm untouched by plunder or blight, for there was peace round about.

Apollus had heard much evil concerning Sammas and was thus suspicious of his designs and his summons. There had been no such pledge of troth to Cadaras for over a generation and Apollus was loath to put the fair vales and rills of Asylia under the despotism of Sammas. Therefore he delayed in coming east. When the other lords of Asylia saw that Apollus failed to do homage to Sammas, they likewise did not go unto Cadaras, nor did any of the Periorids who were dwelling throughout the land. Neither did the sons of Necho or the house of Elphas of the southlands go up. Only the Hazerites of An Erras hearkened to the summons of Sammas and went east to pledge fealty to him.

Word soon reached Sammas of the refusal of the lords of the west to do him homage. Sammas inquired of some of his counselors and said, "Who are these arrogant lords of the west who refuse to pay honor to the sacred ties that perpetually bind Cadarasia to Asylia under the lordship of the King of Cadaras?" He was told by his counselors, "My lord, these men are the remnants of the house of Manissa, which have ever been a bane to the throne of Cadaras." At the sound of Manissa's name Sammas frowned and said, "That name is hateful to my ears. But tell me, what is it about this house that renders it so troublesome?" His lords said, "For many generations they have maintained a claim to the throne of all Elabaea and refuse to recognize either the Council or thy kingship. This view is especially prevalent among those called the Periorids." Then Sammas brooded about the Citadel, for these words greatly displeased him. But he recalled the words of Bakku, his liege-lord of Caeylon, and resolved to put an end to the claims of the house of Manissa.

In the spring of the eighth year of the reign of Sammas, the king summoned a great army upon the Cadarasian plains for the purpose of forcibly subjecting the Asylians west of the Erriad to the crown of Cadaras. Who was mustered there on that great and terrible day, when the King of Cadaras resolved to make war upon their ancient allies? First was the king himself, Sammas-Anthalus, who donned a cloak of blazing red and a helm of glittering bronze with a plume of white horsehair. In his left hand he bore up his sturdy spear, and in his right the shield that he had borne into battle against Azael. How terrible and mighty he appeared that day, armored and seated on his steed, his dark eyes glaring hatefully beneath the shadow of his helm towards the west, towards fair Asylia and the land of his desire!

With Sammas rode three thousand horsemen mustered from the regions of An Hered and An Danara east of Cadaras. He also brought forth a legion of Badoan hillmen from the southern mountains, fifteen hundred in all, each ragged and unkept but armed, thirsty for blood and pillage. Also mustered on the dusty plains of Cadaras were two thousand spearmen from the south who were loyal to Cadaras, as well as one thousand from the regions in the immediate environs of the city. He also had in his force five hundred mercenaries of Ituria and a thousand Marudan soldiers which had been lent him by his kin in Caeylon, on the agreement that one third of all booty should be sent as a gift to King Bakku. Thus the army mustered by King Sammas was nine thousand men. Unlike Adaran of old who had marched his forces west in a great mass, Sammas divided his legions up into three columns: one to enter Asylia in the north by the fords of the Sehu bordering Epidymia, one to cross into the west through the land of An Erras (which Sammas led himself), and another to take the southernly route through the foothills and the Nimru Pass.

Apollus was returning from the hunt when his servants brought him word that Sammas was mustering an army.

Apollus was incredulous, and said to his servants, "Can it really be that the King of Cadaras would make war on the Lord of Asylia? Never in the days of my father or our forebears has Cadaras ever made war on Asylia! Nay, this is some ruse for the purpose of compelling us to swear obedience to that viper Sammas. True is the proverb which says:

> *From one whose name*
> *Said front and back the same,*
> *Let one speedily fly*
> *For evil is his eye.*

"Let us call the bluff of this Sammas and see if his threats do not fade away like the mist at the breaking of the dawn." Thus Apollus disregarded the rumors of Sammas's intentions until some other word should come from the east.

But it was not many days after that the armies of Sammas began crossing over the Erriad. At that time the Hazerites were dwelling in An Erras, where since the days of Hadrior their house had been established. The heads of their clans were Idoreth, grandson of Erras, and Rommoss, son of Pelarus, who was seventy years of age and blind (it was he who tended the shrine upon the Hill of Pelaroth and offered incense over the tombs of Hazer and Iyla perpetually). Idoreth had four sons and many brothers, and the kin of Rommoss were also many, so that the house of Hazer was very great in An Erras. When the Hazerites saw the army of Sammas passing through An Erras, a great many of them came out to greet him, for they had pledged loyalty to the king and knew nothing of his designs against the house of Manissa. As the Hazerites were approaching the train of Sammas with wreaths and timbrels, Sammas's counselors said, "These Hazerites are treacherous, for in the days when Perior, son of Manissa, came against the Cadaras, it was these who sheltered him from the wrath of the lords." So Sammas cried, "Slay them all; let not a man among them escape!" Then the riders of Sammas burst forth from their ranks and rode the Hazerites down where they stood, spearing some and trampling others. No man among them was armed, for they had come forth in festive garb with musical instruments to bless the king as he passed by. When the dust had cleared and the sound of slaughter ceased, it was found that thirty-five Hazerites had been slain, with many women and children among them. Yet the heads of the house, Idoreth and Rommoss, were not among the dead.

Then Sammas motioned south, towards Ar Pelaroth, and said, "Destroy that beacon of treason and all who guard it!" So the men of Sammas came against Ar Pelaroth, the poplar covered hill where once Hazer had dwelt in former days. Hoary-headed Rommoss was within the shrine offering incense to Manissa over the tombs of Hazer and Iyla and was told by his sons, "Father! Make haste, for we are under siege!" But old Rommoss was blind and could move only with great sloth. Though his sons attempted to spirit him away it was to no avail, for the men of Sammas charged the hill and took it. The sons of Rommoss they ran through, their white linen garments bloodied with grime as they fell dead upon the dirt. Then Rommoss was seized and treated roughly by the soldiers, who mocked him and struck him with the butts of their spears. But old Rommoss said, "Do you not fear the dreaded curse that Fate will visit upon you for the treachery you have wrought this day? Though Manissa has long since departed the world of mortals, her spear is still sharp and whetted for death, and it is trained upon you and your half-breed usurper before whom you grovel like dogs!" This enraged the soldiers, and they threw old Rommoss to the ground and thrust their spears through him in many places, till the floor of the shrine was full of blood. Then many men ascended the hill and demolished the shrine, burning the wooden beams with fire and hurling down the blocks thereof.

When Idoreth heard what had become of his uncle Rommoss and of the slaying of the Hazerites at An Erras, he gathered his sons to him and said, "A vile deed has been done in Asylia, for the King of Cadaras who reigns from Manissa's throne has used his authority to put to death our kindred, all of them as innocent and gentle as our forebear, Hazer. We must flee this land, west to the court of Apollus our kinsman before we, too, are slain." But the sons of Idoreth said, "Nay, we will stay and fight to avenge our kin." Idoreth said, "My sons, the Hazerites have never been men of war, but rather poets and composers of beautiful songs and melodies, and though you are in the prime of youth, you will not stand up to Sammas the Usurper. What shall it profit you to hurl your lives away so recklessly? Come away with me to the west." But the blood of the sons of Idoreth was young and hot and they would not listen, so after many hours of dispute it came to pass that Idoreth bid them farewell, saying, "All of you are men, even the least. Do what seems best to you. My wife, thy mother, has preceded me in death by many years and I fear not for what may become of me, but I go away from you grieving, for I fear I shall not see you again." They said, "Nay father, for we shall soon meet again." So Idoreth kissed his sons and blessed them before riding swiftly west upon his stallion.

So the sons of Idoreth rode through the lonely moors and hillocks of the heather covered lands just west of the Erriad, north of An Erras, until they came upon the column of Sammas marching through An Erras towards Asylia. They marveled and said, "Has Sammas brought forth so many to slay so few?" and realized the futility of their quest. Nevertheless, the brothers cried "Cruacha!" and charged the lines of Sammas with great fury, spears lowered and eager for death and honor. But Sammas laughed when he saw the four young men charging and said, "Is this the hope of the Hazerites?" Then his archers fired a volley of arrows and sent the brothers and their steeds tumbling to the earth in death. Thus perished the sons of Idoreth.

Sammas grimaced from behind his helm and said, "Go throughout the valleys and the regions of An Erras; slay every Hazerite who dwells therein, the young with the old, the men with the women, the mother with the suckling babe.* Put them all to the sword." So the men of Sammas assented to all that he said and spread out over the land like devouring ants, led by the black robed captains which Sammas had brought over from Maruda. Every cottage and dwelling they came to they cried out, "Sons of Hazer, come forth, for your king is in need of your aid!" Then whomever came forth was thrust through with a spear and the cottage burned; all who were found within were put to death. For seven days Sammas tarried in the western marches of An Erras while the Hazerites were slaughtered. Some tried to defend themselves and were overtaken in combat, while others were slain weaponless. Many other men of the region who were not Hazerites were also killed, for they attempted to come to their aid or were otherwise in proximity to them; these, too, Sammas ordered to be put to death. At the end of seven days his captains returned to him and laid their gore covered spears before his feet and told him, "The house of Hazer is no more."

Meanwhile Idoreth came unto Asylia and the hall of Apollus, and collapsing at the feet of Apollus, cried out, "My kinsman! An unspeakable crime has been committed against us, for Sammas, King of Cadaras and lord of the east, has crossed the Erriad with a great host and has put a great many of my kin to death!" As he was speaking, other servants and runners came into the hall confirming the words of Idoreth and telling Apollus of the slaying of Rommoss and the destruction of the shrine on Ar Pelaroth. Then Apollus said grimly, "We have seen what mettle this Sammas has, for he shrinks not even from killing his own people! This is dire, indeed." Idoreth said, "Apollus, my kinsman and my lord, tarry no longer! Walk not in the way of Baldor your ancestor, who despite his strength and prowess was like a reed shaken in the wind. Act, and act boldly, for Sammas will not cease with the slaughter of the Hazerites but will seek to make an end of all Manissa's house!" Apollus said, "What would you have me to do?" Idoreth said, "Summon all the house of Manissa to the Hill of Cruachan, that the sons of her womb may be united and make war against Sammas as one man; Periorid with Hazerite, descendants of Baldor with sons of Mariammné, Elphas and Necho side by side with the people of Secum's house as well." Then Apollus trembled at the words of Idoreth and the greatness of the thought, for never had all the house of Manissa been united in such a manner.

Apollus sent his most trustworthy servants on his swiftest steeds to the uttermost corners of Elabaea: to fair and verdant Lugaria in the west, where the sons of Mariammné held sway, to the northern wilds of Ituria and Cyrenaica, where many of the Periorids were dwelling, as well as some of the Secumites. They rode even far south into Badoa and the regions around Engor, where the houses of Necho and Elphas ruled. His messengers bore his words to the head of each house, saying, "Let every son of Manissa's blood gather forthwith at the Hill of Cruachan, for Sammas, King of Cadaras, had usurped the throne and is making war upon the peoples of Asylia and the house of Manissa, our blessed forebear."

When this message had gone forth, Apollus marshalled all the riders of Asylia upon the windswept plains beneath the shadows of the Cyrian Highlands, and after three days they numbered some six thousand men who could swing a sword or cast a spear. Then he took the arm of his kinsman Idoreth and said, "Now let us ride east to put an end to this foul Marudan fiend who calls himself King of All Elabaea." So Apollus and Idoreth mounted their steeds and led the riders of Asylia into the wilderness towards the Hill of Cruachan. They went forth on the seventh day of the tenth month, when the frost was upon the grasses of the field, the earth hard from the chill of night, and the breath of the Asylian horses visible in the gray of the morning.

But when they came to the Hill of Cruachan, Idoreth and Apollus were dismayed, for none but forty riders from the house of Mariammné came to them. Apollus was wrathful, and calling to the captain of the riders, said, "My lord, from whence have you come?" And he replied, "From Karanak, my lord Apollus, to fight for the glory of Mariammné and the house of Manissa. I am Eranor, son of Servius, son of Ancus, who was the eldest son of Cygnus and Mariammné, daughter of Blessed Manissa." Apollus said, "You are welcome here, my lord Eranor. But the house of Mariammné is very great in Lugaria; why have so few come?" Eranor said, "My elder brother, Erasinus, rules as king in the pillared halls of Karanak, and great is his authority over the house of Mariammné. He said unto me, 'Why should the kingdom of Lugaria risk provoking Sammas even more by aiding the Manissans? This is a feud between Cadaras and Asylia in which Lugaria has no part.' But I recalled the strife of our Blessed Lady and the common blood that runs through our veins. Then I said, 'Let every man who would fight for Manissa come with me,' and lo, these forty alone followed." Then Apollus and Idoreth wept, for they knew they had not enough men to defeat Sammas.

Meanwhile, the army of Sammas marched through the countryside south of Kerion and came upon the Hill of Cruachan. Seeing the six thousand warriors of Apollus encamped upon it, they made haste across the plain and surrounded the hill so as to lay siege to the Asylians. Yet Apollus did not charge the army of Sammas, nor did Sammas try to ascend the hill, for Sammas hoped to obtain the surrender of Apollus without bloodshed. But the northern column of Sammas's army, under a Marudan called Javad, came into the environs of Asylia. When the people of the city of Asylia saw the soldiers of Javad approaching, marching rank on rank across the plains with spears glittering and banners blowing in the frigid autumn air, they wept with despair, for all of the men of the city were away, gathered with Apollus on Cruachan. When Javad approached the city and encompassed it about, he saw that it was devoid of men, but was populated solely by women, youths, and the old. Therefore he called out in broken Asylian, "Come, why should you all perish? We seek not your destruction, but only the submission of Apollus, your lord. Yet since he is absent, we will take as hostages the kin of Apollus, both the small and the great. Therefore, send forth from the city all those of the house of Baldor, the young with the old, the men with the women, the youth with the suckling babe. Give these over as hostages, and the city and all within shall be spared."

The Asylians wept bitterly at these terms, for they had little faith in Javad the Marudan and less in Sammas. Some said, "No, let us fight to the bitter end against these tyrants!" But the women of the house of Baldor said, "Nay, for it is our house alone they seek. We will go of our own accord, that the rest of you may be spared to live on peaceably." So after some deliberations, the house of Baldor agreed to the demands of Javad and yielded themselves up willingly to his hand. They came out of the city gates dressed in black, for they mourned and wept for Asylia and the house of Manissa, singing dirges and throwing dirt into the air as they gave themselves into the hands of Javad, some seventy-two persons in all. Then Javad ordered his men to tear down the walls of Asylia and pull up their foundations, so that the city should not be defensible anymore.* Thus the Asylians stood by trembling, fearing for their lives and the lives of the hostages while the men of Javad demolished the walls of the city. This having been accomplished, Javad turned south to find the legion of King Sammas.

Meanwhile, the men of Apollus were penned up on the Hill of Cruachan, surrounded by the army of Sammas. The two armies were of equal size and faced each other for several days. For this reason, Sammas was timid and desired not to charge the hill if he could lure Apollus down by some other stratagem. It was while he was deliberating these things that Javad and his men came to them, strengthening their numbers and brining him tidings of what had been done at Asylia. Then Sammas grinned and said, "Bring the hostages out." So Sammas came to the foot of Cruachan and called forth to Apollus, saying, "Apollus, lord of Asylia, will you not come to terms with me?" Apollus came forth from the top of the hill and said, "We have no faith in one who has put to death the people of Hazer, who had hitherto pledged fealty to your throne. Your word gives us no security, and your promises are as dung."

Then Sammas brought forth the kin of Apollus and said, "See these hostages, seventy-two in all? Before you stands bound the entire house of Baldor, which we have taken from Asylia as a surety of your good will. Therefore, hear these terms: you shall give yourself and your army into my hands by tomorrow at nightfall, or else I will behead these seventy-two hostages here before you, the young with the old, the men with the women, the youth with the suckling babe; all alike shall die, and the house of Baldor will utterly perish from the earth." Idoreth said, "'Tis a despicable bluff, my lord! Can these really be thy kin from Asylia?" But Apollus and his men gazed upon the hostages and recognized them as their own. Then there was a deep lament upon Cruachan, for they saw their dilemma and doubted not that Sammas would carry out his word. So Apollus called down and said, "We will give you an answer on the morrow." Sammas said, "Very well. But take heed; do not think to play the trickster with me! If you think to outwit me by some cunning, they will die. If you attempt to make a sortie off the hill and break through our lines, I will slay them. If anything goes amiss, they will pay for your folly with their heads." Thus Apollus and Sammas departed to their tents for the evening.

Then Apollus and Idoreth were in great turmoil, and all the men with them, for they knew the treachery of Sammas and had little trust that he would keep faith with them if they laid down arms, yet they feared what would become of their children and womenfolk if they failed to surrender themselves. After much argument, Apollus said, "If we do not turn ourselves over, he will put our kin to the sword. When he has done this, he will take this hill and we will all die here just the same. But if we deliver ourselves over to him, he may slay us or let us live; who knows what he shall do with our kin? Therefore, though it colors us with a dishonor from which our house may never recover, let us hand ourselves over to him for the sake of our little ones." Then the soldiers all wept and said, "Aye, for our little ones."

But during the night, it came to pass that some of the Periorids who had heard the summons of Apollus came upon the Hill of Cruachan, about thirty in all. The Periorids were hotblooded and eager for battle, for besides desiring to aid Apollus and their kinsmen at Cruachan they were also seeking to defend the place, for the hill held the bones of Perior, entombed there in olden times when the nine sons of Perior fled west after the burning of Cadaras. They arrived near midnight, and seeing the place encompassed about by the army of Sammas and the captains of Maruda, were full of wrath. They crept through the lines of Sammas, coming at last to the crest of the hill and the camp the Asylians. The Asylians were wearied with the toil of the siege and with much grief and told the Periorids of the ultimatum of Sammas. But the Periorids said to Apollus, "Has the house of Baldor utterly lost its nerve? Where is the fury that possessed Baldor before the gates of Thán, when outnumbered and alone he destroyed the three sons of Endumion and took the city for Hadrior?"

Apollus was irritated by their words and said, "We lack no boldness, sons of Perior, for if it were a matter of our own lives only we would throw them away at the first cry of battle to avenge the wrongs done to us and give honor to Manissa. But our womenfolk and little ones are in their hands, and they force us to come to terms." So the Periorids went out from him grumbling.

As they went out into the night from the tent of Apollus, one of the Periorids, Pictor of the house of Semnos, said, "Why should we come unto this hill to fight this evening only to be compelled to surrender on the morrow? Who knows what this Sammas will do? Let us muster the great strength that has ever resided with our house and charge the lines of Sammas. By Manx, we will give him a thrashing he won't soon forget!" So the thirty Periorids clutched their swords in hand and crept down the Hill of Cruachan, to the tent where the hostages were kept. Before them at the rock-strewn base of the hill stood a picket of a dozen men. Pictor said, "Let your blood flow hot, sons of Perior. Daring deeds await us!" Then they lunged forth from the shadows and struck the guards with a great fury, slaying them all before they had time to raise the alarm. But when they came into the camp they were sighted, and men cried out, "The Asylians are upon us!" A troop of soldiers came forth against the Periorids and they soon found themselves enmeshed in battle. The din of war filled the camp, and all the watchfires were lit. The Periorids fought savagely, slaying many of the men who came against them. Pictor yelled, "Get to the tent and usher the womenfolk up the hill to the Asylian camp!"

But when they fought their way to the tent, they found it empty. Sammas had suspected some treachery on the part of the Asylians, and so had removed the hostages to another place farther from the hill. Then the full force of Sammas's army came upon the Periorids and pressed them hotly. The cold night air was full of the cries of captains and footmen shouting, the sounds of spears breaking upon shields, and of bodies crumpling upon the frosty moonlit grass. When it seemed that they could fight no longer, Pictor cried "Perior é Manissé!" and all the Periorids shouted likewise. Then they crashed forth with a mighty charge and trampled the soldiers of Sammas before them, grinding some into the icy mud and cleaving others with their cruel blades in hopes of cutting a clearing back to the hill. It was only slowly and with much bloodshed that the Periorids took to the hill; when they paused to refresh themselves behind the rocks they found that they had lost half their number in the camp. Then Pictor sat down and wept as the stars began to fade by the gentle gray light of autumn's dawn.

Sammas came forth, fully arrayed in his cloak of red and his terrible brazen helm, eyes aflame with fury and teeth gnashed in cruelty. He held his spear aloft in his left hand and cried, "Is this how you propose to deal with me, sons of Manissa? Did I not say what I would do if you attempted something so foolish?" But Apollus was ignorant of the sortie of the Periorids and was at a loss for words when Sammas spoke. Then Sammas brought the hostages out, seventy-two, women and little ones, and had them beheaded upon the rocks at the foot of the Hill of Cruachan. No one was spared, neither nursing mother nor suckling babe; all alike were bound and had their heads struck off upon the rocks, till the stones were covered in gore and filth.

When Apollus saw this, his eyes blazed with fire and he roared like an angry lion, like a bear deprived of its cubs. He cried out with a voice terrifying and thunderous, "To the wind with caution now, my beloved brethren! Cruacha! I say, Cruacha! Slay Sammas and water the earth with his blood!" All the Asylians crashed their sturdy spears against their massive shields and cried "Cruacha!" while wiping the stinging tears from their eyes. How glorious were the riders of Apollus that autumn morn, as the sun dyed the horizon pink and the blasting winter gales pressed upon the barren plains? Glorious and resplendent were they in power and fury as they raged down the hillside upon their steeds, teeth gnashing, hair trailing behind in the wind, spears lowered and ready for their gruesome work. The Asylians crashed into the Cadarasian camp, trampling the foot soldiers of Sammas down, their bloodied faces ground into the frosty mud. In that moment Apollus was as marvelous as Baldor in the days of his glory and as terrifying as Arrax the Mighty on the day when he humbled the pride of Adaran in Arcoria's woods. His spear ripped flesh and spilled blood everywhere he turned, and the army of Sammas was in utter terror of him. Eranor and the forty riders of Lugaria, the kin of Mariammné, rode beside him and also wrought destruction among the ranks of Sammas.

But while the battle raged thick, the Periorids said to one another, "If we fight, we may be killed by the men of Sammas; if we prevail and Apollus wins, he will surely seek our lives in that he will hold us responsible for the death of his kin. Therefore, let us take advantage of the fray to flee to the north." So Pictor and the Periorids hacked their way from the melee and escaped into the northern wildernesses by Ituria.

As the Asylians were pushing back the Cadarasians at every side, Sammas cried to Javad, "Bring up your riders and halt their advance!" So Javad called, and his riders came forth to engage Apollus. But Apollus took his sturdy shaft in hand and heaved it upon his shoulder, his gnarled knuckles whitened in his iron grip. Javad rode to him, his black cloak billowing behind, thinking to unhorse the heir to the seat of Baldor. Yet it was not to be, for Apollus let fly the heavy beam with the strength of a cyclone. A devastating hit! The cruel blade crashed into the breast of Javad, smashing through bone and piercing flesh as Javad tumbled from his horse into the mire. He tried to speak, but blood issued forth from his mouth. Apollus brought his horse round and pulled the blade out of the breast of Javad, saying, "Though I may perish this gray and unhappy morn, today will not be the day that the heir to the house of Manissa is felled on his own earth by a swarthy Marudan." Then Javad's eyes closed as darkness overtook him.

But the army of Sammas was twice as great as the army of Apollus, and as the Asylians were slicing through the Cadarasian lines, it came to pass that the third column of Sammas, the legion which had marched by a southwesterly route through Nimru, came upon the plain and beheld the fray. They were commanded by another Marudan, Amira, who wheeled them about and brought them due north, two thousand fresh riders, and poured them into the battle to aid Sammas against Apollus. It was then that Apollus began to be fiercely pressed, for try as he may, he found himself outflanked on all sides with many arrows and javelins raining down upon him continually. Then Idoreth, who rode beside him, was suddenly struck by an arrow in the throat and fell from his steed. Apollus leapt down to aid him, trying to staunch the wound, but he could not halt the tide of crimson blood that continually poured from his throat. Thus perished Idoreth, grandson of Erras and the last of the Hazerites.

Next fell Eranor, son of Servius of the house of Mariammné, who had fought beside Apollus. In the midst of the fray a certain captain of Sammas, Immorath by name, took sight of Apollus and cast his spear at him. Eranor shouted and lunged between Apollus and Immorath, bearing the force of the throw squarely in the chest. The spear tip punctured his armor and crashed through flesh and bone, sinking deep into his breast. Eranor gasped and fell to the earth, the shaft of hardened ash protruding from him with its brazen spearhead buried deep within. The warriors of the house of Mariammné surrounded him to drag his body away, but Immorath and the Cadarasians fell upon them in hopes of securing the armor of Eranor for a trophy. Then was there a bitter fight over the body of Eranor, biting spearheads gouging flesh on both sides. Every man of the house of Mariammné closed in around the body of Eranor, fighting desperately to keep their captain from being stripped; but the Cadarasians under Immorath pressed hard. Then the kin of Eranor began to falter and were cut down, for Immorath had a great number of fighters with him. This only made them fight all the harder, and nowhere was the battle so hot as around the body of Eranor. But Immorath closed in with his spearman and thrust through the men defending Eranor, so that all forty of Lugarian warriors fell defending the body of their captain. Then Eranor's body was stripped, and his arms taken by Immorath as a trophy.

Apollus cried out and raged, and rallying the Asylians about him, said, "Shall Eranor die unavenged?" Then the blood of Baldor boiled hot in him, and he cast his spear at Immorath. The shaft split the air with its swiftness and tore into the flank of Immorath, opening his side. He cried and tumbled from his horse upon the slippery grass, blood spewing from the wound as his life drained away. This gave hope to the Asylians, but even so their numbers diminished by the moment, and everywhere Apollus looked he saw Asylians being struck down with arrow and spear and collapsing onto the hard earth. Then Apollus looked and saw Sammas, mounted upon a gray horse directing the battle from some distance away. Then he prayed, "Blessed Manissa, mother of our people and protector of all who are upright, grant me this one boon before I die, that I may strike down this beast!" Then Apollus roared furiously and cast his bloody spear at Sammas. The king heard the roar of Apollus but saw not the cast of the spear; as he heard the cry he turned his head, so that the point of the spear struck him in the back of the head near the nape. He tumbled from his horse into the muck and was dragged off the field by his servants.

But Apollus was surrounded and pressed hard from every side, till only ten men stood beside him. Yet how boldly they fought, for even when pressed so desperately Apollus took up a sword and struck off the head of Sammas's other captain, Amira, who had foolishly gotten himself too close to the din in hopes of bringing down Apollus. One by one the companions of Apollus fell, speared through and collapsing about his feet. Finally Apollus stood alone, buried to his knees in Asylian and Cadarasian corpses, knowing he was the very last of the house of Baldor. In that moment he gazed up at the northern sky, just when the stars of the constellation Laoön—the sign of the spear—faded into the azure folds of the heavens as the sun finally burst fully upon the earth. Then his foes ran him through the belly with their spears, and as soon as he was thus transfixed they speared him innumerable times before he had even yet fallen upon the earth. They fell about him in a rage and speared him until all his blood was poured out upon the frosted soil and no part of his body remained unwounded. Then they beheaded him and marched the head of Apollus about the camp on a spear in victory.

Thus perished the entire houses of Baldor and of Hazer, man and woman alike, young and old, the youth with the suckling babe. All were slain, so that those houses were utterly extinct from the earth. And neither strength of Baldor nor song of Hazerite has been found in the land since.

Sammas, however, was severely wounded. He lingered for three days on the threshold of death, for the spear of Apollus had struck him in the back of the head and wounded him grievously. When the spearhead was removed, his head poured forth a torrent of blood from the frightful wound. But the Marudan physicians who attended him bound up his wound and kept his tent filled with incense for several days, chanting incantations and spells to the gods of the east. On the third day King Sammas opened his eyes and began to speak, and by the fifth day was able to walk and move about. When the men of the camp saw Sammas walking about and administering his affairs after surviving a spear to the head by Apollus, they marveled and said, "Who among the sons of Elabaea or Maruda is like Sammas? Behold how he has triumphed even over the house of Baldor! Who can make war with him and survive?" Word of Sammas's victory and his remarkable recovery spread far and wide throughout the land, so that he was held in great esteem by the people. Even those who were sympathetic to the houses of Baldor and Hazer were puzzled, saying, "Perhaps Fate is one his side, for if he were not in the right, why would such a disaster been permitted to overtake Apollus?"

Yet Sammas did not retire to Cadaras for the winter, for in his recovery he was even more vicious than before. He said, "I shall not rest so long as even one descendant of Manissa breathes." So he brought his armies up from Cruachan into Ituria and the regions around Cyrenaica. Now Cyrenaica was home to some of the Periorids, but the house of Secum also dwelt there. Since the days when Orius, son of Secum, was spirited away west from Cadaras in the care of Cilla his mother, the Secumites had resided peacefully in Cyrenaica. But when Sammas approached the people they were sorely afraid, and he told them, "Deliver up to me all the Secumites, the young and the old, the men and the women, the youth with the suckling babe and I shall spare your cities; but if you do not do this, I will burn them all and put every person to the sword." Thus the people of Cyrenaica betrayed the Secumites and bound them, delivering them up to Sammas on the plains outside Thán near the spot where Baldor had slain Imbrossé in olden days. When the Secumites had been delivered to Sammas, about twenty persons in all, Sammas took them down to Lapidoth and murdered them upon the stone there. Thus the house of Secum was wiped out and was no more. Sammas would have then turned west and pursued the Periorids, for whom he bore a special hatred, but they were too spread out in the wilderness and too elusive for his armies or his scouts. Therefore Sammas retired to Cadaras for the winter, encamping the army in the plains between Cadaras and the ruins of Danath Hered.

Now the houses of Elphas and Necho were very great in the south, in the plains around Engor and Anentora going all the way down to Corbalund, where the sons of Pilux still ruled over Badoa. Because they were distant from Asylia, word did not come to the south concerning Sammas's treachery until Apollus was already besieged at Cruachan. There was great debate in Anentora about what should be done, the lords of the house of Elphas arguing that they should come to the aid of Apollus, the sons of Necho preferring to stay out of the fighting and see how things settled. But as autumn turned to winter and word passed to the south about the slaughter at Cruachan and the death of Apollus with all his house, the lord of the house of Elphas, Ornax son of Anaxor, said, "Have you not heard what this beast of a king has done to the houses of Baldor and Hazer? This cannot be tolerated, for even if he means to leave us in peace, how can we not avenge our kin?" But the lord of the house of Necho, Eidareth son of Aroth said, "And will you triumph where the house of Baldor has failed? Let us rather fortify our cities in the south, build up our lands in might and declare our own kingdom apart from the power of Cadaras and the chair of Sammas." Ornax said, "Do as you will my kinsman. Whether you fight or not is something I cannot persuade you one way or the other; but I will not do as you say, for I will not sunder the unity of the south from the throne of Cadaras. It was our forebears, mighty Elphas and glorious Necho, who won these lands for our people from the Illyrs in the days of Anaxandra. They were given unto her by Baldor, Necho and Elphas, and I will not take for myself what was given once and for all to Anaxandra and her successors." So Ornax and Eidareth had a great many such disputes about what to do concerning Sammas.

When the spring came and the snows began to melt off the plains between Engor and Cadarasia, Sammas came forth from the Citadel and marched his army south into the grasslands going towards Engor. When Ornax and Eidareth heard that Sammas was bringing his army south, they held counsel at Engor, for they deduced that Sammas was hoping to wipe out the houses of Necho and Elphas as he had done to Baldor, Secum, and Hazer. But there arose no little dissension among them, for Ornax was in favor of marching north and engaging Sammas upon the open plains before he should come to Engor, but Eidareth was in favor of retreating south, towards Corbalund, and allying with the sons of Pilux and the people of Badoa.

Ornax said, "Do you not see that if we give ground to Sammas and do not engage him at once that he will only gain in strength while we will be driven to the frontiers of our own kingdoms?" Eidareth said, "Sammas's armies are greater than what we can muster; if we engage him, we shall meet the same fate as Apollus. Furthermore, we ought to recall that the Cadarasians are not our enemies, for until this day we have been as one people with them. Perhaps if we remove to the south we can have words with the lords of that land and induce them to betray or slay Sammas themselves and save us the effort." Ornax scoffed and said, "As for me, my enemy is whomever steps in front of me and gets in the path of my spear, that is all I know. I put no faith in the lords, for it is they who carry out the designs of Sammas by obeying his dictates. If they should be induced to betray him, then why not us as well? No my kinsman, I will lead the sons of Elphas north to engage Sammas in the open." After much debate it was agreed that Ornax would lead the men of Engor and its environs north to engage Sammas upon the plains while Eidareth would remain with the house of Necho in Anentora in readiness to come to the aid of Ornax if things should go ill in the battle. Thus they embraced and parted ways at the oak of Gemurath near Engor.

Then Ornax raised the battle cry throughout Engor and its environs, and every sword-bearing man of the house of Elphas and bloodline of Manissa came forth to go to war, one hundred forty-five men in all and each one a lord. With them came scores of riders, rugged spearmen of the plains, for they had heard what Sammas did to Apollus and feared for their own homes. Every man took his spear and shield and joined Ornax on the plains in the shadow of the hill of Mimmoth by Engor, until by the time the last of the snows were melted he had mustered three thousand hardened warriors. Every man that came to Engor brought with him his wife and kin, for word had spread of how Sammas had went throughout the lands and destroyed the Hazerites, and should the battle go ill no man wished his family to be left alone in the countryside. Therefore Engor was swollen with refugees from the surrounding plains and the foothills of the Bados, especially those of the house of Elphas.

Not long after this, scouts came to Ornax in Engor and told him, "Sammas is upon the plains with eight thousand men and is but four days north of Engor." The captains of Ornax remonstrated with him and said, "The three thousand mustered here will not be enough to break the ranks of Sammas." But Ornax said, "We need not break him, only wear him down and drain his spirit. Then we shall send riders forth to Anentora and summon Eidareth. The house of Necho will come from the east and smash the army of Sammas upon the dusty plain when he is already wearied." This plan bade ill with the captains, for they did not trust Eidareth to reinforce Ornax. But they said nothing and assented to all that Ornax proposed.

Now Sammas was intent upon wiping out the houses of Elphas and Necho, for he thought, "As long as the sons of Manissa hold power anywhere my throne will never be secure."* He therefore mustered his armies at the first lengthening of the days and arrayed them upon the plain between Cadaras and the ruins of Danath Hered, counting seven thousand men who could throw a spear or wield a sword. They marched in early spring, when the snows melted from Cadarasia's fair vales and the Cadar was swollen with the overflow of the highlands. The march from Cadarasia to Engor was only seven days by horseback, but the army tarried for some time on the southern borders of Cadaras until Sammas should be joined by a legion of Caeylonic infantry coming from the east and a troupe of hillmen from Bados in the west, so that when he again departed after a fortnight his numbers were some eight thousand men, most of them mounted.

In the fertile plains north of Engor there is a certain place called Migdalim wherein are many gently rolling slopes covered in choice wheat, which at every harvest put forth golden heads of immense size and richness. There is a dusty road which leads north through Migdalim into southernmost Cadarasia, and at its southern end, opens out into the vast flatlands that border the environs of Engor. Though the wheat is thick and the hillsides golden at harvest time, in the spring its slopes are barren and grey, having only recently been freed from snow cover and still bearing the stubble from the previous year's harvest. Such were the fields of Migdalim that spring day when Ornax first sighted the approach of the armies of Sammas coming up along the road from the north only three leagues from his own position. When Ornax saw the immense size of the army of Sammas, his heart quaked and he summoned his swiftest riders, saying, "Ride quickly to Anentora and tell my kinsman Eidareth that we are in dire need of the swords of the house of Necho. Let him make haste to Migdalim to aid us!" So the riders were dispatched to summon the people of Necho before the first strike was landed or ever spear rattled upon shield. Then Ornax arrayed his men along the crests of some low-lying hills and stretched his line out for nearly a half league.

Sammas beheld the forces of Ornax and saw them lining upon the hilltop. He summoned his captains and said, "See how the people of Elphas stretch their line so thinly upon the ridge! Behold, their numbers are few and their position is weak. If we can drive them from the ridge and down the slope beyond, we shall take the day." But some of the men did not approve of charging the hills, wishing to instead stretch out their own lines and attempt to outflank Ornax. So Sammas summoned some priests of Shamash and made a sacrifice of a crow upon the field of Migdalim. When the augurs had been summoned and examined the entrails of the bird, they said, "Let the king do as he pleases, for the day is given to him." So Sammas ordered his men into companies ten lines deep and brought them up within a half mile from the hills occupied by Ornax, and there pitched camp for the night.

When daylight broke upon the fields, Sammas ordered his men forward, two thousand cavalry leading the assault up the slope. The three thousand warriors of Ornax stood their ground at first, bringing many of Sammas's riders down to with their deadly casts. But the cavalry of Sammas struck the line several times, so that the army of Ornax began to falter as breaches were opened in the line. When Sammas saw this, he blew a horn, and the legions of infantry charged the slopes, spears leveled and intent on bringing doom to Ornax and his people. The assault was far too great for the men of Ornax to withstand, and they yielded the ridge to Sammas, fleeing down the southern slopes to escape the charge. Ornax cried, "Let every man take a stand upon the hill! Do not let them press us into the gulley!" But the horsemen of Sammas crested the ridge and pursued the fleeing men hotly, harassing them with spear and arrow, so that the warriors of Ornax could not form up on the hillside, but were driven down into the broad gulley which ran along the base of the hills. Ornax saw his men thus entrapped and turned to take a stand upon the southern slope, hoping to rally his men to retake the hillside. But as he was raising his spear aloft and crying out, an arrow struck him in the eye and killed him.

The riders of Sammas rained missiles upon the army of Ornax until the latter were in utter disarray. With the hill cleared and Ornax slain, the infantry of Sammas surged down the southern slope and fell upon the men pinned down in the gulley, striking them with a great slaughter until midday. Thus did all the men of Elphas perish; not a man of them escaped. When Sammas came afterwards to see the place of the battle, the gulley was filled with the blood of the men slain there. Thus was that gulley in Migdalim ever after called *Canakkalé*, which means "Ditch of Blood."

In the meantime, the riders of Ornax came unto the city of Anentora and brought word to Eidareth of the house of Necho that Ornax had requested his aid against Sammas. Then was Eidareth sorely troubled, for he said, "If Ornax requests my aid then he must be in a place of grave necessity; shall the men of Anentora be able to save him? Who can make war on Sammas and prevail?" So he was deeply disturbed and did not immediately muster his people. But in two days another rider came from the west and told him of the utter destruction of the army of Ornax and of Ornax's death. Then Eidareth wept and tore his garments, saying, "Woe to thee, Ornax, my kinsman, valiant in life and noble in death! But shall I save thee now? What profit is there in consigning my own kin to doom?" So Eidareth mustered all the people of Necho together at Anentora, some three hundred persons in all, and with them fled south, into Corbalund and the regions around Badoa where the descendants of Pilux, son of Necho, were reigning peacefully.

But Engor was left unguarded, for all its sword-bearing men had fallen at Canakkalé. The people of Engor were in grave terror and distress when they heard of the fall of their menfolk and saw the army of Sammas marching upon the city from the north. Sammas surrounded the city and proclaimed the same words he had delivered before Thán, saying, "Deliver up to me all the house of Elphas, the young and the old, the men and the women, the youth with the suckling babe and I shall spare your city; but if you do not do this, I will burn it with fire and put every person to the sword." But whereas the Cyrenaicans were affrighted and had delivered up the Secumites at Sammas's threats, the womenfolk of Engor said, "Shall we disgrace the deaths of our husbands and sons by committing such treachery? We will fight beside the house of Elphas in their defense till our very life is snuffed out in blood and flame." So they spurned the words of Sammas and dared him to strike the city.

Sammas advanced his legions upon Engor and took it after only three days, for only youths, women, and the old and infirm remained in the city. Then the city was torched with a terrible conflagration and all the people therein put to the sword, the young with the old, the men and the women, the youth with the suckling babe. Sammas left none remaining but slew them all alike, save for fourteen youths of the house of Elphas whom he removed alive to offer as sacrifices to Neb. When he had utterly overthrown and burned the city he went some ways north, to the great oak of Gemurath. There he chopped down the ancient tree and said, "Where is the amity of Elphas and Necho? Are not the ancient alliances utterly sundered?" Then he erected a hard, brazen altar to Neb, cruel and cold, and there slew upon it the fourteen youths whom he had taken from Engor, sons of nobles all of them, whose blood spilled down the sides of the vile altar. So Gemurath became a place of blood and weeping, for there the house of Elphas was utterly wiped out and removed from the face of the earth. Thereafter was that place called *Kalétha*, "Deeds of Blood."

When Sammas was told that Eidareth and the people of Necho had removed themselves to Corbalund, he desired to march onward and do to them as he had done to the house of Elphas, but his captains protested that Corbalund was too distant and that they were ill equipped for a campaign so far from home. So Sammas reluctantly returned north to Cadarasia for the remainder of that year. Yet he was not idle, for he immediately began laying plans to come south the following spring with more men and supplies for the destruction of the house of Necho and the subjection of Corbalund. Yet it was not to be, for it came to pass that very year that the wickedness of Sammas was requited upon him, for the spear of Manissa which was trained upon him for all his evil was finally cast.

There was a certain man in the court of Sammas, Ninós, who was a lesser captain in the guard of the king. Now King Sammas was arrogant and cruel to all his lords and captains, for he compelled all of them to prostrate themselves before him in his presence and to address him with many great and pompous titles, such as *Most Exalted Lord* and *Master of Fate* and similar names which the Manissans were not accustomed to giving to their sovereigns. But of all the lords and captains, Ninós suffered worst, for he spoke with a stutter and was often mocked by Sammas at the royal banquets. Nor did the other lords ease his trouble, for they sought to win the approbation of the king and likewise heaped abuse upon Ninós if they saw it pleased Sammas and made him laugh.

One evening, in the dead of winter, when all Asylia lay quiet under thick snow, Sammas was reclining at table in his palace at the Citadel with his lords and captains. It was late in the night and the Marudan guards who typically protected the king were weary with wine. Laughter roared from the couch of Sammas and the lords gathered at his table, for the mood was merry. Then Sammas, full of drink, saw Ninós and began to taunt him and mock his stuttering speech. He called for him and said, "Ninós, bring me another f,f,f,flagon of w,w,w,wine." And all the lords roared with laughter as the king's jesting. Ninós was greatly put out at this insult, and of being asked to perform the task of a servant. So he went to the storeroom to fetch a flagon, but while there concealed a dagger in his cloak. Then he returned to the king's chambers and drew near him to hand him the flagon. But when Sammas reached out to grasp it, Ninós drew forth his dagger and thrust it deep between the king's ribs, piercing his lungs.

Sammas gasped and blood spewed from his mouth as he tried to cry out. Ninós said, "Say it again, my king, for thou art stuttering and I cannot understand thee!" and he twisted the dagger within the king's breast. Then Sammas plummeted from his throne and collapsed upon the table, his regal robes drenched with hot blood and the crown of Cadaras ringing upon the pavement. The lords rose to seize Ninós, but he took the dagger with which he stabbed the king and thrust it into his own breast, thus escaping the wrath of the king's companions. King Sammas was eight and thirty years old when he died. He had reigned nine years over Cadaras, having polluted the land with much blood and committed many unspeakable crimes. Are not all the wicked deeds of his reign, how he destroyed the sacred places, slew the sons of Manissa, persecuted the holy virgins and brought foreign gods into Asylia all written of in the bitter histories of those days?* Thus Sammas died and was buried in the Citadel at Cadaras. He was succeeded by Karax.

Giannor

nhappy were the days of old when the land of Asylia was overrun by the foreign gods and cults that had been established under the reign of the detestable King Sammas. The sons of Manissa abandoned the land, for the house of Mariammné remained west in the kingdom of Lugaria, concerning themselves not with the troubles of Asylia or Cadaras. The Periorids were dispersed and wandered hither and thither throughout the desolate wildernesses; the house of Necho remained in the uttermost south, in the regions of Corbalund, where they prospered and grew but remained aloof from the affairs of Asylia. The cults of the Illyrs spread from the south even to the remotest north, so that shrines and altars were set up to every manner of god and spirit, from the vast fields of the south around Anentora even to the verdant pasturelands of the Erriad and the wastes of Cyria. Men neglected the gods of their fathers, and some even forgot the language of Asylia.* The old cities were abandoned; many men took up their belongings and came east to Cadaras. Kerion and Paros, where stood the hearths of hot-blooded Arrax and other ancient men of renown, were no more, and became as ruins. Old Asylia waned as the shadow of age fell over its wooden palisades and its hallowed mounds, so that it dwindled, and its lords were of little account.* Men grew weak and of feeble mind, so that the greatness of former days was found no more.

And everywhere evil spirits and vile creatures came forth and troubled the people of the land.*

In those dark days there was of the house of Mariammné one called Giannor who dwelt on the far side of the Erriad in the wilderness east of Enna, where the heather clad hills sit somber beneath the churning grey clouds of the south. This man Giannor had the power of Manissa in him, for to him was given the strength to cast out spirits and to have dominion over them. When any farmer or herdsman was in need of purifying some vale or grove, they summoned Giannor, and he came and cast the evil spirit out of the place. This Giannor was greatly beloved by the Manissans, for their land was plagued by spirits in those days so that the once bold men of Asylia feared to traverse the wilderness alone or be found upon the roads after sunset.

It came to pass that, as the caravans came west on their return from Cadaras, the merchants told of a frightful spirit that dwelt in the Nimru Pass and was hampering those who wished to go through it. So frightful was this spirit that many traders and merchants feared to travel to or from Cadaras. So Giannor said, "I will go to Nimru and cast out this vile spirit which plagues the pass." Thus Giannor arose, took his staff, and set off on the stony road which leads eastward towards Nimru.

Now the Nimru Pass is situated in the northernmost foothills of Bados and runs through an ancient and dried out riverbed cut deep between two cliffs of sandstone, so that by following the pass one can come into Cadarasia by a direct route rather than passing north and fording the Erriad or traversing over the mountains. When Giannor came unto the entrance of the pass, he perceived a great evil coming from within and said, "Such strength I have not seen in all my days." Then begging the aid of Manissa, he entered the shadows of the pass.

When he had come some way into the pass, a mighty force struck him and hurled him violently to the ground. Then a fierce presence surrounded him, and a deep fear and a terror fell upon him, so that he was thrown into the midst of a dense darkness. Giannor cried out, "Who are you and for what reason do you torment me so?" A voice cried out of the pitch, "I know thee, son of Manissa, and why thou hast come. Turn back or perish!" Giannor said, "I shall not turn back but have come to drive thee from this pass and into the nether regions." Then the darkness pressed upon him, becoming like a smothering blanket. But Giannor cried out "Manissé ena elotha imurié!" and struck out at the darkness with his staff.

Then the spirit came to him in the form of a great bear and roared voraciously at Giannor, trying to frighten him off; but Giannor said, "Though you roar and tear the very mountains asunder, I will not depart from here." So the spirit came to him in the form of a vile serpent, dreadful and immense in length and girth, and surrounded Giannor in its coils; but Giannor called upon Manissa and told the spirit, "Though you crush me in your hideous coils and poison me with your dripping fangs I will not depart from here." So the spirit came to Giannor in the form of great dog, rabid and frothing, and growled and leapt at Giannor; but Giannor raised his staff and said, "Though you tear my limbs and feast on my pulsing heart still hot in my breast, I will not depart from here." So the spirit raged and swirled about him but could not persuade him to depart.

Then Giannor took his staff and struck the floor of the pass in rage, crying out, "Where is the fury of Manissa and the power of her house?" Then a great light blazed and burned upon the earth before Giannor with great intensity, so that the spirit was cowed and subdued in fear.

Giannor said, "Tell me thy name, foul spirit." The spirit said, "Behold the fallen, son of Manissa! For once I was called Gygas, brave son of Gela, who did ride in the company of King

Ioclus and gaze upon the fair face of Manissa in the days when she was in the flesh." Giannor said, "I know thee, Gygas the Betrayer, for it was you who did sell the house of Ioclus into the hand of Arahaz the Marudan for the promise of the hand of Manissa; yet did your evil deeds go awry, for Manissa escaped the ambuscade meant to destroy her and took vengeance upon you with her flaming spear." Gygas said, "It is as you say, and for this great treachery I am doomed to roam the earth in penance until the end of time, in punishment for my sin. I haunt this valley and all who pass through, for it was in this lonely vale that it first entered my heart to betray my lord in the dark watches of the night."

Then Giannor pressed his face near the flame, so that he might see the form of Gygas on the other side, but Gygas said, "Come no closer, son of Manissa. Shall you bind me here at thy will or will you release me?" Giannor said, "It is not for me to commute the decrees of Fate concerning your sentence, fiend! But inasmuch as the betrayal of Manissa and her house began with thee, so shall the vindication and triumph of the heirs of Ioclus begin with thee as well." Then the breath and words of Manissa entered Giannor, and he prophesied mightily and spoke many words of power, so that the spirit of Gygas cried out and fled from the place.

Thus was the spirit of Gygas driven out of the Nimru Pass, to roam and haunt the desolate wastes of the world where no man has seen or pitched his tent. Then did men again pass to and fro from Cadaras to the purple hills of the west without fear, and there was peace in that region all the days of Giannor.

Lorion and Eira

❧❧❧ ❧❧❧ ❧❧❧

In the days when the four houses of Manissa were purged from the land through the wickedness of Sammas, there was a certain man called Lorion of the house of Mariammné. Lorion was but a boy when Eranor went forth to aid Apollus at the Hill of Cruachan and therefore escaped the slaughter of Sammas. During the reign of Karax he made his way into Cadarasia and from thence into the south, dwelling in the rugged foothills of the Bados with the hill-people who populate those regions. In those days the houses of Manissa that survived the purge of Sammas were scattered and weakened, for Sammas had wrought great destruction among them.

Lorion was tall and comely, with curled hair of brown and a good frame. When he came into the hill country, the people of the Bados welcomed him and give him land on the northernmost edges of their territory to establish his house. So Lorion laid the foundations of a great hall and hauled stone from the nearby mountains to set up the walls. He harnessed a plough to his oxen, plowed out the furrows of his land, and hewed sturdy beams for his hall from the cedars which were spread out upon the rugged hills of that place. He worked in solitude for many days establishing his house, furnishing it, and seeding his fields, so that all of the wild Badoans in the region came down from the hills to marvel at Lorion's industriousness and at the splendid hall he was raising. After some time, the hall was complete and Lorion called the place he had erected *Arialor*, but the hill-people called it *Halicor* because of the great cedar beams which Lorion had used in the construction of the place. So Halicor became a mighty bastion in the land. Many of the Badoans flocked to the hall of Lorion to seek his judgments, labor in his fields, and pledge fealty to him. Thus Lorion became a great lord among the Badoans. His estate was vast and plentiful, so that he amassed hundreds of sheep and cattle and employed an equal number of servants and hired hands at the harvest every autumn.

Lorion also established in that place a shrine to Manissa, where every month he offered prayers and sacrifices for the good of the land. A company of virgins was brought down from Cadaras to tend the fire at the shrine and to offer prayers continually. In those days there was a great spirit of piety and austerity about Halicor and it greatly prospered in the early years of Lorion. So men of that region called Lorion and his house blessed.

Every autumn, in the waning days of the harvest, it was Lorion's custom to don his cloak, take up his spear, and venture some days into the wilds of the Bados mountains to hunt game. Brown bear, elk, the red fox, and many fur-bearing creatures he pursued and slew with his hardened spear of ash, bringing them back to Halicor at the time of the first snowfall and making from them beautiful cloaks of fur which were admired throughout the land. Thus it was, when the frosts began to settle and the grass turned crisp in the morning air, that Lorion donned his cloak, and taking up his spear, departed by foot into the hills west of Halicor.

When he had wandered several days into the mountains and found little game, Lorion spied a certain promontory jutting out atop the ridge of a steep hill, the uppermost reaches of which were clustered round about in thick rhododendron, with their delicate violet blossoms, and topped with dense alder trees that obscured the promontory's top. His curiosity was aroused; he said to himself, "Is it not autumn upon the land? How does the rhododendron then blossom so late in the year? I shall ascend the hill to the top of the promontory to investigate this further, and perhaps see what is concealed behind this barrier of tree and bush." So he made his way up the stony hillside, but could only go up with great difficulty, for the hill was steep and the stones loose beneath his feet.

When he had struggled up the rocky bluff for the better part of an hour, Lorion at last came to the top of the ascent, and thrusting his way through the thick rhododendrons, collapsed upon the ground. To his astonishment, he found that atop the promontory was a small grove, shaded and enclosed by the great alders and the thick bushes, in the midst of which bubbled forth a pure fount of crystal water from the depths of the hilltop, pooling up and watering the grove, which allowed for it to be so densely wooded round about. But sitting upon the grass at the fount he was amazed and affrighted to see a young woman bathing her hair in the waters of the pool. Her hair was long and black and spiraled off into a multitude of delicate curls; her skin was pale and cold, her demeanor stern yet alluring. Lorion stood in awe of her as she bathed her hair in the spring. Then, taking notice of Lorion, she looked up and said calmly, "From whence have you come, son of Manissa?" Lorion marveled and said, "How do you know who I am and from what house I descend?" She said, "I beheld you in the pool before you ascended the hillside, and from this pool I can see things both near and afar."

Lorion furled his brow and said, "You are some sort of enchantress, I perceive. Even so, your beauty and fair form hold me bound here, for never have I gazed upon one as lovely as you, my lady. By what name are you called?" She said, "I am called many names by many peoples, but among the peoples of the Bados I am called Eira. And you need not fear me, man of valor, for I have worked no enchantment upon you." But her enchantment was wound through her flesh and wrapped within her voice, like a ribbon wrapped within a braid.

"I have never spied this fair glade before," said Lorion. "Do you see herein anything you fancy?" said Eira. "Indeed, I do," breathed Lorion, his bones enflamed for the woman. So Lorion was taken with Eira, and forgetting the hunt, gathered her into his arms while her hair was still wet and made love to her there beside the enchanted pool. Then he bore her up and returned with her to Halicor, smitten by her.

There was much confusion at Halicor when Lorion was sighted upon the trail only a brief time after his departure, returning with no game but with black-haired Eira at his side. He established Eira in his house and gave her many fine things to wear as well as servants of her own to command, for he intended to wed her at the next full moon. But many persons from Bados and the districts round about Halicor came to told him, "Master Lorion, put this woman away, for she is a Badoan witch, exiled from her own lands west of the mountains for her sorceries. This is common knowledge among the people here, and they are greatly scandalized by her presence at Halicor. Nothing good will come from her." Lorion's heart was troubled at these words, for he did indeed perceive something amiss about Eira. But whenever he went in to gaze at her, he was smitten anew by her lovely appearance and his doubts vanished like mist at the breaking of the sun. So it was that at the next full moon Lorion was wed to black-haired Eira in the great hall at Halicor. Thus was sung of Lorion and Eira:

> *Noble Lorion was smitten*
> *By alluring Eira's eyes*
> *And brought her home in mirth*
> *To Halicor 'neath blazing skies*

Eira was adored by Lorion, and for a time Halicor and the estates of Lorion were blessed with abundant rain and rich harvests. Eira bore Lorion three sons: the eldest were Dimmoth and Vinos, and the youngest Lothar, who was in the image of his father Lorion.

But the peoples around Halicor never put off their suspicion of Eira, for they murmured always that she was a witch who worshipped the dark powers in secret. Many laborers and traders who came to Halicor claimed to have seen her roaming the windswept ridges of the hills round Halicor by light, her hair disheveled, her voice crying shrill upon the wind of the evening like that of a banshee or spirit. Lorion was aware of these grumblings and forbid any man of his estate to speak ill of Eira; and any man caught doing so was beaten with ten lashes.

Nevertheless, it came to pass that in the fifteenth year after Lorion was wed to Eira that he took ill, and though many sages and physicians were summoned from as far as Cadaras, they were unable to restore him to health. They were at a loss as to what ailed him, and whatever remedy they prescribed only seemed to make him worse. Thus he wasted away and perished, being about thirty-eight years in age and having reigned eighteen years from Halicor. So there was mourning throughout the land, for Lorion was much beloved by the Manissans and the Badoan peoples alike. His bier was born into the hills and his body entombed at the sacred shrine of Manissa which he had caused to be erected some distance from Halicor. Thus it was sung of in those days:

> *Lorion closed his eyes in death*
> *When soul from body flies*
> *And was entombed in sorrow*
> *At Halicor 'neath troubled skies*

Thus perished Lorion. But yet when he died there was no peace, for the people round about Halicor all suspected Eira of some witchcraft or vex which was responsible for their lord's sudden passing. Thus the people murmured and cast suspicion upon Eira, for they had never ceased to consider her a bearer of bad luck and worker of ill.

Lothar

At the time of Lorion's passing, Eira became mistress of Halicor and all its lands. But the natives of that region would not suffer her to rule over them, nor could they acquiesce to her sitting in Lorion's chair at Halicor. Many of the servants and laborers murmured against her and stopped coming unto the halls of Halicor. She in turn showed herself to be cruel and spiteful and treated the servants and workers wretchedly, causing some to be flogged and others to be sold into slavery in Caeylon if they displeased her. Her elder sons, Dimmoth and Vinos, were carried away in her wickedness and aided her in her misdeeds; but the youngest Lothar, who was only ten, cherished the memory of his father and despised the injustices of his mother and elder brothers. Yet he was but a youth and remained silent.

But in the sixth year after the passing of Lorion, when the walls of Halicor began to crack from neglect and the fields round about to turn wild from lack of laborers to work them, it came to pass that the people in the hills and vales about Halicor purposed to rise and drive Eira out of the land. So they came to Halicor by night, several hundred in all, bearing torches and spears and clamoring for the head of Eira. Dimmoth and Vinos came to their mother in the great hall and said, "The people of the land rise up against you, mother, and are seeking your blood!" She scoffed and said, "In my youth was I thus run out of the wilds of Bados in the west; I shall not relinquish these fair lands or the shadowed hall of Halicor so easily!"

So Eira came forth from Halicor and confronted the assembled crowd of Badoans who had come out against her. Then she cried out, "Thou foolish and craven folk! By what right do you come here and attempt to eject me from the estate lawfully bequeathed to me by my late husband, the Lord Lorion?" The crowd said, "By the same right by which the people of the Bados ejected you from those domains: namely, that thou art a witch and a foul fiend and did yourself put our master and lord Lorion to death. Therefore you and your sons shall depart this place at once or else we will drag thee out and put you to a wretched death."

This enraged Eira, and she said, "Shall you indeed do these things? Behold my power!" Then her eyes became like fire, and lightning and flashes issued forth from her fingertips, so that many of those gathered about were stunned and frightened. Then she cried out in a strange tongue, and at the sound of her voice a wild bear came forth from the brush and mauled some of those standing about, so that many dropped their torches and fled. But Eira again stretched forth her hand and spoke, so that hideous serpents came forth from the earth and crawled among the people, biting some of them and bringing panic. Eira laughed and said, "Yet once more shall I convince thee, so that there be no doubt as to my power over you!" Then she breathed upon the wind, and her breath became foul and brought forth swarms of gnats that flew into the nostrils and eyes of the people and pestered them sorely. Thus there was great disarray among the assembled crowd.

When she saw that they were in disarray, she said to her sons Dimmoth, Vinos, and Lothar, "Take up your swords! Go out among these people and strike them so that they shall never again raise the torch of rebellion against us." But Lothar was afraid and did not accede to his mother's wishes, and so in the confusion fled from Halicor and took refuge in the hills west of there. But Dimmoth and Vinos went throughout the crowd with their swords drawn, stabbing and slaying men at random until the mob turned and fled from Halicor after many had been slain by the brothers or by the evils that Eira called down upon them by the powers of darkness.

When the bloody work was complete and the people cowed into submission, Eira searched for her son Lothar but found him not. Then she realized he had fled and was greatly incensed and filled with great hatred for her son and for Lorion, in whose image Lothar appeared. Dimmoth and Vinos were also incensed at Lothar and pledged that they should kill him if he ever returned to Halicor.

After this, Eira sent her sons to tear down the shrine of Manissa that her husband Lorion had built. In its place she erected a shrine to Makur, a god of the night once worshipped by the Illyrs. She expelled the virgins who tended the grave of Lorion and permitted it to become tangled and overgrown with briars. Then she compelled all the Badoans in the region who served under her or came to Halicor to pay homage to Makur at the shrine she erected.

The people of the Bados were in terror of Eira and her witcheries and assented to all she commanded, bowing their faces to the ground before the grotesque idol of Makur and doing the bidding of Eira in whatsoever she ordered. Her sons Dimmoth and Vinos lorded their authority over the people of the Bados and treated them very harshly. Instead of lords they became plunderers of the land. So Halicor became a place of lamentation and sorrow.

But Lothar fled west, passing over the foothills and into the treacherous granite peaks and snow choked passes of the Bados Mountains. Lothar was a month in the inhabitable passes of the Bados, exposed to the perpetual snows and frigid gales that blast through them. After tremendous suffering, he passed out into the northwest, coming up into the verdant lands bordering Enna on the east with their many hamlets and villages. There he sought Giannor of the house of Mariammné, who was old and advanced in years. He sought for Giannor that the sage might come at once to Halicor and prevail over the power of Eira his mother, who had bewitched the people of the Bados and was afflicting them. "For," he reasoned, "this Giannor has power over spirits and may triumph in contest with her." But Giannor would not make the journey, for his body was wracked with pain and his eyesight was dim because of his great age. He told Lothar, "Go unto the city of Cadaras, the city of the great king, and offer your services to him there. Before too long you will accomplish the will of our Lady." So Lothar went to go to Cadaras, but Giannor said, "Take heed that you remain as you are and do not take a wife from among the daughters of that city, for you have been set aside for a special work. Though righteousness will prevail, it will not come without great sorrow, which must be borne alone." So Lothar thanked Giannor and went east to Cadaras, pondering these words in his heart.

At that time Alcidus was ruling in Cadaras upon the throne of Manissa. This Alcidus was a good-natured man who had won glory in war against the Epidymians. Lothar came unto Cadaras and attached himself to the court of Alcidus, calling himself Telendor. Thus he served King Alcidus as Telendor, no one knowing of his origin, neither the king nor any of the lords of the court. Five years Lothar served in the court of Alcidus, so that Alcidus came to love him greatly and bestowed on him many lands in the northern marches near the Plains of Anorel. Lothar also went out with Alcidus on many campaigns against the Epidymians and won much glory, for he struck off the arm of an Epidymian champion who meant to spear the king in battle. For this feat King Alcidus commanded Lothar to take for himself any one of the maidens of Cadaras to be his wife, and Lothar chose Ornis, a delicate and lovely daughter of the Lord of Andanor. In this he did not recall the words of Giannor or heed them, for he said to himself, "Perhaps the evils of Halicor are forgotten and the shame of my mother will be no more." So he took Ornis into his house but told her not of Halicor or of his mother, nor did he reveal his true name to her.

But meanwhile the fortunes of Halicor waned, for Dimmoth and Vinos, the elder brothers of Lothar, did not work or labor at Halicor but instead tyrannized the hill people and consumed the inheritance left behind by the thrift of Lorion. Nor did Eira prohibit them from acting such; on the contrary, she encouraged their rapaciousness, so that the people of the hill country began to curse the name of Halicor. They would have risen and thrown out Eira and her sons but for their great fear of her evil powers. And so Halicor fell more into ruin until it became a crumbling haunt where Eira brooded about its dim chambers alone by night, uttering incantations to the powers of darkness and seducing her sons to do vile deeds.

When Lothar had been in the court of Alcidus some time, it came to pass that the king purposed to find for himself a bride from among the maidens of Cadaras, for he was in the prime of life and had yet to take a wife. When it became known abroad that Alcidus was seeking a wife, Dimmoth and Vinos came to their mother Eira and said, "Mother, why content thyself to be mistress of a dying estate when you could be queen over all Cadarasia? Behold, King Alcidus seeks a maiden from among the women of this country to take to be his bride and reign as queen." Eira scoffed and said, "And would he choose me, a woman who has birthed three sons and is past the flower of youth?" They said, "You are yet beautiful; is not your hair rich and dark? But if you doubt that it could be so, let an enchantment be placed upon the king, that he may be smitten with you and overlook your age. Thus, preferring you to even the most buxom virgin of the land, you shall be exalted and sit enthroned in the pillared halls of the Citadel."

Eira mused upon the words of her sons and said, "Let it be as you have said." Then she took for herself a gleaming necklace of finely wrought gold and placed a curse upon it, so that the eyes of the king would be fixed upon her, and by it his heart held captive. So they departed from Halicor and came north to Cadaras and the court of King Alcidus. But they did not know that Lothar was dwelling there, nor that he was known by the name Telendor.

Many maidens came from all Cadarasia to present themselves before Alcidus in hopes of becoming his bride, but Alcidus was an indecisive and particular man and had difficulty selecting one. But when Eira presented herself before him, decked in fine silks with her black hair done up in plaits and the cursed band of delicate gold adorning her white neck, he was smitten with burning desire for her. This was not so much because of the great beauty of Eira (for it was obvious to all the court that she was nigh forty years old) but because of the cursed band. Immediately he said, "Bring no more maidens before me! Never until this day have I seen such beauty and pleasantness of form among all the women of this kingdom. This woman at once shall I take to wife to be my bride and queen."

Some of the attendants of Alcidus said, "Sir, what do you mean by choosing this woman, who, though lovely, is beyond childbearing age? How will she secure the continuation of thy house?" But Alcidus silenced them with anger, being unwilling to tolerate any word against his choice of Eira.

Lothar, however, was attending upon the king and recognized his mother and brothers (though they knew him not) and said to himself, "Trouble comes to Cadaras this day, and the woes of Halicor have followed me north." But he kept his counsel to himself, for he knew the king was enchanted and would not heed reason. So Lothar was in turmoil as to what course of action to pursue.

Meanwhile the betrothals of Eira and Alcidus were announced, and the time of the marriage fixed for the next full moon, some three weeks hence. King Alcidus was enraptured by Eira and presented her with many gifts of gold and finery. He also exalted the sons of Eira, Dimmoth and Vinos, making them captains in his army. Then Eira saw the bronze statue of Mardu in the courtyard of the Citadel that had stood since the days of Sammas and asked the king, "What is this?" The king said, "This was erected in the days of King Sammas when he ruled from the white halls of the Citadel."* So Eira petitioned Alcidus and said, "Erect for me a statue of my god, as well." Alcidus, being a good man, would not have conceded to her request had he been in his right mind, but because his heart was held prisoner by her, he assented. Then a great statue of Makur, the vile god of the Illyrs, was set up next to that of Mardu. Each morning Eira went out and offered incense before the idol and spoke in frenzied words.* Many of the people, seeing Eira do these things and knowing her to be the one whom Alcidus would make queen, imitated her, and thus made obeisance to Makur. So the people of Cadaras were led into wickedness by the example of Eira.

Yet not all Cadaras succumbed to her influence, and many of the people were grieved at Eira's presence at court and her patronage of Makur. Some of the king's companions again said to him, "My lord, what do you mean by taking this aged woman to be thy bride when there are virgins a plenty throughout the land? Are none of the daughters of thy lords pleasant enough for you? Do their eyes lack depth or their figures lack fullness that you turn to a widow from beyond?" But Alcidus was held fast to Eira by the spell which she wrought upon him and heeded them not. Therefore the men of the court came unto Lothar as he sat in his gardens at the side of lovely Ornis, his wife. They said unto him, "Telendor, you alone have the grace and shrewdness to prevail with the king. Go unto him and tell him the folly of his ways. Will the king raise up sons by her? Will their lives not be endangered by Dimmoth and Vinos, who will certainly put them out of their way and claim the throne for themselves?" The lords pressed upon Lothar until he said, "I will act! By the gods I will act, though I cannot see how things shall end."

When Alcidus next summoned his court to hear the regular petitions that were brought before him, Lothar stood up and said, "My king, I have a petition to present before thee." Alcidus said, "Say on, noble Telendor." Now Eira and her sons were seated near the king.

Lothar addressed the king and the court, saying, "My lord, the court and people of Cadaras are in great anxiety over this woman, Eira, whom you have known only little more than a fortnight and yet propose to elevate to the queenship. Shall you so quickly decide the fate of the kingdom upon so brief a betrothal? And does it not trouble you that this woman has already two grown sons, whom she arrogantly brings into your presence and who parade about as if they were already princes? If you should somehow bear up children by her, will not her elder sons hold thy sons in scorn? It sits not right with me, my lord; I perceive some witchcraft in this. Inquire of her and ask from whence she came and by whom she fathered her sons, for as of yet she has spoken nothing of her origin or of the father of her sons." Eira glared at Lothar in hatred and perplexity, for his form and voice seemed familiar to her, but Manissa prevented her from discerning her son.

Alcidus, not taking his eyes from Eira, said, "Peace, Telendor. Is it not written that Arrax the Bold was smitten by such love for Erissa upon their first meeting? As to her lineage and origins, I care not and will suffer it not to be questioned. Eira shall surely be queen." The court was sorely troubled by this answer, for ever before had Alcidus been patient and calculating in his decisions, not rash and haughty. Therefore, when Lothar perceived that the mind of Alcidus was gone and that he would not listen to reason, he cried out, "My King

Alcidus! I have a charge to bring against this woman whom thou wouldst take to wife." Then the mouths of all the court were stopped, and Alcidus stood up in a rage, fury in his eyes at Lothar, who had dared to speak ill of Eira.

Lothar spoke boldly and said, "I accuse this woman of sorcery and witchcraft, and of her sons as accomplices of her crimes, for she assuredly is a witch from Bados and even now holds the heart of the king under and evil spell. Furthermore, I accuse her before thy majesty and the lords of this house of the murder of her first husband, Lord Lorion of Halicor." Eira shrieked a foul cry; Dimmoth and Vinos drew swords. The king said, "Telendor, thou shalt die for these words!" Lothar said, "My king, shall this matter not be investigated in the least? Is it custom to put to death a man before the truthfulness of his words have been tested? Speak to this woman and ask her from whence she has come and of the father of her sons."

Eira scoffed and said, "I do not know this man, this whelp Telendor, nor from whence he comes or by what right he makes these accusations. I will answer nothing he poses to me." Alcidus, enchanted by Eira, said, "No questions shall be posed to the lady. Let Telendor be taken out and burned to death for this false accusation!" Lothar cried out, saying, "If thou wilt not judge, I commend my case to our Lady, glorious Manissa, who judges all things rightly and casts her blazing spear without error. Let our Lady decide and prove my words by some ordeal or trial!"*

When Lothar said these words and invoked the name of Manissa, the king's companions and the whole court of Alcidus cried out with one voice, "Yea! An ordeal! An ordeal! Let Lothar be put to the ordeal!" Alcidus said, "Very well! You have asked for an ordeal—so shall you be tried! But how shall it be done? By fire, or water perhaps? Or shall we find some champion to cross swords with you?" Then the sons of Eira, Dimmoth and Vinos, stood up angrily and said, "Let us come to blows with him in the ordeal, for he has spoken ill of our mother and shamed our names before the entire court." Alcidus said, "Let it be so. Telendor will cross blades with Dimmoth and Vinos, but because of the severity of his accusations he shall fight them both at once." This the king said because he wanted to ensure Lothar's death. Lothar's companions cried out at the injustice of the sentence, but Lothar said, "Let it be so. Our Lady will cast her spear and cause justice to prevail."

Lothar and the sons of Eira were immediately taken out into the courtyard of the Citadel and made to fight to the death. King Alcidus took his place upon the steps of the Citadel, near the tomb of Secum, with black-haired Eira seated beside him. All the lords of the court and servants of the Citadel with the entire garrison also came forth to watch Lothar do battle with the sons of Eira, his brothers. Alcidus said, "Let it be known that no man can evade the spear of Manissa. If Telendor prevails over Dimmoth and Vinos, we shall surely know that there is truth in his words. But if Telendor is slain, then the good name of Eira shall be secured for all time."

Then Dimmoth drew his sword and charged for Lothar across the flagstone of the courtyard, Vinos circling to the side to outflank him. But Lothar was swift, and Manissa guided his steps, so that he easily dodged the charge of Dimmoth and parried the strikes of Vinos. Vinos swung swift and desperate against Lothar; the courtyard echoed with the ringing of swords and the scuffling of the feet of the combatants on the flagstone. Dimmoth sought to run Lothar through from behind, but Lothar caught him in his eye. Turning skillfully, he swung out behind with his blade and struck the face of Dimmoth, separating his jaw from his skull. The sword of Dimmoth fell clattering to the ground as Dimmoth collapsed in blood. At the sight of the mighty blow, some of the Asylians in the court yelled "Cruacha!" and roared in approval of Lothar.

White-knuckled Eira sat grimly motionless beside Alcidus, brooding upon the battle.

This did not deter Vinos but further enraged him, so that he struck fierce and wild against Lothar, pressing him back to the wall of the Citadel. As Lothar gave ground, he saw that the attacks of Vinos were clumsily landed by reason of his great fury. Vinos tried to land a great blow upon the head of Lothar, but Lothar rolled his body. Then, dashing to the side, he brought his blade down upon the skull of Vinos and split it in two. A gruesome crack! With a splattering of brains, Vinos tumbled lifelessly to the ground. When Dimmoth saw his brother slain, he stood aloft despite his pain and charged Lothar in rage. Lothar grounded his feet upon the ground, called upon his Blessed ancestress, and met the onslaught of Dimmoth. Dimmoth's blade was turned aside easily, and Lothar sunk his sword point into the belly of Dimmoth till it came forth from his back. Dimmoth gurgled and fell into darkness as his body struck the floor of the Citadel. Lothar stood alone.

Eira's countenance fell, and her breath failed her, for in that moment the veil was lifted from her eyes, and she knew her son Lothar. Before she could think what to do, Lothar rushed to the steps of the Citadel where Alcidus and Eira were seated and tore from Eira's neck the cursed band of gold. Immediately the eyes of Alcidus were opened. Then Lothar put his blade to the throat of Eira and said, "Now I will speak, and you will all listen. This woman Eira is my mother, for I am not Telendor but Lothar, son of Lorion, of the house of Mariammné and a descendant of Blessed Manissa, who has aided me this day in vindicating my cause. This woman is assuredly a witch, for though from her womb did I spring I know her heart to be wicked. Some years ago, she caused to die my father, Lorion, and took over his estate, fair Halicor in Bados. There she enslaved the people of the foothills, put many of them to death, and worshiped the heathen gods of the

Illyrs, which were stomped out of our land in the happy days of Anaxandra. I fled from her evil in my youth and have ever since dwelt here in the service of my king, hoping to put those evil days behind me forever. Thus it was until she came to Cadaras, and by means of her foul witcheries, vexed the heart of the king, holding him enslaved to her will. And these things she did in Halicor she would have assuredly done in Cadaras.

Alcidus stood up, his eyes flames of rage, and cried out, "Let this woman Eira be taken without the city immediately and burned to death!" Then all the lords and people assembled cried out with one voice, "Yea! Let her be burned!" But Eira's eyes became black as pitch, and her voice like a howling wind upon the moors of Bados. She shrieked and called upon the powers of darkness, so that a thick mist of darkness fell upon the Citadel and caused much confusion. Then Lothar cried out, "*Manissé crua dior!*" which means "Manissa, assist thy children!" Immediately the sun beat down fiercely upon the mist and dispersed it; but Eira was nowhere to be found.

Then the people of Cadaras thronged the Citadel and said, "What shall we do?" Noble-hearted King Alcidus said, "Purge the evil from the Citadel and the temple!" So the people went to the great bronze idol of Mardu which Sammas had set up in the days of old and hurled it to the ground, shattering it into hundreds of pieces. They also took up axes and mattocks and hewed apart the statue of Makur which Eira had erected. The priests of the Nergalim were ejected from the temple and the priests of Adar were hurled down from the towers of the Citadel, their bodies broken upon the stone. The various cults of Neb and Innana which had been allowed to prosper in the verdant gardens of Cadaras were ejected, and the high priest of Neb, a Caeylonic called Shazu who had bloodied his hands with many sacrifices of infants and virgins, was taken out and burned in the Valley of Danathor east of the city. All the vile shrines to the gods of Maruda and Illyrana that had been allowed to prosper in Cadaras since the days of Sammas were destroyed and defiled.

Then Alcidus took the hand of Lothar and said, "Beloved Lothar, son of glory, ask whatsoever you will, and it will be granted unto you."* Lothar said, "Great king, only that I may be confirmed in the lordship of fair Halicor, the estate founded by my father Lorion of happy memory." Alcidus said, "Go, receive the lordship of Halicor." So Lothar blessed the king in the name of Manissa, and taking up Ornis his wife, returned to Halicor rejoicing. Thus the peoples of the Bados sung of the glorious return of the son of Lorion to Halicor:

> *Lorion rejoicing evermore*
> *Whose splendor never dies*
> *At his noble son's return*
> *To Halicor 'neath golden skies*

Then was Halicor blessed and prosperous again. The shrine of Makur that stood there was torn down and the virgins again established at Halicor. Then there was peace and prosperity in all the land round about in the just and wise administration of Lothar.

But Ornis remained barren, and Lothar was full of sorrow at this, for he desired to raise up sons for himself. When many years had gone by and Ornis had not conceived, he saddled his horse and rode northwest, through the Nimru Pass, to the abode of Giannor, who was blind and bedridden. Lothar said, "Wise Giannor, seer of the ways of our Lady and the gods beyond, why is my house cursed with barrenness? Did I not do a good thing in expunging the evil of my mother from the land?" Giannor said, "Aye, it is as you say, but in so doing you have committed a great sin, for you have slain your blood brothers. Hadrior was accursed in the days of old for the blood of Erogel, who was only a remote cousin. How much more shall you bear the curse for the blood of thy brothers?"

Lothar tore his garments and said, "Crooked are the ways of Fate! Shall I be ordained to deliver the Manissans by the slaying of my evil brothers and then condemned because I did what was ordained?"*

Giannor said, "Do not despair. Because thou did slay them righteously, the sin of your house can be atoned for. Go into the remotest south, past the plains of Engor, into the wilds of Corbalund bordering the land of the Enlilim. There do penance in solitude for a period of three years and the sins of your house shall be forgiven." Lothar wept, "Three years!? Is there no other way? What of my wife, beautiful Ornis, who waits even now for my return in white-halled Halicor? Giannor said, "Did I not tell you your days would be burdened and that you should not take a wife? Yet did you disregard my words and accounted the decrees of Fate as of little value." So Lothar went back to Halicor mourning and weeping. Then Giannor breathed his last and died, being about one hundred and four years of age.

So Lothar did as Giannor commanded, removing himself to the far south, into Corbalund, and sought a place among the endless fields where there were boulders and rocks strewn about. He found for himself a mass of rock with a small cave worn out at the bottom, and there he dwelt in solitude and penance. But Ornis his wife would not be comforted, and leaving Halicor, followed him south in weeping and lamentation. Every night she collapsed upon the soft grasses of Corbalund and wept bitterly, so that a small lake sprung up wherever her tears fell. These lakes of Corbalund are even today called the Tears of Ornis.

But Lothar would not permit her to dwell with him or abide near him, and so she took a place atop a rock some distance from him, where she was near enough to see the cave of Lothar but too far off to see his form. She said, "If Lothar is condemned to suffer so, I shall suffer as well." So she perched herself atop the rock and remained through sun and cloud,

wind and rain, summer and winter. And in this condition
Lothar and Ornis abode in Corbalund for three years.

When the three years of penance were completed they
returned to Halicor, and Ornis conceived. She bore to Lothar a
son, called Marí, which means "labored," because they labored
for three years to atone for the blood of Dimmoth and Vinos
and for the sins of Eira.* Thus the house of Lothar was blessed.
When Lothar and Ornis grew old and departed, Marí became
Lord of Halicor. It was in the days of Marí that the hill people
of Bados put away the gods of the mountain folk and began to
pay honor to Manissa and the gods of the north, so that from
the time of Marí on the peoples of the eastern Bados were
reckoned among the Manissans.

But it was never known nor heard of what became of
Eira, though some of the peasants of the distant mountain
villages say she is still seen roaming the vales of the Bados at
night, black-haired and fair, gliding ghostlike over the moonlit
rocks.*

Oros

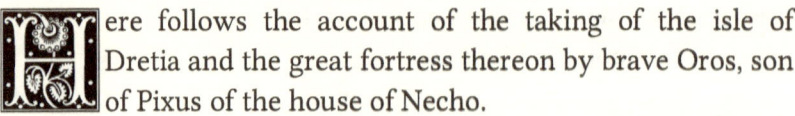

H ere follows the account of the taking of the isle of Dretia and the great fortress thereon by brave Oros, son of Pixus of the house of Necho.

It came to pass that the house of Necho waxed strong in the regions around Engor and Corbalund, especially in the west around the district of Halicor and the foothills of the Bados. In the days after the passing of Marí, son of Lothar, the hillmen of Bados were converted one and all from the ways of their fathers to the manner of living and worship of the Manissans, and thus the great lords of the Manissans extended to them the hand of fellowship. Then many of the house of Necho came up from the plains to settle around Halicor and the foothills of the Bados and intermarried with the folk there, so that the region became densely populated. And in those days the lordship of Halicor was considered the greatest lordship of the south.

Year by year the Manissans of Halicor, whether of Asylian and Badoan stock, ventured further west into the mountains of Bados, where the hills give way to steep granite cliffs that form valleys verdant in the summer but impassible in the winter. They grazed their flocks upon the slopes of the mountains, hunted in the forested vales, and took wood from the hillsides. It was in this manner that they first encountered the Dretians, a wild and fierce people who occupied the peaks and valleys of the Bados. Their clothing and manner of living was

248

rustic, but they were skilled workers of stone, having constructed many solid fortifications in the valley passes so that no one could venture through the mountains to the sea without their leave. They also established fortresses and strongholds along the western coast on the Bay of Norn, commanding the shoreline for hundreds of miles both north and south. They took their name from the great island of Dretia, that isle which sits in the Bay of Norn on the sea. This island had been in possession of the Dretians for many centuries and, according to their lore, was their first homeland.

Yet the Dretians were at that time in decline, for their line of kings had gone extinct, and a fearsome plague had ravaged them for some years. Therefore they gave ground before the Manissans who were ever coming west, ceding the mountain passes and pleasant, sloping hillsides year after year until there remained to them only the narrow strip of territory upon the sea and the great isle of Dretia in the midst of the bay. As the Manissans pressed westward, many of the people of Dretia removed themselves to the island, which was a little more than a league into the sea from the coast and visible from the mainland on any clear day. Thus there was peace between the Manissans and the Dretians for a time.

But when the Manissans had been in the land many years and had taken over from the Dretians all the fortresses and strongholds commanding the mountain passes, the Dretians began to regret that they had given way before the Manissans. They regretted that they had allowed themselves to be penned up on the rugged coasts of the land and upon the island. Therefore they called secret councils by night upon the desolate peaks of the most foreboding mountains of the Bados, and there plotted to blot out the Manissans from the land. The Manissans knew not of these plans, for the Dretians were masters of doubletalk and treachery and gave no indication of their hostile intent.

Then came the year of war, for the Dretians raised the torch of battle from the barren heights of the Bados, descending upon the Manissan settlements with great fury. They came upon the villages by night with torch and spear, burning the habitations of the Manissans, slaying many, and sending the survivors fleeing east towards Halicor. In the following weeks they fanned out throughout all the Bados, engaging the Manissans in the narrow mountain passes and putting them to rout from the south even to the north. Most of the Manissans were hardy mountain folk and managed to escape the Dretian attacks, but no small number were slain as well.

These raids quickened the Manissans and made their blood run hot, for they had enjoyed peace for many generations and there was few among them had ever marched to war or borne their spear aloft in battle. Word spread quickly to Halicor and beyond—to Engor and Corbalund, Cadaras, and Asylia, and all throughout the lands of the Manissans—of the Dretian treachery. And everywhere the word went, there were men eager to take up the spear to win glory in battle, as they had heard in the tales of their forefathers.

But the kings of Cadaras were weak in those days, for the city was in decline and the king could command little save for the environs immediately surrounding it. Each region was in the hand of its own lords who did as they pleased, swearing fealty to the king but ruling their own territories alone. Thus the king in Cadaras could muster no warriors to come and aid the Manissans of the Bados, instead bidding them defend themselves the best they knew how. Therefore many of the lesser lords of the land—from lower Cadarasia, Greystone, Asylia, Engor, Corbalund, Badoa, and Anentora—all mustered their men and came together by the Brook of Teruel in the shadow of the foothills. There, by the waters of Teruel, they raised the cry of war in defense of the Manissans of the Bados and pledged to do what they could for the succor of their countrymen, the king having provided no aid. They gathered there under their respective standards in the spring, after the second winter of raiding and slaughter by the Dretians.

Who were the great men among the lords who raised their spears in the glittering sun by fair Teruel's watery course? From Cadarasia came Dindar, a powerful lord of great renown and of the royal house of that city. In his youth he had killed a Caeylonic captain in a raid that won him much glory, and at Teruel he boasted that he would drive the Dretians into the sea. Dindar brought with him two thousand men from Cadarasia, Avlos, Elos, and its environs.

From An Hered and An Danara in the east came Corax and Beruah, two men of noble disposition with strong sword arms whose families had been strong in those regions for many generations; Corax and Beruah brought with them to Teruel fifteen hundred men who drew the sword, all of them experienced in raiding and skirmishing against the Caeylonics and Elamites.

From Halicor came grim Durmius, lord of Halicor from youth and a descendant of Marí, son of Lothar, of the house of Mariammné. Durmius stood head and shoulders above all other men and wielded a spear of cedar five cubits in length with a blade as long as a man's forearm. Durmius had been out to defend the Manissans of the Bados before and was experienced in fighting the Dretians. Thus was he accounted an important captain in the campaign and by some the most important lord of all Elabaea. He brought from Halicor and its lands three thousand warriors, more than half of them of Badoan stock who were thirsty for the blood of the Dretians, whom they regarded as their ancient enemies. When Durmius's towering form was seen approaching Teruel at the head of his column of warriors, a joyful cheer erupted from the Manissans, who clashed their spears upon their shields and shouted, "Aüe Durmius nomé Lotharé!" which means, "Hail Durmius, son of Lothar!"

From Anentora came three captains: first among them was Oros, son of Pixus of the house of Necho, a lord of exceptional wisdom and might whose aim with the spear was praised all over the east. Also from Anentora came Oros's companions, bold Urmax and Imloss the One-Eyed; the lords of Anentora brought with them eighteen hundred men, all wielding the spear and the sword and grinning for war and plunder.

Tanus, lord of Engor and a distant kinsman of Oros, came forth with a thousand men, as did two lords from Greystone, Carus and Sirmius, who brought seven hundred warriors. From Corbalund marched lord Solax with five hundred hardened plainsmen, as well as Ermarius, Prince of Badoa. Ermarius was the son of King Panasted of Badoa (which in those days was not yet united to the throne of the Manissans) and a descendant of Necho through Pilux; Ermarius brought a thousand men. Finally, from old Asylia came proud Antylos, who brought five hundred riders from the rugged northern plains, each long-haired and equipped with deadly ashen spears. Also mustered at Teruel were Anax and Urbus, two chiefs among the Badoans who were reckoned among the Manissans.* They brought with them twelve hundred Badoans from the hill country, all of whom had scores to settle with the Dretians.* Thus the total number of men who drew the sword that mustered at Teruel was thirteen thousand two hundred.

But almost immediately a violent dispute broke out as to who would be chosen to lead the campaign, for in the absence of the king there was no clear ruler. Each legion shouted and clamored for its own lord, men sometimes coming to blows with each other over the matter. After several days of violent quarrelling, three men were settled upon: Dindar, by virtue of his relation to the king at Cadaras; Durmius, by right of the importance of the lordship of Halicor and his imposing stature; and Oros of Anentora, by virtue of the quality of his character, the wisdom of his words, and his deadly aim with the spear. Yet even among these three no one could agree on who should take command, so it was proposed that Dindar, Durmius, and Oros should all possess the leadership together. The three lords assented to this, but each one privately hoped to win the most glory by outdoing the others in valorous and daring feats. So the army of the Manissans swore obedience to Dindar, Durmius, and Oros by the gentle course of Teruel. Then priests were brought forth to offer sacrifices and discern the will of Manissa. The birds were slain, the auguries taken, and the setting forth of the army set for the next full moon, nine days hence.*

The grand army of the Manissans set forth on the twentieth day of the third month in the second year after the Dretians began their offensive in the mountains. They went up into the foothills by way of the Durimor Pass, following the pass up through the dwellings of the Badoan-Manissans without incident until coming after seven days into the region where the foothills fall away before the foreboding granite slopes of the Bados. Here there was a disagreement, for Dindar proposed turning along a northernly route to come upon the land of the Dretians in a roundabout way, but Durmius and Oros proposed heading west to engage the Dretians head on. The captains quarrelled late into the night, pacing about the tent of Durmius in agitated conversation. "Master Dindar," said grim-faced Durmius as he raised the steaming chalice of spiced wine to his lips, "is it not true that attacking the Dretians from the north, as you propose, will only drive them away from us to the south and give them opportunity for withdrawal? The Dretians are a folk both crafty and brave and will seek any means of escape which we provide for them. Is it not so?"

Haughty Dindar scoffed and said, "They will not know we are upon them, lord Durmius, for we shall move with stealth and strike them suddenly before they have time to organize their retreat. In this way we will come upon them unawares and smite them where they dwell." Lordly Oros laughed and spoke in his deep and thoughtful manner, saying, "And do you suppose, my lord Dindar, that thirteen thousand warriors moving through the mountain passes will go unnoticed by the Dretians, especially in a time of war? Nay, this would be laughable to assert if its consequences not so disastrous were we to heed thy words. Moving the army round north will bring forth what Durmius suggests, and we will find the better part of the campaign season spent chasing phantoms and shadows in these boulder-strewn passes."

Durmius said, "Then would the Dretians move against us at the first snowfall, when we are wearied from months of fruitless marching and low on provisions. We would be forced to winter in some forsaken and snow-choked mountain pass while the Dretians kill us at their leisure from the peaks. Nay, Dindar, we shall by no means do as you suggest. If we move straight on as has been our course until this point, we shall come against the Dretians like a moving wall, rolling them westward with the cliffs and the sea at their back. Thus shall they be blotted out of the land."

But haughty Dindar said, "And what will stop them from retreating to the north and to the south if we act thus?" Oros said, "It is true that they may still flee, but at least we shall divide them in two, some to the north of us and some to the south, and thus divided they will be twice as weak and that much easier to subdue." They proposed many such arguments and counter arguments throughout the night until Durmius and Oros prevailed upon Dindar to accede to the westerly route. Yet Dindar was full of spite against Oros and Durmius and brooded in his heart, saying, "I will yet win glory over these two arrogant pretenders and establish the honor of my house." So he pondered how he could win glory at the expense of Oros and Durmius.

Thus the army pushed west through the rugged passes of the Bados, marching under the foreboding cliff shadows in vigilance and attentiveness, lest the Dretians espy them from the peaks or cliffside paths and entrap the Manissans in some ambuscade. Every man slept in his armor with his spear by his side lest they be surprised and murdered in the night, for the fear of attack was constantly upon them. Yet it was not until the third week in the mountains that the Manissans engaged the Dretians, for Oros led the army into a broad valley between two great ranges and found it swarming with Dretian warriors. The Dretians flooded down the hillsides and assaulted the Manissans fiercely, encompassing them both on the west and the east so that the main body of warriors was cut off from the rear. The Dretians howled and thrust their biting javelins at the Manissans; any man who dared to stretch his arm outside the shield wall or lift his head to look for an opening was pierced. If the Manissans turned to strike the east they were assaulted that much more fiercely from the west; if they turned to the west they were pressed from the east, and thus began to be in dire straits.

But Oros crashed his spear upon his shield and roared with fury, and with his iron arm hurled his hardened shaft at one of the Dretian chiefs, a large man of war with his face dyed many colors. The deadly spear crashed into the skull of the haughty chief, sending bits of bone flying and exposing brain to sun and sky. When the Manissans saw this they rallied and cried, "Curcua! Curcua Manissé!" Then Oros called to Durmius, "Let every man train his spear outward, so that we at once defend front and rear. Form the men into a circle so that there is no weak spot found in our lines!" Durmius thus harangued the men and turned them to ward off the blows of the Dretians, Oros and Dindar doing likewise. Then the Dretians began to weary of the assault, for they saw that they could in nowise break the Manissan shield wall so long as grim Durmius and noble Oros held the command. By the falling of the dusk they moved off and withdrew to the west, going towards the coast, leaving the Manissans in possession of the valley. Then the men elevated Oros upon their shields and heaped glory and honor upon him for the victory.*

The army encamped in the valley for two days before moving off again to the west. They came into the wilds of the Bados where there is neither path nor road through the mountainous terrain and treacherous gorges and deadly cliffs made the travel exceedingly difficult for the mounted men of Asylia under Antylos. Oft it happened that some ill-fated rider, perhaps caught napping or otherwise inattentive in the saddle, allowed his steed to stumble upon loose stone and plummeted from the deadly heights, horse and all, to be dashed apart upon the cruel and jagged stones of the canyon floor. Furthermore, the paths and footholds upon which Oros led the men were so narrow that the army was compelled to divide into several columns, each taking a disparate route around various mountains and over differing cliffs, so that within a few days the bulk of the army had been sundered from one another. Durmius said to Oros, "This does not sit well with me, lord Oros, for lord Dindar with Corax, Beruah, and the Cadarasian men have gone off on a more northerly route around these perilous cliffs. I fear he means to abandon the remainder of us and win some notable victory over the Dretians alone." Oros laughed and said, "Let Fate order all things as she wills."

The passing over those mountains took weeks and wearied the Manissans exceedingly, so that many began to regret that they had left the fair plains of Asylia or the bounteous fields of Corbalund to face calamity in the merciless mountains of the desolate Bados, so far from the warmth of hearth or the familiar faces of kin. They were further hindered by the Dretians, who made raids and ambushes upon their columns frequently, picking off stragglers or striking men upon the narrowest paths with arrows or falling stones, so that no man was ever sure of his safety. Yet by and by they pressed ever westward and came to those regions of the Bados where the jagged granite peaks that reach ever heavenward begin to recede, and the foreboding mountain passes give way to wider vales, regions more pleasant and hospitable to human habitation. Then it was that they approached the great fortress of Ardilla, which stood upon a narrow space of flatland betwixt two great mountain ranges on the westernmost side of the Bados.

As the grand army of the Manissans came out into the valley floor they heard a roaring and tumult from the distance beyond the fortress. Durmius clasped his spear and said, "My lord Oros, 'tis the sound of the Dretians falling upon us from west of Ardilla!" But Oros laughed and said, "Fear not, brave Durmius; the tumult we hear is neither the army of the Dretians nor anything to be feared, but is the tossing of the turbulent waters of the Bay of Norn upon the cliffsides." Then all the men rejoiced, for they had traversed the mountains and reached the sea. The army pitched camp at the entrance to the valley, about a league east of Ardilla, at the place called Evlas. There they bided their time to scout the fortress of Ardilla and see whether Dindar would rejoin himself to them with his forces.

But the fortress of Ardilla was at that time manned by no more than three thousand Dretians, the greater number of them having moved off to the north and to the south to search for the column of Dindar, whom they knew to be encumbered in the mountain passes. Therefore the scouts of Oros said, "My lord, compared to our numbers the fortress is weakly defended." Durmius said, "Let us press the attack now, Oros, while the greater number of them are gone!" Oros said, "Summon Antylos, as well as Urmax and Imloss the One-Eyed." When these lords presented themselves at the tent of Oros, he said unto them, "My lords, to thee to I entrust the taking of Ardilla, which our Lady has delivered into our hands." So Antylos of Asylia, with Urmax and Imloss, took their men, about two thousand infantry and another five hundred mounted, and assaulted Ardilla with great ferocity. The Dretians held them off for two days, but on the third day the fortress was taken and Antylos brought back a train of prisoners to present to Oros and Durmius, two thousand in all. Then the fortress was overthrown and demolished.

It was at this time that Dindar came upon the Manissan camp. His men were wearied and in a foul mood by reason of the many days of laborious marching they had endured through the northern passes, for Dindar had become turned around and added four days more to their march than what it would have been had they pursued the same route as Oros. Furthermore, no small number of them had perished on the journey upon the loose footing of the treacherous cliffs. Therefore, when they came into the valley and heard how Oros and Durmius had taken Ardilla without their aid, they were greatly incensed. Then Corax and Beruah said to Dindar, "Cursed be thy arrogance, Dindar, for in following thee over Oros we have forfeited the plunder of Ardilla!" Enraged at the insults he suffered from his own men, Dindar came to the tent of Oros and argued with him to his face before all the other captains of Asylia. So fierce became their words that those who stood around feared that blood would be shed. But then stout-hearted Durmius came into the tent and cried, "Let these words be reserved for another day my lords, for the Dretians are upon us!"

Oros came forth from the tent and beheld several companies of Dretians swarming into the valley from the hillsides round about. They perceived that Ardilla had been overthrown and their comrades slain or imprisoned and were filled with wrath. The Manissans had little time to form up, for it was midday and many were relaxing or taking their noontide meal. Oros ran throughout the camp shouting, "To arms, to arms! Our foes press us and seek to drive us out of the valley! To arms or perish!" Durmius likewise rallied the men, as did all the Manissan captains. But the men under Dindar and his captains had only been in the camp for a few hours and had yet found little rest. They were greatly unnerved at the call to arms and grumbled against Dindar.

The Dretians came upon the Manissans like a wave, running in a vast line and wielding swords of beaten bronze. But Durmius took the front, as did lord Tanus of Engor. Both lords won glory that day, for the Dretians broke upon the Manissan spears like waves upon the cliffside. The Manissans formed a great wall of spears and greeted the Dretian charge with flesh-rending thrusts, skewering many of them upon their whetted blades. Durmius roared and pressed them on, the great Manissan phalanx pushing forward and driving the Dretians back. When Oros saw that Tanus and Durmius had broken the charge, he called, "Brave Antylos! Let them feel the pounding of the steeds of Asylia!" So Antylos blew his horn and led forth his riders, scores upon scores of hardened warriors from the rugged Asylian plains. Each man bore a death-dealing shaft of hard ash and a shield overlaid with hide, rimmed with silver studs. They rode out fiercely, auburn locks trailing upon the winds behind them as they thundered into the Dretian lines. The Dretians were unaccustomed to warring against cavalry and turned in flight at the approach of Antylos. The Asylian riders hurled their spears and trampled their foes unopposed, making short work of the first Dretian attack.

But the victory was yet turned to bitterness, for as the Dretians fled, they turned and fired a final volley upon the pursuing horsemen, and noble Antylos was struck in the throat with a barbed arrow. He tumbled from his charger and crashed upon the beaten grass, his blood spurting from the hideous wound. His captains bore him aloft and carried him from the field, but when he was laid at the feet of Oros his life had departed him. Then the men of Asylia wept for brave Antylos and swore vengeance for his blood.

Meanwhile another mass of Dretians pressed the Manissan camp, this one more numerous than the first and with many archers among them. Missiles fell among the men of Tanus and Durmius, striking the spearmen and weakening the line. The Manissans shuddered at the blistering war-cry of the Dretian warriors, who crashed again into the Manissan lines and cleaved flesh with their dreadful brazen blades. Then Prince Ermarius, the son of King Panastes from Badoa, said, "Lord Oros, entrust the relief of Durmius and Tanus to my warriors who are yet fresh and ready for the din of war!" Oros said, "Win glory, beloved prince." Therefore Ermarius cried out and raised his glittering blade, bringing his Badoan thousand into the fray. Yet at the same time a third assault from the Dretians broke upon the camp, for another horde of them had swept into the valley from the north, west of the ruins of Ardilla. These skirted the flanks of Tanus, pressing further into the camp than either of the other two attacks, and fell hard upon the men under Dindar, who were already weary. The Dretians did great damage to the men of Dindar, especially those of Corax and Beruah, for the Dretians were well rested and zealous for war while the men of Dindar were weary. In this assault Beruah, lord of An Danara, was slain, for he attempted to rally his men and form a line against the Dretians but had his head cloven in two by a heavy Dretian longsword. Some of the men under Dindar fled to Oros, saying, "Our flanks collapse under the Dretian assault!"

Oros summoned his own captains and companions, Urmax and one-eyed Imloss and told them, "Come, my lords! Let us relieve Dindar and the Cadarasians who are hotly pressed." But Anax and Urbus, chiefs of the hillmen of Bados, and also Solax of Corbalund, whom he had kept in reserve, he sent forward to aid Ermarius, Durmius, and Tanus. Thus every lord was engaged and every last man among the Manissans fought hotly with spear and sword for possession of the valley. The hillmen of Anax and Urbus raged among the Dretian lines, strengthening the will of the Manissans and rallying their comrades. They moved with agility and dexterity, striking this way and that with their long, thin spears and piercing the Dretians wherever they tried to advance. Some Dretians were in great fear of them and threw down their arms, but the hillmen would not be halted, and thrust these men through where they stood, for the hillmen were ancient foes of the Dretians and wanted nothing less than to blot them out of the land entirely.

The Dretian advance began to falter, and Prince Ermarius charged their lines, at which they turned and fled. Then Durmius roared, "We have them! By our Lady's locks, they are in flight!" So the wearied men of Durmius and Tanus joined with those of Ermarius and the hillmen to pursue the fleeing

Dretians, striking them as far as the western end of the valley where the land falls away before the dreadful cliffs that overlook misty Norn and the lonely isle.

Yet the fight was not yet won, for Oros was hotly engaged on the right flank. Dindar's men were in disarray and many were hit in the back with spears or arrows while they fled. But Oros brought his companies into the fray and charged the Dretian advance. The Dretians were ill prepared for the fury of Oros's charge and were sliced and broken upon the Manissan spears. Oros won glory in this engagement, for he slew no less than twenty men with his relentless strokes and killed in single combat a Dretian chief who was foolhardy enough to cross blades with him. Then the Dretians began to flee to the hills and mountain slopes, Urmax and Imloss pursuing them for almost three furlongs until the stragglers escaped into the mountains. But Dindar was found lying wounded upon the battlefield, for a Dretian javelin had pierced him in the shoulder.

The victory was very great, for Oros's scouts reported that no less than six thousand Dretians were lying slain upon the bloodied grass of the valley floor. Yet it was not won without great cost, for two lords, Antylos of Asylia and Beruah of An Danara, had fallen, and Dindar was wounded grievously. Furthermore, a dozen lesser captains had fallen slain, as well as two thousand of the common men. The men were silent that evening, the still of the mountain night was broken only by the baleful dirges sung at the pyres of Beruah and Anytlos. But Dindar brooded upon his sickbed, for his envy and malice against Oros was hot.

In the morning the Manissans beheld a wondrous sight, for Oros and Durmius brought the men down to the cliffside to gaze upon the Bay of Norn and the isle of Dretia in the midst of Norn's deep blue waters. How lovely was the green isle when the Manissans set eyes upon it for the first time, as the mists parted, and the sun blazed upon the gentle waters of the bay that morning! The sight of the pleasant isle sitting proudly in the midst of Norn like a jewel in the bosom of the sea moved the men immensely, and Oros, being filled with wonder and praise, lifted up his head and sang this verse:

Jewel of the sea! O crown of the west!
Thou blessed abode of a people noble and fair-
May thy fields be verdant and thy harvests unfailing
O isle of pleasantness, haven of rest. *

And with many such songs and hymns did the Manissans praise the beauty of the isle as they knelt in the bedewed grass upon the cliffside of Ardilla by Norn.

Then Oros began to tremble, and his eyes were lifted up to the island, for a grand vision unfolded in his noble heart. He cried out with a loud voice, "Men of Manissé, we have these many weeks battled our way through the cruel passes of the Bados to the very sea, scattering the Dretians and overthrowing their mighty stronghold of Ardilla. Yet shall we cease at this? Shall we come to this cliff to hear the crashing of the sea upon the shore and gaze at this happy isle across Norn's pleasant waters only to turn back and leave the Dretians in possession of their most well defended stronghold? Hear me, O men who go by Manissa's name and those of her house! We shall never be secure in these hills or in the pleasant valleys of Halicor so long as the Dretians possess this island, from which they can make raids and sorties to the mainland at their leisure and retreat there in the face of any expedition against them. Therefore do I tremble at the words I speak today: let us go forth upon Norn's waters and plant our feet and the dominion of Manissé upon the land of the Dretian's own isle. Let us swear a covenant here, in the sight of the isle and in the sight of Manissa, never to turn back to rest until, by the bloody work of spear and sword, we secure the island and become ourselves masters of Norn." Oros spoke with the very fire of Manissa in his bosom; at his words all assembled with one accord crashed their spears and swords upon their shields and cried out, "Yea, let it be so! By the gods we so swear it! To the isle or to doom!" Thus they all vowed to continue the campaign until the island of the Dretians should be seized.*

Yet the lords were not of one accord on how to capture the island, for the Manissans encamped near the cliffs for many days and beheld the waters of the Norn frequently traversed by the Dretians, who navigated it in small crafts. The region around the cliffs was sparsely wooded and provided no means for the fashioning of boats. Furthermore, the cliffs were treacherous and of a great height, falling immediately down to the coast at a severe incline, so that if any retreat was called or if the Dretians pursued the Manissans back to the shore there would be no escape. Therefore Oros said, "Let us follow the coastline north and west until the mountains of Bados fall away and we are not so near the sight of the Dretians. There we can fashion crafts and make for the isle in one attempt without working under their very eyes."

Dindar was much opposed to this, for he said, "The way north out of the Bados is at least a march of a fortnight and a half, not even considering the time needed to construct boats and crafts to carry us to the island. By then the summer will be over and the chill winds of fall will drive hard against us. Men's hearts will turn towards their homes and much time will have been wasted. Let us rather plan to make but a few boats from such materials as we have on hand, enough only to transport a few hundred men; in any case no more than one thousand. Then let the boats and a few picked men make an attempt down the cliffside by night and take to the water. Then let the picked men row by cover of darkness to the shores of the island and there set up an encampment, so that we shall have a foothold there. Then we can construct more boats from the abundant wood of the island, and sending this back to the main camp here, build enough vessels to enable the remainder to come over in a timely manner and begin the siege of the fortresses there. All this can be accomplished in much less time than marching the long route out of the Bados."

All the lords protested against this plan, for they doubted that the Dretians would suffer a company of a thousand to remain unmolested upon their shores long enough to fell timber and send it back to the mainland. But Dindar thought their opposition was due to the influence of Oros and said to himself, "They speak thus only to rob me of glory and humiliate me." He therefore vociferously insisted his plan to be the best and declared that he would make the attempt himself with or without the aid of the other lords. Oros said, "Lord Dindar, far be it from us to compel you to sunder your own efforts from those of the rest our company. By Teruel's pleasant banks did we not vow to fight and die together as one? If you will put yourself forward to lead this treacherous descent down the cliffs and bold crossing of the Norn by nightfall, then I for one will maintain my warriors in readiness to support the landing if it should be successful. Is it not written in our histories that the great fortress of Danath Hered was taken from the Marudans by a similar daring effort?" Dindar cast haughty eyes upon Oros and said, "I shall lead the attack myself." All the other lords scoffed in disbelief at the audacity of Dindar's words. Dindar did not heed them but took his leave to prepare for the assault. Durmius said to Oros, "I fear the efforts of Dindar shall come to a disastrous end." Oros said, "Fate shall decide. If he succeeds, we shall have captured the island. But if he fails, we shall be rid of a troublesome and divisive gadfly." Durmius said, "And what of the brave lads who shall be taken in Dindar's folly? Do they deserve such a fate?" Oros said, "What can be done? As goes the nest, so goes the eggs."

But the heart of Dindar was arrogant; he set his face to put Oros and Durmius to shame by seizing Dretia unaided.* He stormed back to his tent in a fury and immediately summoned Corax, his most trusted captain, and told him of the plan. Corax said, "My lord, far be it from me to turn coward or to go back on the great oath which we all swore by the cliffside, to seize the fair island for our own. But my heart wrenches and my stomach drops at the plan you propose. What if we were to be sighted by the Dretians and assaulted while making our way down the cliffside? To where would we go, or how should we fight them off? We would be utterly exposed."

Dindar scoffed haughtily and said, "Where is the boldness of Corax? We shall move quickly and with stealth, taking the coast before ever a Dretian eye perceives what we do." But Corax said, "My lord, you have only now been wounded in the shoulder and are even now still bearing the bandage of your wound. Will you descend the cliff in such a state?" Envy burned in the eyes of Dindar and he said, "Fate will give me strength, for it is given to me to seize this isle alone and win the glory for myself, thus putting the pride of dimwitted Durmius and arrogant Oros to shame." Corax said, "I have sworn fealty to you, my lord, and thus will I follow you in life or in death; but I could not go to the grave content unless I speak my mind here and now. This plan is plain folly, which any man born of woman can see, and which is only veiled from your sight by the blinding jealousy which you bear against Oros and Durmius."

Dindar was enraged, and shaking his spear violently at Corax, cried out, "The shades take you Corax, friend of fruitful days and opponent in trial!" But Corax said, "I have spoken my peace, my lord, and will say no more. Come, let us make ready to take the cliff."

Then did Dindar, with the blessing of Oros, caused all the carts and supply wagons to be dismantled and set craftsmen to work constructing small boats from the planks, enough to transport two hundred men in all. The crafts were made by night so that the Dretians of the mountains would not see what was being fashioned, while by day Dindar and the men chosen to accompany them down the cliff scouted the precipice, debating the best route to take in the nocturnal descent. Meanwhile, Corax went throughout the camp gathering ropes and knotting them together for the lowering of the boats. But Oros sat daily upon a stool in the midst of his tent and would not go out. The servants of Dindar came to him and said, "Will you not aid Dindar in the attack of the isle?" Oros said, "I have told Dindar that we will aid him how we can, and so we shall if he makes it as far as the isle. But this past night a vision came to me in my sleep, terrifying and ghastly, and showed unto me to what end this endeavor will come.* Therefore I will not move from this spot until Dindar either sets foot on the isle or perishes, for I have seen what will befall and will not take part in Dindar's doom." The servants of Dindar were perplexed and told their master all Oros had spoken. Dindar only brooded and worked all the more feverishly.

Finally, the preparations for the assault were complete and the evening came upon which Dindar was to make his descent. The servants of Dindar again came to the tent of Oros, saying, "Will you not come forth this evening at least to observe the descent of brave Dindar down the cliffside?" Oros said, "My friends, courage must be tempered with prudence and humility, else it becomes courage no longer but foolishness and coarse bravado, benefiting nobody and serving only to inflate vanity. Come unto me no more until Dindar either takes the isle or is slain in the attempt, for I will not until then come forth from my tent." So the servants went away perplexed.

As darkness fell, Corax began to lead the first scores of men down the cliffside. The night was clear and warm but windy, and the route down the cliff torturously slow. The cliff was treacherous; each man went with his spear and shield strapped to his back and upon precious little foothold, clinging to the ropes as to life. After some time Dindar himself led the second group over the side, following the path taken by Corax. The rest of the Manissan camp gathered about the top of the cliff to see what would become of the endeavor. But Oros remained in his tent.*

It happened, however, that Dindar had grossly misconstrued the effort required for the endeavor and how long it would take his men to scale the cliff, for the company of Corax was not yet halfway down and already the men were wearied to the point of exhaustion by the hard descent. Many men clung tightly to the rocky precipice and made only the slowest progress for the fear that was upon them by virtue of the darkness, the great height, and the constant crashing of the sea upon the rocks below. Corax saw that his men were exceedingly weary and in need of rest, and so called up to Dindar to halt the descent until his men could recover their strength. But Dindar called down and ordered him to continue.

The men upon the top of the cliff, hearing the shouting of Corax and Dindar, thought these were the shouts to let down the boats, and so the men began lowering the boats down the cliffside slowly by rope. Yet because of the darkness they could not see the men of Corax and Dindar still upon the cliffside. The boats thus dropped down upon the men of Dindar suddenly, knocking a few from their footholds and causing those ill-fated souls to plummet to their doom. When Dindar realized that the boats were being let down prematurely he shouted and screamed in anger, as did all the men upon the cliff. But this furor, and the clamor of the men being dashed upon the rocks, rang out loud across the Norn and caused some of the Dretian crafts lurking in the bay to take notice and light their lanterns. Straightaway the dark waters of the bay were illuminated by first one, then dozens of lanterns from the Dretian crafts upon the bay. Corax saw this and cried out, "My lord, the bay swarms with Dretian ships! We must make haste!" So Corax urged his men on and began making his descent swiftly.

Dindar, when he realized what was happening, also cried, "Haste, haste!" and urged his men on downward; but the men above thought he was asking that the boats be lowered down with greater haste and so again began lowering the boats by rope, this time at a greater speed. Again the boats came down, knocking several from the cliff, and paralyzing the rest of the men with fear. But in their great haste to lower the crafts, the workmen at the top of the cliff became careless and let the ropes slip so that one of the boats fell freely down the entire face of the cliffside. It struck several men of Dindar and Corax off the sheer side of the precipice and shattered upon the jagged rocks at the cliff base. At this sound the Dretian boats in the bay began to move swiftly, converging upon the shore not far from where Corax was attempting his descent.

Then was there a horrific sound, the rattling of arrows off the stone as archers from the Dretian boats began firing upon the men. There was great panic upon the cliff, for many of the men of Dindar and Corax tried to don their shields against the arrows. Some lost their bearing and fell to their death; still others huddled upon the scanty footholds and nooks offered by the precipice and defended themselves the best they could. Corax and some of his company succeeded in reaching the shore at the base of the cliff, but not before several boatloads of Dretians came upon the land at that point. There was a fierce battle upon the shore between Corax and the Dretians, each clanging deadly blades together in the mist, ankle-deep in foam. Yet was Corax overpowered and all those with him slain, those valiant souls who braved the treacherous cliffside for a fleeting glory. But Corax they bound and took back to the island to be made prisoner.

At this time the number of Dretians upon the shore was very great; they fired arrows and threw spears at the Manissans still struggling upon the cliffside. The Manissans atop the cliff were in intense anxiety, for though they knew their comrades were suffering attacks from below they could neither fire arrows down themselves nor throw rocks, for the night was dark and they feared striking their own comrades. Thus the Dretian arrows struck men one by one; the Manissans above in the camp gnashed their teeth in agony as every few minutes the cries of some valiant young son of Manissé plummeting into the darkness rang out across the bay. It was only very late that Dindar realized how dire his situation was and attempted to climb back up the cliff in order to retreat. He found, however, that his shoulder was sorely troubled by reason of the wound he had recently taken and that he was in nowise strong enough to ascend.

At this time there was two young Dretians upon the shore engaged in the fight against the Manissans upon the cliffside. When they perceived Dindar stationary upon the precipice, they made a wager as to whether he was within distance of a stone's throw and hurled two stones at him. Neither stone hit its mark, but they struck the rock beside him and jarred him so that his grip loosened, and Dindar dropped from the cliffside. He plummeted down the façade of the cliff and was broken upon the rocks with a hideous crack. Thus perished Dindar in the calamity he visited upon his own head by his pride.

As for the other young men upon the cliff, it was a woeful and pitiful sight, for the Manissans found them too far out of reach to aid effectively. Though they tried to lower more ropes down to aid their escape, they found the men were too tired to make the attempt. Thus it was that they were picked off over the course of the night by the Dretians, each being dislodged from the cliff face to endure death by either arrow point or bone-breaking rock upon the ground. All the men of the expedition were cut off; not even one survived save Corax, who was taken away by boat to Dretia.

At that time word was brought to Oros in his tent, saying, "Dindar has perished upon the crags and the expedition has failed." It was then that Oros arose and came forth from his tent, noble and recollected. He cried out, "Make haste to the cliffside! Perhaps we can avenge our brethren's deaths!" So as the dawn began to creep over the eastern horizon the men of Oros came to the cliff, but the Dretians had already taken to their crafts and set out towards the island when they saw the coming of day depriving them of the shadows. So Oros was told, "They have departed, my lord." Then Oros and the Manissans sang a dirge beside the sea and lamented the folly of Dindar and the bitter doom of those who went over the cliffside. When the mourning for the folly of Dindar and the taking of Corax was ended, Oros said, "Thus has Fate settled for us what by words the lord Dindar and I were unable to come to terms on. Therefore we shall march north, through the mountains and up the coast, until we come out of the range of the Bados and their shadowy vales. When we have come into the regions around Greystone we will hew wood, assemble boats, and take Dretia, not piecemeal as Dindar proposed, but as one." Then all the men and lords said, "Aye," for after beholding the fate of Dindar they were of no mind to try another descent down the cliffside. But the place where the assault of Dindar was thwarted was ever after called Dindar's Folly.

It was on the first day of the eighth month that the armies of the Manissans mustered upon the plains outside the ruin of Ardilla. Durmius strode among the warriors, noble and godlike in his glistening armor, towering above every other man, speaking words of encouragement, haranguing them to be bold and courageous for the long march and rigors to come. Oros moved this way and that, now here and now there, delivering instructions to his captains and seeing that all things were ready for the army to move off to the north. The army of the Manissans gradually formed up upon the windswept heights, each man under his lord and each lord bold and strengthened by the oaths sworn at Teruel and upon the cliffside at Norn. When all things had been settled, stout-hearted Oros gave the word and the grand army of Manissé began their long march north out of the mountains. Ten thousand men marched under the banners of Oros, Durmius, and the other lords, one thousand under the hill chiefs Anax and Urbus being left behind to garrison Ardilla, rebuild its ruins, and subjugate the Dretians remaining in the surrounding hills. With Anax and Urbus were sent the prisoners taken from the battle in the valley, which were broken up and sent to serve as slaves to the hill people in the eastern foothills of the Bados, though Oros retained some to bear burdens for the army.

The Manissans went up from that place into the rugged foothills along the northern shores of the Norn and from there into the midst of the towering peaks and deep granite valleys of the northern Bados. After twenty-one days they came out of the mountains into the rugged, sloping country that goes down from the Norn's northernmost waters, a placed called Galmura by the peoples of Bados. The army rested for some time at Galmura, sending forth scouts under Ermarius to find a path into the peninsula of Greystone. After seven days Ermarius returned to Oros and proposed the sea road, which would take them into Greystone in the briefest time and with the fewest obstacles, though the road was rugged and washed out in many places. Yet did Oros and Durmius agree that a washed-out road was better than the wilderness, and so led the army onward along the sea road of Galmura going north. The region round about was harsh and inhospitable, for the soil was shallow and the earth rocky with shale and slate. The terrain was uneven and dipping, and little vegetation grew there, save for the hard grass and mosses that flourished upon the stones. The wind blew up bitterly from the sea, the violent gales flying up upon the coast and stinging the men despite that it was still summer. Thus all the army was wet and wearied from the uneven road and the dearth of beauty in that land.

With rejoicing and song did they pass out of the region of Galmura after nine days and came into more pleasant lands in the southeastern marches of Greystone, where the soil became somewhat richer, the grasses longer, and hawthorn and hornbeam trees began to be found along the roadside and upon the gentle green slopes round about. Carus and Sirmius, two lords native to the region, told Oros that the place was called Buturlüe.* But, as this was a Mogul word, it was difficult for

Oros or the Manissans to pronounce, so Oros called the place Betulia. Thus have the Manissans ever called the region Betulia.

Finding the land pleasant and wild game abundant, Oros encamped in Betulia for a fortnight until the men were well rested and again eager for the march. But Carus and Sirmius, lords of Greystone who knew the land well, he sent on ahead to find a spot wherein there was much wood and water where the army might wait out the winter. They returned after a fortnight, near the time when the army was making ready to depart Betulia, and said, "There is a spot not seven days march northwest of here where the hills slope up from the sea and terminate in a broad plateau. The plateau is about a league distant from the ocean and overlooks it, as well as the countryside roundabout. The slopes are covered in pine and oak and a small river runs from the highlands down the gulley upon the east side of the hill. From this place we can encamp for the winter and find a ready supply of timber for the ships you propose to construct." Oros was well pleased with these words and gave unto Carus and Sirmius each a bar of pure silver. Then the army broke camp and marched north and west from Betulia.

After nine days they came unto the place described by Carus and Sirmius and found it as they had said. When Oros saw the place, he said to Carus and Sirmius, "This shall serve us well as a place of encampment and defense for the coming months." Therefore was that place called *Adlor*, which means "defense."*

Thus they occupied the heights of Adlor and encamped there on the second to last day of the ninth month, when the sun burns hot in the noon sky, but the breezes of night bring blustering autumn winds from over the sea. They spent the autumn and winter of that year felling the trees of the slope, fashioning them into planks, forming the hulls of the ships, and knitting sails together from a variety of material collected around the camp. Still others were charged with forming wagons and barrels (for many had been dismantled when Dindar attempted his haughty descent down the cliffside) while others were engaged in the hunt or in going to and from the city of Greystone in the north to gather provisions. All that winter the men labored under the scrutinizing eye of Oros, who saw to it that no task was done shabbily, and no detail left undone. By midwinter they exhausted all the trees on the hillside and were compelled to wander further from Adlor to find suitable trees. When all the boats were completed, the men made pitch from the resin of the trees and sealed the crafts with it.

As soon as the ice began to break up from the shore, they dragged the crafts down and tested their seaworthiness, and finding them well constructed and resilient, Oros gave the command that the men prepare to embark from Adlor to the isle of Dretia upon the fifteenth day of the third month, a fortnight hence. When the appointed day came and the men had made sacrifice at the beachside, the army of the Manissans took to the boats and set off from the encampment at Adlor for the isle of Dretia. The men from Asylia were loath to board the crafts, for they disliked the seas; they had also been commanded to leave their steeds behind, something that did not sit well with the noble horsemen. But Durmius reminded them of their oath and of the death of brave Antylos by Dretian hands, and by his words they were convinced to leave their horses and board the crafts with the rest of the Manissans. The crafts were neither small nor large, being about forty feet in length and propelled by a single mast and sail along with a single row of oarsmen. The coast of Adlor for two leagues was choked with boats setting forth into the open waters, for the Manissans had constructed no less than one hundred fifty crafts, each manned by seventy-five men.

The fleet of the Manissans was graced with favorable winds and was three days upon the sea before pressing into the waters of Norn and the region about the isle of Dretia. It was the early morn of the fourth day when the fleet came upon some Dretian crafts scouting the bay, only three and each manned by less than ten men. They attempted to flee, but the Manissans overtook them and captured them. Oros pressed them and was told that the isle was but a single day south by sea. He also learned that the Dretians supposed the Manissans had retreated east for the winter following the slaying of Dindar. Oros said to them, "And what of the lord Corax? Does he live?" They told him, "He lives, my lord, and is a prisoner in our great fortress of Cumala in the midst of the isle." Then they told Oros much of the island, its peoples, terrain, and of the impenetrable fortress of Cumala, which means "mound" in the Dretian tongue. They told Oros a great deal, for they trembled for their lives in the presence of the Manissans under Oros's the stern scowl.

So the Manissan fleet idled in the waters there for another day before hoisting their sails and making south at noon of the following day, so as to approach Dretia by night and land under cloak of darkness, if possible. The grey dusk was falling over Norn's dark waters as the island began to be visible, and Oros sent word to all the ships that lanterns and torches be extinguished. Sails were taken down, and the fleet glided silently across the bay moved by the oarsmen alone, drawing nearer to the black island looming ahead. Oros was in great consternation lest they run afoul of some Dretian crafts and lose the secrecy of their assault by the din of war, but when he saw the sign of spear in the northern sky he commended the cause to Manissa, She Who Guides Fortunes, and prepared for the landing.

The fleet came unto the very coast of the isle with no difficulty, the crafts grounding upon the northeastern shores shortly after midnight. The men leapt from their boats, hearts trembling, spears clutched in their white-knuckled hands. Stout-hearted Oros was first overboard, knees in the frigid foaming surf, spear in hand leading the men in dragging their boats upon the shore and forming a picket of defense around the place. Surrounded by the brave men of Oros, a wall of bristling spearheads glimmering in the quiet starlight, the other crafts gradually came to shore. The entire army of Manissé had formed up upon the cold and sandy beachhead shortly before the rising of the sun.

It was at dawn that the Manissans were first sighted by the Dretians, for a group of women had come down to the seashore to gather mussels and saw the Manissans grouped by their hundreds and their thousands upon the beach. The women shrieked and fled, and though the scouts of Oros pursued them, were unable to capture them. Oros said to his captains, "Prepare ye all for a clamor, for they shall try to drive us into the sea before we make any further progress towards Cumala." It was as Oros said, for it was near noon when a small legion of Dretian fighters came upon the Manissans from the lightly wooded hillside a half league south of the beach, about a thousand men in all armed with bows and spears. Oros cried, "Their numbers are small, but we are weary from four days upon the sea and no sleep this night. Engage them hotly! Do not let them press our backs to the water!"

It was grim Durmius who roared and bore up his great spear first, a cedar shaft of five cubits topped with a flesh-goring point a forearm in length. The men of Durmius cried out and clashed their spears to their shields, following their towering lord up the beach to the grassy slope to engage the Dretians. Woe to those foolhardy souls who thought to bring down grim Durmius of Halicor! Woe to those who stood betwixt the men of Manissé and their sworn plunder! Durmius roared like a bear and crashed into the Dretians, his men behind him and each hot for blood. So close were the Manissans engaged with the Dretians that the Dretian archers could not fire. Man grappled with man upon the grassy slope, spears thrusting to the left and the right and the gruesome sound of gouging flesh and deadly strikes filled the noontide air. No man who engaged Durmius could stand, for the fierce son of Lothar wielded his death-dealing spear with fatal accuracy and felled every man who crossed his path. After only a quarter hour the remaining Dretians were in full retreat, vanishing back into the woods.

Durmius raised his dripping spear to the heavens and hollered a cry of victory.

Oros summoned his men and said, "Word shall spread of what has been done here. Though our eyes burn from watchfulness through the long night and our bodies ache for sweet repose, we must rouse ourselves and take heart at the victory won by bold Durmius. Let us make haste and depart from this place, for though battle is inevitable we must press inland as far as time permits before engaging the mass of the Dretians, lest our numbers dwindle through skirmishing while giving them time to reinforce and defend Cumala!" The Manissans all shouted their assent and moved out from the beach, marching south up the slopes and into the lightly wooded highland from whence the Dretians had attacked. Oros led the main column, placing grim Durmius as the fore guard and entrusting the rearguard to Tanus of Engor.

The forest soon fell away before a series of pleasant hills crowned with looming cypresses. The army moved swiftly along the gullies at the base of the hills, some of which were marked by gently rippling streams that tumbled over rock and sand down to the sea. They came upon several Dretians homesteads, small villages upon the hillsides, but found all abandoned. By dusk the army had come from the gentle hill country into a more rugged terrain of steep, shrubby ascents covered in basalt stone. Seeing the difficult march ahead, Oros permitted the men sleep for a time, but roused them before dawn to begin the ascent. It took the army the better part of a day to come up the sharp incline, which was several hundred feet at most points. Yet when they came to the top they found themselves upon a broad and pleasant plateau which constituted the central highlands of the island. From where they stood they could descry rolling fields for many leagues distant, as well as lush forests and a few roads that seemed to wind among the fields going south.

But as the men gazed upon the countryside from the top of the ascent, Ermarius of Badoa perceived a company of

Dretians massing on the plains some distance away. He said to Oros, "My lord, we are sighted by the Dretians and will soon come under attack!" Oros said to his men and captains, "This is indeed a bind! Though we are worn from the climb we cannot rest, lest we be caught in a battle with our rear to these treacherous slopes. Yet if we advance we find ourselves giving battle on an open field with no high ground to fortify and no knowledge of what lies to our south, from whence our enemies come!" Tanus of Engor, the captain of the rearguard, said, "Let us make haste and at least take possession of the road which seems to cross these fields some distance to the south. If nothing else it will give us sure footing upon which to give combat and a vantage point to see from where our foes come."

This advice seemed good. So Durmius was sent forward with his men and seized the road, the rest of the men under Oros following shortly behind. The road was found to run east to west, veering off towards the south near the place where the Dretians were massing. Tanus of Engor and the men attached to him were placed upon road facing west, so as to ensure no one came upon the Manissans from the rear. The Dretians marched with great speed towards the Manissans upon the road. As they approached, Oros discerned their numbers to be about four thousand under three chiefs, and most of them armed with spears and bows. Oros crashed his spear upon his shield and cried out, "They are going to sorely test us, my brethren! Let us give them doom!" All the Manissans from the greatest to the least clashed their weapons to their shields and roared, "Aye! Give them doom!"

When the Dretians saw the Manissans in possession of the road and formed up for battle they howled, doubled their pace, and began firing their arrows. The fearless men of Durmius, whom Oros put in the foremost position, bore up their shields and deflected most of the missiles, though stray arrows fell here and there among the men and wounded some. The Dretian chiefs saw that the Manissans were well equipped with bronze shields and gave the command to engage them hand to hand, thereafter falling swiftly upon the Manissan lines. Grim Durmius saw their approach and cried, "Now my companions, bring them down to the grave in blood!" Then with one accord the men of Durmius took aim and hurled their ashen spears. A deadly cast! Each man picked his target and hurled his shaft skillfully with their iron arms; each spear end found its place in the breast of some Dretian fighter, bringing at once hundreds to the ground writhing as pigs impaled on the spit after the hunt.

The Dretians held back, for the Manissan cast downed a very great number of them. But their chief, a hulking giant of a man whom they called Umba (which means "tower" in the Dretian tongue) raised aloft his battle sword and urged them forward. The Manissans drew their swords and awaited the Dretian onslaught with knuckles white and teeth gnashing in dread. The Dretians hurled themselves with frenzied fury into the lines of Durmius, their spears gouging and biting wherever exposed flesh was found. The air was filled with the din of battle, the crash of arms and the cries of men locked in relentless struggling to the bitter end, both Dretian and Manissan. At that time fell Myrilus, one of the captains of Durmius, who was struck in the belly with a Dretian spear. He groaned in pain, doubled over, and collapsed upon the dusty road, blood and dirt upon his lips. Also slain was Maximoss, a young lad whose father was a vassal of Durmius. This Maximoss was caught between two Dretian fighters and, finding himself unable to keep them both at bay, was run through the back and sides with many spears. Thus perished young Maximoss in the flower of his youth.

But grim Durmius, who towered above all other men on the battlefield and whose stature blotted out the very sun from the eyes of his foes, cried out, "Ten for Myrilus and one hundred for Maximoss! We shall see how these savages do when I run my spear through their chieftain!" The men of Durmius snarled and dug their heels into the dirt, smashing the Dretian advance with their shields and gouging them with their spears. Durmius gnashed his teeth and lunged his flesh-biting spearhead at a Dretian captain called Aruvax and caught him unaware, thrusting his spear through the Dretian's belly as the latter gave directives to his men. The Manissans rallied and cried, "Aüe Durmius nomé Lotharé!" and then threw themselves against the Dretians with renewed fury. Durmius led the charge, immovable as a tree trunk and deadly as a wounded bear. He raged this way and that, striking out with his great arms and downing scores of Dretian fighters with his gore-soaked spear.

But the captain of the Dretian attack, the one they called Umba, stroked his matted beard and caught Durmius in the dark gaze of his eyes. He raised his gleaming sword and strode after Durmius, seeking to halt the Manissan advance by slaying the grim and mighty lord of Halicor. Durmius saw his advance and shook his spear menacingly at the Dretian giant, crying out, "Shall grim Durmius of the house of Lothar be affrighted by your size? Behold, I shall make your size good for nothing you vile beast!" Then he took aim and hurled his death-bringing spear at Umba with the fury of a whirlwind. The spear's path was true; it struck Umba in the breast, smashing armor, flesh and collar bone and dropping the Dretian giant where he stood, still some distance from Durmius. Umba groaned and clutched his breast, his fingers vainly trying to hold in the crimson life that was pouring forth from his wound. Durmius advanced upon him and wrenched the slimy shaft from his broken body, so that his fallen foe was left with a gaping hole through his breast to his very back. Then Umba, the tower, fell forward and collapsed with his face upon the dirt, grim Durmius standing upon him in victory.

When Oros saw this, he called his captains Urmax and one-eyed Imloss, saying, "Come, my lords, let us aid brave Durmius in impaling these Dretians upon our spearheads!" So Oros led his men, mighty men of the plains from Anentora, and brought them up to reinforce Durmius. They shouted, clashing their spears and swords to their shields, and caught those

Dretians before them in a surge of doom, just as a great wave rolls away whatever stands before it. The Dretians stood behind their chiefs and tried to make some defense, but they could not put enough distance between themselves and the Manissans to make use of their archers and so were cut down where they stood. The Dretian ranks were thrown into confusion; some under the captain in the rear attempted to wheel about to flee back up the road. But stout-hearted Oros took aim and hurled his javelin at the man. Such a throw was never seen among the sons of Manissa until that day nor has been seen since, for the spear flew straight and sure almost a half-league and struck the Dretian captain squarely in the back, sending him to the earth howling in the throes of death. When the Dretians saw that he had been struck from such a great distance, they feared that they fought gods rather than men and began to flee as the shadow of panic cast its pall over them.

The Manissans pursued the Dretians and struck them with the edge of the sword all the way across the hill country as far as the opening of the great valley which leads on towards Cumala, a half-day journey by foot. The Manissans put the Dretians to rout and did not cease striking them until the chill of night fell over the countryside. Tanus of Engor came up from the rear and told Oros, "My lord, the scouts have found three thousand Dretians slain and of our own men only six hundred." Durmius marveled and said, "Such an unequal victory has never been seen since the night our Lady struck the Marudans with the spear in the dark groves of Adarwood and slew ten thousand of them!" Then all the lords and the men of Manissé offered sacrifice and made oblations of thanksgiving for the marvelous victory. They encamped in that place for the evening and sung songs of the mighty throw of Oros and the slaying of Umba by Durmius, and thus warmed their hearts by the watch fires even as the bitter gusts of early spring chilled their bodies.

Oros permitted them rest until midday on the morrow but then broke camp. They entered the broad valley which lies at the center of the isle, the valley which stretches out and then up towards the fortress of Cumala, the heart of the island. Oros said, "We know not what lies before us, nor how formidable be the defenses of this fortress or even how many Dretians we may find protecting it. Therefore, let us sing hymns and make petition to our Lady to deliver this place into our hands this day, so that the spear and standard of Manissé may be established in this land." So the grand army of the Manissans formed themselves into a mighty procession, several thousand long and stretching out a great distance. Each man removed his helm from his head and walked with his face cast down, chanting the ancient hymns of Asylia and intoning prayers of petition in the solemn, sonorous melodies of the days of old. Oros and Durmius each took turns leading the responses with their booming, cavernous voices, so that across the whole valley was heard the songs of old Asylia as the column came upon the very region of Cumala itself. It was this song which poured from the lips of Oros at the moment when the Manissans sighted Cumala upon the distant ridge for the first time:

> *O Manissa, defender of your people,*
> *Taken from the holy mount in radiance,*
> *You are glorified among the immortals,*
> *And seated in splendor.*
> *Aüe! Aüe! Nomé Manissé!*

> *O Manissa, our Lady of the Spear,*
> *Your majesty is great,*
> *To that of the sons of men unequaled,*
> *Because you watch from above the clouds.*
> *Aüe! Aüe! Nomé Manissé!*

> *O Manissa, just and radiant,*
> *Give us help in our bitter struggle,*

Make our hearts bold and our spears sure,
Remember Manissé forever.
Aüe! Aüe! Nomé Manissé!

When stout-hearted Oros was intoning the third versicle of the hymn, he lifted up his eyes and beheld the outline of Cumala before him. It was a mighty and imposing fortress, seated high upon a great earthen mound and of such a height that no man could throw a spear or fire an arrow over its hulking walls. Before the ramparts of Cumala the great mound sloped downward into a pleasant and grassy hill, and from thence into the broad valley that now lay before Oros and the Manissans, a vale pleasant with hardy meadow grasses in the first blossoms of the spring. When the Manissans sighted Cumala, they collapsed to their knees upon the plain and gave thanks for their preservation through so many trials and hardships.

Oros summoned Durmius and said, "The fortress appears to be sealed, for by now they have certainly heard of our coming. Let us cross this valley as quickly as possible and commence the siege." Durmius said, "Aye, let us cross the valley with haste, lest we be taken and cut off in the midst of it." So the entire army of Manissé marched with determination and celerity, and making their way quickly across the grassy lowlands, came to rest at the base of the hill which goes up towards the great mound of Cumala. They encamped at the base of the mound upon which the fortress of Cumala sits, finding the stronghold sealed as Oros said and garrisoned with a very large number of Dretian warriors. Then did Oros and Durmius puzzle over how to take the place, for it seemed impregnable. The fortress was constructed at the top of a very large hill and was defended by seven towers; the walls were thick and of considerable height and could only be passed through by a single gate on the eastern side of the wall. When the Dretians perceived that the Manissans had come to the base of the hill but were at a loss as to how to besiege the fortress, they began to jeer and taunt them. They also harassed the Manissans by firing random volleys of arrows from the ramparts at sundry times, forcing Oros to withdraw the encampment some distance back to bring it out of bowshot.

Oros was downcast because of the excellent defenses of Cumala, but Ermarius, the thoughtful prince of Badoa, said, "Fear not, noble Oros. Do we not surround the fortress with a great host? If they wish to make it a siege we shall show them a siege. Let us fortify our camp here and wait them out." Durmius roared with approval and said, "May the gods do so to me and more if the men of Cumala are not wasted away with starvation by the time we make an end of them!" Oros said, "Thy counsel is true, good Ermarius. Let grim Durmius see to it that the hill and fortress are thoroughly surrounded." Durmius nodded and said, "The fool who comes forth from Cumala, whether it be to fire arrow or gather sticks, that same man shall die by our spears." Thus was the fortress of Cumala put under siege, completely cut off from the countryside by the Manissans.

Yet the Manissans were not idle while besieging Cumala, for Oros sent expeditions out under Tanus and Ermarius to subdue the island and bring the Dretians roundabout into submission. There were raids and skirmishes all that spring across the island, the Manissans taking everything from the lowlands in the east to the rugged wilderness in the west, from the verdant pastures of the north to the dark forests of the south. The Dretians put up a fierce resistance at first, but afterwards fled and took to the wilderness and the high places of the island to escape the Manissan onslaught. Meanwhile Oros and Durmius kept up the siege of Cumala unabated.

But the fortress had an abundantly greater store of provisions than the Manissans had thought, so that the siege of Cumala dragged on through the spring and into the summer. So long did it continue that the Manissan army began to run low on supplies before the city, so that the men began to grumble against Oros because of the excessive duration of the siege. Finally, Oros called his two captains, Imloss and Urmax, and told them, "Go forth into the verdant pastures in the northernmost region of the isle and bring back as many provisions as you can take on, for if we cannot provision ourselves we shall have to quit the island in a fortnight and return to Adlor." So Urmax and one-eyed Imloss took a thousand men and went forth to scavenge, plunder and hunt. But while they were out the mood of the Manissans further soured, and even grim Durmius began to forget the oath he had sworn by the cliffs of Norn and turned his heart towards home and the proud halls of Halicor. The men grew lax and the guard around the fortress slackened, so that several Dretian runners escaped by night into the countryside, coming to their countrymen in hiding and rallying them to arms against the Manissans.

So it was that Urmax and Imloss, while taking the north road into the farm district, were waylaid by a column of Dretian men bearing spears and mattocks. Being unprepared for any pitched battle and burdened with many provisions and much plunder, they were slow to put up a firm resistance and suffered much at the hands of the Dretian spearmen. Then scores of Dretians began pouring out of the fields and woods, hurling themselves recklessly into battle and demolishing the Manissan defenses. The lines of Urmax and one-eyed Imloss were overrun and utterly put to rout. Then Urmax was slain, pierced in the breast by a crude Dretian spear. When Imloss saw his comrade fallen, his men in rout and his escape cut off, he fell upon his sword and killed himself. Thus was the expedition of Urmax and Imloss utterly overthrown, and the provisions so desperately needed by Oros were seized by the Dretians. After the battle the Dretians beheaded Urmax and Imloss and sent their heads all throughout the region, rallying their brethren to arms and saying, "Behold the heads of the Manissan captains! Rise up and drive the foreigners into the sea!" But Oros,

Durmius, and the men at Cumala knew nothing of the disaster and grew more wearied with hunger and boredom with every passing day.

Meanwhile the Dretians massed upon various parts of the island, roused by the slaying of Urmax and Imloss, and converged upon the crossroads a day south of Cumala. Men from all parts of the island had come out to fight, as well as from the mainland and even some Dretian womenfolk, who were reputed to be as fierce as the men. These all gathered by the crossroads with eyes flaming for vengeance and spears trained for doom, some twelve thousand in all. Once they had come together they began moving northward towards Cumala, intent on making a complete end of the Manissans in the shadow of the fortress. Thus the crossroads where they massed has ever since that day been called *Crodurus*, which means "Crossroads of Doom."

When the Dretian warriors were sighted coming up the road, the Manissans gave a great cheer, for they assumed it to be Urmax and Imloss returning with provisions. But their rejoicing was soon turned to bitter lamentation when they perceived it was an army of Dretians rather than Manissans, and that the rotting heads of Urmax and Imloss were born aloft on pikes at the forefront of the mob. Then the Dretians within Cumala erupted in uproarious cheer, for they saw their countrymen coming to their aid and fully anticipated to see the army of Manissé destroyed before their eyes. Oros roused his men furiously, haranguing them and shouting, "Stand fast, men of Manissé! Have our victories till this day been in vain? Have the bold sons of Manissa, noble sons of glory, begotten you as gods upon the earth only to perish on this forsaken hill? Does Manissa walk among the fire of the stars and hurl down vengeance like lightning for nothing? Therefore, I tell you stand, and bring them doom!" So the men steadied themselves, leveling their flesh-ripping spears and preparing for slaughter. Oros called upon Tanus of Engor and Ermarius of Badoa to take the front, placing himself and Durmius in the center and Solax of Corbalund in reserve with Carus and Sirmius.

The Dretians closed with the Manissans and hurled the heads of Imloss and Urmax into the Manissan camp with savage fury, following with a barrage of spears and stones that caught the wearied Manissans unprepared, wreaking havoc upon the lines of Tanus and Ermarius. The Dretians charged the Manissans with barbarian rage, pressing them against the hillside and driving them from their lines. Many men fell in the advance; even brave Ermarius was wounded grievously in the shoulder with a lance. Durmius and Oros stayed the withdrawal and strengthened the front, but the Dretians spread out and encompassed the Manissans, striking them to the left and to the right and biting their flanks; even Solax, Sirmius, and Carus were drawn into the fray, so that there was no safe place on the battlefield or anywhere where the Manissans were not engaged. Then fear began to fall upon the Manissans.

Seeing their plight, Oros cried out to the men to form circle, and thus defend themselves roundabout with bristling spearheads. The Manissans, from the commanders down to the lowest man, did as Oros called and formed up into a great circle at the base of the hill before Cumala. Thus arranged, they defended themselves the best they could and made deadly thrusts outward at any Dretian foolish enough to come within an arm's length, for even surrounded and wearied the men of Manissé could still deal fatal blows with terrible swiftness.

Yet once the Manissans had formed into a circle, the Dretians easily encompassed them round about and pressed on them from every side, hurling javelins into the lines, firing arrows and hacking at exposed limbs or fingers with their mattocks. When the besieged within Cumala saw the Manissans thus surrounded, a mighty roar of victory went up from the fortress. Then did the Manissans hear the dreadful sound of the gates of Cumala creaking open and the sallying forth of the garrison, for the men within the fortress, thinking to make an end of the Manissans, had sortied out to join their countrymen in the final assault. Durmius cried out, "Steady thy hearts, men of Manissé, for it seems that we shall not fulfill our oaths but shall rather crouch in the bitter dust before Cumala's looming bulwarks. But blood for blood! If we shall go down to death, let us bring them with us!" So the Manissans fought furiously, hurling their spears at their foes and striking with their swords. The air was bitter with the clanging of sword upon shield, the breaking of spears and the cries of men tasting the cruel pang of sliced flesh and bodies thrust through. Yet after a time did the Manissan circle shrink, for mighty was the assault of the Dretians upon them, and they found their numbers declining as scores of them fell dead or wounded onto the hot dirt.

Then did noble Durmius, tallest and fiercest of all the Manissans, like a bear in fury and a lion in his wrath, take a spear thrust into his back from a Dretian fighter, a young whelp of a boy. The giant of Halicor howled bitterly as the blade of the Dretian spear found its way between his shoulders, dropping him to his knees. But Durmius would not give his consent to be dragged away to the stillness of death in such a manner; he roared and steadied himself, then with the javelin still protruding from his back, wheeled around and struck at his assailant with his mighty spear. Pitiful whelp! The boy thought to win glory among his people by killing the giant Durmius with so treacherous a blow. But Durmius turned on him and thrust his own spear with his iron arms, crying out, "I will show you how it is done!" The blade sunk into the breast of the boy, splintering bone, severing flesh, and bringing a dark mist before his eyes. Durmius withdrew his gore-covered spear and the Dretian whelp closed his eyes in death before he even fell to the earth. But when the boy had been slain, Durmius faltered and collapsed from his wound. His aides came to him and withdrew the spear from his back, then bore the wounded captain as far from the fighting as they could.

When Oros and the other Manissans saw Durmius taken out of the fight and their numbers shrinking all around they began to despair, and some even began to talk of falling upon their swords. Then noble Oros, ever pious, withdrew from the battle lines and knelt upon the cold earth, crying out, "O Manissa, blessed forebear and protectress of all the peoples of Manissé who are called by thy name, show thyself strong and vigilant and deliver us this day from the fury of the barbarians who encompass us about! Remember us and defend us as in the day of Arcoria, thy great victory, or in the day of Lothar when you gave him strength to slay his foes, though they were his very kin! Give us the might of Perior on the day he threw down the towers of Cadaras in vengeance! O blessed Lady, have mercy on us, the sons of your womb!" Then all the Manissans gathered about him cried, "Aye!"

Then did something marvelous happen that had never been seen among the peoples of Manissé nor has yet been seen to this very day. Behold! From the midst of the Dretian hordes came a frightful cry of panic and rout. Oros stood aloft and marveled, for it seemed suddenly that the entire Dretian assault was thrown into confusion. There was heard a thunderous crashing of arms and a tumult among the Dretians, and then the collapsing of bodies and the piercing of flesh. Oros and the Manissans strained to discern who was now assaulting the Dretians or what force could be bringing such consternation upon them. At first they saw nothing but the panic of the Dretian fighters, but then by and by a green cloak was sighted dashing here and there amongst the barbarian hordes. Then was the glittering of an Asylian spearhead seen, glorious and dreadful in the brilliance of the sunlight. The spearhead flashed and whirled this way and that, following the cloak, and wheresoever it flashed scores of Dretians fell slain, their bodies sliced in two, or their limbs hewn off entirely.

The Manissans stared dumb, knowing not what or who was so ravaging their opponents' lines. Then was heard arising from the fray a single voice, that of a woman, crying, "Cruacha!" The Manissans marveled and said to one another, "Can it be our Lady?" They pressed towards the battle lines and strained to get some clear view of the one behind the cloak and the gleaming spear, but always their view was obscured; they could not get any clear sight of the woman.

But noble-hearted Oros held his sword aloft and cried out, "Marvel of marvels and of all wonders most glorious! Our Lady has returned from her sojourn among the heavens to deliver her people this day! Arise, men of Manissé! Fulfill your vows to the taking of Cumala and the doom of the Dretians!" Then all the Manissans were strengthened and refreshed in their souls, from the greatest to the very least, and did all arise and press upon the Dretians with a raging furor, crying, "Curcua!" The Dretians were thrown into a panic by the green cloaked warrioress who appeared here and there among them bringing death and were in nowise prepared for the vehement counterattack made by the Manissans.

What seemed a desperate plight only moments before now became a slaughter for the Manissans, for a thick dread and a terror fell upon the Dretians. Their hands became heavy and their knees like water. Then did the Manissans hurl themselves at their enemies with relentless violence and cut them down as the workers cut down the grain with a scythe at the time of the harvest. The Dretians utterly collapsed before the Manissans, led now by fierce Oros, mouth wide open and roaring like a lion, beard dripping with sweat and blood. With his deadly sword he cut great swaths in the Dretian position, and like a woodsman making a path through the dense forest with his axe did mighty Oros hack openings in the Dretian lines wherever he went. And all the men of Manissé rallied behind him, mouths shouting cries of doom and blades trembling for vengeance.

Like fog before the burning rays of the noontide sun did the Dretians evaporate before the furious drive of the Manissans. The Dretians began to flee in every which way, seeking only to escape the rage of Oros and the men of Manissé. Some thus escaped, but any Dretian who attempted to give battle to the Manissans, or who fell wounded or paused to minister to a fallen comrade or for any other cause stopped their retreat, the same was fallen upon by the grim Manissan hordes and speared to death mercilessly, for great was the anger of Oros on that burning day of wrath.

Then Oros looked up and beheld the gates of Cumala still swinging open, for the Dretians had sortied out in their arrogance and failed to seal their fortress, so confident were they in the overthrow of the Manissans. Oros cried, "To the fortress! Let us all be accounted cowards if we do not dine in Cumala this very evening!" So the Manissans rallied behind Oros and stormed the hill, straightaway taking the fortress and striking the remaining garrison with the edge of the sword. The men under Oros came to a certain tower, and therein found the Cadarasian captain Corax still imprisoned and in a miserable state. They unbound him and brought him forth into the light, praising Fate for delivering him safely. Then Corax, still clothed in his filthy prison rags, threw himself at the feet of Oros and said, "By our Lady and all the gods, I so swear fealty to thee this day, noble and stout-hearted Oros, son of Pixus, for I owe thee my life and my honor.* With you truly is the lordship of Manissé." Oros accepted the fealty of Corax and had him bathed and clothed in garments of honor. Then ever after did Corax serve Oros as a vassal, who greatly loved him in return.

By nightfall the grand fortress of Cumala was in the possession of the Manissans, all the Dretians having been slain, captured, or scattered to the hills and woods. Then Oros told his captains, "Go throughout the men, both the Manissans and those prisoners of the Dretians, and inquire whether or not any knows the identity of the glorious woman in green who saved our armies this day." But though Oros sought and inquired, the green cloaked warrioress was not to be found, nor could anyone, Dretian or Manissan, be brought forward who had gazed upon her face. So the Manissans said, "It was our Lady." So Oros declared a great feast in honor of *Manissa Tualitha*, "Manissa Who Delivers."* And thus Oros and the men of Manissé feasted with great revelry, and the deeds of Manissa were read aloud before the sacrificial fires.*

But while the deeds of Manissa were being read aloud, Oros cast his gaze into the flame of the fires and seemed lost as in a mist. Tanus said, "My lord, what thought seizes you so? The men roar with cheer at the taking of the fortress and yet you gaze off if taken away in a cloud." Oros said, "Our Lady has appeared and walked again among us for so to deliver us from the sword, and in so doing has secured the establishment of a great throne for all ages. But when she next appears again among us, it shall be not for our glory but for our humility, and a great day of doom." Then all the men fell silent and pondered Oros's words, for they perceived that he had uttered a prophecy.*

The great fortress of Cumala rests atop a mighty hill or mound, for in the Dretian tongue Cumala means "mound." Its gates face eastward, and the stronghold is encompassed about by seven towers. Thus were the seven towers called for the seven captains of Manissé who took the city: in the east on either side of the gates were the Durmius Tower on the southeast and the Corax Tower on the northeast, so named because it was in this tower that Corax languished in prison. Then in the north the Carus Tower and Sirmius Tower, and likewise in the south, the towers called Solax and Tanus. But in the west, and standing alone, was the Tower Ermarius, after brave Ermarius of Badoa. But the gates of Cumala themselves were called for Oros, for it was Oros who first espied them flying open when the Dretians were in rout, and it was noble Oros who led the men of Manissé up the ascent to the fortress and whose foot first stepped inside the grand fortress. Thus were the gates ever after called the Gates of Oros.

So the land of the Dretians, from the mountains of the Bados as far as the regions bordering Corbalund and as far north as Greystone, was subjected to the dominion of Manissé, even the pleasant isle of Dretia and the marvelously wrought fortress of Cumala. Then by acclamation Oros was proclaimed Lord of the Isle and was elevated upon the shields of his men who cried "Aüe Oros!" Ermarius of Badoa and all the other lords present swore oaths of friendship and fealty to Oros, promising to follow him in peace or war to whatever end. Also did Anax and Urbus, those chiefs of the hillmen who had been left to garrison Ardilla, come over to Dretia and swear oaths to Oros, rejoicing in his fortune. But Durmius, who was still swoon from his injury, was not present and swore no oaths to Oros.*

Soon messengers came from the king in Cadaras confirming Oros in his lordship of Dretia and praising him for his valor. So Oros became a mighty lord and Cumala a great city, for many men from all the regions of Manissé came out to see the splendid isle and marvel and the conquests of Oros; many of these chose to submit themselves to Oros and dwell in Cumala. It was not many years before the island was populated by Manissans and the seed of the Dretians waned. Then did the Manissans cultivate the fair isle, making it into a region of great beauty and fruitfulness. They planted fields and gardens about it, erected shrines, and other splendid buildings, and built stately roads of gleaming white gravel. The sons of Manissé formed the isle into a rustic paradise, a mirror of old Asylia in the days of its splendor. The city of Cumala began to be called no longer by its Dretian name but was called "The Grand City of Manissé," or the City of Manis, for from that city were Oros and the Lords of the Isle able to extend their power over the coasts of Norn, the entire shoreline of the Greystone peninsula, and the lands round about for many miles.

In the latter days it came to pass that the Lord of the Isles became the greatest of all the lords of Manissé, so that even the kings of Cadaras removed the seat of their authority from

Cadaras, the City on the Plain, and established their dominion in the City of Manis, from whence all Manissan kings have henceforth reigned even unto this day.

So Oros ruled as Lord of the Isles for eighteen years in prosperity and splendor. Then in the eighteenth year of his rule, being the fifty-eighth year of his life, he took ill and died in the cold of a winter's night. There was great mourning throughout all the City of Manis for the death of Oros, that great lord of the house of Necho. So his body was entombed in the forum of the lords before the palace in the City of Manis, where it remains to this day.

Casias & Lyrgoné

𝔖ing in me, O spirit of song, the tale of brave Casias and sad Lyrgoné, lovers for a season, but doomed, in the end, to a bitter parting before their time, like a star which, when falling from the heavens, burns brightly for but a moment before its glowing plume vanishes and is seen no more among the celestial bodies.* Thus did the spirits of Casias and Lyrgoné shine and burn out before men, glorious in their days, tragic in their downfall, ever memorable in their passion.

It came to pass in those days, when noble Oros had not yet set his heart on the spoils of Dretia, that wise King Arytos, ruling in white-halled Cadaras, sent a delegation west to forge an alliance with the stout-hearted men of Tabia, those distant sons of Samnor who made their homes at the world's end, beyond the vast forest of Adarwood. Wise Artyos reasoned, "The Tabians are a plentiful and powerful race, hardy and seafaring, whose commerce will bring much wealth to Elabaea." Besides this, he was at that time hoping to enlist their aid against the Lugarians, who in those days had become hostile to the Manissans.

Therefore did King Arytos summon forty of the wisest and most refined of all the Manissans, men known for pleasant speech and golden tongues, all skilled in the ways of diplomacy; for some of the forty he chose priests, and for others, nobles or advisors to the royal court. At the head of the forty he placed

Prastor, a grizzled old priest of excellent knowledge and prudence who had spent the better part of his days on such errands for Arytos and the father of Arytos before him. King Arytos summoned Prastor to his chambers and said to him, "Prastor, priest of our Lady and most crafty of all Manissans, go west to the land of the Tabians to forge an alliance with them, so that the Manissans may be enriched and the Lugarians beset by adversaries to the east and the west. Perhaps, when the alliance is sealed, they will go forth to war with us against the haughty Lugars. Show forth to them the might and splendor of the king at Cadaras, manifest the greatness and power of the Manissan peoples, and teach them of the religion and ritual handed on to us by our forefathers; perhaps they, too, will be numbered among the peoples of Manissé."*

Old Prastor said, "It shall be done, wise King Arytos." So Prastor made ready and departed at the head of the delegation. With the forty he took Casias, a prince of Cadaras of the house of Mariammné, to be head over the armed men that were to escort the delegation into the west. Casias in turn took with him Myrax, another prince of Mariammné's blood, though of lesser renown than Casias. These two were placed in charge of seventy hardened warriors from Cyrenaica, each bearing sturdy shafts of ash and shields of beaten bronze. So all the men who went forth in the company of Prastor were one hundred and twelve.

In such manner they ventured forth, spears and banners in hand, that glorious and ill-fated expedition, westward across the pleasant and windswept plains of Asylia that spread out towards the horizon, going west over the Erriad. From there they moved into the environs round about old Asylia, then pressed northward, traversing the desolate highlands of Cyria under the relentless sun of the north Elabaean summer, coming after fifteen days to the fertile regions of Arcoria in the shadow of that venerable and ancient forest called Adarwood. From the sylvan glades of Arcoria the band turned north, towards the scorching northernmost coasts of Elabaea and the undying blue sky, moving forward in the shadow of Adarwood for ten days further until arriving at the deep blue expanse of sea. There wise Prastor took his bearing from the stars, for they were now in uncertain lands, and after consulting the heavens and the sign of the Spear, they turned due west and marched toward Tabia and the setting sun, keeping the sea to their right and the ascent that rises up towards Adarwood on their left.* Thus did the expedition of Prastor and Casias follow this route for many days, traveling beside the sea's salty billows by the light of day and resting upon the virgin sands by night.

In those days Tabia was ruled by white-haired King Eurastes, a king possessed of great wisdom and prudence. This Eurastes had held the kingship for thirty years, tracing his descent through many centuries back to Samnor, son of Laban, who was the father of all the western peoples. Joyous was the heart of Eurastes in those days, for the entire kingdom of Tabia was in celebration at the betrothal of Lysias, only son of Eurastes, to yellow-haired Lyrgoné, a distant kinswoman of the royal house and of all the noble maidens of Tabia the most splendid and delicate. Throngs of people crowded the wide lanes of Tabés and acclaimed the union of Lysias and Lyrgoné, strewing flowers about the city in celebration. There did Lyrgoné meet Lysias beneath the pillared portico before the royal house and lay her hand into his, pledging troth and fealty before all the people of Tabés and before their king, old Eurastes. A day of happiness and rejoicing, though woefully short lived, for the petals were still fresh upon the ground when word was brought to King Eurastes that foreigners were coming upon the city from the north.

Eurastes and his councilors came to the tower by the gates of Tabés and looked out, beholding the column of Manissans under Prastor and Casias snaking across the arid plain. Then spoke the king's counselor Dario, "My lord, the raiment and look of these men are strange to me. From what land do they come?" Eurastes said, "Unless I am deceived, these are Manissans. It has been a generation since they were seen near our borders, for in the time of my father some of the men of Manissé joined themselves to our own warriors to make war on Lugaria. I was only a child then, yet will I never forget their long locks and ashen spears all my days. These are indeed Manissans from the east."

Dario said, "They are too few for war, for they are led by priests and ministers; only those handful in the rear bear arms." King Eurastes furled his ancient brow in thought and then cried out, "Let them be admitted! Let us greet them and hear their words!" So Prastor and the Manissans came under the gates of Tabés and did homage to Eurastes, saying, "Hail Eurastes, King and Lord of the Tabians." Eurastes ushered the men into his great hall, and seating himself before them on his throne of ivory, said, "Good tidings, sons of Manissé. From whence have you come and to what do we owe the honor of thy visit to the court of Tabés?"

Prastor said, "My lord, we have come across many weeks of wilderness to bring thee tokens of the good will of our people in order to forge an alliance with thee and thy people, for we are sent by none other than King Arytos of Cadaras himself." Eurastes said, "And what benefit can be had from an alliance between two peoples whose lands are as distant as those of Cadaras and Tabia? Surely it cannot be for trade, as our lands are far too distant." Prastor said, "Nay my lord, but to make war on the people of Lugaria, that haughty and savage race who dwell between our two kingdoms in the south. Thus say King Arytos, 'Let us renew the alliance of previous generations in making war upon the cruel Lugarians and in subjugating them.'" There was a murmur of approval throughout the hall, for the men of Tabia had no love for the Lugars.

But Eurastes said, "Why, good Prastor, does Arytos send priests and ministers to conduct this arrangement? Why does he not send some lord or man of war? Does he think so little of Tabia to send men of common birth?" Prastor replied, "That you might know that we come in peace, and that, if such an allowance is made, we might speak of our religion and rituals and set up a temple here for sacrifices and prayers to our Lady, and that we may teach all who are willing of the glories of mysteries of Manissé." At this there were murmurs of anger throughout the hall. Dario said to King Eurastes in a reserved voice, "My lord, let this not be so. It is known far and wide that the Manissans, once they are allowed to bring their cult into the land, go forth like lions and seek to do away with the customs and traditions of the peoples amongst whom they dwell as foreigners. Then, when they have become great enough in strength and number, they seize power themselves and compel all the people of the land to do homage to Manissa, their immortal foundress. The cults of the other gods they suppress."

Eurastes said to Prastor, "Conduct an alliance and a war we may, but you shall not call upon your deities nor set up any place of honor to Manissa in our lands, for we have our traditions and our god, Succo, the great spirit of the earth, and his servants, the Manes, the Silent Watchers who lurk in the shadows.* Therefore we have no need of your Manissa or your ritual." Thus Eurastes sent the Manissans away and vowed to speak more on the alliance again, though he in nowise would be persuaded to grant them any concessions regarding their worship.

But that night Eurastes had a dream. He awoke, panicked and short of breath, and his wife Eryice was greatly affrighted. But by and by he came to his senses and said, "Dearest wife, a vision this night has stolen the very breath from my soul, so terrible and frightening was it to witness. Even now my flesh trembles and the hairs of my neck stand on end." Gentle Eryice consoled him and said, "Tell me of the vision." Eurastes said, "I beheld the gates of the city, and before them stood a gentle lamb which bleated and cried, for it was lost and besought its master. My heart took pity on the poor creature, so I commanded the gates to be opened for it and led it in behind me." Eryice said,

"This is what has terrorized you so?" But Eurastes said, "Nay, for once it was within the city, it grew and became a terrible beast, so large and horrible that scores of the bravest men of the city fell in battle with it. Then it was overcome with a great anger and a rage, and it smashed the royal houses with its tail and ground up the city walls in its teeth. Then all the people were exceedingly troubled, for there was nowhere left to flee. And the beast devoured everything before it until there was nothing left, neither warrior nor maiden."

Eryice said, "May it never be so! May you go down to the grave in peace before such a thing ever befalls fair Tabés!" But Eurastes was troubled in spirit and said, "I fear that I have as of late let this beast in by welcoming the Manissans." Yet he kept his counsel to himself, for the time continuing to meet with Prastor and the ministers of King Arytos in the following days to come to an agreement about the alliance against Lugaria.

Yet during this time, while grizzled Prastor and the ministers of Arytos met in council with Eurastes, Casias, Myrax and the armed men of the company were idle and moved freely about the city. Casias and Myrax, inseparable companions, were especially fond of the Vâlcea Bridge, a marvelous footbridge which stretched over the pleasant course of the River Soldara. This river winds gently through Tabia, crosses the coastal lowlands, and drains into the western sea, so that those who stand upon Vâlcea Bridge at dusk behold the sun setting behind the sphere of the world at the edge of the sea.* Among the Tabians it was said to be one of the most beautiful places in the world, for at dusk the whited marble and alabaster ornaments of the bridge were bathed in the dull red glow of the sun as it dipped below the rim of the horizon. Casias and Myrax lingered about the gardens and places near the Vâlcea Bridge, idling about there admiring the city, its buildings, and pleasantness of the place.

It was at the Vâlcea Bridge that Casias happened upon yellow-haired Lyrgoné one afternoon, for she, too, was accustomed at certain times to walk upon the bridge with her ladies in waiting at the close of the day. She did this to pass the time, since her betrothed, Lysias, spent all his days in council with King Eurastes and the Manissan dignitaries and had not called upon the king in several days. Gentle Lyrgoné and her maidens glided delicately upon the flagstones of the bridge, coming into the presence of Casias, who with Myrax, beheld her in hushed wonder. She, too, beheld him curiously, for though she had heard of the Manissans she had never seen one.

Yellow-haired Lyrgoné said to him, "Who might you be, you who wear your hair long and whose hands are rugged from much labor? You need not say, for I perceive you are a man of Manissé, from far off Cadarasia. Is it not so?" Casias marveled and said, "It is so, my lady." Lyrgoné said, "Why do you marvel at me so? Your gaze absently as though you have never set eyes on a woman before!" Casias said, "May my lady forgive me this offense, for I stare only because in our country it is custom for men to call upon maidens first, not for maids to approach the menfolk." As he spoke, the heart of Casias was enflamed with desire for Lyrgoné, who appeared to him as one exotic and enticing.*

But Lyrgoné said, "Ah, well there you are, for I am no maid, but betrothed, for I am Lyrgoné, the fairest woman of all Tabia, or so they say. The one who is to be my husband is none other than Prince Lysias, who even now sits beside grave Eurastes in council with Prastor and the ministers of your king." The heart of Casias fell at the mention of the betrothal and of Lysias, and he said, "True is it said that you are the loveliest of all women of the west. Regrettably you are spoken for, though not yet bound by nature's irrevocable chain!" The ladies of Lyrgoné were amused by the wit of Casias and turned red with laughter. Then Lyrgoné said, "Tell me thy name, crafty Manissan." Casias said, "I am called Casias, son of Carius, of the house of Mariammné. My companion is Myrax of Cadaras." Lyrgoné said, "I see you are of royal lineage, for some of the descendants of Mariammné still hold power in Lugaria." Casias said, "Such may be true in Lugaria, fair maiden, but in Cadaras the sons of Manissa regrettably serve other kings not of their lineage."

Lyrgoné said, "Casias son of Carius and Myrax of Cadaras, shall I show you the wondrous city of Tabés and all its marvels?" The men assented gladly, for they found Lyrgoné and her maidens beautiful and were desirous of their company. So Lyrgoné and her maids found laughter and gaiety all that afternoon with Casias and Myrax, whom they led about the city, beginning at Vâlcea Bridge. All that day were Casias and Lyrgoné as one, for as she guided him about the city their hearts began to burn, and their souls were welded together in the intense heat of love. Yet neither spoke of it, even as their smiles and glances from one to the other betrayed the hidden union being forged within their hearts.

But not all was well, for in the grove near the Vâlcea Bridge was hidden one Gallo, the brother of Lyrgoné and companion of Lysias. By reason of the king's troubling dream, Eurastes had bidden Gallo to secretly observe the actions of Casias, for the king perceived him to be a powerful warrior and of a noble lineage. Thus Gallo shadowed Casias, Lyrgoné and their companions throughout all that day and took in all their words.

As the sun dipped behind the western sea, Lyrgoné and Casias parted ways near the garden where Prastor, Casias, and the Manissans were lodging. Casias said, "My lady, I shall treasure this day always. I thank thee for your graciousness." Lyrgoné returned thanks to Casias and the two parted ways, though their hearts were heavy afterward. Myrax, observing his friend's sorrow, said, "Bitter is the wound of the heart and of love unobtainable." Casias brooded and said, "Say you love unobtainable? You ought rather to say, 'love forbidden,' for to be unobtainable and to be forbidden are not one and the same. Is she one whom I cannot have, or is she one whom I am forbidden to have? And if forbidden, then by whom? What law or custom or cruel tyrant keeps her from me? And, supposing it were Fate that we are to be joined together in love, then what kind of man would I be if I did not press on against all obstacle to make her mine? Are not all things forgiven when done for love?"

But Myrax laughed and said, "Return, my friend, from the treacherous domains where your heart has led you. Return from cloudy heights of passion to the clear daylight of reason, for such thoughts will lead to ruin and such words to bitterness." So Casias kept silent about the matter, but from that day forward his heart was fixed on Lyrgoné and he pined away with sorrow in her absence. Lyrgoné likewise brooded upon her bed at night and fixed the will of her heart upon Casias, so that she no longer found pleasure in her maidens, nor in her walks to Vâlcea over the placid waters of Soldara, nor even in the companionship of Lysias her betrothed.

But Gallo, brother of Lyrgoné, skulked back to the royal palace and came by night to Lysias, who was awaiting word from Gallo on the intentions of the Manissans that he might report to his father the king. He saw his friend Gallo coming up the causeway to the courtyard and called out, "Is all well, noble Gallo?" Gallo drew near to Lysias and tore his garments, whispering, "Woe to us, my fair prince, for sorrow has come to your house this day!" Lysias was alarmed and drew his sword, saying, "Make haste and tell me, faithful Gallo, do they mean to make war on us?" Gallo fell at the feet of Lysias trembling and said, "Nay, my lord, a treachery deeper and a bitterer wound!" Lysias said, "I am puzzled, Gallo, for if they plan no attack then what can be graver?" Gallo said, "My very bones quake at the thought of telling thee, my prince, for I know you to be rash and quick to anger."

When he had said this, Lysias's countenance fell, and he seized Gallo roughly, saying, "By the name of my good father Eurastes and by the Watchers who avenge those who are done ill to, I charge thee to tell me all and to omit nothing, lest I run thee through this very moment!" Gallo, still trembling and stammering, said, "It appears that Casias, captain of the Manissans, is taken with Lyrgoné thy beloved." Upon hearing this, Lysias stood motionless as a statue, his face flushed with anger. Gallo said, "And even more so, my prince, for it seems that Lyrgoné has returned his affections; in point of fact, it was she who made overtures to him first and who led him about the city all day, with carefree footfalls and glowing countenance."

"Enough!" cried Lysias, the bitter knife of envy striking his heart. "Let us keep this news from my father, good Eurastes, for the time being. We shall chastise these arrogant Manissans ourselves, these foreigners who presume to come with the hand extended in peace but in truth seek to supplant our gods and rob us of our women. Come; let us plot evil against this Casias." So Lysias and Gallo went off and laid a snare for Casias.

Meanwhile Casias was conferring with Prastor the priest in the Manissan quarters. Old Prastor lamented, "These Tabians are stubborn and suspicious of our motives. Though Eurastes speaks well of Arytos and feigns interest in attacking the Lugars, he says such things only to rid himself of us, for he will by no means allow himself to be tied down by treaty, nor will he relent in allowing us to offer the sacrifices and rituals to our Lady in these lands. It is my judgment that if we cannot press Eurastes to pledge a certain number of men and arms by three days hence that we retire to Cadaras."

These words stung Casias, for he was at that time desperately pining over Lyrgoné, thinking of some way to possess her and would not return to Cadaras without her. The thought of return was hateful to Casias, for his mind had turned and his heart crossed over a barrier from longing to willing; no longer content to merely love Lyrgoné from afar, he was determined to take her from Lysias and have her for himself. "Today is the only day one has," he mused. "One must act, else life be nothing but a string of adventures untaken, of bridges never crossed." He prospected within himself all sorts of ruses and plots by which he could convince her to leave the city with him without detection. Thus he fell into a restless and anxious sleep, for his heart was filled with affections for Lyrgoné and his head swirled with intrigues and stratagems.

The following day, shortly after Prastor had left to call upon King Eurastes, a Tabian servant came to the quarters of the Manissans. "I seek Casias, son of Carius," said the servant. "I am he," said Casias. The servant said, "I come as a messenger of the fair Lyrgoné, maid of Tabia, who bids you to come to her this evening."

The heart of Casias erupted in passion and he said, "Truly Fate has sent thee, dear servant, for at this very moment was the lady Lyrgoné upon my heart. Where does my lady bid this? Speak, and it shall be so!" The servant said, "Let my lord come to the Gardens of Jura near the Vâlcea Bridge where you first met, says my lady. Only take care to come by cover of darkness, for my lady fears to be seen with my lord by reason of her betrothal to Lysias." Casias rejoiced, for he thought, "The lady's affections for me are as mine to her." Then he said, "Go, faithful servant, and tell fair Lyrgoné that stout-hearted Casias shall come as she bids." Then he gave the messenger a bracelet of finely hammered gold and sent him to bear the word to Lyrgoné that he would come to her.

Then servant said, "My lady says, 'Take care that you most assuredly come, for I shall be saddened and angered if you do not appear.'" This enflamed the passion of Casias even more and he cried out, "Say to my lady that Casias will indeed come to her without fail. If it be not so, may I suffer an ignoble shame!"*

But his companion Myrax thought ill of the plan and said, "Do you yet tempt Fate, you arrogant and wanton flatterer? Do you not know that you come here under the charge of Prastor and in the service of King Arytos? What would the Tabians say if it were made known to them that you court the betrothed of their prince?" Casias, wrathful with Myrax, said, "Can human words turn away the leading of the heart? Will your reason alter my inflexible course? Keep thy counsel to thyself and speak to me not of Prastor and Arytos, of Fate and duty. Perhaps Fate has so willed that the union of our two kingdoms shall come about by the union of Lyrgoné and Casias in marriage." Myrax scoffed and said, "Thus the union of you and the woman you have known not yet two days is now decreed by Fate and written in the courses of the stars? Do you not hear your own arrogance? You have become so overwhelmed by your own desire that you fail to see the enormity of the obstacles that stand between you and the success of your plans."

Thus the two argued vehemently and with increasing violence until Casias said, "Till this day have I called you friend, brave Myrax, and friend not only, but also kinsman, for we both descend from fair Mariammné, eldest of Manissa. Yet you sour my disposition towards you with your words, you who would thwart my intentions and rob me of what I have purposed in my heart to possess. Get thee hence from my sight, for after we return to Cadaras I will see thee no more." So Myrax went off and wept for the folly of Casias.

Yet while Myrax was out he came upon old Prastor, who was returning from the royal chambers. Prastor said, "Good Myrax, why is your countenance so downcast? What has befallen you?" So Myrax told Prastor all that Casias had said and planned to do regarding Lyrgoné. Then old Prastor trembled with rage, and coming into the quarters of Casias, confronted him, saying, "Thou base knave and fool, unworthy of the name of thy house! Do you seek to bring us all to ruin by your philandering? Have you no shame! Thou debauched and wanton seducer!" Casias remonstrated with him, scoffing, and saying, "Will you, too, act the role of father and mother in telling me how to conduct my own affairs?" But Prastor said, "How can a son of Manissa not know how hateful such a thing is to Fate as you now propose to undertake? Do you not know that the bond of betrothal is sacred? Did not doom come upon Caeylon because Belthazre had sought to seize maidens for himself who were rightfully pledged to others? Was not Asaph son of Hazer struck down in vengeance because he dared to make love to the wife of Belabret, King of Epidymia? You conduct is an abomination to the gods and a defamation of the holy memory of Manissa."

After Prastor and Casias had argued for a time, Prastor said, "I command you, under the sacred obedience which you owe to me as one put in charge by our lord Arytos, and by the reverence that all Manissans owe priests of our Lady, that you by no means leave these quarters this evening but shall abide here. I also forbid you from seeing again the fair and yellow-haired Lyrgoné, lest your mind be further carried away into madness than it already is. If you disobey me, you shall incur the displeasure of the king and of our Lady." Casias was enraged even more by Prastor's words, but because of the authority the old priest bore he could make no further remonstrance. So he brooded, swallowed his anger, and said, "It shall be so."

Prastor and Myrax turned to leave, but as Myrax was departing, Casias said, "Myrax, if thou hast ever held me in any esteem or born any love for me, I ask of thee one boon before we part ways." Myrax said, "Say on." Casias said, "Go in my place to these Gardens of Jura to meet fair Lyrgoné. Convey to her my sorrow, tell her of the commands of Prastor, and make it known to her that we shall not see one another again." Myrax pitied Casias because of the great sadness he saw in his eyes, and said, "It shall be done my old friend." Myrax departed and Casias wept.

Sing of the sorrow and remorse of Casias, O spirit of song! Sing of the mysterious and twisted paths of fortune! Ah, cruel Fate! Bitter destiny! For though it was Casias who had plotted iniquity, nevertheless, was doom decreed for innocent Myrax. Unbeknownst to Casias or Myrax, the servant whose message had stirred up the passions of Casias came not from Lyrgoné, but from Lysias and Gallo, who had sent the message with the intent of luring Casias out and slaying him in the night. And so Myrax, not Casias, came unto the Gardens of Jura by cover of darkness, cloaked in black and seeking the maiden Lyrgoné. He dashed to and fro amongst the apple trees and poplars of the garden, calling out for the lady Lyrgoné, seeking to catch some glimpse of her. But Lysias and Gallo were concealed behind a stone wall lying in wait. When the cloaked figure of Myrax came into the garden, Gallo said to Lysias, "See, here is Casias seeking to find thy beloved by dark of night. Do you have any more doubt of his wicked intentions?" The heart of Lysias burned and he said, "Fall upon him!" Then Lysias and Gallo leaped from their place of concealment, each bearing long and dreadful daggers. They fell upon Myrax and thrust him through in many places so that he perished before his warm body fell upon the grass.

But when Gallo pulled the cloak from their victim's face, he saw that it was not Casias but Myrax. Then he howled, "Ah! My lord, we have been deceived, for this is not Casias but his faithful friend and companion, Myrax!" When Lysias realized that he had slain the wrong man, his stomach sank and his heart quaked. "Let us flee," he said to Gallo, "for Casias may come seeking him and find Myrax thus with ourselves leaning over the body. Then that rage and power which flows in the veins of the sons of Manissa may rise up in him and enable him to slay us. Let us make haste and return to the royal palace!" So Lysias and Gallo fled, leaving the body of faithful Myrax torn and bloodied upon the garden turf.

The following morning the gardeners found the body of Myrax, and, judging from his attire, discerned that he was one of the Manissans. They faithfully brought his body to the house of Prastor, who wept when he saw it. Then Casias came and beheld the lifeless form of his friend and was shaken with remorse. He pounded his mighty fists upon the floor and cried out, "Ah, Myrax! Why did my last words with you need be so harsh? Now you have gone into shadow and will never more be seen among the fair fields of Asylia or the whited lanes of Cadaras! Never again will we ride together through the foaming waves that ever lap the shores of Cyrenaica! Would that I could retrieve the words I spoke, or that we could at least converse pleasantly once more as we were wont to do in the days of old, in the days when we idled by the tumbling waters of the Cadar in our youth and spoke of battles and maids and glory to be won. Would that your countenance last to me would have been a smile! Now you leave me in bitterness; yet shall I find thy killers and bring them down to the grave in blood."

Prastor, too, was full of anger, and said to Casias, "Stand up like a man, Casias! Who could have done such a treacherous thing to thy friend and mine, to thy companion and my companion? Who would have chafed at the attention you gave unto Lyrgoné, so much so that they laid a snare for you beneath Jura's peaceful canopy to put you to death? Who would have had the gall and the strength to overpower and slay noble Myrax? Could it be anyone but Prince Lysias, who must have known of your affections for Lyrgoné and sought your blood? Would anyone other than Lysias have so envied you so as to wish you dead?"

Casias leaped to his feet and said, "Yes, Lysias! By the locks of our Lady, it is he who has engineered this treachery! By the gods I will make him pay!" So Casias took up his sword and stormed out. Prastor followed some way behind, crying out, "Only Fate can restrain thee now, Casias! Ah, Lysias will rue the day he was born! Yet take caution, for Fate works mysteriously. It was thy impropriety which brought forth this chain of events, so that thou, too, are guilty of the blood of Myrax." Casias called back, saying, "Cursed be Lysias and Fate along with him! In renouncing beautiful Lyrgoné I am deprived of faithful Myrax. I know not how this affair will end, but the one certainty I hold is that some damned Tabian will pay in blood!" So Prastor trembled at the thought of the rage of Casias and followed along some ways behind, desiring to see how things unfolded, but fearful of how they would end.

Thus did Casias come angrily to the court of Eurastes, demanding audience before the great King of Tabia. When Eurastes heard that Casias demanded to be heard and would not be turned away, he said to Dario his attendant, "Is it not the priest Prastor that we deal with? On what occasion does this war captain demand our attention?" Dario said, "I know not, your majesty." But Lysias came quaking before his father Eurastes, saying, "Father, my king and my lord, I fear it is on my account that the Manissan presses for your attention." Eurastes gazed at him sternly and said, "Tell me everything, my son, and withhold nothing, though it brings shame to our house." But before Lysias could speak, Casias leaped past the sentries, charging boldly into the presence of the king and his court. Lyrgoné was also present, standing near the throne of the king.

"Treacherous swine!" cried Casias to the face of Eurastes and his court. "Vile murderers! Thieves who lure the innocent out by trickery and lay in wait for guiltless blood!" Shouts and jeers went up from the court at the hard words of Casias. Dario withstood Casias and said, "How is it that you dare to make such accusations before our lord the king? Perhaps King Arytos allows himself to be spoken to in such a manner in Cadaras, but in Tabés such things are done by none save barbarians and the ignorant." Laughter erupted from the court at this jest, but Lysias skulked behind the throne of his father, for he knew on what business Casias had come and was in dreadful fear of the Manissan war captain's angry spear.

Casias pounded his chest and cried, "My cause is just and my intentions noble. I come to lay an accusation before the throne of Eurastes for a crime committed against one of our company by a nobleman of this very court." Dario said, "Master Casias, if you need to make a legal claim, there are times and occasions appointed for such things." Casias would not be silenced, however, and went on, saying, "This past night, while the whole land lay under the cover of darkness, my kinsman Myrax, a man most innocent and upright among all the sons of men, went out to the Gardens of Jura on an errand of mine. I had been summoned to meet a certain person by darkness in the said garden. But being detained by the command of Prastor my priest and elder, I regretfully sent Myrax in my place to bear this news to the one I was to meet. Poor soul! When he reached his destination he was treacherously set upon, slain by murderous rogues, men sent by one in this court—or perhaps themselves men of the court!" The whole court fell silent and grave, wondering whom Casias would accuse and what the king would do.

Eurastes stroked his grizzled beard and furled his whited brow, turning over the words of Casias in his mind. Finally he said, "Hot-headed Casias, this is a serious charge you make to accuse anyone of the noble court of Tabia of such a base thing as you narrate. But come, leave us in doubt no longer; who is it that you name as perpetrator of this wicked deed?" Casias said, "I accuse Lysias, son of Eurastes."

The court erupted in anger, the temper of the Tabian nobles flaring at the words of Casias. Dario said to him, "Casias, you have gone too far. For this insult you shall be punished." But King Eurastes restrained Dario, for he recalled the words of Lysias before Casias presented himself. Eurastes silenced the hall, saying, "Brethren, you seek to condemn this Manissan for his accusation against my son, our prince. But I say let the prince himself answer these charges. Lysias, what have you to say to the accusations of Casias? Is it as he says? Are you indeed guilty of the blood of his companion?"

Lysias stepped forward and said, "I will answer this charge if Casias will first answer one question." Casias said, "Ask what you will, for I have no secrets." Lysias said, "Before I say my part in this affair, you will tell the king and the court exactly whom it was that you were hoping to meet, whom you sent Myrax to with such regret?" Then Casias stood dumb, for he reasoned within himself that if he revealed that he had intended to meet the lady Lyrgoné, the suspicion of the court would be aroused against him, and Lysias would appear justified in Myrax's killing. Furthermore, the honor of Lyrgoné would be imperiled, for she would be shamed before the entire court. Therefore Casias said nothing, seeking to protect his claim and defend the honor of Lyrgoné.

Lysias goaded him, saying, "Where are your rash words now, Manissan? You have arrogantly raged into our court like a mad dog leveling ungrounded accusations at the royal house; now that you are cross-examined, will you say nothing?" But Casias was unwilling to reveal the name of Lyrgoné, and responded at length, "I will not name them."

Then the court broke forth into laughter and jeering, all the nobles heaping insult and reprobation upon Casias. Lysias, too, jeered at the crestfallen Manissan. But Eurastes's face was grave and anxious. Finally, Dario silenced the hall and said, "Casias, until you are willing to name your party in this affair, we cannot take seriously so grave a charge as you level against Prince Lysias." Eurastes arose and said, "Good Dario speaks the truth, Manissan. Shall I deliver my flesh and blood to your justice when half the tale remains untold? Therefore let this affair be concluded, as well as the whole sorry presence of your delegation within our city, which was happy and content until the day you arrived. This I decree: that neither you nor Prastor nor any Manissan come to seek audience with me again, neither for the purpose of forging an alliance, nor for the promotion of your religion, nor for this matter before us now. Were you a citizen of my kingdom I would have you flogged with thirty lashes for such a rash accusation as you have today leveled; perhaps even drowned in the Soldana. But because of the honor I bear to your King Arytos, I give only the command that you and your kinsmen make haste and depart Tabia within two days' time."

Casias was incensed and said, "How can you not take the charge seriously when my comrade and kinsman lays dead? To whom shall I appeal for judgment?" Eurastes said, "You shall have no judgment from us till you reveal whom you were meeting in the Gardens of Jura and on what business." Casias was mute and departed, full of anger and panged with remorse. The court rejoiced and mocked Casias, but Eurastes retired to his chambers and brooded, for he suspected his son to be involved in the affair regarding Myrax but was yet uncertain. His wife, delicate Eryice, said, "You ought to have had nothing to do with that Manissan." But Eurastes said, "Then should I allow him to make such charges against our son without answering him?" But both Eurastes and Eryice were filled with anxiety over the matter and fell into a troubled and restless sleep.

Lysias, however, stole away and came to the chambers of Lyrgoné by night. She came out to him and said curtly, "What have you to say, you coward and weakling?" Lysias scoffed, saying, "Don't banter words with me, you whore and daughter of a whore! Do I not know of your unfaithfulness? Do I not know of your fondness for Casias and your pining away for him? It is the scandal of the palace!" Lyrgoné said, "Get thee out of my sight, for when you refused to answer the charge of Casias I knew at once of your guilt, you envious and hateful creature." Lysias cried, "Shall a man not envy his betrothed when she dallies about the city with another man?" But Lyrgoné wept and withdrew to her quarters, for the sting of Lysias's words was bitter.

Casias returned to his quarters and brooded, though Prastor comforted him as best he could, saying, "Come Casias, let us leave the woe and bitterness of this city behind and return east, to the gentle hills of Asylia and the broad plains of Cadaras. Eurastes has broken off discussion because of this matter and there is nothing more we can do here." But Casias moaned, saying, "Shall we go home in peace and leave the killer of Myrax unavenged? Behold, a certainty firmer than the solidity of the earth beneath my feet tells my heart that Lysias was behind Myrax's unhappy end. By our Lady's cloak, I shall make him pay, even if I cannot name him before the court for fear of exposing Lyrgoné to shame." Thus Casias persuaded Prastor and the delegation to abide in Tabia despite the edict of Eurastes compelling their withdrawal within two days.

By the time the pink rays of the dying sun cast their glow over the streets and towers of Tabés on the dusk of the second day, word had already spread throughout the city that Prastor, Casias, and the Manissans had not departed, but lingered in hopes of finding justice for the killing of Myrax. This unnerved Eurastes, and he told Dario his attendant, "Most trusted Dario, take with you fifty men and be prepared to make an arrest of the Manissans if they do not depart the city by nightfall." Lyrgoné, who stood nearby in the court of Eurastes, heard this and fled at once in hopes of seeing Casias again, that she might warn him of the coming of Dario.

She came in tears to the house of Prastor and fell to the ground weeping. Clutching the knees of Casias, she besought him, saying, "Most noble son of Manissé, I beg thee by whatever affection you may have held for me, arise and flee this place, for even now Dario approaches with fifty men to take you and your company prisoner for refusing to abandon the kingdom within the time allotted by the king." Casias looked at Lyrgoné, loving her, and said, "Let him come, my lady, for I will by no means leave this city until justice is done for the killing of Myrax."

Lyrgoné said, "I know by surety that he has been slain by Lysias, my betrothed, along with Gallo my brother, though it tears my soul to say it, for I know you are a fierce but noble man who will require blood for blood and bereave me at once of beloved and kinsman alike." Casias snorted and said, "Then why do you tell me at all?" She said, "Because from the moment I saw thee at the Vâlcea Bridge I have pined for thee. Though I am pledged to another I cannot restrain my heart nor forget the comeliness of thy form. I know I ought not; I know I cannot. But

I see in thee the nobleness and power that in Lysias is but petty jealousy and craftiness. I love thee and would see no harm come to thee; therefore, depart at once, I bid you! For the sake of the love I bear for you and you bear for me, take what little time has been granted to us and bear it away east, where at least you may love me in peace from afar. Stay here and all shall end in cold, bitter doom."

Casias was moved with passion and declared, "And how can I depart now that you have declared your love for me? How can I remove myself from thy presence now that you have set me afire even more by your affections? Can a flame remove itself from the wood it consumes? Can a wave, once propelled by the wind, arise and remove itself from the sea? Neither so can I remove myself from thee now that you declare yourself to me and me to you. By the gods I will not depart. Far be it from me to do so! I will abide, come what may." With tearful eyes Lyrgoné pounded her fists on his breast and said, "Get out of here you beautiful, stupid man!" Casias, however, would in no wise listen, but remonstrated with her, declaring again his devotion.

As he was speaking, Dario arrived at the house of the Manissans with fifty men seeking to arrest Prastor, Casias, and all their companions. But Casias, expecting them, called out for the seventy hardened warriors who accompanied him, saying, "Rise up, men, for we are ensnared!" Then the Manissans rose in a fury and slew Dario and the fifty men, for many of the Manissans were Periorids and fought mightily. When Casias saw Dario and the men lying slain in the street, he cried out, "Blood for blood! To battle, men of Manissé!" And all the Manissans roared for Casias and for war; but old Prastor wept bitterly.

Lyrgoné shook at the sight of what Casias had done and said, "Casias, you put me in a hard place, for if I return home my betrothed all the court will know that you were able to slay Dario because I forewarned you. I shall be cast out as a traitor, or perhaps drowned in the depths of the merciless sea, as was custom in days past when women broke faith."* Old Prastor said,

"Then you shall abide with us, dearest lady, leaving your people and your city to come east into the fair dominions of the Manissans, where you will be ever welcome." So Prastor, Casias and Lyrgoné, the seventy Manissan warriors, the ministers, and all the priests fled the city by night, exiting by the south gate. They traveled with little food or sleep for four days until they came into the sandy dunes that border Tabés to the south. There, in the protection afforded by the dunes and the tall sand grasses, the company took their rest by the light of the stars at nightfall of the fourth day.

But once sheltered behind the great dune they fell into despondency, for they were many weeks from their homeland and in the midst of a hostile people. So they struck up camp near the dune and debated what course of action to take.

Meanwhile word of the slaying of Dario and his company reached King Eurastes. He moaned and said, "Thus the vision I saw in the night comes to pass, for the Manissans have shed blood within our city." Lysias pressured his father to be given leave to take a company of soldiers out to the countryside to find the Manissans and slay them. But when it was known that Lyrgoné also had also went out with Casias, Gallo her brother pleaded with the king and said, "My lord, though our blood be hot for the slaying of Dario, let us not yet send out the soldiers as Lysias proposes. Yellow-haired Lyrgoné is among the Manissans now; my sister, the betrothed of Lysias, and one day queen of our realm. The Manissans hold a valuable pearl, for whose sake we cannot act too hastily."

Eurastes said, "Gallo, I concur with thy judgment. Therefore, go out to the Manissans under a flag of truce. Our scouts tell us they are encamped some distance from the city in the region of the dunes. Bear this message; let all be forgiven and let them depart our realms in peace, only relinquish fair Lyrgoné to her people and her betrothed. Perhaps a brother's entreaties will move them." So Gallo took with him only a few servants and went out of the city into the arid plains of the south, seeking the Manissans by the dunes.

It was on the third day of the Manissans sojourn beneath the shadow of the dunes that they saw Gallo approaching under flag of truce. Lyrgoné said to Casias, "Tis Gallo, brother of mine and companion of Lysias. He comes under the flag of truce." Casias grimaced and said, "A companion of Lysias, the one whom I hold answerable for the death of innocent Myrax? I shall indeed have words with this one!" But Lyrgoné clasped the hem of his cloak and pleaded with him, "Have mercy on him, my love, for he is my flesh and blood!" Casias said, "If he is innocent of the blood of Myrax, I swear he shall have nothing to fear. But I have sworn by our Lady to make those pay who slew noble Myrax, and inasmuch as no vow sworn in our Lady's name can be broken, then likewise I cannot vouchsafe your brother's life if he has partaken in the blood of my companion. I pray for thy sake he is innocent." With these words stern Casias went out to meet Gallo, leaving Lyrgoné trembling in the encampment.

Face to face upon the dust choked plain before the dunes, Gallo spoke to vengeful Casias, saying, "Thus says Eurastes, King of Tabia, 'Let all be forgiven to the Manissans and let them depart in peace to their own land; only leave behind fair Lyrgoné and restore her to her people and her betrothed.'" Casias said, "So, the brother of Lyrgoné comes asking for the return of his fair sister?" Gallo spoke and said, "Kin sendeth for kin, and blood for blood! Though you Manissans are fierce and hardened by war, perhaps you will be moved by the entreaties of a brother for his kin? Surely even you barbarians understand such things. What say you to the offer of our generous king?"

Casias replied, "Blood for blood, indeed! Well-spoken Gallo, for it recalls that it was on account of blood that we now find ourselves here upon this plain, for it was my companion and kinsman Myrax whose blood I sought justice for in coming before Eurastes." Gallo said, "Do you still seek to avenge the death of your friend? Take the king's generous terms! Leave our lands and return to the fair and verdant fields of Manissé while you can! Do you not know that if you do not heed our king's words and return yellow-haired Lyrgoné that you will face doom here in the wilderness? Forget Myrax! Let the dead bury the dead and return to the east, to the hearth of kith and kin."

This angered Casias. "You know not what you speak, Gallo! Lyrgoné stays here of her own freedom and by no constraint. She is no prisoner; I have not carried her off like the spoils of war. It is for love of me that she abides among us and will by no means consent to be wed to that scoundrel Lysias, that murderer and whelp of a man. Go back and tell your king and your companion Lysias that it is Casias whom Lyrgoné loves. She has declared her love for me, and I likewise have declared my love for her. She will return with me to Manissé and will be seen among the white spires of Tabés no more."

Gallo shook with rage at the words of Casias, indignant that his sister should betray his companion Lysias and love a Manissan. Therefore he cried out, "So, destroy our peace with such ill tidings, will you son of Manissé? Then I will destroy thy peace! I tell you, it was none other than Prince Lysias who did slay thy friend Myrax, and that with my aid! We lay in wait for him at Jura, thinking he was you. When he came out we fell upon him and ran him through with many wounds and savored his dying cries! With smiles upon our faces and mirth in our hearts did we butcher him on the grass. What say you to that, you beast of a man?"

Casias frothed in anger and drew his sword; Gallo likewise took up arms and threw himself at Casias, hoping to slay him. Yet he had spoken imprudently, thinking too little of the might of Casias and the power of the sons of Manissa, for he found that though he struck mighty blows, he could not make Casias give even the smallest bit of ground. Battle-hardened Casias easily deflected all the blows of Gallo and pressed the Tabian back towards the dune. When Gallo saw himself pushed back and knew he could not prevail against Casias, he attempted to flee, but Casias leaped after him and pursued him at his heels. Finally Gallo could run no longer and collapsed upon the dry earth, crying out, "Thus am I repaid for the taking of innocent life!" Having said this, he dropped his head. Casias fell upon him and with one cruel stroke took the off the head of Gallo, sending it tumbling down upon the parched earth.

Lyrgoné came forth weeping violently for her brother, saying, "Ah, poor Gallo! O Gallo, why did you tempt Fate by lying in wait for innocent blood?" Then she cried forth a torrent of tears, first for the death of her brother, second for the folly of Lysias and Gallo in scheming to murder Myrax, third for the dilemma she now found herself in, and fourth for Casias, whom she at once loved fiercely and despised for slaying her brother.* Anger smoldered in the heart of Casias against Lysias as he sought a way to avenge himself upon the prince.

The servants of Gallo fled back the city to tell King Eurastes what had befallen him in the wilderness. Then Casias attempted to comfort Lyrgoné, but she beat her hands violently against him, struck his face, and refused his overtures. Casias grimaced, and motioning to the severed head of Gallo lying in the bloodied sand, said to Lyrgoné, "What think you of the nobleness of the sons of Manissa now?" But Lyrgoné only wept and found no relief.

Eurastes, Lysias, and the court of Tabés were thrown into grief and consternation by the report brought back by the servants of Gallo. Lysias at once demanded that he be put in command of a great squadron of men to go forth to the dunes to slay Casias and bring back Lyrgoné. Yet old Eurastes faltered, for he said, "My heart yearns for justice, as done yours, my son. Yet what will become of all this? Where will it end? I ache at this news of the death of Gallo, thy friend, and Dario, my trusted servant of many years. Even so, I am pained by the words brought back by Gallo's servants that he has confessed to the murder of Myrax and named you as the accomplice. Tell me, my son, have you truly done this thing?" Lysias, heavy with trepidation, said, "It is so, father." Then Eurastes became full of anger and struck his son Lysias across the face with the back of his hand. And all the court fell silent at his public disgrace. "Stupid boy!" the king raged. "Stupid, petty boy! Is this the way princes settle their scores? Have you no sense? Have you no propriety? Even though Casias was first in the wrong by dallying with your betrothed, it was you who acted vilely by planning to lay in wait by cover of dark to slay him! Casias has acted nobly in bringing his charge to me before all the court. He acts in the light while you cringe in the darkness, you reckless fool! And now not only is innocent Myrax slain, but loyal Gallo and faithful Dario as well, two of the greatest men of our kingdom! What will come of it all? And what position have you left me in? If I do not pursue this Casias and overtake him, I shall appear weak and contemptible in the eyes of my people. Yet if I do pursue him, I am sure to court war with the Manissans, for Casias and Prastor are among the most respected men of their realm. Do you not see the chain of doom you have bound me with? Do you not see you've tethered me to a stone cast into the sea?"

The face of Lysias was flushed with humiliation and rage as he bore his shame before the whole court. Then he cried in anger, "It is true that this matter began with me father! Yet with me let it also end. Give me leave to take two thousand picked men of the city garrison to go out to the dunes and annihilate these Manissans. Though Casias and Prastor be important men in their realm, we must not let the slaying of Gallo and Dario go unanswered, nor can we permit these foreigners to flee the realm with Lyrgoné in their company."

Eurastes brooded heavily, his great beard tumbling down his breast as he furled his old brows in thought. Finally he said, "Lysias my son, and all lords and nobles of Tabia, let it be as you say. We must not let these wrongs go unavenged, nor can we give up yellow-haired Lyrgoné to them in this manner. Go, my son, taking with you two thousand picked men of the city garrison. May our god Succo give you strength and cause you to prevail over the Manissans and their hallowed protectress." Lysias rejoiced and said, "I shall not return until I have vindicated my name and the name of our city," but Eurastes only said, "We shall see if thou returnest at all."

So Lysias summoned two thousand picked men of the city garrison and placed them under twenty trusted and battle-hardened captains, each captain commanding one hundred men. Then they departed Tabés towards the arid and sandy regions south of the city where Casias, Prastor, and the Manissans were encamped with Lyrgoné among them.

Meanwhile Lyrgoné, Casias and the Manissans were encamped in the shadow of the dunes some distance south of the city. Casias had sent forth two men to keep watch to the north for the coming of the Tabians, which the Manissans were in dread of hourly. Yet it was not until dusk of the third day after the slaying of Gallo that the scouts returned to Casias and said, "Brave Casias, Prince Lysias marches out of Tabés with two thousand men under arms!" When Casias heard this, he removed himself and his people from the shadow of the dune to its height and attempted to fortify the place with what stone and dead wood was to be found in the vicinity, though it was not much. When they had made such fortifications as they could, they called the place *Eleftaia*, which means "Last Hope." Some men were in great fear and pressed Casias to retreat into the wilderness, but Casias said, "To do so would only be to trade one doom for another, for we have fled from the city in haste and have no provisions with us for an extended sojourn in the wilderness, nor is there any game or water for us in this arid place; even now our provisions are close to running out. Nay, we shall take our stand here as did Apollos against the hordes of Sammas and see what lot Fate will deal us. In any case, our Lady will judge all things rightly." This settled the hearts of the men and resigned them to accept whatever lot befell them.

Yet sorrow and misery was the lot of delicate Lyrgoné,

for she fell to the earth beneath the shade of the hastily erected tent that served as Casias's dwelling and wept. Casias spoke tenderly to her and tried to comfort her in her affliction, but to no avail, for the grief in her heart was deep. So Casias was perturbed in spirit and went out from her to see Prastor. The old priest was sitting upon a log at the opposite side of the encampment. Night had fallen upon the land and Prastor was offering up the prayers said at the rising of the stars, his gaze turned towards the north. Casias said to him, "It is enough to tell a man to harden his spine and put away his fear with death lurks nearby, but what words can one say to a weeping woman who is overtaken with such a calamity as has swallowed up fair Lyrgoné? What words of comfort or courage can one impart to her?" Prastor said, "No words, dear Casias, but only the grace that comes through the right and lawful union of man and woman in the bonds of matrimony. If all things are to end for us tomorrow, then go into the life to come with this grace upon your soul, that you have pledged undying troth and affection for Lyrgoné and she to you before the stars and the watchful eyes of our Lady." These words brought comfort to Casias. He returned to bitter Lyrgoné and repeated to her the counsel of Prastor. She quietly acceded to all things he said, finding comfort in the wise priest's admonition.

Thus the whole company of the Manissans assembled and witnessed the union of Casias and Lyrgoné beneath the stars, officiated by old Prastor. When all present had uttered their yeas to the union and witnessed the solemn exchange of vows, they returned to their watches. But Casias retired to his tent with Lyrgoné for the evening, finding peace once and only once in the warm embrace of she for whom he had suffered so much. Then did Casias and Lyrgoné find rest from their sorrows in one solitary night of sweet love and repose.

How brief was that warm respite! How fleeting the comfort of love's long sought reward and the pleasure of a lover's embrace! Soon, too soon, did the mingling of flesh end.

The men of Lysias approached the encampment of Casias with banners unfurled and spearheads whetted for doom even as the sky was dyed pink with the first glimmer of that baleful day's son. Lysias peered ahead, beholding the meager defenses of the Manissans and the smoke arising from their watchfires and said, "Behold, they have taken defense upon that hillside. Quickly! Let us encompass it about and cut off their retreat." So the trumpets of the Tabians blared and the fleet-footed men under Lysias and his captains advanced and formed a perimeter around the small hillside, some one hundred meters out around the base of the dune, so that no there was no means of flight. Then he said, "Let us now bide our time and see what rash Casias will do." So the Tabians set up pickets and drove sharpened stakes into the earth, entrenching themselves and waiting upon Casias to take some action.

Casias was roused from his carefree slumber at the waning of the night, beholding with sorrow the arrival of Lysias and the Tabians. With sighs and deep groanings he heard the blast of the trumpet and the forming of lines around the hillside. In sorrow and against the pull of nature he roused himself, gently removing the bare arms of Lyrgoné from off his chest. Thus he went out from her to the cruel contest.

Lyrgoné awoke alone in the tent of Casias and went out to seek her husband, and finding him beholding the forces of the Tabians, despaired when she saw the multitude and quality of those arrayed against them. Casias was amazed at this and said, "Why do you lose hope, beloved? Think you not that some five-score Manissans are sufficient to deal with these two thousand of thy kinsmen?" Lyrgoné protested, "Has madness overtaken you, dear husband? These are the best warriors of the city arrayed under the renowned Prince Lysias, of late my betrothed, who has won great glory in many battles and whose forces outnumber ours by twenty to one!" Casias laughed in scorn and said, "Be it so, though I vouch they have never waged war against the sons of Manissa before! Know that we are not like other men, but are mighty men of renown, called by some *paladins*, which means in our tongue 'sons of glory.' Know you not that our Lady, Blessed Manissa, once slew twenty thousand Marudans with a force not more than half the size and with casualties that could be counted on the fingers? Surely you have heard even in Tabia of the deeds of mighty Perior who alone destroyed the gates of Cadaras and slew thousands of his foes? Or of his sons who, being only nine, razed that city to the ground and put its inhabitants to the sword? Or what of glorious Apollos of undying fame, who made Sammas the tyrant rue the day he thought to subdue the house of Baldor upon Cruachan's bloody heights? In all these engagements and more did the blood of Manissa boil hot in her descendants and cause them to rise up with great ferocity to deliver doom to the enemies of her house. Even now my spine turns to iron and my arms tremble with wrath at the deeds that will be done here today and the blood that will be spilled, for though we may perish and see fair Manissé never again, we will most certainly execute a vengeance upon these Tabians that will make Eurastes weak in the knees and will cause the tongues of his court to wag, for though we die they shall know that the glorious sons of Manissa have not yet perished from the earth and that the wrath of Manissé is bitter!" Then all the Manissans assented to Casias' words and cried, "Curcua! For Manissé and Myrax! Curcua!"

Then Prastor and his company of priests offered up burnt offerings, invoking the memory of Manissa and the strength of Perior in the struggle to come, chanting the somber hymns and dirges that were heard in old Asylia in the ancient days, some of which were written by Hazer, son of Manissa.* When the pink sun began its slow ascent in the east and the long shadows of night fled away, Lysias came to the fore of the Tabian defenses and cried out, "Hear me, O son of Manissa, lord Casias! Should so many perish when it is you alone whom I contend with? See, you have nowhere to flee and no hope of victory in arms. Therefore I say this, that if you should but turn over to me Lyrgoné, my betrothed, you and your men shall go free and return in peace to Manissé."

Many of the Manissans thought the terms generous and urged Casias to deliver Lyrgoné to Lysias, but Casias said to Lysias, "Nay, it cannot be so, for this very evening have I taken to wife this Lyrgoné according to rites of Manissé, and before this entire camp as witnesses. I have held her in my embrace in the intimacy of the bed. Should I give her up now, I would be delivering up my own flesh and blood to you who have no further claim on her. But I now make this offer to you, that if you should turn back from bloodshed and allow us to return to Manissé in peace with Lyrgoné I will not only forgive the treacherous slaying of Myrax but will pay thee compensation for the loss of thy betrothed at any amount you should set, for I have acted dishonorably in pilfering her from your charge."

Many of the Tabians thought the words of Casias wise and urged Lysias to heed them, but upon hearing that Casias had lawfully wed Lyrgoné his ears became stopped up and his eyes fell red with consuming envy. "To war!" shouted Lysias. "There is nothing left but the cracking of shields, the splintering of spears, and the rending of flesh for this outrage. Curse the day the men of Manissé were sighted in our lands and welcomed into our city! To arms, brave Tabians!"

But being men of honor, the Tabians permitted the Manissans to send away Prastor with the priests and ministers in his charge, forty men in all, before they brought the hill under siege. With tearful embraces did Casias and his men of arms bid farewell to Prastor and his company. Prastor wept on the shoulder of Casias and said, "That you would have stayed away from the fair Tabian maiden and minded your place! Now all has come undone! Yet will I remember you in my oblations and lift your name up in the smoking incense of the daily offering." Casias said, "It matters not, my old friend, for I sense greater things are at play here. The only course left to us is to fight gallantly to do honor to our kin and our kingdom." Then Casias took Lyrgoné his bride and donned her in the cloak of a priest, covering her head and hiding her among the company of Prastor. She protested and would not be removed from his company, but he entrusted her to Prastor, saying, "Take Lyrgoné among you and spirit her away from here. If we should be found victorious this day, I will find you in old Asylia and claim her there. If we should fall and not find you at Asylia by the next full moon, it remains to you only to bear word of our disaster to King Arytos who reigns from white-walled Cadaras. Either way, please take Lyrgoné from this place of doom." So Prastor and all the Manissan priests left the hill of Eleftaia with Lyrgoné hidden in their company. When they had left, the anger of Casias waxed hot, his hair bristled like a wild dog, and the power of the sons of Manissa arose in him.

Then was there a clashing of arms and a din of battle such as never was heard of in the fair land of Tabia since the ancient days, for charging the sandy hill of Eleftaia whereupon the Manissans stood their ground came Lysias and the Tabians, two thousand all, bent on slaughter and vengeance. Their cries were fierce and the throws of their spears powerful, so that the Manissan shields rang out across the dunes in the gentle morning sun of the west. Yet did the Manissans maintain their ground at that terrifying charge, for the Tabians fought uphill upon sand while the Manissans had only to hold their places and not fall back. Thus Lysias drew his men off to regroup, and upon doing so found that he left behind over a hundred of his company dead in the sand. Lysias cried, "Have seventy warriors slain a hundred of our own? Let it not be so, my brethren! Where is your pride? Rise and take the hill! Let the foreigner be blotted out from our land!" So the Tabians again charged Eleftaia.

But Casias called to his men, saying, "Let each of you men cast your spear when I shall give the call!" So the Manissans awaited the onslaught of the Tabians and withheld their spears until their foes were nearly upon them. Then Casias roared with a resounding cry, the men of Manissé yelled, "Curcua!" and cast their deadly shafts as one. The air was rent with the whirring of whetted spears that blotted out the sun; the barrage of death crashed into the Tabian ranks and toppled men to the earth, both the young man and the hardened warrior, for the Manissan spears made no distinction, piercing all flesh equally. Then Casias cried, "Draw swords, brave men of Manissé! Run them from the hill!" So the Manissans drew their hardened brazen blades and lunged down the hillside, hacking great swaths in the Tabian ranks and splattering the sand with gore. The Tabians fled down the hill in frenzied disarray, giving no thought to strategy or honor but seeking only to escape the cutting blades of the Manissans. Thus they retreated a second time, leaving behind them another two hundred slain upon the white sands. But not a man among the Manissans had yet fallen or was even wounded.

Lysias hurled his helm down in anger and raged about the Tabian camp, saying, "Is there no commander among us who can drive these seventy men from this wretched hill?" Then came forward one Andelor, a grim and brooding captain, who said, "I will drive them from the hill." So Andelor took charge of the Tabian fighters and made a third attempt at the hill, though this time the ranks were spread thinner so that the Manissans found them more difficult to strike. Then there was bitter hand to hand combat on the dune, sword upon shield ringing out in the mid-morning sun or Tabian grappling with Manissan in the bloodied sand for life and honor. Casias found his little band increasingly encircled, for if he turned to strike one way he heard shouts and cries from his men behind him imploring his aid, so that everywhere the Manissans were sorely pressed. Then some of the men of Manissé began to be pierced and fall.

Casias said to himself, "Even the loss of one of our men is severe, for our numbers are few. I must bring down this gallant captain who seeks our destruction!" So Casias caught Andelor in his sight and hurled a spear at him; the blade punched through the Tabian's armor and struck him in the gut, sending him toppling over onto the sand. When the Manissans saw Andelor fall, they cried "Curcua!" with one accord and struck out with renewed vigor, as if iron flowed in their veins and strengthened their arms. Then the Tabians retreated behind their line, leaving over three hundred slain upon the hillside, among them Andelor, the most experienced of all the Tabian captains.

Finally Lysias himself came forward and said, "I see now that these Manissans have some valiance in them yet! Men of Tabia, gather around me! Let your spears be lowered for doom and your eyes each set upon his man, for I myself shall lead us up this time!" So every Tabian man came to the banner of Lysias—even those who had been wounded—and rallied about him, crying out threats to the Manissans and frothing for vengeance. But Casias only said, "Let us meet them," and entrusted himself to She Who Judges Justly.

Then the Tabians roared and came crashing against the hillside, a wave of bitter spearheads and glittering helms in the noontide sun. The fighting was desperate and dreadful, and neither side gave ground, the Manissans knowing that the struggle was to the very end and the Tabians smarting from shame and fury that so many of them had yet been bested by so few men of Manissé. Though the Manissans slew many Tabians and wreaked havoc upon their lines as the latter struggled up the sandy ascent, nevertheless the Tabians gradually overwhelmed the Manissans by their immense numbers and began to kill a great many of them, though not without bitter loss. Seeing men falling around him and the lines rapidly shrinking, Casias said, "May Manissa Dylydia, the Avenger, guide my spear and bring me into the halls of my fathers in glorious light!"* Then he caught haughty Lysias in his sight and hurled his spear. Even as he hurled he was overwhelmed by Tabian swordsmen and run through in many places, drenching the sand with his blood. Thus perished Casias, son of Carius, of the house of Mariammné. But

his spear found its mark and struck Lysias in the throat, rending the tender flesh and spilling his hot blood over his burnished armor and down upon the gore-soaked sand. Lysias fell and thrashed about in the throes of death, vainly trying to cry out, but breath and speech eluded him. His retainers tried to staunch the wound, but the gash was too grievous. His flesh paled, his eyes turned up and all became dark. So perished Lysias, Prince of Tabés, upon the blood bespattered sand, even as the Tabian warriors were rejoicing at the death of Casias. Thus the Tabian cries of victory were turned to mourning, for Lysias was the only son of King Eurastes and sole heir to the Tabian throne.

The Tabians slew every last Manissan and left no one alive. When they had finished their gruesome slaughter, they ransacked the tents of the little camp, thinking therein to find Lyrgoné hidden away. But great was their consternation when they could by no means find her and realized that she had escaped with the priests. Then they wailed and moaned, for they said, "We have suffered and fought in vain, for Lyrgoné is not here! In vain has Prince Lysias died and in vain do over a thousand of our brethren also litter the sand in this place of death!" Some wanted to pursue the priests and overtake them, but many were in fear to venture any further from Tabés with so few men, most of whom were wounded and exhausted. So they bore up the body of Lysias and returned unto Tabés with great mourning.

But Lyrgoné, who was with Prastor and his company some distance away, began to feel pangs of sorrow and longing for Casias and was taken with great curiosity concerning his fate. When she could no longer bear her anguish she slipped away from Prastor by night and hurried alone through the wilderness, back to the sandy wastes and dunes that border Tabés to the south. But when she came unto the place of the Manissan camp, wracked with hunger and famished from thirst and weeping, she saw only the bodies of men scattered all over the place, Tabian and Manissan alike, all food for carrion. She saw the Manissan tents ravaged, and the Manissan corpses piled and burned; she took in the stench in her nostrils. Then she beheld the body of Casias upon the hillside of Eleftaia, exposed to sun and bird of prey, pierced with many wounds. She wept and drove the birds away with a stick; then, when she had anointed the body of Casias and wept over it, she took from the folds of her gown a cruel and deadly dagger and thrust it into her breast, and falling down upon the body of Casias, died upon her husband.

When Eurastes saw the Tabian stragglers returning with the body of Lysias upon a bier, he tore out his hair and rent his garments in weeping. Then the entire city did likewise, and the maidens sung this dirge:

> *A doom! A doom upon our prince!*
> *A doom! A doom upon our people!*
> *For the hope of the people is cut off,*
> *And the fruit of Eurastes' loins rots.*

So all the people lamented the death of Lysias and the loss of Lyrgoné for many days, but none so bitterly as Eurastes. Some of his counselors came to him and said, "Let the king not worry; let him send envoys to King Arytos and seek the return of Lyrgoné to our people. Offer in exchange the alliance which Prastor came to secure!" But Eurastes said, "You do not know the Manissans, O counselors of foolishness. Do you not know what they will do? They are a people hardy and populous, a people who raise their spears hastily and do not turn back from the slaughter until they have destroyed their foes from the land. No, there shall be no peace now. I will tell you what shall befall us in the latter days: behold, the Manissans will rally around the standard of Casias, who shall now become their martyr. They will muster their men, small and great, from all across the land to make war upon us, as they did to the Illyrs when fair Elifanora was ravished. Then they will come here by their thousands and their tens of thousands and will wage war on us in city and country, in the north and in the south, until we are utterly blotted out of the land. Our cities and our holy places will be burned with fire, our nobles put to the sword and our kingdom will be utterly overthrown." The counselors of Eurastes said, "Nay lord, it shall never be!" But Eurastes only wept.

When Prastor found Lyrgoné to be missing from among his number, he ordered his priests to turn back and return unto the region from whence they had fled. When he came upon the destruction upon the hill of Eleftaia and found the bodies of Casias and Lyrgoné, he sung a bitter lament. Then he ordered his priests to inter their bodies in the side of the hill where they were found. So the priests took the bodies of Casias and Lyrgoné and dressed them in white linen garments. Then, singing the dirges of old Asylia, they interred the bodies of the two lovers in shallow graves upon the sandy hillside of Eleftaia. When Prastor had made sacrifices and prayers, he said, "Let us now return with haste to Manissé, lest the Tabians find us here and put us to a wretched end." So Prastor and the priests went forth from that place in sorrow and haste. But the place on Eleftaia in which he buried Casias and Lyrgoné he called the *Lygonea.**

[*The following epilogue, though not originally part of the tale of Casias and Lyrgoné, was nevertheless appended to the end of this paladology relatively early on as a more satisfactory conclusion than the one described above, also serving to fulfill the prophecy of Eurastes. It is found in all the ancient manuscripts of the Paladologies and is believed to be the gloss of a scribe writing in or around Cadaras at least a century and a half after the events it describes, though it no doubt finds its origin in a much older oral history.*]

In the spring of the tenth year of Arytos, king at white-walled Cadaras, the City on the Plain, the armies of Manissé mustered in the valley outside of the city under their captains and their chieftains. Upon being counted, they were found to be ninety thousand in number, all equipped with armor and spear and sword for the conquest of Tabia, in vengeance for the blood of Casias. They set forth on the twenty-fifth day of the third month and came unto the west by way of Lugaria, encamping at Lygonea on the first day of the sixth month, there paying honor to Casias and Lyrgoné, his beloved. Then they went forth and overthrew the city of Tabés with a great destruction. The city they razed to the ground and did capture and put to death all the nobles and counselors of that great city. They also laid hands on Eurastes, king of that place, and struck him with the sword so that he died. But the Queen Eryice was not taken but found to have killed herself in her chambers. Then the shrines of Succo and the Manes were overthrown, and the peoples put under the tribute of and vassalage of Manissé. Thus did all the lands of Tabia come into the dominion of Manissé.

Fragments of Adrius

❦❧ ❦❧ ❦❧

Adrius is considered the "missing" Paladology, inasmuch as it was expunged from the traditional canon during the centuries when the various texts and oral traditions of the paladins were being compiled. The original tale of Adrius concerns the efforts of one Adrius of the house of Necho to remove a hereditary curse his family incurred in the time of his grandfather Adurax, who slew a Manissan priest and tried to defile a temple at Greystone. In the tale, the paladin Adrius, grandson of Adurax, can only atone for the sins of his family by slaying his own father, Malech, who had apostatized from the Manissan religious tradition and organized a sect to the vile sun god Dakor. Horrified by the human sacrifices and the practice of holding wives in common by Malech and the followers of Dakor, Adrius raises an army in Lemur, marches on Malech's stronghold of Molcha, and puts all the followers of Dakor to the sword, including his own father. Yet because he is now a parricide, Adrius finds the curse of Adurax still hangs heavy on him; nevertheless, Manissa appears in a vision and shows him that he can be purified of his deeds by establishing a shrine to her honor, which becomes the famed Oracle of Orale in Lugaria.

The original paladology of Adrius was very popular in the regions bordering Lugaria for several centuries but is believed to have been expunged from the Paladologies sometime after the reign of King Palereus, later Manissan sentiment being uncomfortable with the concept of exalting a parricide. Nevertheless, the editors and redactors of Palereus's time retained what they thought was the most important part of the tale: the founding of the Oracle of Orale, which was the most popular pilgrimage destination in Manis from the time of Adrius (c. 2940 AR?) until the middle Lesalian period, around 1500 AR. The fragments below tell of the founding of the Oracle on divine commission following the slaying of Malech and destruction of the cult of Dakor and are believed to be only the conclusion of what was once a much longer paladology.

...It came to pass after the burning of Molcha and the slaughter of the Dakorites that Adrius was visited by a dream. In the dream, Manissa appeared before Adrius standing upon a rock, her hand extended gesturing west and saying, "Go and return to the west from whence you came. There in the shadow of the forest called Adarwood, establish a shrine to my honor."

But Adrius said, "O Lady, how shall I know where to build this shrine?" Manissa said to him, "Knowledge will burn heavy within you, and you will know with certainty the spot I shall choose." After hearing this, Adrius awoke from his dream and knew that Manissa had spoken to him. So he left the regions around Molcha and headed west, into Lugaria and the lands around Lemur.

He wandered to and fro throughout the wilderness bordering Lugaria, going up towards Adarwood. Nowhere did he find a site suitable for the shrine, but neither could he rest, for the words of Manissa and the lingering shadow of the curse of Adurax weighed heavily upon him. Thus he wandered and roamed the countryside for three years, searching every shaded glen and hillside for the spot which our Lady should indicate to him. Yet his efforts were in vain, for he found nothing and had no certainty, only restlessness and the weight of the curse pushing him ever onward.

One day, while crossing a verdant field that spread across the wilderness, he looked up and saw a dense grove of poplars at the crest of a gently sloping hill, which went up to the north from the meadow as one goes up from Lugaria. Being very weary from his travels, Adrius thought that perhaps he could find in the grove some mulberries or crab-apples to sustain him. So he aroused himself and went out to the poplars, ascending the hillock and coming upon the grove from the south. As he approached the grove he descried the remains of an old and broken road that had once run through the field up the hillside, though little remained save some cracked stones and a depression in the ground where the lane once ran. Adrius followed the old lane to the cluster of poplars, and, upon entering the grove, found it to be the site of some ruins of great antiquity.

To his delight, Adrius found that the grove concealed a small pool issuing forth from a spring deep in the earth. This pool bubbled up in the midst of the grove and dispersed in several directions, trickling down through the tall grasses and watering the meadow round about. Around the pool were old stones, remains of tumbled down pillars, and other signs of ancient habitation by men.*

Though he found nothing to sustain him in the grove, the water was cold to the touch and clear as fine crystal, so that Adrius desired to slake his thirst by it. He knelt to drink and was startled to see lying near him a large and excellently wrought cup of gleaming bronze which seemed to appear suddenly, for he had not noticed it before. He therefore took the bronze cup, plunged it into the crystal fountain, and took a deep draught from the spring's refreshing waters. Having done this, he immediately collapsed before the pool and fell into a deep sleep.

In his sleep, behold! He was shown a vision. In the vision he saw a very large tree with seven great branches. Off these branches grew many smaller branches. But a great many of the branches were dead and rotting, though they still clung to the tree and made it ugly to look upon. Then Adrius looked and saw a woman coming towards him; she was of great beauty, but also moved with authority. She said, "What do you think of this tree,

Adrius, son of Necho?" Adrius said, "It is in woeful shape, my lady, for many of its branches are dead and rotting." The woman said to him, "Adrius, son of Necho, what must be done?" Adrius said, "My lady, someone must prune the tree and remove these dead and dying limbs." Then the lady brought forth a small axe, exquisitely wrought with a handle of ivory inlaid with gold and a blade exceedingly sharp. Then she said, "To you, Adrius of the house of Necho, do I entrust this axe to prune my tree and remove the rotten branches so that the tree may flourish and live again." So Adrius took the axe in hand and hacked all of the dead branches from the tree until it had been completely pruned.

When he had done this, Manissa appeared to him and said, "So shall the sons of Manissa do to my house, which has grown corrupt and weak. Therefore, establish the shrine of which I have commanded you at this place, that evermore men from all the ends of Manissé may come and find clarity of heart at these healing waters."

When Adrius woke he felt himself refreshed, but also cleansed of body and spirit, as if all the vigor and hope of youth had flooded back into him, bursting the chambers of his heart with vitality and joy. Then he knew with certainty that the curse of Adurax had been lifted, and that this was assuredly the place chosen by Manissa for the shrine. Then did he trim back the overgrowth and pull up the brambles from that grove, planting in their stead lovely wildflowers and fruit-bearing bushes to beautify the spot. He enclosed the spring in a small pool, rimmed in by bricks hewed of marble, and set about the pool flagstones, forming with them a pathway that led down from the grove into the meadow below. When he had done this, Adrius set up the pillars that had fallen around that place, when necessary sending his servants to Karanak to purchase materials to repair those that were too damaged. After all this Adrius erected a small altar to Manissa, and beside the altar he set up a marble pillar to which he fastened the bronze cup with a chain, the selfsame cup with which he had drank when he first came to the grove.

When all this work was completed, Adrius offered sacrifices upon the newly erected altar for the lifting of the curse of Adurax. He called the place *Orale*, which means "dreams," for he said, "In a dream was I commanded to build this sacred shrine, and in a dream was this place revealed to me." Then he constructed for himself a hut beside Orale and dwelt there for the remainder of his days, just as Hazer in days of old had settled upon the hill of Ar Pelaroth and refused to be moved; in the same way Adrius dwelt for the rest of his days at the Oracle of Orale and ministered there. Many persons from all over Manis came to drink of the miraculous waters of Orale, for it was said that whoever came to the shrine with any difficulty or question and should drink from the waters of Orale out of the bronze cup would be shown in a dream the solution to their problem. And as many came to the shrine in the days of Adrius to drink of the mystical water likewise received dreams and visions in which our Lady made known to them many things. Thus the road to Orale from Lemur became the most frequented in all of Lugaria. Men came even from as far away as Anentora and An Hered to seek out the waters of Orale.

When Adrius had ministered at Orale for thirty-seven years he fell ill and died in the sixty-eighth year of his life. Some wanted to bury him there at Orale, but others said, "No, it is a sacred place and ought not to be filled with the bones of the dead." Thus the body of Adrius was carried away to Lemur and entombed at that place. His tomb is still there to this day in the Tower of Sur.

Ezion[*]

⚚⚚⚚

During the long reign of Eumaios the kingdom of Manis had rest from all of the wars and disorders that had plagued it for many generations. Wise Eumaios appointed capable and industrious men to govern the affairs of the kingdom and was solicitous in the attention he paid to the reports that came to him from the farthest reaches of his dominions, whether of distant Lygon in the north or Badoa in the south. He fortified the great City of Manis with bulwarks and towers and established laws throughout all the kingdom, so that men took their grievances to the king's courts and no longer ruled by custom. He also destroyed many of the fortified places that stood here and there throughout the kingdom, either demolishing them or seizing them from the hands of their lords, so that only the king should have possession of the fortified places. To reduce the power of the lords, he oppressed Cadaras with heavy taxes and compelled the lords of the north to do homage to him for their lands. Furthermore, he instituted games to be celebrated every five years upon the plains outside of the City of Manis, so that men of prowess and agility from all over the kingdom came to compete before Eumaios and win honor. Thus Eumaios consolidated the Manissan peoples and ruled with great splendor all his days.

Now Eumaios begat two sons: Erius the elder and Eydor the younger. He also begat a daughter, Eloë, who was fair and industrious but also bold of spirit, for she despised the confines of the Manissan capital and instead made her home in Greystone, dwelling with her cousins. There Eloë saw mighty Embor, a Periorid from the north who came often to Greystone to trade. Embor was bold and handsome, and the fire of Manissa was in his eyes. He enthralled young Eloë, for she had never seen one of the houses of Manissa, though she was familiar from youth with the tales of their exploits. By and by he came to love Embor, and Embor in turn was charmed by her comely form, nobility of manner, and boldness of heart.

But when Eloë petitioned her father King Eumaios for leave to wed Embor, Eumaios refused, who wrote to her, saying, "The sons of Manissa are a two-edged sword, sometimes turned toward good, sometimes to lawlessness. Have nothing to do with this wild Periorid; find for yourself a well-respected prince from Cadaras or from here at the court." Eloë disregarded her father's letter, however, eloping and wedding Embor at Greystone despite Eumaios's wishes. After this she went north with her husband to dwell with him in the hinterlands of An Erras, going up towards Cyrenaica and Ituria, the domain the clans of Perior. There she conceived and gave birth to a son, whom she called Ezion. Her father Eumaios was wrathful with her on this account.

But soon after this the two sons of Eumaios, Erius and Eydor, perished at sea. Eumaios was plunged into grief for the loss of his sons, and all Manissé mourned their passing, for they were of excellent character and comely appearance. Yet was the grief of Eumaios doubled, for besides weeping for the death of his sons he wept because he was bereaved of heirs to the kingdom. He wandered about the battlements of the City of Manis by night, wailing and crying out, "In a single day my house has been extinguished! I am undone!"

After the customary period of grieving was over, Eumaios summoned his counselors and said to them, "Men of Manissé and counselors of my throne, tell me, who shall succeed me to the throne of Manis since my sons Erius and Eydor have been so cruelly wrenched from me?" His counselors urged him to name as heir his nephew Thalon, son of his brother Argoss who ruled as lord in the fair city of Engor upon the eastern plains. But Eumaios said, "Shall I name a nephew as heir when a grandson of my own loins lives, Ezion, son of Eloë by Embor the Periorid?" The lords and counselors were bitterly opposed to naming Ezion as heir, for they said, "The blood of Perior runs in the veins of Ezion. Were he to succeed to the kingship, the throne of Manis would undoubtedly pass into the house of Perior." They said this because they regarded the Periorids with disdain and thought ill of Eloë for her union with Embor.

After hearing all opinions and weighing them prudently, Eumaios stood, silenced his counsel, and said, "Thy counsels I have heard and thy opinions in this matter considered, but by all right the throne ought to pass to Ezion, my grandson by Eloë. Therefore I will recall him to the City of Manis and have him brought up in all things pertaining to prudent government and the responsibilities of the kingship. Thus have I spoken." So the counselors were silenced and assented to Eumaios's judgment, but on the condition that only Ezion should be recalled and Embor and Eloë remain in An Erras. This way, isolated from the influence of his mother, he should be more easily molded according to manner prescribed by the king. Eumaios considered this a fair proposal and thus sent out the decree summoning Ezion to the court.

Ezion was at that time seven years of age and dwelt in An Erras with Embor his father and Eloë his mother. From his mother he learned the gentle refinement and mannerisms of the noble house of Eumaios, for Eloë taught young Ezion upon her knee the script and language of ancient Asylia and had him commit to memory the lays of the Manissans. But from his father, Embor, Ezion learned the ways of the wilderness, of holding the spear and casting it skillfully, of tracking game and bringing it down, and of making war. At times Embor would bring Ezion with him into the wilds of Cyrenaica and beyond, where many of the Periorids were still dwelling. From these relatives of his father Ezion learned of the might of the house of Perior and of the great deeds of his ancestors.

When word came of Eumaois's decree summoning Ezion to the court to be named heir, Embor was set against it, for he said, "Does not Thalon, son of Argoss, live in Engor? This is a plot by the house of Argoss to seize and slay Ezion to clear the way for Thalon to take the throne." Therefore Ezion was not sent south. But not too long after this, Eumaios sent a delegation in person to retrieve the boy. When Eloë and Embor saw the delegation they knew that the matter was indeed from the king himself and reluctantly parted with Ezion, bidding him farewell with many tears. Thus was the boy Ezion brought down to Isle of Dretia and the City of Manis, there to be brought up as heir to Eumaios.

Then was Ezion crowned as prince and heir apparent of the throne of Eumaios with great pomp and splendor in the glorious Temple of Manissa, which stands in the great City of Manis. All the lords and nobles of the kingdom stood about Ezion in the court as the high priest anointed him, placing the royal diadem upon his tender brow. The high priest called out the *Erí Septalë*, the seven-fold blessing:

Might of flame
Fire of speech
Breath of knowledge
Wisdom of wealth
Spear of tidings
Song of bitter edge
Light of life

Then Eumaios, the high priest, and all those present cried, "Blessings upon Prince Ezion! May his days be long! May the wisdom of Eumaios be with him always!"

When Argoss, brother of Ezion, heard of the coronation of Ezion, he refused to make the journey west to the court to pledge fealty to him, for he was envious of Ezion and thought the throne by right should pass to his own son, Thalon. So Argoss and Thalon grumbled against Eumaios and Ezion and refused to come west to pay homage to the new prince. Eumaios entreated them to come, but they would by no means do homage to the son of Embor. After that Eumaios had no more words with Argoss, so anger and resentment smoldered in the hearts of Thalon and Argoss against Eumaios and Ezion.

Nevertheless those days held blessings for Ezion, for he quickly excelled in his studies as well as in feats of physical prowess. As he grew in stature his wisdom increased, as did his comeliness, and there was none at the court that could best him in the hurling of the javelin or the racing of chariots. His tutors praised his wisdom and his trainers his strength, and Eumaios and the people of Manis rejoiced that they had been graced by Fate with such a prudent and handsome heir. Even so, are not the most fruitful trees still blighted by rotten fruit? The counselors of Eumaios and some of the other lords of the realm despised Ezion as a Periorid. They did not rejoice in his good fortune; on the contrary, the more he was exalted, the further they were distressed and spoke ill of him, for Ezion put the cowardly to shame by his fortitude and the avaricious to shame by his generosity. Thus these men of the city grumbled about Ezion and the manner in which old Eumaios exalted him, though none dared voice their opinions before the king.

In Ezion's sixteenth year, it came to pass that Eumaios summoned the great lords, nobles, and counselors of the kingdom for the purpose of holding a grand council, such as had never been convened in the lands of Manissé since the beginning.* By this council he hoped to hear the advice of the great men of Manissé for the purpose of extending the reforms as the king had begun early in his reign. Thus every lord was present in the great City of Manis: lords of Lygon in the farthest west and Anentora bordering Caeylon; grizzled old warlords from Asylia and the refined and courtly nobles of Cadaras; the lords of Cyrenaica under the eternal blue sky and the hardy warrior lords of the southlands. Every dominion was represented before the king. Argoss, the brother of Eumaios and lord of Engor, also was in attendance, along with Thalon, his son, though they did not speak with Eumaios nor see him privately. Yet Embor, father of Ezion, was not summoned, for though Eumaios thought highly of the lad Ezion, he allowed his mind to be poisoned against Embor by his counselors. He alone of the notable men of the kingdom was excluded.

The city was swollen with the entourages of the great men of Manissé, abuzz with excitement and anticipation of the great works the king would accomplish through this grand council. But before Eumaios could convoke the council, he fell ill with a fever and passed away suddenly, to the great astonishment of all the lords and great men gathered in the city. The prince Ezion was at that time returning from the temple at the hour of the evening offering when word was brought to him that his grandfather Eumaios had died. He was at once conveyed to the royal apartments within the palace to await his installation as king, following the instructions given by Eumaios and ratified by all the counselors and lords of the kingdom. But Argoss, brother of Eumaios, knew that there were powerful men and persons of the king's counsel who disliked Ezion. Therefore he said to them, "What stake have we in the son of Embor? Let us drive him from the kingdom and anoint in his place my son Thalon as king, for he is closer to the king's blood than Ezion." Then the counselors of Eumaios and all those who had resented the elevation of Ezion conspired together to deprive him of the throne and make Thalon king in his stead. But Ezion as of yet knew none of this.

Then Thalon, son of Argoss, was summoned and brought before the king's counselors in the great hall of the palace. Argoss set a crown upon his son's head and cried, "Long live

King Thalon! May his reign be blessed!" And all the counselors, nobles and men of the city gathered there cried, "Long love King Thalon!" But the priests of Manissa protested, for they had all sworn solemn oaths to Ezion in the presence of Eumaios on the day when the son of Embor was invested with the princely office. These fled from the presence of Argoss, Thalon, and the conspirators and went to the apartment of Ezion, where they found the lad assisting the ministers of the royal house in the funeral rites and prayers for the dead for king.

The priests told Ezion, "Son, you must flee, for Thalon has been made king by the counselors of Eumaios and even now conspire against your majesty." So Ezion fled by night, taking with him but one servant, and made for the village of Dula on the north shore of the island. There he found a craft, and taking flight from the island of Dretia, and went to Adlor, upon the peninsula of Greystone. From thence removed himself to the north to seek his father's house.

At the breaking of the dawn, Argoss, Thalon, and all their confederates assembled at the Temple of Manissa and demanded the high priest anoint Thalon with the sacred oil, bless him, and proclaim him king. But when the high priest refused, Argoss tore the man's garments from him and had him beaten with rods. Then they took one of their own kin, a worthless fellow called Silius, and made him high priest instead. When Silius had donned the garments of the high priest, he brought forth the sacred oil from the sanctuary and anointed Thalon in the courtyard before all assembled, proclaiming him king and heir to the throne of Manissa.

When he had been crowned, Thalon said, "Bring forth Ezion, son of Embor the Periorid, and let us put him to death." But Ezion could not be found, for he had fled. Thalon was enraged, and upon finding that several priests of the temple had spirited him away, seized such as had aided Ezion and had them beheaded in the courtyard. This was the first sin of Thalon, which he committed while the coronation oil was still moist on his brow.

Argoss said to Thalon, "The lad has certainly fled the island and will try to reach his kin in An Erras! Listen my boy and do not delay, for your throne may depend upon the course of action you choose for yourself this day: send word by your fastest couriers to your friends and agents at Greystone and Cadaras; tell them that Ezion has been declared an outlaw and the house of Embor has turned traitor. Then encourage them to lay waste the estate of Embor and put its males to the sword." Thalon dispatched this message as his father had suggested, so that soon companies of royal soldiers departed from Greystone and Cadaras for An Erras and the estate of Embor. This was the second sin of Thalon.

Would that young Ezion could have followed the straight course from Greystone up to An Erras and warned his father of the calamity that had befallen him, or that he could have gazed once more upon the tender countenance of his mother Eloë! But Fate had not decreed this for Ezion, for though he was a wise young man and full of knowledge and cleverness, it had been many years since he had been in the wilderness, since the days when brave Embor taught his son the ways of the Periorids. Therefore was he weary, exhausted, and lost his way more than once in the emerald grasslands that roll out endlessly east of Greystone. There he labored for a fortnight, lost and starving, taking his bearing by the stars at night but losing his way again every day, sometimes doubling around back, sometimes going west or east and sometimes making no progress at all for want of food. Finally he came into the region around Enna and fair Eidyllion, there finding rest and nourishment in the home of a kindly shepherd, one Pontus.

But the riders sent from Cadaras came at once into the region of An Erras and sped quickly to the estate of Embor. Embor they found in the valley, directing the work of his laborers in the reaping of the grain harvest. The riders of

Cadaras flooded into the valley and struck down Embor with the sword and burned his crop. Then they went to the home of Embor and found therein gentle Eloë, daughter of Eumaios, who was spinning at the wheel by the pink rays of the falling sun. She beheld the killing of Embor from her balcony, and upon the entrance of the assassins into her chambers cried, "In doing this you commit the greatest crime that has been heard of in these lands since the tyrant Sammas put to death the Hazerites! A curse be upon you!" But the riders were moved by neither appeals to honor, fright of curses nor the pity usually elicited by the pleas of the fair sex; upon hearing the curse of Eloë they cut her throat and left her to spill her life out upon the floor of her chamber. Then the home of Embor and Eloë was burned to the ground, and as many servants and maids of the house as could be apprehended were likewise killed.

Ezion, meanwhile, recovered his strength in the care of Pontus, the kind old shepherd of Enna. He spent several days resting, but frequently went out to make prayers and supplications to heaven beneath a terebinth tree that rose from the wilds some distance from the home of Pontus. Upon returning one evening, Pontus said to him, "Know ye the history of that mighty tree?" Ezion said, "Nay, good shepherd, though I perceive it to be of some antiquity." Pontus said, "Aye, for it is the terebinth of Osseia, sister of our Lady. There she used to weep and lament for her virginity in the days before war broke upon the land in times of old." Then Ezion marveled and said, "As Osseia and the house of Ioclus reposed here in times of sorrow, even so has Fate guided me to this hallowed tree in my hour of woe." Pontus said, "Even as Fate raised up Manissa to deliver the Asylians from their distress, perhaps so shall you find good fortune in days to come?" Then Ezion rejoiced and said, "Thy words enkindle hope in me again, good Pontus. Let it be as you have said." Then, when he had rested fully and was restored to health, Ezion departed the house of Pontus bound for the pleasant vales of An Erras.

But when he came unto An Erras and the house of Embor his father, he saw only smoke and destruction round about. After weeping and howling with agony the lad took the bodies of his parents and entombed them in a shaded glade upon the side of the valley and called the place *Molissum*, for he said, "This place has become my Lissus."* Then he opened his mouth and sang these words over the tombs of Embor and Eloë:

> *Sing it not round Engor's plains*
> *Inscribe it not in Merona's marbled halls*
> *Tell it not in Lygon's streets*
> *Nor proclaim it upon the Citadel's walls of stone*
>
> *Slain, the servant of Embor's land*
> *And slain, fair Eloë, from her linen bed*
> *Man and beast cut off alike*
> *A day of darkness for Antyas's noble house*

But even as he sang there came upon that spot a mounted rider of hardy disposition, cloaked in green and staring intently at Ezion. Ezion gazed up at the stranger upon his steed of black and said, "Sir, do you come in kindness to a boy who has just been bereaved of his parents and grandfather in so brief a time, or have you come in vengeance to finish the work which was begun here?" The man said, "By the melodious singing that came forth from you I descry that you are of the house of Manissa." Ezion said, "Indeed, for I am Ezion, son of Embor, a Periorid by blood and heir to the throne of Manis by virtue of the decree of Eumaios, late king of this realm."

The man dismounted and bowed before Ezion, saying, "I thought to find you here, my lord, and for this purpose was I sent." Ezion said, "You puzzle me, sir; by whom were you sent and for what end?" The man stood upright again and said, "I am called Eldax, a Periorid of the house of Antyas and kinsman of your father. I knew you when you were but a stripling and used to accompany good Embor north into the wildernesses around Cyrenaica."

Ezion said, "Grace and peace be unto you, dear Eldax, for thy love of my father and your solicitude for his house. But who has laid waste the estate of my father and put my parents to the sword?" Eldax said, "Do you doubt that it was Thalon, the usurper who calls himself King of Manis and rules in the citadel of Manis upon the island of Dretia? When you fled the isle, he decreed doom for your father, for he feared an uprising of the north under the Periorids. Even now, the name of Perior strikes fear into the hearts of baser men." Ezion was appalled and in disbelief; Eldax said, "Has the whole kingdom heard of these things but you yourself have not?"

Then Ezion said, "Good Eldax, to where shall I flee to escape the hand of my cousin Thalon, who seeks my life?" Eldax said, "I have been sent by our clan to take charge of you and bear you north, into the country of the Periorids, and there shelter you from the long sword of Thalon until the appointed time." Ezion puzzled about this and said, "What appointed time?"

Eldax said, "It is a queer matter, for not more than a fortnight ago I was shaken by a terrible dream in which I was being roused by a great wolf.* The wolf dragged me from sleep and led me into a valley, where I beheld a great fire and a child trapped within the flames. Then the wolf spoke to me, saying, 'This child is Ezion, son of Embor your kinsman, who even now is persecuted by Thalon his cousin who has usurped the throne. Go to the house of Embor in An Erras and find him there. Then bear him away north until the appointed time.' When I told this dream to the sages of our clan, they with one accord appointed me to come south to An Erras and see if the vision would come to pass. I thought it all foolishness myself until the moment I saw you standing by these charred ruins. Yet now I know that Fate has spared you and sent you here to me and that our Lady has cloaked you in her mantle of protection."

Eldax took charge of Ezion from that day and bore him away, to the land of Cyrenaica. This was the domain of the Periorids, lands Ezion had visited as a young child in the company of Embor, his father. In the hardy Cyrenaican wilderness Ezion dwelt again with his kinfolk, Periorids of the clans of Antyas, Crastor, and Erytas, bands of rugged men who lived according to the old ways and knew nothing of the royal court on the island of Dretia or of the laws of the realm. Ezion slept countless nights beneath the stars upon the broken plains around Beru as he accompanied his kinsmen on the hunt. He spent numberless days herding the sheep of the clan Antyas across the broad and desolate steppes of the northern wastes, going days and even fortnights without the companionship of men. In those days he raised his voice in prayer and song and turned his thoughts towards the contemplation of things celestial. And so Ezion lost the refinement of the court and grew into a man of a rugged and grim exterior, though internally he was ever absorbed in thoughts broad and deep. This was in contradistinction to most of the people he had known at the court of Eumaios, who were always of a refined exterior but of minds shallow and frivolous.

After some time Thalon sent spies up into Cyrenaica seeking Ezion among the Periorids, but Eldax spirited Ezion away to Mount Sligo in the uttermost west.* Sligo was a great mound rising off the plains, held by the clan of Crastor, from the heights of which could be seen both the crystal sea to the north and the shadowy green boughs of Adarwood to the west. It was called the Cruachan of the north, for from ancient days it had been the rallying point of the men of Crastor in times of danger, and a place of assembly where important judgments were rendered. The hill was full of caves and hallows round about to which the Crastorids would remove themselves in inclement weather or danger of attack. Here Eldax left Ezion till such a time when it would be safe to return to Cyrenaica, and for five years Ezion existed in the jagged caves and upon the wind-beaten heights of Sligo, hunting and shepherding with the people of Crastor, growing all the while in fortitude, strength, and wisdom, hidden from the eyes of Thalon and of all men.

It was at Sligo that Ezion first manifested the power of Manissa that flowed in his veins, for it became known that he was graced with a mind that could inerrantly discern the truth in every matter. If anyone tried to lie to Ezion or lead him astray in anything, he immediately knew of the deception and exposed it at once. It became known that no man could lie or deceive Ezion, for his heart was ever fixed on truth and he detested falsehood.

After five years Ezion returned to Cyrenaica and the dwelling of Eldax, for Thalon had called off the hunt for him.

But it came to pass, in the second year after Ezion returned from Sligo, being the ninth year of his sojourn among the Periorids, that Thalon, King of Manis, aroused the ire of the people of Cadaras and provoked an insurrection in that city. The lord of Cadaras had died heirless, and Thalon sought to install one of his own companions as lord—a youth who was not of the Cadarasian nobility and knew nothing of the affairs of the region.* This provoked an outcry from the people of Cadaras, who barricaded themselves up within the city and refused to admit the ambassadors of the king who were sent to install the new lord. The ambassadors went away in great anger, reporting to Thalon all that had been done and how the Cadarasians refused to admit them or recognize the king's companion as lord of Cadaras.

Thalon's father Argoss said, "Will you let the greatest city of your realm, the jewel of the north, treat you in this manner? If mighty Cadaras will raise its haughty head against you, what will prevent the other cities of our realm from doing likewise?" Thus Argoss bent the mind of Thalon towards vengeance, and the king began assembling an army to march north and chastise Cadaras for its insubordination.

When word reached Cyrenaica of all that had come to pass regarding Cadaras and the king's plans to chasten the city,

Eldax came at once to Ezion while the latter was ploughing and told him, "Have you not heard that the people of Cadaras are in revolt against the tyrant Thalon?" Ezion said, "What has this to do with me? Of what concern are the troubles of Cadaras?" Eldax said, "Listen to me, Ezion, and thou shalt reclaim thy throne. Behold, all Cadaras is in revolt against Thalon, even more so since it has become known that he plans to chastise them for their disobedience. Nine years hast thou been in my charge, and I tell thee that now is the time appointed by Fate to see thy rising; by our Lady, I can feel it in my bones! Therefore, let us summon together the lords of the Periorids and ride at once to Cadaras. Declare yourself openly to the Cadarasians and they will embrace you as a sure ally against Thalon."

Ezion was indignant and said, "Shall I do naught but ride to the gates of Cadaras, declare myself, and assume lordship over the greatest city in the kingdom of Manissé? Why should they embrace me, who am but dust and ashes?" Eldax said, "Think ye that it is for nothing that you have scratched out a life among the north men for so many years? Have your days among the men of Perior caused you to forget that you are a prince of Manis, adopted son of Eumaios himself? For what reason did Fate raise you up to such an exalted position in the court of the king, or why were you preserved alive in the wilderness and granted the gift of discerning truth in all men? Was it for nothing? Have you not learned to trust in Fate's hand and the providence of our Lady in your affairs?" So Ezion acceded to all that Eldax proposed and went to a place called Dimmura to see who among his people would heed the call to arms.

Then did the cry ring out over the expanses of the north, from Cyrenaica and the fair city of Thán as far as the shaded glades of Zurlina in the east, all the way to the stubbled plains of Periath in the west and the desolate heights of Sligo. All throughout the dominion of the Periorids riders went forth bearing the message, "Let every spear-bearing man who can ride gather at the oak of Dimmura by the borders of Ituria, for Ezion, heir to Eumaios and son of Embor, seeks the lordship of Cadaras!" At the call to arms the hearts of the Periorids were stirred, both by the desire to put one of their own into power and by the memory of the ancient deeds of their house that burned like a flame in their breasts.

Who came to heed the call of Ezion? Down the dusty trails that wind out from Cyrenaica and the endless blue skies of the north came the grim men of the clan of Antyas, led by Danion, a kinsman of Eldax. They passed silently and resolutely down into An Erras and the oak of Dimmura, each cloaked in green and bearing a deadly spear of hardened ash. These were Ezion's own kinsfolk, men his father Embor had known, and all full of zeal for the cause of Ezion. All the men of Antyas that came down with Danion were about two thousand.

Next in loyalty to Ezion were the Crastorids, who dwelt in the uttermost west around Periath, Sligo, and the borders of Adarwood, and as far east as Beru. It was these same Crastorids whom Ezion had dwelt among for five years upon Sligo's weather-beaten slopes. At the sound of the horn, they emerged from their caves, roared at the sun, and hastened across the heather-clad plains by night and by day to be found ready for battle beneath the shade of Dimmura's venerable oak. They came by their tens and their hundreds, over a thousand in all, wielding spears and battle axes and following the lead of their captain Mannax, a titan of a man whose axe was five cubits long.

The clans of Erytas and Marax also heeded the call, four thousand souls who drew the sword under command of their chiefs Amoroth and Prato. The men of Erytas and Marax were experienced warriors of fierce disposition and broad shoulders. They dwelt in the northernmost reaches of the kingdom of Manis, near the border of Zurlina north of Ituria. For many generations the clans of Erytas and Marax had been at war with the Iturs and were trained from tenderest youth in casting a spear, striking with the sword, and using the shield. Amoroth and Prato, upon arriving at Dimmura, fell to their knees before Ezion and pledged him undying troth.

The lesser clans also made a showing: men of Echol and Semnos from the lands round Paros and Kerion, three thousand in all; skilled horse masters of the clan of Aïos who hail from the plains round Asylia, Cyria, and the region of the Manruthim, one thousand six hundred; from the east in the arid regions around Elam and Tilmindor, warriors of the house of Arrax marching under the banner of their lord Gennasius, heir to the lands of Ithaross, about seven hundred in number; from the far distant lands of Albia and the regions north of Adarwood bordering Lygon came five hundred wild men from the clan of Cassos, each with eyes of fire and breasts of bronze.

But also came many Manissans who were not of Manissa's house but nevertheless despised Thalon as a tyrant and usurper and who cherished Ezion and the memory of Eumaios: two thousand mounted Asylian warriors, the long-haired riders of the west; three thousand Moguls from Greystone who were oppressed by the cruel taxes imposed upon them by Thalon; men of An Erras, Enna, Badoa, Halicor, and as far away as Anentora heard the summons of Ezion and mustered at Dimmura, some five thousand in all.

So the total number who came to the standard of Ezion at Dimmura were around twenty-four thousand men who drew the sword. When all the clans had been assembled under their standards and according to their father's houses, the heads of each clan came and pledged fealty and obedience to Ezion and his house forever, saying:

May your throne endure forever!
May you be mighty like Baldor of old and wise like Secum the
blessed!
May sons flow from thy loins like the sons of Necho!
May the zeal of Elphas ever move you!
May you possess the grace of Mariammné, the strength of Perior,

and glimpse that everlasting beauty sung of by Hazer!
May your reign be blessed and your enemies bow before you!*

Then all assembled cried, "Curcua! Hail Ezion, Prince and King of Manis and heir of Manissa's house!" Thus was Ezion first acclaimed king by the oak of Dimmura in An Erras.

On the twenty-fifth day of the third month Eldax said to Ezion, "Let us wait no more, my lord, but proceed at once to Cadaras." So Ezion gave the word and the army departed Gimmura and An Erras, making east for Cadaras. They crossed over the Erriad on the first day of the fourth month, just as the last snows were receding from the pleasantly rolling banks that hedge the Erriad's gently tumbling course.

But Thalon was not ignorant of the massing army, for his spies had brought him word that Ezion still lived and was raising the Periorids in revolt. So Thalon set one of his companions, Attus of Halicor, over an army of six thousand and dispatched him at once to seize the fords of the Erriad and entrench his men in the valley with Cadaras behind them, thus placing themselves between Ezion and Cadaras. But Attus underestimated the celerity with which the army of Ezion moved, for upon coming into Cadarasia he found Ezion already across the Erriad and only three days west of the city. Upon learning this, Attus put his army under forced march, moving night and day with only moments for rest, and thus came to Cadaras before Ezion, but with his men greatly wearied and dispirited from the march.

The army of Attus was not a full day before the walls of Cadaras before the advance scouts of Ezion were first sighted coming up the plain, led by the mounted riders of Asylia. Attus saw the ranks of the horsemen and mistook them to be the entirety of Ezion's force, not knowing that the majority of the Periorids and their allies were still over a day distant from Cadaras. Attus commanded his skirmishers forward to engage the riders and keep them from the valley before the city, meanwhile ordering the remainder of his men to advance up behind. Thus the Asylian riders clashed with the men of Attus all that day at the entrance to the Valley of Cadar with neither side inflicting heavy losses on the other.

But during the evening the main forces of Ezion began to arrive, and flowing into the Asylian encampment all that night, swelled the numbers facing Attus. When Attus awoke the next morning and beheld the myriads of men arrayed against him, he began to tremble and said to his men, "Shall we die here today to secure the throne of the upstart Thalon? Why throw away our lives recklessly?" Therefore Attus came over to the encampment of Ezion under the flag of truce and delivered up his command, pleading for the clemency of the noble son of Embor.

Ezion, relieved at the gesture of Attus, said, "Arise, good Attus, for you shall certainly be spared, you and all yours, for this day you have acted honorably in preferring to lay down your command rather than lead Manissan against Manissan in bloody combat. You have merited my affection and maintained your honor." Then Ezion proclaimed clemency for the men serving under Attus, so long as they swore an oath to never take up arms against him again. When the men of Attus heard these terms they were overjoyed at the prince's generosity and solemnly swore an oath that under no circumstances should they ever take up arms against Ezion again. They also swore many oaths proclaiming Ezion the right and true King of Manis and confirmed these with sacrifices. Thus the army of Attus disbanded and many returned to their homes; but a good many besought Ezion to be taken into his army, and as many as did so were received with joy. Then Attus was given the right hand of fellowship with Ezion and the two men became companions from that day forward.

When the men of Cadaras saw that the army sent against them was no more and heard of the oaths sworn to Ezion, they threw open the gates of the city and welcomed Ezion with rejoicing and festivities. The maidens of Cadaras came forth in festal garments of white, bearing bouquets of blooming trianta roses and brilliant yellow crocuses, singing hymns of praise and merriment as Ezion processed into the city mounted upon his silver charger. When Ezion and his entourage came to the Citadel at the heart of the city, the rulers of Cadaras came forth and did homage. Then they said, "Come, bring forth those men who support Thalon and let them be killed here before the eyes of the lord Ezion." But Ezion said, "Nay, spill no blood on my account, for this day is a day of happiness, glorious in my sight. Let us atone for the bloodletting of the tyrant Sammas, who ruled here in days of old. Let us make amends for the wickedness done by the kings Egol and Pirox in the days when valiant Gilgax and innocent Secum were slain. I have come not to slay but to proclaim peace in all Manissé, an end to the usurpation of Thalon and Argoss and the restoration of the glorious house of Manissa." All present bowed before Ezion in deference to his mercy, and it seemed that Ezion shone with a brightness celestial. His countenance appeared both fair and stern, so that all were in awe of him. Then Ezion venerated the tombs of Secum and Elora which were within the Citadel, and all his entourage did likewise.

Ezion lingered for some time at Cadaras, for every city and district round about for many miles sent delegations bearing him gifts and pledging fealty. Word spread throughout the land that Ezion of the house of Perior had come forth to claim the throne, and all the countryside was fraught with excitement and zeal. The priests of Merona's temple in Cadaras held special vigils of prayer on behalf of Ezion's cause, with hymns intoned day and night for the glorious prince. Eldax marveled at the outpourings of loyalty and affection showered daily upon Ezion and said, "Truly, the authority abdicated by the house of Manissa the day Baldor hurled the spear of Ioclus into the sea in fury has today been restored!" Lords from as far away as Lygon, Thán, Asylia in the west, and An Danara and Elam in the east came and cast their crowns, scepters, and signs of authority at the feet of Ezion, saying, "Come into thy inheritance, son of Manissa." So every day Ezion was exalted more and more in the sight of the people. Yet, his mind was not puffed up, nor did he succumb to pride, but in all things acted with the prudence and humility befitting a prince.

Meanwhile word returned to Thalon at his court on the island of Dretia of the defection of Attus, the loss of the northern army, the taking of Cadaras, and the exaltation of Ezion. His father, Argoss, said, "My son, this Ezion is a treacherous fox! Mobilize your forces at once and strike this bastard Periorid before his insurrection spreads!" But Thalon said, "Ezion is a whelp and the son of a traitor. Is it a great feat to be welcomed into a city that was already in revolt? He shall see how fickle a thing is the loyalty of Cadaras! I will treat with the rulers of Cadaras and offer them their desired liberties in exchange for the head of Ezion." So Thalon sent a dispatch to Cadaras secretly, bearing a letter to the effect that he would forgive the indiscretion of the Cadarasians and grant them certain liberties with regards to taxation and the selection of their own lord if they should but slay Ezion and deliver his head to the court at the City of Manis by midsummer's eve.

Yet when the delegation of Thalon arrived at Cadaras they were in such awe of the esteem in which Ezion was held and the vast numbers of forces that he commanded that they trembled and feared to even deliver the letter of Thalon. Instead, they tore the letter up and threw it in the Brook of Cadar. Then they penned this message and sent it back to Thalon at Manis:

King Thalon-

Let it be known that the things you have lately heard of Ezion, son of Embor, are greater than you have been told. The people of Cadaras embrace him with affection and will by no means suffer any ill word or deed to be made against him. All the great cities of the north have pledged allegiance to him, as well as many of the poorer country districts. Great king, the whole north of the kingdom is in open and general insurrection against you. The army commanded by Ezion is immense and powerful, led by the bravest and mightiest among the Periorids. Let our lord the king do what seems best given the conditions here.

Having sent this letter by courier south, the men arose and fled east to Caeylon where they dwelt until the end of Thalon's reign.*

Thalon raged about the shadowy halls of the palace, saying, "Will nobody be found to rid me of this upstart Periorid?" His father Argoss said, "My son, the time is come for action! Let us put aside the effeminate subtleties of diplomacy and the dark path of treachery and assassination! Muster the armies of Manissé and make open war on Ezion, putting an end to him once and for all. Such is the only way to settle this issue." Thalon, who loved power but was fearful of leading men into combat, disliked the thought of making war on Ezion; yet Argoss harangued and taunted him until finally he relented, saying, "Let it be as you have said, father; but the attack shall be made from Engor, the ancestral seat of our house."

It was around midsummer when the word of Thalon went forth ordering the mustering of the armies of Manissé at the city of Engor upon the southern plains. Of that city, more than six thousand men came forth bearing the sword to fight on behalf of Thalon, whose house had ruled Engor for many generations. A multitude of hillmen from Bados and Halicor, Attus's city, came also to the summons of Thalon, as did two thousand men of Corbalund. Badoa sent three thousand men, and an equal number came from Cadarasia, loyalists to Thalon who were fleeing after Ezion's takeover of the city. Thalon himself came to Engor by way of Bados, bringing in his train two thousand hardened men from the capital garrison. Finally, the men of Greystone sent several thousand spearmen, for ever do the people of Greystone ally themselves with the City of Manis if there is discord in the kingdom. When Thalon and Argoss mustered the men according to their hundreds and their thousands they found twenty-two thousand sword-bearing men in their company.

Argoss said to his son Thalon, "My son, march at once north and besiege Ezion while he holds court in Cadaras! Hedge his army in and do not let them break away into the countryside!" But Thalon ignored the words of his father, instead setting up court at Engor and spending many days receiving delegations from the south, entertaining visiting delegates, receiving gifts, and drinking in the flattery of men. Meanwhile his armies sat idle on the plains outside the city.*

But Ezion was not idle, for Eldax came and said, "My prince, the armies of Thalon are gathered at Engor to make war on us! Quickly, let us march out of Cadaras and into the open country before he brings his armies up and besieges us here!" Ezion concurred with the judgment of green-cloaked Eldax and at once departed the city of Cadaras, marching his army south through the rock-strewn barrens of Molossia, coming finally into the open plains near Halicor after seven days. Thus Ezion escaped into the open country and himself sought to lay siege to Thalon at Engor.

At that time Argoss came to Thalon at Engor, exasperated, and said, "My son, the initiative has escaped us, for Ezion has departed from Cadaras! Up, now, with all thy men, and meet him upon the plains before any more of the kingdom slips out of thy hands." Thalon was still reluctant to take up arms, yet he relented at the urging of his father and his captains, who were eager for battle. Thus he gave the command to put the army in order and prepare to depart Engor. Thalon summoned his pages and donned his armor, a suit of finely wrought mail forged in the smithies of Adlor, adorned with bronze rings and platelets gilded with silver. Then, taking up his battle spear and war helm, he went out to his army encamped about Engor and brought it to order, departing from that place the following morn as the pink robe of the dawn crept up from the eastern horizon. Thalon led out twenty-thousand men, leaving his father Argoss at Engor with two thousand garrisoned men from that city and instructions to fortify the gates and prepare for a siege should he fall in battle.

The grand army of Ezion was six days out of Halicor when they came to a very good land bordering the environs of Engor on the north. The place was a gently rolling pastureland full of wildflowers in full bloom: shining daisies, delicate yarrow, and vast tracts of clover and thistle that blanketed the sloping hillsides and illuminated the land for miles around like a glorious tapestry beneath the brilliant deep blue of the southern sky. Noble Ezion, mounted upon his steed of gray, cast his gaze over the wide vistas that spread out before him and said, "Behold this country, Eldax! Never have I laid sight on any land fairer, neither in the vales of An Erras or the hamlets of Dretia, nor in the wilds of Cyrenaica and Sligo. By what name is this place called?" Eldax said, "My lord, this place is called An Parthas in the old Asylian tongue, but the locals call it Iontaré."*

Even as they were speaking Attus, he who had defected from Thalon at Cadaras, said, "My lord, behold, the armies of Thalon are sighted upon the hills!" Ezion cast his eyes over the gently rolling slopes of Iontaré and espied the movements of troops bearing the banner of Thalon on the distant ridges. Ezion furled his princely brow and said, "They are yet some distance away and perhaps will not be here until tomorrow morning at the earliest. Good Eldax, let us make haste and put our army in order! By Fate, 'tis a shame to have to spoil with blood so fair a ground as Iontaré!" Eldax said, "If it must needs be spoiled, let it be spoiled by the blood of our foes!" So Eldax departed and put the army in order according to the commands of Ezion.

How were the men of Ezion mustered that day at Iontaré? In what order were they called up? The men of the clan Antyas, kinsmen of Ezion under their grim chief Danion, Eldax placed in the center, immediately behind those under the prince. As for Attus, Ezion retained him in the front and set the men under him at the fore of the battle so they should prove their loyalty by bearing the brunt of Thalon's assault. Attus took up the position willingly, saying, "May this noble act blot out the memory of my fealty to the rogue Thalon." Ezion smiled and said, "Do so and win my undying affection."

The Crastorids under their brutish leader Mannax were spread out along the right flank while the clans of Erytas and Marax were likewise spread along the left, going out for half a league until the pleasantly rolling hills of Iontaré drift away into the eastern farm districts. Of the rest who fought with Ezion— the Moguls, men of Cadaras, mounted Asylians and Elamites— these were placed in reserve, along with the men of Echol, Semnos and Arrax, under the command of Gennasius.

Meanwhile Thalon had moved his men in among the hills and sighted Ezion's army forming up as he approached. "So, he aims to give us battle here," said haughty Thalon. "Very well; let him choose his own ground to die upon." Then Thalon commanded half his army to occupy the crests of the low-lying hills of Iontaré as reserves and led the remainder north, some eleven thousand, hoping to engage Ezion before the latter drew any closer to Engor. The men groaned as the banners were unfurled and the legions of Thalon marched out upon the gentle slopes of Iontaré, trampling the wildflowers beneath their heavy steps whilst the sun sank down in the west.

Attus said to Ezion, "My lord, it looks as if Thalon seeks to give battle this very evening, for behold how he marches his troops up with great alacrity!" Ezion said, "Let it be so. Let it be so." At this time Eldax returned and said, "My lord Ezion, all things are arranged as you have commanded. The men are ready to give battle and bring haughty Thalon to his grave." Ezion said, "May it be as you have said, good Eldax. Now, before the enemy approaches too closely, let us ride forth a bit and reconnoiter the ground before us, upon which we will give battle." So Eldax and

Ezion rode out some ways ahead of the army and diligently studied the terrain of Iontaré, now bathed in pink by the dying sun.

Ezion, looking out upon the land and the beauty therein, sighed heavily. Eldax was troubled and said, "Does my lord doubt our victory? Are we not more than Thalon and of firmer mettle?" Ezion said, "I doubt not the resolve of our men, only my own, for despite coming to this point there is one lesson I have yet to learn: to kill a man in combat." Eldax said, "May you learn this one lesson well then!" Ezion pondered within himself and said, "Must it be so? Perhaps if I go forth to speak with Thalon we can come to some terms? Surely even now we can avoid shedding the blood of so many good Manissan men. Must it be so, dear Eldax?"

Eldax drew himself up and said, "Good prince, you mistake trepidation for virtue. Ever has it been the vice of the sons of Manissa to be timid when boldness is called for and bold when prudence is required. We are a peculiar people, throwing spears in anger when a willing ear is needed and then negotiating when we ought to be making our blades drunk with blood. This has been the ruin of our house. Yet it must not be so with you! Be prudent, but do not forsake courage and daring! Be decisive and wield your blade in might, but forget not clemency, wisdom, and humility. If thou can mingle in thine own flesh humility and power, glory and wisdom, courage and prudence, then by our Lady's cloak, you will approach perfection as close as any man. As for this day, the time for talking is past. It is wisdom to know when to grasp the hand of a foe and try, if possible, to turn him to reason. But it is also wisdom to know in thyself when to set your eye on him and hurl a blazing spear through his breast if he will not submit. Thus is the way of the world."

Ezion sighed and said, "You speak the truth, good Eldax. Even still, how I wish it were not so." Eldax, gazing stoically over the flower-spotted hillsides of Iontaré, said, "As do I, my lord. But if there is any other way, it has not been revealed to the sons of Manissé. Therefore, let the brave conquer, the spears go forth, the blood flow, and the bold triumph." Thus did Ezion and Eldax speak as dusk settled over Iontaré and the men settled down to await the coming onslaught they were expecting moment by moment.

But Thalon did not bring his army up to face Ezion until dark had already fallen, and thus had to postpone his assault until first light. His resolve began to waver, for he could see plainly that Ezion had more men than he; he also feared the wrath of the Periorids. Therefore he thought, "Perhaps he can be taken by treachery, as his forefather Perior was in the ancient days." He summoned a certain runner called Diptos and said, "Good Diptos, bear this message to Ezion, that pretender who musters his rebels on Iontaré's flowered hillocks: 'Thus says Thalon, King of Manis: why should you and I be at odds? Is not Manis a great kingdom? Let us come to terms and rule as dual monarchs, you ruling the lands of Cadaras and old Asylia from the north, and I ruling Badoa, Corbalund, Engor, and Dretia from the south. Why should Manissan slay Manissan?'" Diptos said, "Does my lord intend to rend the kingdom asunder to appease this rebel?" Thalon said, "Nay, good Diptos, for it is but a ruse to lure Ezion from his men so that, once in my hands, I may strike him as surely as Hadrior struck the son of Arrax. Thus may I be rid of him once and for all." Then Diptos said, "Let it be so, my lord," and went away to bear the deceitful message to Ezion.

Diptos the trickster crept stealthily through the darkened grasses as the last rays of light disappeared behind the hills; he came to Ezion's camp and presented himself cautiously to the sentries under a flag of truce. He was at once brought to Eldax, who in turn brought the runner into the presence of Ezion and announced him. Ezion was reclining in his tent after having said the evening prayers; he beheld Diptos and said, "What word does that rogue Thalon send at this late hour?" Diptos said, "My lord, King Thalon has no desire for thy blood, nor that Manissan should slay Manissan. He says therefore, 'Let us meet together, you and I, that we may come to terms.'" But Ezion, who could in nowise be lied to, perceived the deception in Diptos's speech and said, "Did you think to deceive me so easily, whose ears can bear no falsehood? Is it not true that you seek to lure me into the hand of Thalon under a ruse in order that he may slay me while I am away from my men?"

Diptos was speechless, for he knew not how Ezion could have so easily discerned his intentions. Then Ezion called out and said, "Eldax! Strike this man! Do not hesitate!" And Eldax came and struck Diptos with the edge of the sword so that he died. Then Ezion said, "Send the head of this deceiver back to Thalon that he may know that we see through his crooked ways." So the head of Diptos was sent to Thalon.

It was shortly before dawn when Thalon received the head of Diptos. He gnashed his teeth and said, "If it is war they demand then by the gods they shall have it!" As soon as daylight broke he gave the command for his advance guard to move up and prepare to charge the slope held by Ezion and Attus. Ezion beheld the marching of the hordes of Thalon and the unfurling of their banners in the red light of the dawn and said, "There is no turning back now! Who will go down to greet our foes?" Attus cried, "Let me now prove my worth, good prince!" and having said this led his men down the slope to break the charge of Thalon's infantry. The men of Attus clashed violently with the men of Thalon; sounds of swords ringing and shields splintering filled the morning air. The men of Thalon proved resilient, for all of them were men of Manis and of fierce character. Nevertheless, Attus came to prevail, for he hurled a spear at one of the enemy's captains and struck him in squarely in the breast. For a time the men of Thalon were thrown into confusion at the fall of their captain; Attus roared and pressed his opponents savagely, driving them back down the hill. Ezion sat motionless upon his mount watching the battle unfold from atop the hillside. When he beheld Attus sweep the men of

Thalon from the hill, he clapped his hands with delight and said, "Thou art proven, good Attus."

When Thalon saw his men losing ground, he panicked. Then he gave the command for the entirety of his army to mass around him and press up the slope, for Thalon reasoned that since Ezion held the high ground a frontal charge of overwhelming power was needed to dislodge him. Ezion cried to all his captains, "Stand firm, men of Manissé! Curcua!" Then all the men cried, "Curcua!" and lowered their deadly spears and whetted blades for the slaughter.

Who can sing of that baleful day of slaughter that begrimed the fair hillocks of Iontaré with gore? A sad day! A dark day! A day of bitterness and lamentation, Manissan killing Manissan in the cool of the morning. What noble souls of Manis fell that dreadful day? Grim Danion, chief of the men of Antyas, struck off the head of one Cestus, a brave young captain who was a companion of Thalon and chief of the palace guards at the court. He had foolishly crossed swords with the relentless Periorid and exposed his head for but a moment, long enough for hawk-eyed Danion to close with him and strike it from his shoulders in a single blow. The men of Cestus were thrown into panic and fell to the slaughter; Danion's folk roared and cut many of them down as they fled.

What of Mannax, the giant of the Crastorids? With his great axe he cut huge swaths of destruction through the enemy's lines, wreaking confusion and chaos all about him. Gennasius of the house of Arrax also slew many men, killing one Neralus, a captain of Thalon, and stripping him of his armor.

When Thalon saw that his forces were again being pushed back he leaped upon his horse and rallied his men, crying, "Come, will you all be driven from this place by these Periorids? To glory!" Then the men of Thalon began to prevail. With his spear Thalon slew Marcellus, a Cadarasian lord who had come over to Ezion with Attus. This Marcellus had seen Thalon and tried to drag him down from his steed as he came up the slope, but Thalon resisted him and ran him through with his spear, skewering him like a pig upon the spit. Thalon also slew Prato, the chief of the clan Marax. Prato had sighted Thalon upon his steed and hurled a spear at him in hopes of slaying the king; Thalon easily dodged the cast, threw his spear in turn at Prato, and struck the chieftain through the eye. Prato's servants dragged him from the battle to tend to him but found he had expired in their arms. Thus Thalon slew many great men of Ezion's captains, and by this rallied his own faltering army.

Then there began to be a very fierce struggle all throughout the gentle slopes of Iontaré. The men of Thalon spread themselves out along the entirety of Ezion's line, pressing especially hard upon the left flank, where the clan of Marax suffered after being deprived of their leader, Prato. In the bloody clashing of arms Amoroth, chief of the clan of Erytas, was also lost, for a stray spear struck him in the throat while he harangued his men; Amoroth gurgled and collapsed to the grass in bloody doom. Then the whole eastern flank of Ezion's army began to collapse.

At this time Ezion was still withdrawn some distance from the battle, witnessing the fighting of the men of Attus and the clan of Antyas from a distance. Eldax flew to his side and said, "Now is the time for action, my prince! The clans of Erytas and Marax are failing; if they fall, we will be outflanked and swept away west with our backs to the mountains! Lead your men into battle!" Ezion reared up upon his steed, lordly and courageous, and cried, "So be it! Curcua!" And in that moment Ezion seemed glorious, no longer a young man but a radiant king, so much so that Eldax backed away from him in awe. Ezion cried with a roar, "To the aid of Erytas and Marax!" Then he charged off on horseback towards the east flank with thousands of sword and spear bearing men in his wake, each eager for glory.

What wonders did Ezion do that terrible day? Though he had never yet drawn the blood of any man, he reared up like an enraged lion and fought as well as any of his illustrious ancestors. From his steed he swung his fearsome sword and struck off the head of Dimoss, one of Thalon's captains, who was leading the charge against the eastern flank; this was the first kill of Ezion. Then he roared and led his troops into the fray, splintering shields and splitting heads with his terrible blows. The men under Ezion poured into the right flank and reinforced the clans of Erytas and Marax, hurling angry javelins at their opponents and driving them back with their stinging blades. After some time their enemies withdrew down the slope, wounded and leaving several thousand slain upon the trampled grass.

But the greatest glory of the battle was won by noble Eldax, that high captain of Antyas's regal clan, for it was his fate to cross swords with Thalon in battle. When Ezion had moved to reinforce the east flank, Thalon saw that the center was weakened and struck at it with renewed vigor, slaying some of Ezion's compatriots. Eldax perceived that the center was weakening and dashed off to stall the advance of Thalon, his green cloak billowing behind him in the morning wind as he closed with the king. The Manissan king struck out bitterly against Eldax with his doom-bringing spear, but Eldax was swift and dodged the blows leveled at him by Thalon. Then did Eldax turn and feign retreat, with Thalon pursuing him furiously across the hillside. But when Eldax had led Thalon on some distance, he suddenly wheeled, faced Thalon, and reared up on his horse. The horse of Thalon stopped suddenly and stumbled, hurling the king down to the earth. Thalon sprung to his feet and searched frantically for his spear, but Eldax the Periorid was upon him in an instant.

When faced with the death-bringing spear of Eldax and finding himself unarmed, Thalon began to weep and offered Eldax the crown in exchange for his life. Eldax frowned and said, "Perhaps if you made this offer to my master he would have accepted it, for he is clement and a nobler man than I." Having said this, he hurled his spear at Thalon and struck the king in the belly. Thalon groaned and toppled to the earth, crying tears of bitterness, and cursing the house of Perior even as blood and life drained from the gaping wound dealt to him by Eldax; the crown fell from his head and rolled into a nearby bush.

Eldax pulled his spear from the gut of Thalon and with the same spear retrieved the crown from the bush. Then he turned upon his steed and galloped off to find Ezion at once. As he rode through the ranks he cried out, "Thalon is dead! Long live King Ezion!" This cry rallied the men of Ezion and affrighted the men of Thalon, whose knees began to tremble and their resolve to fail. Many of the rear guard dropped their spears and fled from Iontaré back towards Engor. Then the entire force of Thalon, being deprived of their king and seeing their comrades already in flight, panicked and ran from the army of Ezion. Thus was Iontaré given over to Ezion.

Eldax approached Ezion and presented him with the crown of Thalon. Ezion marveled and said, "Why, good Eldax, was it not given to me to slay Thalon? It is my throne which he had usurped and my vengeance which was sought against him." Eldax said, "Fate is a strange thing, my lord; perhaps it is so because it has ever been considered the worst of crimes for a king to kill a king. Now it can never be said that you are guilty of Thalon's blood."

Then there was a glorious site upon the slopes of Iontaré: all the men gathered with Ezion, Periorid or other, and bowed low to the ground doing homage to him, saluting him as king and lord. And Eldax approached, and placed the crown on Manis upon the head of Ezion son of Embor. Then all the army assembled there, from the greatest even to the least, roared, "Hail Ezion, King of Manis! Hail son of Perior, son of glory, regal son of Embor!" Ezion was dragged from his horse, and borne upon the shoulders of Eldax and Attus, was carried about the battlefield in victory to the cheers and adulation of his men. Thus, for the first time in over a thousand years, one of the

direct heirs of Manissa's line held the throne of Manissé.

Yet there was little time for merriment, for the giant Mannax said, "My king, is not Engor still in the hands of thy enemies? Does not the lord Argoss, father of Thalon, still rule that land and hold troops there against thee?" Ezion said, "By the spear of our Lady it is so! Mannax! Eldax! Attus! Rouse the men—no time for rest now! Let us press on to Engor and root our enemies out of the land for good." So the captains of Ezion took charge of their men and proceeded south from Iontaré after only a brief respite. By sunset they were gazing over Engor's fertile plains, beholding the fortified city to the left and the great hill of Mimmoth rising up upon their right with the sun falling quickly away to the west.

Then the army of Ezion attacked Engor and overthrew it, defeating the forces of Argoss and burning the city.* Argoss himself was slain in the city's overthrow, for he locked himself inside a tower and refused to come forth and hand himself over to Ezion. Then the flames already spreading throughout the city came and engulfed the tower so that Argoss and those within (mostly persons of the house of Argoss and kin of Thalon) were burned to death. Thus perished Argoss, lord of Engor.

When morning came, the survivors of Engor and the farmers from all throughout that district came and did homage to Ezion, calling him lord and king and heir to the throne of Eumaios and Manissa.

Then began the blessed days, for Ezion was escorted from Engor into Corbalund by throngs of Manissans from every city and region. They followed him for many days along the road to the coastal city of Badoa and hailed him as king in every place and district. Everywhere men and women, from the greatest to the least, were eager to welcome Ezion. They gave unto him many gifts, and throwing flowers before him, sang this song of victory:

Let thanksgiving ascend to the Lady of our hope, for she has
granted a glorious victory;
The horses of the enemy she has thrown down and their
commanders are confounded;
Her spear has struck justly and elevated the fruit of her womb to
the throne;
She is mighty in war and guides the destiny of the
Manissans forever!
Curcua! Curcua!

From Badoa, Ezion and his entourage sailed to Dretia and were joyfully received in the capital at the time when the fields around the City of Manis are golden and the fruits thereof ready to be harvested. There Ezion was solemnly invested as King of Manis with all the proper rites and rituals; but when the high priest Silius came forth to anoint the king with the sacred oil, Ezion cried, "Seize that impostor and strip him of his sacerdotal garments which he defiles by his wearing!" for Silius had been appointed high priest after Thalon had removed the high priest before him. Thus Silius was thrust out of the office of high priest; in his place Ezion installed Pontus, the shepherd who had aided him as a lad when he fled the island of Dretia after the death of Eumaios, and of whose virtue the king was in no doubt.* Thus was it Pontus who consecrated Ezion with the sacred oil.

Then began the long reign of Ezion the Glorious, the Periorid of the clan of Antyas who became King of Manis. He took to wife Celina, a noble woman of the house of Mariammné. By her he begat four sons: Elios, who would succeed him to the throne, followed by Errion, Eldorus and Marius, all of them powerful lords, glorious in appearance and of exceedingly great wisdom. Thus was Ezion's house firmly established in the kingdom.

In all the days of Ezion did truth reign throughout the land, for no lie could be told in his presence, and in all things the king acted with extraordinary prudence and wisdom. All throughout the kingdom he appointed men both competent and humble to handle his affairs. He was just in the exactions and taxes demanded of his people. Temples and shrines to Manissa were erected from the northern sea as far south as Corbalund and from the eastern environs of Anentora even as far as the sandy shores of Lygon and Ligar. These Ezion funded out of his own wealth, for he was always most solicitous to ensure that the Manissan peoples reverenced and honored Manissa, she who had established their dominion in the ancient days and guides their destiny in accordance with the dictates of Fate. No more did the people turn aside to the vulgar cults of the Illyrs or the Caeylonics, nor did the nobles rise and attempt to drive Ezion from the throne. The land was blessed abundantly: the harvests were never so copious, the rivers and brooks had never teemed with so many fish, and the trees put forth fruits larger and more delectable than any that could be remembered. Thus every man was secure on his land and reaped the benefits thereof, and joy was in the heart of every maiden and child, for everything impure and all wickedness was put away from the land. So the Manissan peoples enjoyed many years of peace and prosperity under Ezion and there was no war all his days. So blessed was the reign of Ezion that people blessed each other by his name, saying, "May the grace of Ezion be upon you!"

In the tenth year of his reign, Ezion sojourned to the wildlands north of Enna in the district of ancient Asylia, to the ancient Hill of Cruachan, and there retrieved the bones of his illustrious ancestor Perior. These he had translated with much pomp to the city of Cadaras where they were buried beside those of Elora and Secum. On the day of the translation of the relics he wept before all the people and said, "Now is the House of Perior vindicated before heaven and earth." Then he decreed a holy day in honor of the event, giving Cadaras and its districts a reprieve from taxation for a period of one year.* This endeared the people of Cadaras to Ezion all the more, and they cried out, "The glory of Manissa reigns in Ezion! Long life and blessings to Ezion our lord!" Everywhere he went he showered blessings and gifts upon his people, not to pander to them out of a base desire to win a perishable reputation, but out of sincere and zealous care for the good of all.

Ezion was blessed with many extraordinary gifts and graces, so many so that were this tale to go on even twice as long the half of them could not be told. Yet of all the marvelous works that followed Ezion, the most marvelous was the length of days granted to him, for he seemed to be ever in the vigor of youth and resisted the ravages of age; his hairs grayed only at age eighty and he maintained a quickness of mind until the very end of his days. His wife Celina and all four of his sons were similarly gifted, so that people marveled and rejoiced in the long life of the king and his house. Four generations lived to be graced by the rays of Ezion's just reign; by the end there were few alive who could remember a time when he had not been reigning in splendor.

Yet eventually his hair did gray, his steps began to slow, and the great king began to go the way of all flesh. One year he fell ill and failed to go on progress throughout the kingdom as he had done every spring for many years. Then the shadow of death began to fall over him. He summoned his son Elios and said, "My son, I have had a long life and been graced with many blessings, though it has also been fraught with many trials. Yet have I learned to see the hand of Providence in all things and to regard my blessings and my trials alike as from the hand of heaven for the working out of the good. I am about to go the way of all flesh, and to where I go I know not, for it has not been revealed to the sons of Manissé. Yet remember always that it is better to do justice and suffer tribulation than to inflict tribulation on others while perverting justice in your own soul, for a man who loses everything but retains a pure heart will be blameless, but a man who gains the whole world but does so at the expense of his integrity has lost everything. Do good and flee from evil; fly from a loose woman and from men of low morals. Seek always to do good and goodness and blessing will follow thee all your days upon this earth. Let the grace of our Lady abide with thee now and evermore." These were the last words of Ezion to his son, Elios.

Thus, when he had reigned ninety-four years in peace, Ezion withdrew to his chambers, surrounded by companions and relatives, and expired, being about one hundred and nineteen years of age. Thus ended the golden reign of Ezion the Glorious, he who reestablished the kingship of Manis in the house of Manissa.

Mantarax
The Twilight of the Paladins

❧ ❧ ❧

I t came to pass in the days of Oros that the power of Manis was removed from Cadaras and established upon the Isle of Dretia; thus from the days of Oros unto this day have all the kings of Manis reigned from the Great City, also called the City of Manis, as is told elsewhere. Then, four hundred and fifty years after this, the throne of Manis devolved upon Ezion of the house of Perior, and thus was the lordship of all Manissé finally invested in the descendants of Manissa after many centuries.* Ezion died and was succeeded by his son, Elios, for so did Ezion establish his dynasty.

But after the sons of Manissa took possession of the throne of Manis, their bloodlines began to falter. The line of Mariammné became thin, for the men of Mariammné intermarried with the Lugarians for several generations, so that their blood became more Lugar than Manissan. Thus the sons of Mariammné grew less until there were few left in the land who could trace their descent back to Manissa.

Likewise the house of Necho, though the most numerous of all the houses, failed to produce any men of renown for many generations, and though their bloodline never went entirely extinct, it became weak, and the powers and marvels seen among the houses of Manissa in the former days failed to appear anymore among the people of Necho.

But the line of Perior remained strong, though many of the Periorids forsook the wildernesses and their ancestral lands in the north to settle among the other peoples of Manis. Some became great lords; some also became sages or set themselves up as yeomen in the countryside. Though Perior's line remained intact, the charisms and powers that had hitherto manifested themselves among the houses of Manissa, and among the Periorids the longest, began to wane. At first many years went by without the appearance of a paladin, and then many decades.

The last paladin to appear was Mantarax, son of Mamura, a Periorid of the house Erytas; his grandfather had been Varius, one of the noblemen of the court of the great and wise Ezion. In the days of his youth Mantarax dwelt in An Erras near Ituria, a pleasant land of fruitful valleys and crystal streams that tumble down from heather-clad slopes and lush forests—a region still free from the blight of great cities, as wild as it was in the days of Hazer.

When he was twenty years of age, great power and might came upon Mantarax, like the might of Baldor sung of in the ancient lays. He took with him but a single companion, Ilos, his shield-bearer, and went north into Ituria to make war on the Iturs who dwelt there, for the Iturs had long plagued the peoples of An Erras and raided their farmsteads frequently. Thus Mantarax and Ilos came into Ituria and made war on the Iturs who dwelt there. The chieftains of the Iturs scoffed at Mantarax and sent various war captains to capture or slay him, but whenever Mantarax was attacked a fierce trembling would come upon him and he would invariably slay all those sent against him, so that no one could prevail over Mantarax in battle.

Then did Mantarax come before the great city of Thon, the seat of the Iturs' power, and was set upon by an army of one thousand Iturs, led by six captains of renown.* Yet again did a fierce trembling come upon Mantarax; he cried, "Curcua!" and lunged at the foes ranged against him. His spear was like a great whirlwind round about him, piercing and slashing in a hundred directions, cutting flesh and drawing out life. Likewise, he wielded his shield with such skill and dexterity that no blow struck against him could land its mark, so that wherever he positioned himself in the battle there was heard the constant clanging of weapons and of arrows glancing off his shield. He thus overwhelmed the Iturs, slaying scores of them and killing all six of their captains.

When the chieftains of the Iturs beheld how a single man overcame an army of one thousand, they grew fearful and sued for peace. Thus was Ituria at last incorporated into the kingdom of the Manissans; Mantarax was established as lord over those lands formerly controlled by the Iturs. Then Mantarax overturned the temple of Achor, the vile god worshiped by the Iturs. The altar of Achor Mantarax defiled and the priests of Achor he slew, for they had been guilty of a great many abominations and blood sacrifices. In place of the temple of Achor, Mantarax set up the city of Hamach and erected a magnificent temple to Manissa therein. After this many Manissans came and dwelt in Ituria, and the Iturs gave up their savage ways and became in many ways like the Manissans who lived among them. Thus did Mantarax rule as lord of Ituria for many years.

But when he was old, the youths of Ituria rose up and rebelled against the Manissans. In every city and village throughout Ituria they took up spears and drove out the Manissans who had made their homes there, killing some and plundering others. Ilos, the companion of Mantarax, said to his master, "Lord Mantarax, let us flee Hamach and return south, for in every city and village the Iturs have driven out the Manissans and are bent on destruction!" But old Mantarax refused to flee; instead, he sent Ilos away with many gifts for his years of service, saying, "Go unto King Palereus, who rules at the great City of Manis, and tell him of all you have seen and heard in this land." So Ilos fled away from his master with many tears; but

Mantarax went into the sanctuary of the Temple of Manissa and offered incense.

Not long after this, the Iturs came to Hamach. They burned many of the homes there and did to the Manissans as they had done in the other cities. Then some of the Iturs said, "Let us burn and defile the Temple of Manissa, which stands upon the place where our forefathers worshiped Achor with sacrifices of blood!" Yet when the mob came to the temple they found old Mantarax standing guard at gates, arrayed in priestly robes. Their anger was aroused against Mantarax, and they said, "Behold, it was this one who first brought the Manissans to our land and who defiled our holy place! Let us put him to death!" So they stoned Mantarax; the old paladin collapsed in a heap and died upon the threshold of the temple. After this they burned the temple with fire and pulled down its stones.

Ilos, meanwhile, came unto the City of Manis and told King Palereus of all that had occurred in Ituria. Then the blood of Palereus boiled hot, and he stood up, declaring, "Has the blood of Manissa yet grown cold? Let us avenge the death of our kinsman Mantarax and put these pagan Iturs to rout once and for all!" Then he sent criers far and wide throughout the kingdom and assembled a glorious army, such as had not been seen since Oros and Durmius mustered the Manissans by the brook of Teruel in days of old. Palereus himself rode forth out of the Gates of Oros to take command of the army, gloriously arrayed in finely wrought armor with a helm of silver upon his head, and upon the helm a delicate band of gold. The army was mustered at Greystone; upon mustering the troops and apportioning them among their commanders it was found that twenty-five thousand men had heeded the king's call and come to do battle for Mantarax the Periorid. Also among the men who mustered were two thousand Periorids from among the various clans.

When King Palereus came over across the Norn and arrived at Greystone, he beheld the grand army and wept, saying, "Mark this day well, you priests and scribes of Manissa! For in days of old it was written that kings and lords despised the men of Perior and did them great harm. Let this never be said again, for behold now the love shown to this Periorid by the king and the whole people of Manis! This day we see Periorid ranked beside Lygonian, and Cadarasian and Asylian bearing arms together as in the days of old; we see hardy plains folk from Anentora and Corbalund fighting beside men of Dretian origin. The peoples of Manissé fight as one and their name is one!" Then all the people there yelled "Curcua!" and acclaimed the words of Palereus.

The army of Palereus went up into Ituria on the fifth day of the fourth month, being about the third month of the rebellion. The Iturs melted away before the glorious armies of Manis, for the Manissans marched rank on rank in order and discipline, five thousand mounted riders of Asylia at the head, followed by a thousand charioteers from Anentora and its environs, and then the mass of the infantry lined up behind these. In most places the Iturs fled without putting up any resistance, though some tried to fight and were quickly dispatched. When the Manissans realized that the entire land lay at their disposal, some grumbled and said, "The land lays bare before us; let us put these Iturs to the sword so they shall trouble us no more." But King Palereus restrained them, saying, "No such thing shall we do! We come to pacify Ituria, not to destroy it. Is it not part of the kingdom of Manis, even as much as Anentora or Lygon?" So the army was restrained from slaughter and bloodshed. When the Iturs saw that Palereus was disposed to clemency, they came and did obeisance to him, repenting of the killing of Mantarax and swearing obedience to the King of Manis from that day forward. This was ratified by an oath sworn between Palereus and the Itur chieftains by the oak of Gura outside Thon.

Thus was Ituria pacified and again brought under Manissan dominion. Manissans again came and dwelt in the rugged Iturian highlands and temples were again raised to Manissa throughout the region. Manissans gave their daughters to the Iturs in marriage and the Iturs likewise gave their daughters to be brides for Manissan men. Thus the people were brought together and mingled, so that within two generations men no longer spoke of the Iturs anymore, but only the Manissans of Ituria.

The body of Mantarax was recovered from the ruins of Hamach. Palereus wept over the remains and said, "Truly, he was the last of the paladins." Then Palereus ordered constructed, out of the ruins of the temple, a great tomb for Mantarax, a sturdy stone building with eight sides and capped with a marvelously wrought dome designed by artisans of the school of Andrior. Inside he erected an altar to Manissa, and within the base of the altar he laid to rest the bones of the paladin Mantarax. Upon the altar he had placed a statue of the paladin; the likeness of the statue was that of Mantarax lying down, as if asleep. Thus it was called *Tereldian*, which loosely translated, means "Shrine of the Sleeping Paladin."* In the latter days men of that region used to say that Mantarax was not dead but only sleeping, and that at the end of the age he would awaken again to pledge his sword for the defense of Manissé. This belief is commonly held by the people of Ituria to this day.

Thus the days of the paladins were ended; they are found no more upon the earth.

Minor Paladologies
(*Anridion Inoré*)

Pilux

☙❧☙❧☙❧

ilux was the son of Necho and Engelé, younger brother to Aïross. It was this Pilux who won glory at Anentora by slaying a Caeylonic captain when still a boy, as is told in other tales. In the days when Elphas reigned at Engor, Pilux ventured south into the vast plains of Corbalund, as that region is called by the Enlilim. When he came into Corbalund he saw that the land was plentiful, the soil good, and the people of that region industrious and hardy. He inquired of them, saying, "Let me buy a parcel of land in this place to set up a farmstead and establish my house." But the people of Corbalund said, "By our laws no foreigner can establish himself here unless he first obtains permission from the King of Badoa." Pilux said, "And how do I get to Badoa?" They told him, "A two-day journey to the west, upon the coast of the emerald sea, sits fair Badoa and her proud king, Darion." So Pilux mounted his steed and rode west, and after two days upon the golden plains of Corbalund, came unto the fair city of Badoa on the sea.

But when Pilux came into Badoa, he found the city in turmoil and the court of King Darion closed to all supplicants. He inquired about the state of the city and was told that everybody was in great fear because of a certain baleful creature that was troubling the people, for in the dark foothills north of Badoa dwelt a fearsome beast, three times the height of a man with a gaping mouth full of cruel teeth.* Shortly before the coming of Pilux, the train of the king's daughter, the Princess Amela, was waylaid outside of Badoa; white-armed Amela was taken away by the creature, who was demanding five hundred talents of gold by sunset that very evening in exchange for her. Pilux said, "Has the amount been raised?" And he was told that neither in Badoa or all the dominions of Caeylon could such a sum be found. Then he was told that if the sum was not delivered that Amela would be devoured.

Pilux burned hot with anger and said, "Shall not the blood of Manissa, she who gazed upon the steeds of Agenor and lived, rise up in me to overcome this vile creature?" So Pilux took up his spear and sought the maiden north of Badoa, in the rocky foothills that were bathed orange in the glow of the dying sun. After searching for some time, he came to a certain cave, no more than a vile hole in a rock. Venturing inside, he found the fair maiden, white-armed Amela, bound securely near the rear of the cave, weeping for her fate and for her maidenhood. In the cave with her was a modest sum of gold coins and various articles of silver and precious metals, some of them engraved with signs and letters that Pilux did not recognize.* It was a handsome sum, but the treasure was all befouled and Pilux touched it not.

Then he addressed the girl, saying, "Fair Amela, weep not, for I shall bear you away safely to your father, noble Darion. No harm shall befall you this night." But she said, "From where have you come that you do not know the curse of our land? If the creature finds me gone at the setting of the sun, when the shadows reach long over the stones, he will come and wreak havoc upon our people, for nobody has the might to stand up to him." Pilux said, "I am no ordinary man, for the blood of the immortals runs in my veins. I am Pilux, son of Necho, of the house of Manissa, that great and noble house which has wrought wonders from here unto the farthest north, and from Cadarasia to the shimmering sea of the remotest west." Amela said, "I have heard marvels of your house, Lord Pilux. May it be as you say. But quickly! Hide thyself, for dusk cometh and the creature emerges from his wanderings to see if the gold has been left here as he commanded." So Pilux concealed himself behind a great stone by the mouth of the cave.

Then the sun sank behind the western ridge, the sky was darkened, and the moon cast its pale light upon the sandstone hills and boulders therein, and the first stars were seen shimmering in the dark, blue expanse of the heavens. A foul odor settled upon the place, and then the beast was heard approaching. What a horrid thing it was, for the very sight of it made Pilux wretch. It stood thrice the height of a man and had flesh like a tanned hide, stretched tightly about its thin but powerful arms. Its fingers and toes were clawed, and its head was somewhat like that of a man but somewhat like a frog or wild boar. It had no hair upon body or head and wore nothing save a filthy rag about its loins. When it came to the mouth of the cave, its eyes glared red in the moonlight, and seeing that no gold had been left for him, he bared his cruel teeth and clambered over to the place where Amela was bound, hungry for flesh.

But then came forth Pilux, son of Necho, brandishing his great spear of hardwood tipped with merciless bronze. He cried, "Come taste death, thou foul fiend of the abyss!" and thrust his spear at the creature. The beast uttered a gurgling cry at Pilux, and stretching out its long arm, struck him roughly upon the head so that he was dazed for a moment. The creature leapt upon him, opening wide its ravenous maw, now attempting to bite off the head of Pilux as it pressed its weight upon him. But Pilux regained his strength and wrestled the creature down. When the creature saw that Pilux was full of strength and power unlike other men, it left him and went to ascend the steep hillside to hide itself among the rocks. But Pilux took up his spear and cast it at the foul monster. A fatal throw! The shaft split the air and sunk into the back of the beast between the shoulder blades, whereupon it lost its grip and tumbled down the stony precipice. Wasting no time and eager to complete his victory, Pilux seized a great stone, greater than most men could bear, and ran swiftly to the place where the creature had fallen. There Pilux found the beast writhing on the stone and spitting blood, wounded grievously. Then Pilux hurled his rock and smashed the skull of the creature, dashing its brains upon the sandstone. Thus did Pilux slay the ogre of Badoa.

Amela was restored unto her father, King Darion, and the people of that region marveled at Pilux and worshipped him as a god. But Pilux said, "I am no god, but a man of the house of Manissa, the great queen of the north." The people of Badoa marveled and said, "We have heard great tales of this Manissa, of whom you descend. Is she still reigning in your land?" So Pilux told them of Manissa's deeds and of her passing from the world, and the Badoans marveled greatly at this. Then they told him, "Stay here and abide among us, and tell us more of the wondrous deeds of your house."

Then there was peace between the Badoans and the Manissans who dwelt in the southern plains near Corbalund. A shrine honoring the passing of Manissa was erected in that region, and the Badoans gave their sons and daughters in marriage to the Manissans, and the Manissans to them. But to Pilux, King Darion gave white-armed Amela, his daughter, saying, "No other man has merited such an honor." Then Pilux was granted that which he sought at first, lands to the east in Corbalund, but so pleased was Darion with Pilux that he gave him the amount of ten thousand hectares of the finest grain fields of Corbalund, as well as five hundred sheep. Then Pilux took Amela his wife and dwelt east in Corbalund, where he became a great lord and had many sons and daughters.

Ennus

ong ago there was born to the house of Baldor a child of exceptional grace and beauty.* From the days of his infancy his delicate manner and handsome appearance caused all to marvel and say, "This is one of the immortals of old come in the flesh, for no countenance of a man has ever been seen as beautiful and grace-filled as his." Therefore his mother named him Ennus, which means "beauty." His mother reared him away from the eyes of men, for Ennus, though beautiful and gentle, was fragile and delicate, and thus his mother was determined that no harm of any kind should befall him. Ennus, therefore, did not learn the ways of war, as was the custom with the men of his house, but rather spent his days indoors learning the poems and epics of old Asylia. He did not wear the rugged woolen clothes donned by most Asylian men, but instead was arrayed in fine linens and garments of silk from Caeylon so that his skin would not be agitated by the ruggedness of the wool. Nor did he ever go out on the hunt with his elder brothers, lest some stray spear or arrow strike him, or lest some animal turn on him and tear his flesh. His beauty was rivaled by his character, for he was known far and wide across the lands of the Manissans for his innocence, wisdom, and virtue.

But when Ennus approached his eighteenth year he began to grow restless in the house of his mother and father and desired to go and make a name for himself. His mother begged him not to depart, for never had he been exposed to danger, and she was in great fear for his life. But he reassured her, and kissing her tenderly, departed his home for the east, to the great city of Cadaras, where he became a tutor to the son of a great lord.

All the great ladies of Cadaras who resided at the court marveled at Ennus and said, "Is he not the handsomest of all the sons of men? Surely this must be Ennus, of the house of Baldor, a descendant of Manissa." So many of the great ladies of the court came to call on Ennus, to speak with him and marvel at his beauty. This went on for some time, so that many of the men and lords of Cadaras mumbled against Ennus, for they said, "It is not right for ladies to dote on him such as they do." But all the women of the court were smitten with Ennus.

But of all the women of Cadaras, the one who loved Ennus most was Rhiana, and after some time Ennus came to love her as well. One day, he came unto the house of Rhiana and in the presence of her father and sisters asked for her hand in marriage. Thus Rhiana was betrothed to Ennus. All the women of Cadaras envied her, for Ennus was regarded as the handsomest and most virtuous of all men.

Yet the companions of Rhiana poisoned her mind against Ennus, saying, "Will you accept his offer for nothing? How can you truly know that he loves you?" Rhiana said, "Ennus is the most beautiful of all men who have walked the earth since the dawn of time. Am I not blessed enough already, or has our Lady not been favorable enough to me? What more shall I ask?" Her companions said, "Never has it been known that a man unproven in war or the hunt should take to wife a great maiden of Cadaras without proving his worth. Would you have the men of Cadarasia calling your husband a coward and weakling?

Rhiana said, "What would you have me ask of him?" They said, "Command him to perform some great feat, some deed of bravery and skill. In this way he will have proven that he is worthy of the honor of wedding a great lady of Cadaras. Besides, this has been the custom in Cadarasia from time immemorial whenever a man seeks to wed a noble lady."*

But Rhiana was fearful of asking anything too great of Ennus, for she knew he was delicate and had never before undertaken any dangerous task. She thought within herself, "I will send him on some effortless task, some mere trifle which will pose him no danger. Then the custom will be satisfied which says I must ask him to perform a deed for me." Thus Rhiana came unto Ennus and said, "Before you can be joined in marriage to me, you must prove your bravery by performing a deed of great worth which I will choose." Ennus was crestfallen and said, "Why have you come to doubt my love that you require this boon of me?" Rhiana said, "Such is the custom of our people. Furthermore, the gossiping tongues of the women of this city will speak poorly of you if you do not, as will the lords. Therefore, do as I ask so that our love may be free from the wagging tongues of scoffers." So Ennus resolved within himself to accomplish the task for love of Rhiana and said, "What shall I do, my lady?"

She brought him to the battlements of the city looking east and said, "Can you see there, a far bowshot from the walls of the city, lies the Brook of Cadar, and about the brook the brambles and bushes which flourish there?" Ennus said, "I see them, my lady." She said, "Go forth and pick for me the white rose, which is called *trianta* in the tongue of our people, which blossoms nowhere else but upon the gentle banks of Cadar.* Bring this flower to me and I shall hold your deed as done." Ennus said, "Is there nothing else, my lady?" Rhiana said, "That is all I require. I will remain here and watch thee from the battlements while you go forth."

So Ennus cheerfully went forth from Cadaras, and crossing over the plain outside of the city, came to the ruins of Danath Hered by the banks of the Cadar. He went on some ways and came to the place where the banks of the brook were overgrown with many bushes and flowering brambles. In the midst of one of the great bushes he saw blooming the white trianta rose which is found in no other place but along the Brook of Cadar. Ennus went to put forth his hand and seize the rose, but lo, in plucking it, he pierced his finger on the thorn of the trianta, whereupon he fell down and died there upon the banks of the Brook of Cadar. Rhiana beheld his fall from the battlements of Cadaras; when she realized what had happened, she ran forth to him and found him dead and cold with the trianta still in his hand. Then she wept bitterly and tore her hair from her head, wailing a fierce lament. When the people of Cadaras found out what had occurred, they all wailed and lamented the passing of Ennus with great mourning.

The men came forth from the city and entombed the young Ennus near the place where he fell. Then Rhiana composed these words:

Love is innocent though fleeting
When arrogance and vanity leading
Cruelly spear its tender heart
Drawing life and love apart

Ianthë

anthë was a fair maiden of the Periorids who was bequeathed to the house of virgins in the city of old Asylia.* There she was assigned to tend the sacred fire at the temple, interceding for the Manissan peoples day and night. She had been pledged a virgin since her youth by her father, Narmoros, a nobleman of Cyrenaica. Ianthë entered the house of the virgins when she was twelve years of age and grew to become both lovely to the eyes and pious of heart, and thus was it said of her:

> Ianthë, O Ianthë, thy flesh ever tender
> Thy eyes ever bright, so dear to behold.
> Ianthë, O Ianthë, thy soul wreathed in splendor
> Thy spirit enamored of mysteries untold.

When she was sixteen, Ianthë was made mistress of the house of virgins in Asylia and took on the duties of her office with dignity and grace. It was around this time that young men began to take notice of her beauty. Many of them came to the temple to gaze upon her, or speak with her upon some pretense, lamenting her virginity and her oaths. But being modest and of good character, Ianthë removed herself from their sight.

When her father, old Narmoros of Cyrenaica, was told how the amorous youths of the city were enamored with her, he came down to Asylia and stood before the gates of the temple.

Holding his spear aloft, he cried out, "Let it be known that the man who makes so bold and foolhardy as to be familiar with my daughter Ianthë and thus mocks her consecration, that same man will I bring down to the pit in blood. This I swear by the locks of our Lady." All Asylia heard of the oath of Narmoros, and from that day henceforth the men stayed away from Ianthë. Thus she ministered in peace.

But one day a great lord of Cadaras, Phantos, was sent to Asylia. This Phantos was a captain of King Tullus, who ruled from the City of Manis on far-off Dretia. Phantos was sent by King Tullus for the purpose of soliciting prayers from the virgins of Asylian for the welfare of the kingdom and the fortune of the king's house.* Phantos was a lordly man of great stature and a magnanimous disposition, both handsome to the eyes and deadly with the spear, one of the greatest peers of the kingdom. When it was known in Asylia that lordly Phantos was coming from the east, the women of the city strung garlands about the streets and the elders prepared a great feast to receive him, for not in many years had such a mighty lord visited old Asylia.*

Phantos arrived in Asylia in the first days of spring, when the brooks are cold from the melting of the highland snows and the flowers have yet to unfold their petals to the returning sun. A cheering throng greeted Phantos at the gates of the city, and the priests offered there an ox in sacrifice. Then he was escorted into the city, his train of mounted men and attendants with him. All the people lauded him and cried out, "Blessed be the gracious Phantos, lord of Cadaras, and blessed be the name and lineage of King Tullus, who sends his lord to us in cheer and gratitude!" So Phantos abided among the Asylians and feasted with them many days.

At length the time came for him to go up to the Temple of Manissa and solicit the prayers of the holy virgins who dwelt there. Phantos came unto the threshold of the temple and was received by the priest of that place, a wizened old man called Cerinthar, who said, "Come, my lord Phantos, into the sanctuary and I will show thee the holy virgins who minister here day and night." So Cerinthar took Phantos within the gates and up the ascent which led to the sanctuary. There Phantos beheld the holy virgins of Asylia in prayer before Manissa's shrine, heads bent to the ground in supplication amidst the fragrant incense of the noontide offering. Upon seeing their prayers and hearing their glorious yet solemn chants he was moved within his soul.

But as the virgins came forth from their prayers and made their way across the courtyard to the place of their dwelling, the eyes of Phantos fell upon soft-skinned Ianthë. Seeing her, he said, "By all the gods, Cerinthar, who is that maiden?" Cerinthar said, "Lord Phantos, that is soft-skinned Ianthë, mistress of the virgins here and of all our maids the loveliest, for her piety and virtue are beyond reproach." Phantos marveled and said, "How did it come to pass that such a delicate flower became mistress of the house?" Cerinthar said, "She was dedicated to Manissa as a virgin at a young age by her father, Narmoros of Cyrenaica, who has vowed to slay any man who makes familiar with her."

So Phantos solicited the prayers of the virgins for the good of the kingdom and the welfare of King Tullus while the priests of Asylia offered pigs and oxen in scores to the establishment of the house of the king, and the blessing of the lands of the Manissans. But after the sacrifices were made Phantos would not depart but lingered about Asylia, for he gazed often at Ianthë going to or from her prayers. At first he admired her beauty from afar, bemoaning her virginity and wishing she were not thus consecrated; yet soon these thoughts led his heart to turn covetous and he began lusting after Ianthë and contemplating how he might draw her away from the temple.

One day he came to the temple and pressed himself against the grate which divides the outer court from the house of virgins, hoping to catch a glimpse of soft-skinned Ianthë. She came forth from the temple after the midday prayers, her delicate feet falling gently on the pavement and her eyes cast down in modesty. Phantos called out, "Noble Ianthë, I bid thee speak with me," but she only turned her gaze from him and proceeded on her way. He did likewise on the following day and on the following, but each time Ianthë refused to come to him or even match eyes with him. But Phantos would not be denied, for he pined away for her with sighs and groanings. Exasperated, Phantos summoned the old priest Cerinthar, saying, "How is it that this maiden refuses my summons? I only wish to have a word with her at the grate!" Cerinthar said, "My lord Phantos, you know that her father has vowed death to any man who courts her. Furthermore, she is consecrated and is not for the eyes of man. Surely you can understand these things, for it was in your own city of Cadaras that the order of virgins was first established by Elora in ancient times."

Phantos scowled and said, "Lecture me not on the history of my own city, priest! I know very well what is spoken of Ianthë's grizzled old father. I fear neither his spear nor his oath; am I not Lord of Cadaras, highest captain of King Tullus? Is not my word as good as law throughout the vast dominions of the north? How is it that this single virgin thinks to affront me in this manner before the people of Asylia?" Cerinthar said, "She does such not to offend thee, my lord, but to maintain her chastity and her vow."

"Damned be her vow!" Phantos erupted. "Do you not know that I have come to secure sacrifices on behalf of our good King Tullus?" Cerinthar replied, "Such sacrifices we have offered." Phantos said, "Yet if the maiden Ianthë is not brought to the grate to speak with me, know that I will tell the king that thou hast spurned me and my good will, and that your tidings towards his majesty are ill." Cerinthar was indignant and said, "Such treachery would not go unrequited, my lord! Can you not respect the vow of the fair lady, soft-skinned Ianthë, and depart our region in peace?"

This angered Phantos all the more, and he said, "Presume not to tell me when to take my leave, old man! On the morrow you shall compel the maiden Ianthë to speak with me at the grate or else I shall make an ill report of thee to my lord the king, and he shall require of all your people restitution for the insult." So Cerinthar fearfully and reluctantly agreed to all that Phantos proposed.

But Ianthë would not go out to him, for she honored her vows and feared her father's oath. But Cerinthar pressed her, saying, "My lady, it is necessary for you to speak with him for the preservation of our people!" She sadly consented, saying, "For the love of Asylia and the place of Manissa's birth shall I do as you propose." Therefore, on the following morning, Ianthë saw Phantos waiting for her at the grate and went out to speak with him. She kept her eyes cast down and said, "Say what you will, lord Phantos. You have me in your power."

Phantos took in her fair form with his eyes, withholding nothing from them.* He said, "Tell me, fairest virgin, what benefit you reap by keeping yourself withdrawn here in the house of virgins? Surely this life bears no happiness for you." Soft-skinned Ianthë replied, "My lord Phantos, tis true that I have not known the intimate embrace of a man; I do not know the joy of children sleeping warmly upon my bosom, nor of the pride that comes with a lordly husband and a fertile field sown skillfully; I have heard the laughter of the women who gather the harvest in autumn and bring the sheaves back rejoicing into the gates, though I have known not the pleasure myself. There are a great many pleasures of this life that have eluded me. Yet despite this I am yet happy, for my pleasures are of unseen and my joy in things interior."

Phantos scoffed and said, "Gray hairs and cold winter mornings for interior pleasures! But you are in the flower of youth and your skin is delicate and fair. Your eyes and bright and have the fire of life in them still; thy hair is dark and alluring and thy flesh is as none I have ever gazed upon. Let not the best days of your life fly away from you behind these walls, in the mournful house of the virgins and the solemn pillared courts of this temple! Come, attach yourself to a husband and reserve interior things for the dusk of life."

Ianthë recoiled, saying, "Shall I reserve for my Lady that which by then will have little value, and be accounted as a sacrifice so slight? No, my lord, for in remaining as I am, I have myself become a sacrifice and even in my flesh send forth the glory of our Lady and of the Immortal Ones. Thus, I am a sign—a sign in flesh to the world and to all men." Then she bid Phantos farewell and returned unto the house of virgins.

But this did not satiate Phantos, for after speaking with Ianthë he was all the more consumed with covetousness and lust. While her gracious words were yet ringing in his ears, he determined to carry her away for himself and cause her to forcibly disavow her oath of virginity. He thus went to the Temple of Manissa by night and concealed himself behind one of the pillars in the sanctuary. When it was around the sixth hour of the watch, in the dead of the night, he heard the bells summoning the virgins to the prayers. He crouched deviously while Ianthë led the holy women in chanting the hymns of old Asylia, praising the seven virtues of Manissa and imploring her immortal blessing upon the kingdom. But when the incense was being offered, Phantos dashed forth from his hiding place and clasped Ianthë, holding her tightly in his arms, and dragged her forth from the temple. The virgins were by oath forbidden from leaving the court of the temple, and so they could do naught but wail and weep. Thus the entire city was awakened by the lamentations pouring forth from the temple, though by that time Phantos was out of Asylia with fairest Ianthë, bound and weeping.

When the people of Asylia heard what Phantos had done, they flew into a rage as fierce as had not been seen since the days of Manissa's war against Maruda. Cerinthar the priest tore his garments, saying, "Why did I allow my foolish words to betray my heart and lure Ianthë into this snare? To your steeds, O' Manissans!" So all the men of Asylia gnashed their teeth, crashed their deadly spears of ash against their oaken shields, and mounted their steeds, crying, "North, to Cyrenaica, O Manissé! Let Narmoros, father of Ianthë, be brought down to execute vengeance upon this upstart from Cadaras who fancies himself a lord!" Thus some of the riders of Asylia sped off for ever-blue skies of Cyrenaica to bring these baleful tidings to lord Narmoros. Yet when they arrived they found lord Narmoros worn down with a fever and bedridden, so that it took him many days to recover.

But some of the Asylians sped off southward to the peninsula of Greystone, and from thence were spirited across the Bay of Norn to the isle of Dretia and the court of King Tullus in the great City of Manis. When King Tullus heard how his ambassador Phantos had treated the Asylian people and carried off no less than a descendant of Manissa, he trembled with rage and stood up before all the court. Then he called for his spear, pledging, "By Manissa and all the gods, I so swear that this Phantos shall die for this crime, though he has fought beside me many times." So King Tullus saddled his stallion and departed north with a small troupe of riders to hunt Phantos, for the king was a good man and desired not that Ianthë should be thus shamed.

After leaving Asylia, Phantos rode east with Ianthë for two days without respite, turning aside in the valleys around An Erras until they came to rest in a hidden vale in the shadow of a dark, heather-clad hill. Ianthë besought Phantos on her knees, saying, "You have done a very wicked thing. It is sung in days of old of how the heathen King of Emeric likewise detained the fair maiden Elifanora against her will, so that in the end the valiant woman faced cruel death rather than give her body over to him. Furthermore, that king was destroyed from the face of the earth with all his people by Baldor and the sons of Manissa. Now you, a Manissan like me, think to do likewise? Assuredly, even if my father finds you not, the blazing spear of Manissa surely will!"

Phantos approached her and said, "It is not my wish to harm thee, fair-skinned Ianthë, for I love thee and would be united to thee in matrimony." Ianthë said, "And is this love as it is practiced in Cadaras? To bear a maiden away by force and then try to win her affection with tender protestations of love and matrimony? If so, it is hateful to me." So Phantos pressured her more to yield herself to him, but she would not indulge his desires. Finally he drew his sword and pressed it to the tender flesh of her throat, saying, "Do you not know that what you will not give unto me by consent I have the power to take by force?" She said, "Though you separate my head from my neck you will not separate my will from the oath I have sworn." Then Phantos was greatly angered, and taking Ianthë, again, mounted his steed and took to the old An Erras road, which runs east toward the Fords of the Erriad going into Cadarasia.

But King Tullus, who had been searching diligently for Phantos, reasoned that Ianthë's abductor would attempt to cross the Erriad and bring the maiden back to Cadarasia. Therefore the king laid in wait near the fords on the western side of the Erriad and waylaid Phantos as he attempted to cross the brook with Ianthë. "Phantos, thou fiend!" the king cried. "Release the fair maiden Ianthë and surrender yourself unto me for judgment!" Phantos, seeing the king in possession of the fords with a dozen mounted men with him, trembled and said, "And what shall be done unto me? Is it exile from fair Cadarasia, or else dispossession of the lands I have inherited? Tell me this before I lay down my blade." The king said, "Neither exile nor forfeiture, but death at my hands is decreed for you and sealed by a vow ratified in heaven. Come and kneel before my death bringing spear!"

Phantos said, "I have sworn allegiance to thee and stood beside thee in battle, but do not think that your control over me is such that you can at a word command me to come to my death. Come, defend yourself the best you can!" Then, with Ianthë still upon his horse with him, he rode hard at Tullus and the fords, his sword raised and gleaming in the sunlight. He reckoned against the king striking at him for fear that Ianthë would be hit instead. But bold Tullus, brash and reckless, took careful aim and hurled his javelin at Phantos. The shaft split the air with its whetted tip and found its mark flawlessly, striking Phantos in the throat above the collarbone. The lord of Cadaras spun and tumbled from the horse, leaving Ianthë upon its back spattered in blood and weeping in terror. He crashed into the waters of the Erriad, his lifeless body draining a flood of crimson into the blue tide of the river. Thus perished Phantos, lord of Cadaras, slain by the hand of King Tullus.

Tullus embraced Ianthë and said, "Fear not, Ianthë, for thy aggressor is slain and is no more. Tell me this only, whether or not you maintained your maidenhead in his keep?" Ianthë said, "Aye, my lord." Then Tullus said, "Then, my fairest lady and most dear virgin, I shall escort thee in person back to Asylia. Have no fear; your days of mourning are behind, and no one will dare molest you in the presence of the king." So Tullus sent some of his men onward to Asylia to bring word that soft-skinned Ianthë was found. He retained for himself only a single guard for the road. Thus they turned to the west and began passing back through An Erras.

But meanwhile, Narmoros, father of Ianthë, had recovered in Cyrenaica and was told of Phantos's treachery by the Asylian riders who attended upon him, for they had not gotten word that Ianthë was safe and Phantos slain. Narmoros leapt to his feet and called for his spear, and stroking his grizzled beard, said, "Ah, Phantos, you will rue the day you crossed my shadow, for before I am finished with thee you will curse the day you were born and curse the mother who brought you into this world of light, from which ye shall soon be departing!"* So Narmoros summoned his riders and thundered off to the south in search of his daughter.

Meanwhile King Tullus and Ianthë were encamped near the crossroads of Croas, not too distant from Asylia. It was at this crossroads in ancient days Baldor parted ways with Perior when the latter went east to Cadaras to execute vengeance on the lords of that city. Tullus said to his attendant, a man called Laius, "Faithful Laius, go into the brush and gather for us some kindling that we might build a blazing fire and warm ourselves here before these desolate crossroads." Laius said, "Aye, my lord," and departed into the brush some distance from the road. But while he was gone, Narmoros and his men came creeping up upon the camp of Ianthë and Tullus. Inasmuch as it was dark they recognized not the person of the king, but Narmoros said, "By the cloak of our Lady! There is my fair Ianthë unless my eyes forget my own flesh and blood!" Then his blood boiled hot, for he witnessed the king acting familiarly with soft-skinned Ianthë and discoursing easily with her. He clutched his spear, and said to his men, "Behold the vengeance of Narmoros on he who though to steal my beloved Ianthë for himself!"

Then Narmoros came thrashing out of the brush, roaring like a wounded lion. The very ground shook with the fury of his cry; the stillness of the night was shattered by its rage. The king turned and beheld the gnarled old warrior lunging for him with whetted spear bearing down. No sooner did the king lay eyes upon Narmoros than the old man plunged the shaft with all the strength he could bear into the body of Tullus. The blade pierced the torso of the king easily, for Narmoros drove it through with such violence that it came bursting out the back, pinning the king to the earth. Tullus could not speak but searched in vain with his eyes for understanding, though he found only cruelty in the face of old Narmoros, who planted his foot upon the breast of the king and twisted the shaft further into Tullus's breast, growling, "Since you thought to enjoy the caress of Ianthë, how do you now find the caress of Narmoros, you dog Phantos!"

But the servant Laius, upon hearing the commotion, ran back to the crossroads and beheld Narmoros grinding the last bit of life out of Tullus, who was pinned to the earth and bleeding his spirit away into the dirt. He cried out, "My lord King Tullus!"

Ianthë also cried out, saying, "Father, thou hast speared the wrong man in your anger! Before you is not Phantos, but the great King Tullus, who himself did slay the fiend Phantos and preserved my purity!" Narmoros stood dumbfounded as the light faded from Tullus's eyes. When Narmoros realized what he had done he dropped his spear and ran back to his men weeping bitterly. Laius took up his spear and followed him to avenge his fallen lord, but Ianthë cried out, "Let it be, Laius. Spill no more blood on my account this day." Laius protested through his tears and said, "What will become of valor, my lady, if I do not slay thy father who so recklessly slew our king while he was reclining beside thee?" Ianthë said, "Let it end here or I fear there will be no end." So Laius relented and escorted Ianthë the remainder of the way back to Asylia, both weeping and singing dirges.

Soft-skinned Ianthë was received back into the house of virgins with rejoicing, though the cries of joy were mingled with lamentation at the news of the death of King Tullus at the hands of Narmoros. Old Narmoros was never seen again by Ianthë, for he wandered in the wilderness for some time in deep agony at being found by Fate to be a king-slayer. He later returned to Cyrenaica but found that friend and kinsman alike swore him off as being eminently unlucky and would not do business with him or have him under their roof, for they feared the ill fortune that Fate allotted to him would fall upon them. Thus Narmoros cursed himself and said, "Why was I ever born, that I who sought by the spear to uphold right have become the worst of murderers?" But still nobody came unto him or befriended him and he was an outcast. One day he summoned all his servants and released them from service after giving them generous gifts. Then he washed and anointed himself, and having set his house in order, went inside his chamber and fell upon his sword. Thus perished Narmoros, father of soft-skinned Ianthë.

As for Ianthë, she remained until the end of her days in the house of virgins in Asylia. Though she was content and found again great joy in her state of life, there was a deep sadness about her that clung to her till old age. But when she finally expired, being about seventy-three years of old, it was said that only then did the sadness of the years vanish from her countenance and was the joy of life again seen in her face.

*Amatós**

Back in the days when the land was at peace, the Lords of Asylia ruling securely from the marbled halls of Cadaras, there was a certain man named Menthor who was of the descendants of Perior. This Menthor dwelt in the region of Marmella south of old Asylia and took a wife from among the people of that region named Mirana. Mirana bore him two children, Amatós, his firstborn, and Pipos. But after some time, Menthor got into a bitter dispute with the Manruthim who were dwelling in Marmella over a certain piece of property he wished to purchase. He quarreled violently with a chief of the Manruthim, and in anger, slew him in the field. When he saw what he had done, Menthor gathered up his family and removed himself from Marmella. Going south, he took up residence in the land of Enna in the shadow of the woods of Eidyllion and there established his home, for he feared the retribution of the Manruthim. There were no others dwelling near the wood, leaving Menthor and his household to live in solitude in the shadow of Eidyllion.

The Asylians who dwelt in the region thought Menthor odd, for the Asylian custom is to dwell on the plains and to not make homes too near forests if it could be helped, for the Asylians feared all the nymphs, sprites, and creatures that were said to inhabit the woods in those days.* But Menthor continued to dwell in the shadow of Eidyllion, and his sons Amatós and Pipos came of age among the trees, becoming skilled woodsmen, knowledgeable in all things pertaining to plants and trees, and excelled in both the hunting and taming of animals. But of the two of them, Amatós loved the solitude of the forest more, and as he grew older he wandered ever further into the glades of Eidyllion.

It came to pass one day that Amatós took his younger brother Pipos and went forth into the depths of Eidyllion, telling their father Menthor that they were off on the hunt. But this was a ruse, for secretly Amatós wanted to show Pipos a clear, cold fountain he had found in the midst of the forest. So they traveled into the shade of the wood all that day, coming unto the fountain and its glade sometime in midafternoon, when the sun is at its softest and the light therefrom fell upon the forest floor in a thousand dappled spotlets. As Amatós showed the fountain to Pipos, it happened that a forest nymph came unto the fountain to drink. She beheld Amatós from behind a cluster of lilacs and was smitten with love for him, for he was exceedingly handsome, young, and ruddy, but also strong and of noble appearance. She pined away with longing for him until she at last resolved to make him hers. Thus she called to the trees, and the forest lurched and caused a great crashing someway off from the brothers, so that Pipos was filled with fright, and looking away, cried, "What comes this way, brother?" But while he was thus distracted, the light-footed nymph swept down upon Amatós and carried him off into the wood. When Pipos turned again, he saw only his brother Amatós flying from him. Pipos pursued him some way, but the nymph easily outdistanced him until his brother Amatós was seen no more. So Pipos returned to his father's house in fright, for he perceived that his brother had been carried away by some nymph. Thus there was mourning in the region north of Eidyllion for many days for Amatós, son of Menthor.

Pipos did not know what became of his brother or who had carried him off. Some tales say the name of the nymph was Aella, but others say it was Kadmeia, and that Amatós was smitten with a deep sleep and taken into the far interior of Eidyllion, among the sprites and satyrs, and there drank of the nectar of the sylvan creatures and became kin to them. Thus, putting on immortality, he was wed to the fair nymph beneath the full moon, foreswearing the habitations of men forever. So the tales say.

Iassos*

⟨⟨⟨ ⟨⟨⟨ ⟨⟨⟨

nce, in the land of Lygon, there dwelt a man of the house of Mariammné called Iassos, who above all others of that age was renowned for prophecy, healing, and many miraculous works. Not infrequently did women bring their sick children to him, and as many as did so had them restored to health. Once, in the wintertime, he was summoned to the city of Lygon to attend to a noblewoman whose daughter was wracked with fever and lingering on the cusp of death. Yet Iassos took several days in coming to Lygon, so that when he arrived the child was dead, and the mother was wrathful with him. He went into the room where the child lay dead and laid himself down on top of the corpse. Thus he laid for three hours, until at the end of the third hour the breath of life returned to the child. She was presented to her mother alive and in good health.

Another time a certain woodsman came to him crying, "Blessed Iassos, help me, for my only son has become lost in the wood! Lo, I have searched these two days for him and found him not. I fear the boy is dead." Iassos said, "Bring me a bow." So the distraught woodsman brought him a bow. Iassos went at once to the edge of the wood where the lad was lost; from there he fired an arrow deep into the trees. Then Iassos said to the woodsman, "Follow the path of the arrow and you will find the boy." The woodsman went into the wood at the place where he saw the arrow fly, and after walking some distance found his son. The boy was wedged in a hole in the earth with a broken leg, affrighted and famished from his ordeal, but otherwise of sound body. The arrow of Iassos the woodsman found stuck in a tree near the hole. He brought his boy forth from the wood rejoicing and marveling at the ways of Iassos. Many such works did Iassos do. Thus he was known all throughout Lygon and the far west for his powers.

Despite his works, Iassos was also known to be an ornery man of ill-disposition and foul temper, for at times he possessed the ability to read hearts and minds and was put out at those who came before him with impure motives, or who otherwise appeared vain or demanding. Once a certain noblewoman of Lygon was with child and was desirous to discern the sex of the infant before it was born. She summoned Iassos to come and attend on her, but Iassos sent her a message saying, "It is not for the vain curiosity of idle women that I have been graced. Go thy way and bear all things with patience." The noblewoman was angered and summoned Iassos again, and again he replied the same. Finally she said, "I will go to him myself and press him until he accedes to my request and tells me what sort of life it is that grows in my womb." So she gathered together her retinue and traveled out of the city to the dwelling place of Iassos.

But Iassos, perceiving what she wanted, would not come forth from his home or speak with her. The woman became furious and beat upon his door, threatening him with all manner of punishments if he would not come forth at once. At last Iassos emerged from his door and said, "Thou hast vexed me sorely, woman, and so shalt thou be vexed, for I tell you that the life in your womb shall be still-born." When the woman heard this she went away scoffing, for she did not believe Iassos and said, "He is merely a fool."

Yet, not long after this, she ceased anymore to feel the movement of the infant in her womb and began to be concerned

But her maids and attendants said, "Even were such a misfortune to befall thee and the infant to be stillborn, it proves nothing. Are not stillbirths common? Put no faith in the words of Iassos, for he speaks of his own authority and not by any prophetic spirit." So the woman heard these words gladly and spoke many boastful things against Iassos. When Iassos heard this, he said, "Stillborn it shall be and even more! May I be cursed and driven from the earth if this child is delivered as other children are, for all from the least to the greatest shall see and marvel. Then all will know that I, Iassos, speak naught but what is revealed to me."

Then came the days for the woman to deliver the child, and she was confined to her bedroom and attended upon by the maids, servants, and midwives. But when she labored and brought forth her child, the midwives and maids cried out and fainted in fright, for they saw that the woman had given birth neither to a boy, nor a girl, nor to any child whatsoever, but to a log of wood, which fell from her womb to the floor. The woman was told that she had given birth to a log, which she refused to believe until the bloody log was taken up from the floor and laid upon her breast. Seeing this, her flesh turned white, and her life left her. The log she delivered was placed in the Temple of Manissa in Lygon as a testament to the power of Iassos and the marvel that his words had brought forth. Then all the people of Lygon were in fear and awe of Iassos.

Now the king in those days was one Irglax, a worthless fellow, a drunkard and a lecher who wasted the inheritance of his fathers and brought shame to the throne of Cadaras.* Because of his lecheries, Manissa smote him with an incurable disease which wasted him away and gave him great pain in his belly. He spent great sums on doctors and witches to heal him but found that he only suffered more. When he heard of the powers of Iassos, he said, "Is not the power to grant life to my flesh residing with this son of Manissa? Let him be brought forthwith to Cadaras." So a detachment of riders was sent to

Lygon, a journey of many weeks, that Iassos might be brought to Cadaras for the healing of Irglax.

Yet Iassos refused to go, saying, "I will by no means heal that lecher Irglax. Let him waste." But the soldiers compelled him and adjured him in the name of the king and of Manissa. Finally Iassos said, "Since you adjure me by the name of my Lady, I will go with you peaceably. But I will by no means bring health to your king. Indeed, I will die before I do any such thing."

Thus Iassos endured the long journey from Lygon all the way to Cadaras and was in a particularly sour mood when he was brought in before King Irglax. Irglax was delighted at the appearance of Iassos before him and commanded him to do some marvel for the court. But Iassos stood silently and would not patronize the king. So the king grew angry, saying, "Do you not know that I command thy allegiance? You will heal me yet, you bastard son of Manissa!" Iassos said, "By the cloak of our Lady, I will not do so." The king was indignant and said, "Then why for did you make this long journey all the way to Cadaras from Lygon?" Iassos said, "It was not of my will that I came." Enraged at his obstinacy, Irglax had Iassos thrown into the dungeon and whipped.

The following day Iassos was again brought forth and again ordered to give healing to the flesh of the king. Again he refused, and again Irglax had him taken to the dungeon and beaten. And likewise again on the third day, and again Irglax sent Iassos to the dungeon, this time had him tormented with hot irons.

But on the fourth day, when Iassos was brought forth bloodied and weakened from days of torment, he said, "My king, I have resolved that I will indeed work a marvel for you, and afterwards will heal your affliction if I am able." Irglax was delighted and said, "Does the court hear these words? Iassos has come to reason! Tell us Iassos, what sign will you work in this court?" Iassos said, "I will make a wager with the king that I can hold in my breath longer than any man of the court, nay, longer than any other man of Cadaras." The king marveled at this and said, "What shall be the price of this wager?" Iassos said, "If I lose, I will not only release the king from his illness but will abide here in Cadaras the rest of my days and do whatever the king asks of me. But if I win, the king will give ten talents of gold to the city of Lygon for the construction of a hospital to tend to the infirm, the pilgrim, and the orphan."

The king's avarice was aroused at the wager of Iassos and he eagerly agreed to the prophet's terms before the court. "We shall see the endurance of Iassos! But first let any others who would challenge you come forth and do so." So many great men and lords of the court came forth and held in their breath, but no man could hold his breath in for longer than a few minutes.

When all who wished to challenge him had done so, Iassos came before the king and held in his breath. The king watched Iassos, curious as to how long he would deny himself of air. Some jested and attempted to distract Iassos, but he gave them no notice and easily surpassed the limit set by the other men. The king applauded, but his servant told him, "Hold thy applause, my king, for Iassos holds in his breath still yet." Then Irglax and the court marveled, for Iassos continued to hold his breath and stand motionless. Irglax said, "How long shall he stand thus?" Some thought that Iassos was breathing through his nose, until Irglax had a clamp placed on the nose of Iassos. This changed nothing, so the king ordered a band of wet leather tied about his mouth. Yet still Iassos held in his breath.

It came to pass that Iassos stood motionless withholding his breath for the duration of the hour, and then two hours more, until his face was grotesque and contorted and his flesh sickly in pallor. The women of the court were in terror of the phenomenon, and finally Irglax cried to his guards, "Enough of this witchcraft! Awaken him!" The guards removed the clamp and leather and shook Iassos, but he would not release his breath. They examined him and said to Irglax, "My king, it appears that Iassos has died and is even now dead upon his feet." Irglax stood up, saying, "This cannot be! Surely it is some jest!" So one of the guards of Irglax took the butt of his spear and knocked Iassos in the head, thinking to rouse him. But instead, the head of Iassos snapped off the neck and fell to the floor as effortlessly as a gourd falls from the vine at the time of the harvest.

Irglax pounded his fists on the floor of his chamber and cried, "Damned be thou, Iassos, son of Manissa!" But the king immediately began to cough blood and took to his sick bed where he was wracked with pain. In the night he cried out and died after much suffering, his belly being greatly bloated and hideous to look at. The guards came to move him from his bed to his coffin and happened to drop his body upon the floor by accident. When they did so, the belly burst open, and it was found that the innards of Irglax were turned to mush, rotted away with worms and vermin.

Iassos and Irglax were buried one beside the other in the Valley of Danathor without the walls of Cadaras. But the lords of Cadaras, remembering the king's wager and fearful of the wrath of Iassos even from beyond the grave, gathered ten talents of gold and sent them to Lygon as promised. The Lygonians constructed there a hospital to service the infirm, the pilgrim, and the orphan, according to the wishes of Iassos. And so the Grand Hospice of Irgallos stands to this day in the fair city of Lygon.

Erixus

෨෧෨ ෨෧෨ ෨෧෨

When the Kings of Manissé removed their thrones from the Citadel of Cadaras to the Isle of Dretia, there was a certain man of the house of Perior called Erixus, who traced his descent to Manissa through the line of Crastor. This Erixus dwelt in the wilds of old Asylia and was a hunter of great renown, for he pursued the stags and the boars of that region across the rugged plains and heather-clad hillocks, sometimes turning into the land of Ituria to hunt the great elk that winter there.

In the days after the kings established themselves at Dretia, word came to Erixus from the king, saying, "Erixus, son of Perior of the noble house of Crastor, some hither to the royal city and be a captain among my fighting men."* But Erixus replied and said, "Shall I forego the life of my ancestors for the confines of the court? Shall I abandon the eternal blue skies of Cyria or the endless pastures of Asylia? Shall I give up my spear to the command of king rather than wield it freely at whom I choose, be it beast or man? Nay, I shall remain in the north as my ancestors the Periorids have ever done, aloof from the affairs of court and king." Thus Erixus scorned the invitation of the king and continued his nomadic life.

Coming into the wilderness west of Cyrenaica one spring, he pitched his camp by the springs of Beru and hunted the game of that place for a fortnight. But the lord of Beru came forth and drove Erixus away, saying, "Do you not know that I hold these lands by the leave of the king? No man may hunt or fish, reap or sow here without my consent." Erixus was put out and said, "Ever have the sons of Perior defended these regions against the encroaching dominion of the corrupt kings who once ruled from Cadaras! Ever have the sons of Perior roamed these wilds freely, hunting and traveling as they please, without leave from any man, least of all a whelp of a captain from Beru." Then the lord of Beru attempted to lay hands on Erixus, but Erixus hurled his spear at him with great fury. The blade crashed into his breast, shattering flesh and bone, dropping him to the grassy earth in bitter death. Then Erixus took up his spear and went forth to hunt the game of that place.

When the people of Beru heard of the killing they were appalled. The lords and great men of that region all gathered at Cyrenaica under the governance of the lord of that mighty city. They declared Erixus an outlaw, exiling him from the realm on pain of death. So the people of Beru and Cyrenaica harried Erixus out of the land, compelling him to withdraw to the southwest until he came to the barren slopes of the Cyrian Highlands. The Manruthim had dwelt there in ages past but had since moved on, so that the land was desolate and devoid of any habitation of man or beast. So Erixus scratched out a living for himself from the roots and seeds abundant in the shade of the highlands and ate the small game that make their homes in the cracks of the rock. But his heart was downcast, for he thought, "Is there no place for liberty and honor anymore? Shall a man take insult and leave it unavenged? Shall the only glory be found in the service of the court? Shall a man seek leave from some lord or captain to dwell in the open bounty of the earth? Shall he be forbidden from claiming his own piece of land to sow and reap without permit of the mighty? Behold, the world has changed since the days of yore, and it is hateful to my soul." So he brooded on these things in the shadow of the highlands.

When Erixus had dwelt there some nine months, it came to pass one evening, as he was reclining upon the earth beneath the setting sun, that he heard the movements of some great beast upon the slopes not far from his dwelling. He donned his cloak and took up his spear, heading forth at once in great curiosity, for in the nine months he had dwelt there he had seen no large game. He cast his eyes northward along the ridge in the shadows of the highlands and beheld a great stag meandering among the crags and wild grasses of the slopes.

Immediately his heart was struck with joy unspeakable, for the stag was no ordinary beast but was of exceptional size and beauty. Its coat was of purest white, whiter than the linens of any launderer; its stature was majestic and noble, its antlers blazing and glorious in the pink of the setting sun. The heart of Erixus was set on fire by the very sight of it, so that he was carried away with himself and thought of nothing other than pursuing the creature. He dashed forth at a furious pace, spear clutched in whitened knuckles, hoping to overtake the stag upon the slopes.

Yet the stag bounded away, covering immense distances with its regal strides, heading up gradually along the slopes towards the highlands. Erixus panted and pursued the creature, his own flaming desire quickening his feet and giving him speed and swiftness unknown to him prior. He pursued the stag upon the desolate highlands, the lonesome ranges of Cyria broken only by the forms of Erixus and the gleaming stag of his desire, which he pursued with single-minded passion. The sun dipped below the western hills, and the stars and heavenly luminaries dotted the deep blue of the night sky, but Erixus and the stag sped along their course over the stubbled plains.

Then it seemed to Erixus as if he were caught up into a dream or vision, for his feet seemed to no longer touch the ground but rather flew over immense distances in single bounds, so that he knew not whether he was running or flying. Whole landscapes passed him by at a moment's time, barren fields and rocky crags, as well as verdant valleys and pasturelands spotted with pleasant rills and glades gleaming white in the light of the risen moon. The world passed Erixus by, and he found himself carried off in a current of desire, unable to cease his pursuit, though he tried. But always the stag bounded on before him, just out of his reach yet driving him ever onward despite his intent. Though he found he could not cease his chase, he acceded to all that befell him, for he found unspeakable joy in the pursuit of the creature.

At last they came to what Erixus thought could be the very edge of the world, the great forest Arcorian, called Adarwood by the Lugarians, which lurched up before him as a vast wall of dark green. The stag sped onward towards the ancient and foreboding wood, and Erixus cried out, "Come blessing or woe, I perceive that I shall not now be parted from thee, O sacred stag of Agenor. Let me come unto the domains of light, to the resting place of my Lady and the everlasting hills." Then Erixus pursued the stag into the depths of dark Adarwood, neither scraping branch nor gentle leaf staying his foot or halting his speed. Night and darkness closed around Erixus, and despair overtook him, for the sight of the stag was lost to his eyes; yet ever onward he dashed, deeper and further into the wood, into the midst of a stifling blackness, darker than anything the eye of man had ever beheld. A momentary terror fell over Erixus. But by and by his heart was lifted, for in the field of his mind's eye a great sunrise broke upon him, warming his spirit and quickening his flesh. Then new and marvelous landscapes opened before his eyes, and a gentle sun that warmed both flesh and spirit and hurt not the eyes, illumining new and wonderous things to him. The stag stood before Erixus, glorious and splendid in radiance. Erixus panted in desperation, reaching out towards the creature, hoping now only to touch its coat. But it bounded onward, deeper into the glory that increasingly surrounded Erixus on all sides, both within and without. And

Erixus dropped his spear and hurled himself after the stag, and henceforth was never seen again among the world of men.*

Thus is it told among the people of Beru and Cyrenaica and whispered among the tents of the Manruthim to this day.

Cyllinus

༄ ༄ ༄

Here is recorded the vision which I, Cyllinus of the house of Arrax, a Periorid by blood, saw in the days when I dwelt by the sea in the land of Cyrenaica in the white-towered city of Thán. It was in the glory of the spring, when the apple blossoms bloom throughout the windy pastures of old Asylia, and the trianta roses glisten white before the pleasant waters of the Brook of Cadar. Then it was that I went forth from white-towered Thán to lift up prayers and make intercession before heaven in the yellow meadows that sweep endlessly across the face of the land southwest of the city. There I fell to the earth and bemoaned the fate of Manissé, saying, "O immortal powers, who govern all things by thy wisdom and who have set among thy number our Blessed Lady, Manissa, to whom has been entrusted the special providence over the people called by her name, how long shall we linger in darkness and despair? For the sons of Manissa remain wanderers and vagabonds upon the earth to this day, noble men, sons of glory, destined for kingship but deprived of all rule and authority. Furthermore, since the days of Eíra the witch and the days of Sammas the Usurper has the land of the Manissans been polluted with foreign gods, gods of the Zhinkanthans, Marudans, Caeylonics, Elamites and Illyrs, and in the name of these idols great wickedness is done all throughout the land. When, O Lady of Good Hope, shall the throne be returned to thy house and the foreign abominations be swept away from the land?" Thus I prayed for three days and took no food or water all this time.

I was thus praying in the meadow at the tenth hour of the third day, when the disc of the sun begins to dip behind the western hills at the world's edge, around the time that the evening prayers are chanted in the temple at Cadaras. Then, behold, I heard a voice calling to me, saying, "Cyllinus, son of Perior." I was greatly unnerved by this and did not at first respond, thinking to have lost my senses. But the voice called again, saying, "Cyllinus, son of Perior." So I said, "Here I am. Who is it who calls to me?" The voice said, "Get thee up while the prayers are yet being chanted. Go upon the old road from the northern gate down to the sea at once. Find the spear of Ioclus which has lain at the bottom of the sea since the ancient days." I marveled at these words, for the spear of Ioclus had not been seen for many generations; but I did not want to disobey the voice. Therefore I stood upright and walked until I came to the seashore by Thán, passing by way of the old road that leads down to the sea, a distance of a furlong.

Then I came to the sanded white beaches to the west of the harbor, which were desolate then, as it was near the closing of the day. The sun had fallen, and the sky was darkened, the first stars of the evening having made their appearance. I looked this way and that and moved to and fro along the beach, even wading some distance into the salty waters of the sea. I looked about the beach for several hours, but despite my efforts I could not find the spear. Seeing the night was fully come, I collapsed upon the seashore and cried out, "I have searched hither for the spear of noble Ioclus of old, cast into the eternal blue depths by the rage of Baldor, son of Manissa, but have found it not!"

Then I heard a voice which said to me, "Look into yonder stars." Then I began to be in a trance, for my soul was quieted and peace came upon me, and I seemed to be lifted out of myself. Then I looked into the sky and beheld the sign of the spear, Laoön, blazing exceedingly bright in the Rua Calidé, that place in the northern sky which was called empty in former days. The stars flared and blazed hot in the heavens, so that the deep blue of the night sky seemed illuminated. Then the starlight became a single great beam and cast its glow down to the earth. I marveled, for the starlight fell upon the waters not far from me, perhaps two hundred yards out from the shoreline midway between the harbor and the point where I was standing. Then the voice said, "There, Cyllinus son of Perior, will you find the spear of Ioclus. Go unto it."

So I waded out into the sea again, the night having fully come but the place being illuminated by the brightness which Laoön cast about. I had gone someway out when I found the water came up to my midsection. Then I began to tremble, for I knew not how to swim; but the voice said, "Have no fear, Cyllinus son of Perior, but go further." Then I went a little further on until the water came above my chest, and I began to be terrified, for there was still some distance to the place indicated by the light; but the voice said, "Have no fear, Cyllinus son of Perior, but go further." So I went on until I could no longer touch the seafloor and waded in the dark waters the best I could, mystified by the brightness and the voice but in terror of the water in which I struggled to stay afloat. Then the voice said again, "Have no fear, Cyllinus son of Perior, but go further yet." At last I came to the place in the water where the light of Laoön fell, to the place indicated by the voice.

Then the voice said, "Cyllinus, son of Perior, go down to the spear of Ioclus." But I said, "My lord, whoever thou art, even now I tread water because of the great depth. How shall I have the endurance to swim down to the deep and retrieve this spear, of which it is told that it took three men to bear it?" The voice said, "Look to your left and to your right." Then I lifted my eyes and, behold, two naiads came unto me, one from the left side and one from the right. Their appearance was azure, like the vault of the heavens; they rode upon chariots of foam and wave, their silvery feet dancing delicately upon the crests. Fully beautiful and enchanting were they, with eyes of crystal and skin as soft as the seafoam. They took me by the hand and brought me into the depths, beneath the shimmering expanse of the waters and into the deep places where men were not meant to dwell or permitted to look upon. Down they took me, through the darkening shades of blue, till all around me was chill and black as pitch, so that I feared for my very life. But they sung a melodious tune and Laoön's light pierced the murky depths, dispelling the gloomy darkness with the radiance of the heavens. Then I saw the barren ocean floor and thereupon it before me was the very spear of Ioclus itself, stuck into the earth as it had landed centuries ago when hurled from the angry arm of Baldor.

I pulled upon the spear but could in nowise loosen it, though I tried until my strength was spent. Then a voice called to me in the depths and said, "Thou hast done well, Cyllinus son of Perior, in finding the spear of Ioclus. But know that the time of its restoration is not yet come, and thus shall it remain as it is." Then I was crestfallen and said, "My lord, why didst thou send me forth to retrieve the spear if it cannot yet be removed?" Then one of the naiads cried out and said, "Behold, the Lady of the Sea!" Then I looked, and behold, the sea parted around me so that I stood upon the dry ground, and all around was a frightful noise and a great tumult, as if the sea, the earth, and the heavens were all being shaken.

Then from the heavens I looked and saw a fearsome storm, such that all the sky was covered over with towering clouds of black and gray, and from which thunder pealed and lightning cracked dreadfully. I trembled and fell to my knees, for I saw in the clouds the figure of our Lady, Blessed Manissa, running and leaping as if in great haste. And all the heights of the clouds and their billowing folds were as mere hills under her feet. The naiads said to me, "It is not given to thee to retrieve the spear, but only to gaze upon it. By this you may know its place and learn of the restoration of the kingdom to the house of Manissa, for by the sign of the spear you shall understand that the authority of Manissa shall be restored; even now she hastens to bring justice to the land, She Who Walks Above the Clouds.* But come, we must show you many more things." So they took me and brought me up again, away from the depths and the spear towards the upper reaches of the sea and the night sky. As they brought me up I cast my eyes back and saw the spear of Ioclus closed up in the impenetrable blackness of the sea bottom once again. Then the vision of Manissa was taken from me.

The naiads brought me up near a strange shore, for there was no land round about as far as the eye could see, save for a mighty mountain that rose out of the watery depths. This mountain was the greatest peak I had ever laid eyes on, for its cliffs were so steep and boulder-strewn that no man could scale them. The height of the mountain was so lofty that I could scarce crane my neck far enough to see its top, and my heart became faint at the sight of its immensity. Then the naiads left me and said, "Fare thee well, son of Perior!" But I cried out and said, "What shall I do?" They said, "Cast thyself upon the shore and go unto the majestic peak you see rising before you, which dominates the sea and sky." No sooner did they leave me than I found myself cast upon the stony shore in the shadow of the mountain and at once fell into a deep slumber.

But my visions continued, for a man in a robe of white awakened me. He said, "Eat this," and gave me a small wafer, and upon eating it I was filled with strength and stood upright. Then I said, "Where are we, sir, and what is this mighty peak whose top is shrouded in cloud and gloom?" The man in white said, "This is Mount Eriar, that mountain whose snow-covered tops are sung of in all the lays of Asylia from days of old." Then he told me, "Cyllinus, son of Perior, climb the mountain." Though I trembled at the thought of ascending so forbidding a peak, I felt strengthened and ennobled by the bread which he had given me and began to ascend the cliffside.

My mind was in constant terror, for the ascent was exceedingly steep, and only with great difficulty could I find footholds upon the cliff. When I had gone but half the way up I became petrified with fear, for I was a great distance from the ground but had yet a long climb to the clouded peak and was weary. But then the man in white appeared to me again upon the cliffside and gave me another of the small wafers to restore my strength. "Sir, what is this food with which you feed me?" He replied, "Sustenance for your journey, the remedy of mortality which will allow you to stand in the presence of the immortals."* So I ate the bread and immediately was renewed, both in strength of body and in courage of spirit. Therefore I began again to ascend the perilous cliff.

After I had climbed what seemed like an immeasurable distance, I saw the clouds parting as I approached the summit. Coming up before me was a great plateau upon the summit of the mountain, upon which was a marvelous hall. I scrambled to the top of the mountain and stood upon the summit before the hall, beholding its glory, for it was a hall greater and more magnificent than any hall of men. It was of an exceedingly great height and made of a stone I knew not, though it was white like marble and smooth like alabaster or porcelain. There were diverse colonnaded galleries and porticoes, so many so that it would have taken me months to explore them all. When I cast my eyes up to see its height, I perceived that it went upward for a great many stories, the number of which I could not tell. The place was resplendent with glory; radiance that shone forth even more the nearer I approached, till I was afraid to come any closer because of the burning brightness of that glorious hall.

Then a man came out to me, radiant, shimmering, and full of power and virtue.* His presence caused me to tremble, and I hid myself behind a stone before the gate of the hall. He called out in a loud voice, "Have no fear Cyllinus, son of Perior, for you have eaten of the sacred and life-giving food and are thus enabled to stand in our presence despite thy mortality. Come, for you have been expected." I came forth cautiously and said, "Who are you, my lord?" He replied, "I am Orix, the son of Manx by the maiden Orianna, whom he took from the fair pastures of Asylia and ravished upon this very mount. From the seed of a god and a woman did I spring, and because I was conceived upon this holy mount it has been granted to me to minister in the golden hall and gaze upon the countenance of the immortals." I bowed, saying, "Tell me, Lord Orix, most mighty and illustrious forebear of the Manissan people and of our Lady, for what reason was I summoned hence?" He said, "I will show thee."

Then Orix reached down and took my hand, trembling though I was, and ushered me up the flight of stairs into the antechamber of that luminous hall. When I entered the hall I cast my gaze forth and saw that the place was much greater on the inside than it had appeared even without, and that though I stretched my eyes I could not see where the hall ended, nor could I perceive its dome or ceiling; rather, the expanse of the whole world seemed to be contained within it. The walls were of many fine and precious jewels: some of deep red and possessing a dark fire, like rubies in appearance; still others were a gentle and soothing emerald; others there were of shimmering white or blazing gold, so that the entire hall was filled with a multitude of various colors, all distinct but harmonious and beautiful in their convergence. I immediately fell on my face and said, "Good Orix, I am not worthy of such sights or such glory." Orix stood me upon my feet and said, "Do you marvel at what you have seen in this, which is only the antechamber? You shall see still greater things within."

Then we went on, though I know not how long we moved nor how far, for it seemed to pass before me in an instant, but an instant that comprised the whole duration of the world from its beginning unto its end. As we moved through the antechamber I saw that the gems burned within with lights that seemed to have breath in them, and from them issued forth a gentle but moving melody. I said, "What is this, my lord?" He said, "These are the souls of the just who sing forever in the halls of the blessed." So I perused this vast array of gems, marveling at their beauty and taking in their melodies as we moved through the hall.

By and by we came to an immense gate of solid gold, spanning at least fifty cubits in breadth and at least twice as many in height. Then Orix said, "Be opened, thou gates of gold, for thy master, Orix, bids thee!"* At his word the colossal gates swung open of their own accord, as effortlessly as if gliding on air, and revealing behind them, if it were possible, an even larger hall of vast size with an even greater glory. This hall blazed with a light brighter than the sun and was filled from end to end with persons of every rank and age, both men and women, young and old, the lowly and the great. Yet they all seemed alike glorious and magnificent, full of power and authority, so that I feared to look upon even one of them, let alone cast my gaze wide and take them all in.

Orix said to me, "These are those heroic souls who have merited to feast forever in hall of our forefathers." I marveled, for each person glared at me sternly, but in their austerity was a compassion and a friendship that seemed to make their severity one of mercy and grace, which flowed out of their very form to overtake me and flood me with thoughts of goodness, till I could in nowise tell their compassion from their severity, for both seemed to mingle together in the blessedness that they exuded continually. Orix said, "Gaze not, for you are brought here not to satiate thine own curiosity but to see the wonders appointed for thee." I gasped and said, "To see wonders? Have I not yet seen them? If these be the halls of the blessed, where the souls of the just go when they fly from their bodies of clay, then shall I willingly leave my own flesh behind and remain here for all ages!" Orix's countenance became red like fire, and he said sternly, "Such has not been ordained for thee, for thou will certainly return from here and finish thy days in exile upon the earth." Then I wept.

So we passed through the crowds who mingled in that great hall, and though I strained my ears to hear their melodious and happy conversations, I was unable to catch but fragments of their words, and even these I could not descry, for it seemed to be a foreign tongue. Then we came after some time to what appeared to be the end of the hall. At the end of the hall was there a great and marvelously wrought table, fashioned with such craftsmanship as I had never known was possible. It was neither of wood nor of stone, but of some material I knew not, though it was decorated minutely with the characters of men, horses, trees, and many other figures. I inspected these figures closely and marveled, for they appeared to move before my very eyes, tiny men engaged in combat with one another, others alone lamenting in the wilderness, and still others ruling in splendor from ornate thrones in glorious palaces, all moving about before me upon the table. I said, "What do these figures mean?" Orix said, "Upon this table and in these figures is depicted the entire history of the Manissan people from the beginning of the world unto its very ending." But I could not tell at which side of the table the history began and at which side it ended.*

Then I said, "Who feasts at this great table?" Orix said, "This is the table at which the children of Manissa will sit with all the kings of Manissé at the end of the world, rejoicing in the honor that is rightfully theirs." Then I said, "Where are the sons of Manissa, great Orix?" Orix said to me, "They will not rest nor sit down at their great table in this hall until the fruit of their loins sits upon the throne." Then Orix motioned to a great gate that stood at the far end of the hall leading outward and said, "Go thither, Cyllinus, and you will see greater things than this." I said, "Will you not accompany me?" He said, "Nay, for others purer than I shall guide thee." So I went forth through the gate and came out into a broad space, which upon entry I saw to be a garden of the most wondrous size.

This garden was exceptionally vast and magnificent; its size alone was so immense that it seemed to stretch from the rising sun in the east to the uttermost west, and its depth seemed to go on to the very horizon. The garden was filled with all variety of fruit bearing trees and fragrant flowers, more glorious than even the rooms of the hall, if this were possible. Everywhere was a most delightful odor that filled my body with wholeness and brought peace to my heart. Yet upon closer inspection of the blossoms of that place I saw that each flower wrought a great mystery: for as I drew near to take in their fragrance, I gazed into their blossoms and perceived grand visions opening before my mind's eye.* Behold, in looking at one single flower I seemed to see in an instant all the brave deeds done in the land by every man since the beginning of time, and forward to the very end. I beheld the cunning stratagems of the hunter seeking his prey, the boldness of men closing in battle with other warriors, the works of mighty men of old in their struggle against tyranny and many other like deeds, of men and women, which seemed to take an entire lifetime to witness.

I know not how long I lingered at that flower, but when I pulled my gaze from it I saw standing before me two maidens of exquisite beauty and grace. I was immediately ashamed in their presence and fell down before them, pressing my head into the grass of that garden and clutching the hems of their gowns. Then said I, "Most noble ladies, the sight of thee fills me with shame, for I am unworthy to even look upon such beauty as you possess." Then one of the women spoke unto me, saying, "Rise, most humble Cyllinus, for you have found favor with the immortals and have been appointed to bear witness to the things you see and hear." So I stood upright on my feet, though I could not look either of the maids in the face because of the radiance that came forth from them continually. With my eyes downcast I said, "Tell me, most excellent ladies of the garden, by what names shall I call you?"

They said, "We are they who were graced in life with great beauty, but with which came much sadness. One of us was taken away from our native land in the tender days of youth to be brought to the heights of Eriar, there to bear a son by Manx who would become the father of all the Asylians. The other, by virtue of her unrivaled beauty, was coveted by the very King of Caeylon and was thus sought by him, and in the lust of the king was born the freedom of all Elabaean peoples, though it came not without a bloody price." Then I understood that those who stood before me were Orianna and Osseia, of all Asylian maidens the most renowned for their exceeding beauty. They continued, "Because we received a bitter lot in the days of our flesh, it has been given to us to find rest forevermore in this garden of happiness. Come and behold the pool at the center of the garden whose waters refresh this place continually."

So they escorted me for some time throughout the garden, explaining to me many wondrous things and showing unto me the various flowers and fruits that grew therein, which they said were figures of all the virtues and powers found among the sons of men. After some time they brought me to a grove which was of such excelling beauty that my breath seemed to fly from me when I beheld it. This splendid grove was surrounded by poplars majestic in size and beauty, within whose circle was found a crystal pool surrounded by many varieties of flowering plants and blossoms. From the pool went out sundry rills and streamlets that flowed out into all parts of the garden and watered the plants therein.

Then, behold, sitting beside the crystal pool I saw a woman of exceeding radiance and marvelous beauty, not as beautiful as Orianna or Osseia but more wonderful to look upon by virtue of the plentitude of power that seemed to dwell within her. She was tender and delicate but seemed at the same time to be immensely powerful and glorious. Upon seeing her, I found that I could not clearly discern her stature, for at times she seemed to be of the normal size for a woman, but at other times she seemed to be very large, almost gigantic, so that if she should stand upright the very vault of the heavens would not be enough to contain her height. She was clothed in a simple gown of white linen and her hair was long and golden-brown. My words falter and fail at describing her countenance and the look of her face, save to say that it was like none I had ever seen before but was also somewhat familiar, as someone one sees in distant youth and remembers only a vague shadow of for the remainder of their days.

Then she looked at me and said, "Cyllinus, my son, do you see what they do?" Then she told me to gaze into the pool, and upon doing so I saw the whole vista of all the lands of Manissé spread out before me. She said, "See what evil has befallen our land!" Then I saw men whom I perceived to be the sons of Manissa, driven from the cities and hounded into the wildlands, persecuted, and hunted like criminals for the fear and dread they inspired in the hearts of tyrants. After these I saw passing before me all the wicked kings who had ever sat in Cadaras and all their evil deeds—and following these the vulgar cults of the foreign gods that clung to the land like leprosy.

Then the lady wept into the pool, her tears causing ripples which upset the water and disturbed the vision. She said, "Even so shall the land be purified, though not without much suffering." Then I marveled, for when the water cleared I saw the images therein change: the wicked kings were thrown down from their thrones and their citadels crumbled and collapsed; the shrines of the pagan gods were burned and defiled, and those who frequented them were smitten with a curse. Then a great water spread out and covered the whole land, making green and verdant the barren heights of Cyria, turning the wilds of Ituria into a garden of delight, and transfiguring the grasslands of Asylia into and endless meadow of divers flowering plants. Cadaras, Engor, and Bados were cleansed with torrents of water, causing their pillared halls and pointed towers to glisten white as the clouds of the northern sky. And in the heart of every Manissan was nothing found other than loyalty, justice, grace, and every virtue. Thus land and people were purified.*

When this had happened I saw one like a child who grew in stature to become a great warrior. He plunged his hands into the depths of the sea and brought forth the spear of Ioclus, glittering in the rising sun and even more glorious than it had seemed in the tales of yore. Then many voices were heard crying, "Thus is dominion returned to the house of Manissa and the fruit of her womb!" By this I understood that the kingship had returned to the house of Manissa.

When I saw this vision it seemed that something fell from my eyes and new insight was given to me. Then I perceived that the woman who sat by the pool was Our Lady herself. I fell at her feet. She stood upright, blazing and full of splendor; the brightness of the sun seemed to be in her gaze while the beauty of the moon and the stars was in her form. No longer was she clothed in a linen gown, but in a beautifully wrought breastplate, intricate and wonderful to behold, and a pair of breeches as shepherds wear. In her hand was a burning spear; lightning issued forth from her eyes. I cried out, "Lady Manissa, let it be as you have shown me in the pool! Let the land be cleansed and power to thy house restored!" She said to me, in a voice that was at once gentle and terrible, "It shall be as you have seen in the pool; nevertheless, it is not given to me to determine the times and seasons of such things."

I said, "My Lady, are you not the highest of all the immortals? If you should resolve to unsheathe your whetted sword, who can stand in your way?" She said, "Ah, Cyllinus, thy heart is noble and good, but thy understanding is still clouded and uncertain." I said, "Grant me wisdom, my Lady." She said, "Do you forget that I myself am of the race of men, born of Ioclus to the fair lady Grianné of Cadaras? In the days of my flesh I travailed, suffered, persevered, and learned wisdom through the trials attendant upon the life of men. I am no god, nor is the immortality granted to me mine by nature, only by a singular grace. Yet for a purpose was I exalted among all Asylians and peoples of the west: to be a protectress, an intercessor, and a patron of thy people and a perpetual sign of unity.* All of this has been entrusted to me. Would you do well and have your days be blessed in the land? Then henceforth let no one called by the name of Manissé forsake the turning of hearts and minds towards my goodness in time of need. For to me alone has been entrusted the care and judgment over all the peoples called by my name."

I said, "My lady, can you bring my mind so near to these ineffable mysteries and not lead my heart on to the fullness of truth? Tell me, if you, being mortal by nature but exalted by grace, have been entrusted with care and judgment over all the peoples of Manissé, who is it who is greater than thee and has entrusted to thee this power?" My Lady said, "I will show thee, though you will not be able to bear the vision." So with much trembling I was led through the garden to the base of a great precipice, the height of which extended upward to the very vault of heaven. At the base of the precipice I saw a figure of exceedingly great size, like a man, though much larger and of immense power. His hoary head was topped with long, whitened hair and he bore upon his countenance a great beard, equally thick and heavy. Despite his vast size, he sat immovable against the precipice and appeared to be sleeping, but my Lady awoke him were her voice, saying, "Awake, O Manx, Lord of Eriar and of old the refuge of the peoples of Asylia!" Then Manx awoke as if from a trance and spoke in a voice of thunder, "Let my lady command what she will and thus will I do."

I marveled and said, "How is it that Manx, who is accounted a god, does the will of Manissa, who by her own words is but a mere mortal?" Manissa said to me, "It would not be far from the truth to call Manx a god, for he is of great antiquity and of power unfathomable to you or to me. He is a great power, one of many, who ruled the world in the ancient days and will rule it again in the age to come, but who now sleeps and awaits the time of his going forth."* These words made little sense to me as I tried to fathom their meaning, but Manissa said, "Trouble yourself not about such things; it is sufficient for you to know that you have gazed upon his form, something no Elabaean has done since the days of Orianna and Orix."

I said, "Grant me one more boon, my Lady, in answering another difficulty that arises in my mind. Now that I have laid eyes upon both Orix and Manx, the father of Orix, I do not understand why the immortal father seems less glorious than the mortal son?" My Lady said, "In this age glory has been given to the sons of men, especially those of my house, and thus does Orix seem more glorious than Manx, who slumbers. Yet in the age to come, Manx and all like him will be exalted and will show forth the glory they possess in their very nature. So great will that glory be that even Orix will prostrate himself on the ground in awe."

When she had finished discoursing with me, she said to Manx, "Mighty Manx, this I command: take us aloft and set us on the highest peak of Eriar." So Manx lifted us aloft in his gnarled, ancient hands and set us on an exceedingly high place covered in snow and ice, so lofty that there could be no higher place in all the world. All the lands of the earth seemed small and contemptible so far below, while around us and beyond to the horizon on all sides stretched an expanse of sky and below us ocean without end.

Manissa said, "You have asked who has exalted me and placed me in the care of the peoples of Manissé? I tell you, look to the north and you shall see." So I gazed out over the sea towards the north, straining to see some sign of what my Lady spoke of; yet did I see nothing. So I said, "My Lady, I see nothing." Then she took me and fed me with the white wafer that had been given to me before I ascended Eriar, saying,

"Cyllinus, thine eyes cannot yet bear such sights, yet eat and look again, for perhaps you shall see some semblance of the truth you seek." So I ate the wafer and was refreshed and ennobled. Then I looked again out over the waters.

Behold! Coming over the waters, at the very horizon where sky and sea touch, I beheld a great light, like the light of the sun. At first its rays were imperceptible, but by and by the rays grew and became great beams, casting their light out over the sea far and wide and falling even on the heights of Eriar where I stood beside my Lady. Then the light emerged from the circle of the world and became blazing and glorious, like another sun in the sky but more so, for beside this light the sun seemed weak and even disappeared in its radiant brightness. Yet it was not unpleasant to gaze upon this light; on the contrary, it seemed to draw my mind and will toward it with a power I found unable to resist. I began to pant and long for that light, seeking to know it, to immerse myself into its purity and to thereby become pure myself, for within it seemed to be not only the ground and summit of all mysteries and truths, but also supreme love, unending bliss, and limitless beauty. All other things seemed as dung before this light and its goodness, and had my Lady not spoke I would have thrown myself from the summit of Eriar into the very sea itself, which was made golden by the purifying rays of the light that seemed to glorify everything it fell upon.

I fell on my face as though dead, but my Lady said, "Cyllinus, see thou this light ineffable? Know therefore that all things are ordered by Providence and that yet will the house of Manissa triumph, as surely as the beams from this great light reach from the horizon even to the farthest corner of the sea." I said to her, "My Lady, I pray thee, send me not back to the dirt and vanity of the world! Let me abide here forever on this holy mount and with thee gaze upon this radiant splendor for all time!" She said, "Nay Cyllinus, thou must return." I said, "Shall I come again when my days are ended and take my place among the halls of the blessed?" She smiled and said to me, "O Cyllinus, you simple minded one! All things that you have seen are but vision and similitude, allegory and type, for what you have seen here is already present in shadow even in the world of men, and its glory attainable to those who have eyes to see it."

I lamented and said, "Then whither shall my soul go when from this form of clay it flies? Shall it fly up to this holy mountain and abide with the souls of the righteous? Shall it pass over the sea to dwell in the unattainable light? Or shall it descend into the underworld as the men of Caeylon teach? Or perhaps the soul of man goes neither up nor down but dissipates like the seeds of the dandelion upon the winds of the summer? Or is it as the Tabians assert—that some souls, passing through the gates of the next world, come again unto this world in bodies anew?"

My Lady laughed and said, "Go thy way, Cyllinus. Let your heart not be troubled about these questions, for it is not given unto thee to know.* Only let thy heart be upright, thy virtue plain for all to see, thy spear be sharp and thy fidelity to my words unshaken, and no anxiety should you bear, for if you will do these things you will go down to the grave in peace and face with confidence what awaits, which, I suspect, shall be no less glorious than what you have seen here. But the faithless man I will burn hot against and drag down to death with my blazing spear."

Here ended my visions which I saw by the beach outside of white-towered Thán on the third day of my prayers. Then I was as one who is dead and was found by some fishermen of that region, who took me unto the city of Thán and cared for me, though I did not speak for many days. But on the seventh day my mouth was opened, and I spoke of the marvels I had witnessed, of the holy mountain and of our Lady. But some scoffed and said, "The man has had too much to drink." Yet on the following day, being the eighth day, our Lady confirmed the vision, for a great star appeared in the heavens over the ocean and illumined the dark waves of the sea, just as I had seen in my vision. The star abided day and night for three days and was seen by all the persons of that region, both great and small; but on the morn of the third day the star vanished. Then the priests of the Temple of Manissa in Thán summoned me and ordered me to recount all the things seen in the vision from the very beginning even to the end, omitting nothing. Therefore I have done so, and this is my testimony.

These things have been written by the scribes Marius and Isrán. I, Nubio, have witnessed and attest to these things. Signed the fourteenth day of the fourth month in the sixth year of Thalus, King in Cadaras.

Pelinós*

After the burning of Tabés during the reign of King Arytos, and the subjection of the Tabians to the dominion of Manissé, it was decreed by the Manissan lords who conquered Tabia that a generous grant of land should be set aside and given to the relatives of Casias, by whose exploits the war with Tabia was first prosecuted, as is told elsewhere. Therefore messengers were sent to Cyrenaica and Cadaras to see if there might still be any kin of Casias living to come west and claim the Tabian lands set aside for that purpose.

Now the nearest kinsman of Casias was a young war captain called Pelinós who dwelt in the environs of Cyrenaica. This Pelinós was a cousin of Casias and had won renown as a navigator in the regions of Cyrenaica, making a name for himself by ridding the coasts of Thán of Caeylonic pirates. So when no other closer relations could be found, the lords bestowed the land upon Pelinós and invited him west to Tabia to come into possession of it.

When Pelinós was told of the land granted to him in the name of his illustrious cousin, he at once left Cyrenaica and made the journey west to settle in the newly founded colony of Lygon, which the Manissans had built up around the resting place of Casias and Lyrgoné. Pelinós was hailed by the men of Lygon as heir to the titles and glory of Casias and was installed as lord over the lands appointed to him, which consisted of two thousand hectares of rolling pastureland west of Lygon going towards the sea. Thus Pelinós ruled as lord of that region and put the Tabians to work as fieldhands, for he harvested wheat and barley, and also grazed a great many sheep. Pelinós also aided the lords of Lygon in building the port of Ligar on the westernmost shores of Tabia and constructed the great road that runs from Ligar to Lygon, thus providing the Manissans with an outlet to the sea, for King Arytos greatly desired to have concourse with Lygon and Tabia by sea, since the overland route was tedious. The lands prospered under Pelinós, for he was industrious, prudent, and just in all his dealings.

But when the Manissans had constructed the harbor of Ligar and began making voyages from the eastern port of Thán, a fearsome serpent was found dwelling in the waters about a day's journey northwest of Ligar. The serpent was fierce and cunning, being about twenty meters in length with a thick head and jaws capable of seizing and swallowing a full-grown man. Several ships were attacked and not a few sailors were devoured, so that all trade between Cadarasia and Tabia came to a halt, for no man dared venture onto the high seas for fear of the loathsome creature. The Tabians were asked of this monster, and they called it *Rahan*, which means "tumult" in the Tabian tongue. But the Manissans called it *Athyrac*, which means "silver demon," for its appearance upon the water was like bolt of silver lightning.

This Rahan caused Pelinós no little harm, for Pelinós derived great profit from the shipping of wheat and wool to and from the east and found himself impoverished due to the lack of trade brought about by the presence of Rahan in the waters. When he saw that no lord of the Manissans or warrior among the Tabians was willing to go out and fight with Rahan, he said, "Let all who are stout-hearted and fearless come to me, for I myself will venture out upon the waters and will slay this foul vermin." But only twelve men could be found who were willing to fight the serpent with Pelinós. Yet Pelinós said, "It is enough and more than enough, for by my lance alone will this foul enemy of mankind be vanquished." So Pelinós and his valiant band of twelve set out by ship for the perilous waters, wherein lurked the cruel fiend Rahan, whose jaws ever quivered for the flesh of men.

He was three days upon the waters when the monster Rahan caught sight of the craft of Pelinós and came forth to attack it. It darted across the waves, silver back gleaming in the sunlight. When the crew saw the beast approaching, one of the twelve, Kaganus, a Lugarian, lost his nerve and said to Pelinós, "Master, let us flee, for this hideous beast will devour us all! Who can stand against it?" But Pelinós said, "Kaganus, because you have doubted my resolve and my spear, we will all certainly return to land so fair; but you shall make your grave at the bottom of the sea."

Then Rahan lunged at the ship, gaping jaws and red teeth reared at Pelinós. But the brave Manissan took his lance in hand and engaged the cunning serpent, striking this way and that so that Rahan could not bring his gaping maw near the craft. The beast hissed and gurgled with fury, attempting to swim beneath the hull of the craft and overturn it. Thus Rahan struck the ship from beneath, five times, till the crew quaked with terror. But Pelinós would not be dismayed, for after the beast struck the fifth time it reared its head above the water. Then did noble Pelinós strike it in the throat with his lance, sending a crimson fountain of blood splashing into the billowing sea foam.

How did Rahan thrash and rage, for never had head of spear or point of lance pierced his hide and gouged his flesh! In mad fury he opened his great and bloody mouth, intent on nothing other than devouring the noble Pelinós, kinsman of Casias, mighty one of Mariammné's house. But Pelinós was recollected and unshakable, even when faced with the mouth of the beast. He took aim skillfully and with purpose, swiftly dashing at Rahan and striking him in the mouth with the lance.

His arm was iron, and his aim was sure; the lance head pierced the tender flesh of Rahan's mouth, tearing tissue, muscle and breaking through bone, ripping through the brains of the beast. Rahan quivered and shook on the end of Pelinós's lance, skewered and writhing midway between the heavens and the sea.

Then Pelinós cried, "Quickly, someone take off its head!" So one of the crewmen, a bold Asylian called Lapax, came and struck the head of Rahan from the torso, leaving only the head affixed to the end of Pelinós's lance. Then a great cheer of victory arose from the men of the ship, they cried, "The silver demon is vanquished by the might of Mariammné!" for Pelinós had engaged and slain the dreadful serpent Rahan. So the men set out for Ligar and the praise of the people.

But the return home was soured by sadness, for that very night tragedy visited the ship of Pelinós. It was the turn of Kaganus to take the first watch of the night, but, wearied by the exhaustion of the day and the stress of the battle, he fell asleep in the look-out atop the mast. Shortly before midnight a violent gale blew upon the ship and tossed Kaganus from the look-out so that he plummeted into the sea and drowned. Immediately after Kaganus was lost, the gale ceased, so that the men murmured fearfully among themselves and said, "The curse of Pelinós has come to pass." Thus was the prophetic word that Pelinós spoke concerning Kaganus fulfilled.

Upon returning to Ligar, Pelinós and the remaining eleven were welcomed and acclaimed with joy and song and given many accolades and treasures, so that each became very wealthy. Pelinós retired to his manor outside Lygon to take up husbandry and the civic affairs of the city. He was wed to a maid called Cayla, daughter of Cerbel, lord of Lygon. But the head of Rahan, the silver demon called Athyrac, was affixed over the gates of the city of Lygon in commemoration of the great deed of Pelinós. Lapax, too, was honored for striking the head off Rahan while it was transfixed on the lance of Pelinós, for Pelinós made him steward of his household and all his possessions till the end of his days. When Lapax died, Pelinós bestowed this office upon his eldest son, so that ever after were the sons of Lapax hereditary stewards of the house of Pelinós and his descendants. Thus has it been even unto this day.*

*Telux and Andrior**

Once, upon the windswept plains west of Anentora in the region of Engor, there were two brothers of the house of Necho, Telux and Andrior by name. The brothers were twins, equal in stature and appearance, for both were slender and comely with hair of burnished auburn and of considerable height. Yet despite their similar appearance, they were of different temperaments, for Telux loved the poems of old Asylia and the lore of the north, and he studied the sayings of Secum and the songs of Hazer and loved above all else wisdom and the pursuit of knowledge. But Andrior was a practical man, for he loved to work with his hands in the construction of things, especially in the working of stone and marble, but also wood and any other medium malleable by the hand of man. Thus they became known in the region of Engor, Telux for his great wisdom and Andrior for his skill in the crafting of things.

When they were still youths, Telux and Andrior were compelled to flee the region of Engor and their home, for there was a feud in that city between the kin of the brothers and some of the sons of Scius, who was then ruling as Lord of Engor. In the heat of the feud, Telux and Andrior had slain one of the sons of Scius, whereupon they fled from Engor lest the house of Scius take vengeance on them for the blood of their kinsman. Thus Telux and Andrior came to Corbalund, but being unwelcome there, continued to wander south until they passed the endless fields of Corbalund and began to venture into lands into which the Manissans had never ventured. This was how they came into the dominion of the Enlilim.

These Enlilim are a very ancient race, for according to their own lore, they have dwelt in the lands south of Corbalund for over a hundred generations before the time of Telux and Andrior. They are not like other men in appearance, for they are all slender and elegant, full of beauty and wisdom and graceful in everything they undertake, whether in their speech or the manner of their clothing or even the construction of their cities, which were not like those of other men. They are virtuous and beautiful, for their songs are full of power and their laughter like the most harmonious music. When Telux and Andrior came into the region of the Enlilim, they took them at first to be demigods or descendants of Anak, so full of splendor did they appear in the eyes of the brothers.

Likewise at first the Enlilim did not know what to make of Telux and Andrior, for they were unlike the men of Caeylon with whom they had dealings in ages past, for the brothers were fair and handsome, and the splendor of Manissa was in their eyes. So one of the Lords of the Enlilim, Númerian, came and said, "Come, dwell among us in the homeland of the Enlilim, the emerald isles of Islindia by the setting sun." So Telux and Andrior were taken west with Númerian, over the Hembraean Bay, to the verdant isles of Islindia, which from remotest antiquity have been the ancestral home of the Enlilim. There Telux and Andrior dwelt in the presence of the Enlilim and lived among them for three years, learning their language and of their customs and some of their lore, though the more they learned of the Enlilim the more they saw there was still to know. Thus they traversed all over the realms of the Enlilim, from the splendid cities of Elgerian on the mainland with its verdant pasturelands, all the way to fair Islindia, whose hundred isles grace the glistening waters of the Bay of Hembraean. The Enlilim delighted in the brothers and called them in their own language *Fathaduann*, which means "children from the north" and rejoiced in them.

When Telux and Andrior had been in those lands for three years, the Lord Númerian summoned them to himself. Telux and Andrior came in before him and bowed low, saying, "What does our lord desire of his servants?" Númerian lifted the brothers up and said, "There is little need for such shows of obeisance as are the custom among men, for though you are not of our race we account you our kin. Even so, three years have you dwelt among our people in these happy lands, which have been blessed both for yourselves and for our own people. Yet it is not meet for the Enlilim to dwell perpetually with men, and thus our happy acquaintance cannot endure forever. Therefore I say to you that the day has come for you to depart and return unto your own people, to verdant Asylia, both rugged and fair, and to its people, both harsh and noble." Telux and Andrior were grieved when they heard this. They earnestly desired to remain among the Enlilim and would have abided there perpetually had it been permitted, for they marveled at how much the Enlilim were advanced in their wisdom and their manner of living, so much so that Asylia seemed savage and rustic by comparison. Seeing their faces had fallen, the heart of Númerian was moved with pity and he said, "Nevertheless, because of the fellowship you have had with our people, and because of the splendor and beauty of your countenances, we desire to grant you a boon hitherto not given to any others among the sons of men: that thou shalt name anything you have seen in our fair lands, whether purest maiden or exquisitely wrought jewel, and it shall be given unto thee to bear away northwards as a token of the esteem of the Enlilim towards thee and thy people."

Were they men of lesser virtue, perhaps the splendid wealth and luxury of the Enlilim could have tempted the brothers; or if not these things, at least their glorious maidens, who are full of beauty and radiance and unlike the women of Asylia, Maruda, or any other kingdom of men. But Telux and Andrior were turned aside neither by the covetousness of the eyes nor by the lust of the flesh and instead chose things of more excellent worth for the benefit of their people. Telux came and bowed before Númerian, saying, "Lord Númerian, ever since the days of my youth I have desired nothing more earnestly than the poems and lore of my people, especially those things that pertain to wisdom and the pursuit of knowledge. Therefore, I ask this boon of thee, that I be granted entrance into the ancient tower at Sorian, which forever blazes white in the resplendence of the southern sun. Grant it to me that I may enter the sacred tower and learn all the lore and wisdom of the Enlilim from the mouths of the sages who minister there continually, for in our three years here I have heard many things but perceive that there are innumerably more secrets which are preserved by the sages at Sorian and of which I have no knowledge. Grant that I, too, may learn at their feet, so that I might bear this treasury of wisdom north to my own people and bless them as the lands of the Enlilim are blessed."

Númerian brooded and said, "This is a hard thing you have asked. What of you, Master Andrior? What boon will you seek?" Then Andrior came and bowed before Númerian, saying, "Lord Númerian, ever since the days of my youth have I loved above all else to work with my hands in the construction of things, especially in the working of stone and marble, but also wood and any other medium malleable by the hand of man. In my days in Islindia and all the domain of the Enlilim I have seen many beautiful buildings, marvelously wrought of earth, stone, and wood and shaped with such skill as is unknown in the wild reaches of north from whence we come. Despite this, I have yet to understand how they are constructed or in what manner the stone, wood and earth are worked to fashion such constructions. Therefore, I ask this boon of thee: that thou initiate me into the secrets of the craftsmen of the Enlilim, that I may understand and comprehend all their sundry methods for the construction of buildings and monuments. Thus enriched by this knowledge, I shall bear it back to Asylia to grace my homeland with such buildings and constructions as are found throughout the dominion of the Enlilim, which is ever happy and glorious."

Númerian furled his ancient brow, saying, "You have both asked hard things, but in that you chose neither wealth nor a maiden for yourselves, your wisdom and virtue are made manifest. May it be as you have requested and may the grace that flows in your blood abide in you and your house forever." So they bowed low and departed the presence of Númerian.

Then Andrior was sent to the master craftsmen of the Enlilim who abide on the sacred isles of Islindia. There he was instructed in the craft of building, which the Enlilim hold to be a sacred art. He was instructed in fashioning both the arch and the column, along with the skill of crafting statues, free standing and in relief, and many other sundry arts of great practical value. But Telux was taken forthwith to the great tower of Sorian in Elgeria and admitted to the mysteries of the sages there. His mind was quickened when he beheld the mysteries of the tower, and he was given to understand all the secrets of the Enlilim. Of the origin of all men and the lore concerning the Enlilim and the Anakim he was instructed, and also of the gods and spirits of the world and of where the souls of men fly to when they perish, as well as all the days of the world and the time of its final consummation.* All these things he was instructed in at Sorian, so that his knowledge and wisdom was greater than any man who had ever lived prior. He was also instructed in the music of the Enlilim, which the sages of that noble people say was given to them by the Sons of Anak in ancient days, and which has the power to elevate or destroy the sons of men.* Thus Telux mastered the music and instruments of the Enlilim, working marvelous sounds upon the flute and lyre and excelling at every mode and scale, both played and sung, so that even the sages of the tower marveled at the beauty of Telux's music. Then Telux said, "With this wisdom and power, Asylia will be restored and flourish like the kingdom of the Enlilim."

So when they had been instructed in the ways of the Enlilim, Telux and Andrior arose and departed for the north after having dwelt among the Enlilim for a period of four years. Yet they could not return home straightaway, for in those days there was war in the regions of Engor and Corbalund.* Therefore Telux and Andrior did not go up by a direct route, but instead traveled in a circumspect manner, traversing the foothills of the Bados so as to stay clear of the main roads and cities of that region.

It came to pass when they were still some ways from home that they sat down to rest for the evening after a difficult day of travel through the rugged foothills. In the spot where they reclined there were many stones and boulders scattered about, so that there was nowhere fitting to recline and sleep save beneath the boughs of a solitary cedar, which stood in the shadow of the cliffs.

Andrior came and took his place beneath the tree, but there was a contention as to who would rest there, for Telux also wanted to recline beneath it and there was but space enough for one of them. After arguing for some time, they decided to cast lots to determine who would sleep beneath the tree for the evening and who would sleep among the rocks. The lots were cast, and the lot fell to Telux. Therefore Andrior grumbled, removing himself from beneath the tree so that Telux took his place. Then they retired for the evening.

But during the night a fierce storm blew up off the plains and lightning struck the tree so that one of its mighty boughs came crashing down and crushed Telux, who was sleeping immediately beneath it. Andrior awoke when he heard the crash and saw his brother pinned beneath the mighty branch, his delicate frame crushed and blood spurting from his mouth. He attempted to remove the branch but found it much too great. Able to do nothing else, he wept beside his brother as Telux lingered between life and death. Then Telux said, "Would that I had been allowed to bear this knowledge away to the north! Surely our people would have put away the spear and shield and dwelt in splendor. Alas, it shall perish with me and be no more found upon the earth." Then Telux gave up his spirit with a loud sigh and died, pinned beneath the mighty branch in the wilderness between Corbalund and Engor. Andrior tore his hair and beat his breast with stones, weeping vehemently. And he cried out, "Why, O fairest brother, with all thy knowledge and wisdom didst thou covet my place beneath the tree?* Did you increase in wisdom but lack charity? Or did the knowledge of the Enlilim cause your heart to be lifted up in pride, so that you became arrogant? By Manissa's spear, had you not set your eyes upon my place it would be you weeping beside my crushed frame; yet at least the splendor of the Enlilim would have lived on in thee to be borne away north!"

After Andrior had performed the burial rites for his brother Telux, he turned about and set his face south for the lands of the Enlilim, hoping again to come to the court of Númerian. He thought to himself, "Perhaps Númerian will have pity on me for the sake of my brother Telux and will teach unto me all the marvels learned by my brother, so that this knowledge may indeed come to bless Asylia." But when he came into the south he could not find the Enlilim, though he wandered to all about the land. He spent a year in his wanderings, which took him from the east to west until his feet stood in the waters on the western sea and his eyes gazed upon the sun setting over the endless waves. But he found neither the Enlilim nor sighted their cities or by-ways. Then he cursed his fate and said, "The magic of the Enlilim shrouds their land from my sight. Alas, the wisdom of Telux is lost forever."

So Andrior returned to Engor with much sadness. As the house of Scius was still reigning there, he removed himself to Anentora and made his abode in that city. When the days for the grieving of Telux were passed, he began to work the marvels that he had learned among the Enlilim, so that Anentora was enriched and beautified by the wondrous works of marble and stone that came from the hand of Andrior. Then all the Manissans throughout the land heard of his skill and were in awe, for he crafted statues and constructed buildings unlike any before seen in the west. So wonderful were his works that men flocked to Anentora from the far reaches of the north to learn the craft of Andrior, and when they had been instructed they likewise took his wisdom back with them to the uttermost ends of the land.

Thus it was that by the time Andrior was old the whole realm of the Manissans was full of exceptional buildings and splendid marvels of engineering: the vaulted dome along with the stately column with ornate capital, wondrous works of marble and statues of alabaster rivaling even the works found in the court of the King of Caeylon. It was in the days of Andrior that the Manissans ceased building their halls of wood and began assembling them of stone and decorating them with beautiful statuary, so that the Manissans became great builders upon the face of the earth, whither soever they journeyed.

When he was advanced in years, Andrior took up his staff and his tools and again went south into the rugged wilderness, between Corbalund and Engor, into the foothills of the Bados. There he found one of the great boulders which are plentiful in that region and worked upon it with his gnarled hands until he formed a marvelously wrought column, eight cubits in height and as big around as an oak. This he decorated at the base with intricate depictions in relief of the deeds of the house of Manissa, and scenes from the legends of the Enlilim about the top. At the summit of the column he carved a likeness of his brother, Telux, and had the pillar set up at the place where his brother had perished. Then he said, "Henceforth shall this pillar be a perpetual reminder of the glories and tragedies of the house of Manissa, the splendor of the Enlilim, and the inestimable loss our people incurred when cruel Fate ripped Telux from the land of the living." Thus did he erect the Pillar of Andrior, which remains there in the wilderness to this day.*

Then Andrior returned northward to Anentora and put his hand to the chisel no more.

Fála and Miross

hen the great Queen Anaxandra ascended to the throne of Cadaras, she made a gift unto Elphas, son of Manissa, of the great shield of Ioclus, which had until that time been an heirloom of the descendants of Arrax the Bold. A firm and unbreakable shield it was: four layers of hide overlayed with beaten bronze and rimmed with delicate silver ornaments round about. Elphas bore this shield with him when he sold his sword to the Marudans and bore it back with to Engor when he was reconciled with his brother Necho. After the death of Necho, when Elphas took up residence upon the hill of Mimmoth, the shield was given over to his sons and remained in the great hall of Necho for a generation until the coming of Sammas. At that time it was spirited away by the people of Engor, and through various turns of fortune, wound up in the custody of the house of Corinos, a noble family of the Periorids who traced their lineage through the clan of Aïos. This house of Corinos was once very prominent in the city of Thán in Cyrenaica, but over the years the line failed to produce any heirs, and eventually all the lands and titles of the house of

Corinos were held by a single wealthy widow called Fála. But
the greatest treasure of Fála was the ancient shield of Ioclus.
This shield she displayed proudly in the great hall of her manor,
a testament to all of the fell and fearsome deeds done by her
illustrious forebears.

But there was in the city of Thán a thief called Miross
who coveted the marvelous shield, for a certain merchant from
Lyson in Caeylon had offered Miross a trunk filled with gold
bars if he could steal the treasured heirloom and deliver it unto
him. Thus Miross entered the estate of the lady Fála one evening,
when the brightness of the moon was obstructed by cloud, and
in the dank blackness of the night, removed the shield of Ioclus
from its hallowed shrine and made off with it.

When Fála awoke the next morning and perceived the
great shield to be missing, she raised the hue and cry and alerted
the magistrates of the city. Yet the word of the theft had not
gone forth for more than a single hour when word was brought
to Fála that the shield had been recovered and the thief
apprehended, and this not more than a furlong from her own
home. Fála greatly marveled at this and went out to the spot
indicated by the people. There she saw Miross the thief in the
custody of the magistrates. He was trembling and in a terrible
fright. When Fála approached, he fell at her feet and confessed
immediately to the theft.

Fála said to him, "Tis a wretched thing you have done
indeed, thinking to deprive the kingdom of the one heirloom of
our Blessed Lady which she left behind upon the earth. You
deserve to be slain for this! Yet tell us what has so affrighted
you, for you look as if you have seen the undead!"

Miross said, "Behold, as I was making my escape down
these lanes with the shield secured to my back, it suddenly
seemed to take on a great weight, becoming denser with his
every step, so much that I could no longer bear it up. I took it
from my back and tried to roll it, yet it became so heavy that I
could neither roll nor even hold it up anymore. I was struggling

to move the great shield from the ground when, marvel of all marvels, I heard it speak unto me!" Those surrounding Miross laughed at this, but Fála bid him continue.

He said, "The shield rang out clearly, and from it proceeded a terrifying voice that said, 'Miross, whither do thou takest me?'* I was stunned, but by and by I said, 'I am taking thee to the port to be given over to the Lysonians in exchange for a trunk of gold.' Then it spoke again and said, 'By what authority do you do this?' and I was speechless. Then it said to me, 'Thou art a thief and a villain, to be sure!' After it said this, I heard footsteps approaching me on the road, though I saw nobody. I thought I was discovered and turned to flee, but some unseen hands took hold of me and held me firmly. Then the shield said, 'You have troubled me this night, so now I will trouble you.' Then the invisible hands held me so tightly that I could scarcely breathe. In this manner was I bound here until the breaking of the dawn. I was not released until the servants of Fála came running and beheld me here on the street with the shield at my feet."

Fála and those assembled were dumbfounded by the tale and knew not what to think of it. Finally Fála said, "Can it possibly be other than Miross has narrated? Why else would he allow himself to be so easily apprehended here on the lane so close to my estate if it were not as he says? Glory to our Lady and the powers that ever flow through her house, even through the things she has once touched, for an unliving shield has worked wonders! Who has heard of such a thing?" Then all those present bowed their heads and reverenced the shield, giving assent to the words of Fála and honor to Manissa.

The shield was returned to the estate of Fála with much pomp and festivity. As for Miross, the magistrates of the city sought to put him to death for his crime, but Fála took pity on him, saying, "The power of the house of Manissa has chastened him enough," and had the magistrates release him. Thus freed, Miross fled away to Lyson and was seen no more among the peoples of Manissé, though to this day the Manissans tell many tales about what adventures he had there.

But the shield of Ioclus remained fixed as an heirloom in Fála's hall within the city of Thán for many generations.*

Loross the Undying

⚭ ⚭ ⚭

Of the most wonderous of all deeds wrought by the sons of Manissa was the marvel worked by Loross, son of Limnos, of the house of Necho, who dwelt in Anentora in olden times. Anentora was transferred from the dominion of Caeylon to the dominion of the Manissans in the days of Elphas, when Elphas and Baldor stormed the city in vengeance for the killing of Necho. Yet though the city came under the dominion of the Manissans, it was also populated by many Caeylonics by virtue of its proximity to the borders of that kingdom. Anentora had been under the lordship of the kin of Oros in days past, but after the removal of Oros's seat to Dretia, the city passed to the descendants of Urmax, who were weak and contemptible. Thus the city was full of lawlessness, evil, and sorcery, for every vile custom and arcane art became practiced in the dark alleys of Anentora.

In the days of Loross, the city was under the sway of a fearsome and powerful mage called Galban. This Galban was Manissan by birth but of Caeylonic descent. He had gained great power and wealth in Anentora by virtue of the fearful magic which he commanded in the name of the vulgar gods of Caeylon and Illyrana. All of the people of Anentora feared him and paid him a handsome amount in gold and silver every year to avert his wrath; furthermore, all the other wizards and mediums of the city were in his power, as were most of the lords and governors, so that no one could exercise any influence in Anentora without the leave and pleasure of Galban, who built for himself a magnificent house on the east side of the city.

But Loross was a humble poet who composed hymns and songs about old Asylia and the glories of Manissa and her house. People came from all quarters of the city to hear the singing of Loross, especially when accompanied by the harp, which Loross could play with dexterity. Loross was fond of singing in the commons in the middle of the city where all who desired to hear him could find space upon the meadow grass to recline. The hymns of Loross were exceedingly beautiful and turned the minds and hearts of the Anentorans away from the vile and despicable practices of the wizards and mediums, directing them to the pure and holy lore of old Asylia. So Loross brought hope and joy to the people of that city.

One day, the carriage of Galban was being drawn through the streets of the city when he passed the commons and heard the songs of Loross floating upon the air, melodic and joy filled. Galban was enraged and cried out, "Who pollutes the air with such horrid verse and such hateful sounds? Who dares to utter such sour notes in my domain?" His servants were puzzled, for everyone with one accord agreed that the singing of Loross was praiseworthy and joyful. Nevertheless, they told him, "The singing comes from Loross, son of Limnos of the house of Necho." Galban scoffed and said, "Ah! A paladin of Manissa's house! They are poison and ever have been, for to have a paladin about is to court disaster." Then Galban came forth from his carriage and made his way across the commons to the place where Loross sung. When the people of Anentora saw the black form of Galban they withdrew from Loross, for they were in great fear of him.

Black-robed Galban glided across the meadow like a shade and stood face to face with Loross, saying, "I command thee, accursed son of Manissa, to cease thy baleful singing that is so hateful to my soul." Loross said, "But Master Galban, how can I not sing of the hope and goodness which is within me? It is my verse alone which preserves any semblance of goodness in this town, which you and your kind have defiled.* I would sooner die than withhold the medicine of life from the people of Anentora, so long made ill by the curse of the wizards, the pollution of the foreign cults, and thine own corruption."

Galban flew into a rage and said, "Do you not know that I am a mighty sorcerer? Do you not know that it is within my power to call down lightning from heaven to char thy very bones, or else to open the earth to swallow you entire? How do you presume to contend with my power with such haughty words?"

Loross withstood Galban, saying, "You speak of power? The power that flows in my veins is greater than the power of your dark craft. Whatever god you call upon, the Immortals who ever guide Asylia through their chosen one Manissa are greater in splendor and might.* To them do I defer and them only do I fear." Then all the people cowered, for they saw a flame of hatred flare in Galban's eye and knew he meant to slay Loross. But the face of Loross was like that of a child, glowing with innocence and goodness. Galban raised his gnarled hand, gathering about a thick blackness, and cried out, "See my power and tremble! Let all know that Galban is supreme!" Then he called out an incantation in the forgotten language of the Illyrs. A blazing thunderbolt flashed from the sky and struck Loross, laying him out dead upon the commons. The people wept and came to his aid, but his flesh was blackened round about, and his form smoked with the stench of death. Then some of the servants of Galban cried out, "Bow before Galban, your ruler and lord!" So all the Anentorans bowed before Galban and did obeisance to him. But Galban told them to leave the body of Loross to rot upon the field. Then the Anentorans returned to their homes, weeping for the death of innocent Loross. And a bitter storm broke upon the land that evening, the heavens weeping for Loross's bitter fate.

But lo, the following morning the people of Anentora were awakened by a melodious strain coming from the town commons. They donned their garments and came to the center of the city, and there beheld Loross son of Limnos standing the midst of the meadow, harp in hand, singing and making melody as he always had done in days past. Some said, "It is a ghost," for all had been there the day before and saw his charred and smoking body upon the grass. Yet a few moments more and they saw it was no ghost, for he was as alive and real as any of them. Most marvelous of all was that his body was not marred in any way, nor was any hair of his head singed or out of place, nor were his garments stained or blackened in the least, for in all things he looked as fresh and new as if he had never run in with Galban. So the people marveled and gave praise to Manissa and the immortals who had brought Loross back from oblivion.

Yet it was not long before Galban was told, "Did you not slay Loross son of Limnos? Behold, he is yet alive and making music in the commons." Galban was perplexed; taking with him six servants armed with clubs, he left his abode and made his way to the commons to see for himself the marvel. He was greatly unnerved to see Loross again singing amidst the people, this time with even more gathered than on the day previous. Galban cried out, "How is it that you have recovered so quickly from the blow I dealt thee the day before? By what witchery do you return here seemingly unscathed?" Loross said, "I recover not from a blow but from cold death itself, for as I told you before, the power which I serve is greater than that which you wield against me!" Galban said, "Yesterday I erred in leaving you unattended and swoon in this field; I shall not so err this day!" Then he turned to his servants and said, "Fall upon him!" So the servants of Galban fell upon Loross with clubs. They beat him sorely about the arms and legs, breaking his hands so that he could not play nor defend himself. When he had fallen beneath their bitter strokes, they smashed his head with their clubs until his skull was shattered and his brains were exposed before the sun and the people standing about. Then the men drew daggers and slashed the brains of Loross, so that they were scattered about the place. So the people wept for Loross's death, but Galban said, "Lest there be any doubt," and taking up a great dagger, sliced off the head of Loross and hurled it into the briar patch near the commons. Then his servants cried out, "Bow before Galban, your ruler and lord!" So all the Anentorans bowed before Galban and did obeisance to him. Then Galban had the body of Loross taken and burned and the ashes scattered to the winds.

But lo, the following morning the people of Anentora were awakened by a melodious strain coming from the town commons. They donned their garments and came to the center of the city, and there beheld Loross son of Limnos standing the midst of the meadow, harp in hand, singing and making melody as he always had done in days past. The people began to tremble with fright, for they had clearly witnessed his head struck off the day before and the body carried away by Galban. Yet here stood Loross, restored and in the prime of health, with neither scar nor wound upon his head or neck. He again took up his harp and began making music and singing, so that every man and woman, young and old, said, "Come, behold the marvel of Loross the Undying who has again been brought back from the netherworld to contend with Galban!" Thus the commons were filled with throngs of people, so much so that there was scarcely room to stand.

Yet it was not long before Galban was told, "Did you not slay Loross son of Limnos? Behold, he is yet alive and making music in the commons." Galban was enraged, but began to tremble, for he knew that there was no room for trickery on the part of Loross. Therefore he summoned several other mages and wizards, along with a detachment of fifty men armed with spears, and made his way from his abode down to the commons.

When he arrived at the commons he forced his way through the crowds, coming face to face with Loross. Galban marveled, saying, "This is beyond trickery, son of Limnos. Is not the grass still wet with your blood? Was not your head hurled violently in yonder briar patch not one day past? By what power do you stand here before us again, polluting the air with your baleful song?" Loross said, "By a power greater than any you can muster against me, thou villain and deceiver." Galban said, "You have somehow eluded death twice, but I shall destroy you yet once more and seal your spirit in the netherworld." Loross said, "It is you who shall go to the netherworld, and this before the sun rises again."

This infuriated Galban, who cried out to his priests and wizards, "Let us destroy this cur and banish his spirit forever from the fair fields of the earth!" Then summoning up all the powers of darkness from his black soul, Galban and his followers chanted a foul and wicked dirge, so hateful and malicious that all the crowds who thronged about trembled in fear and covered their ears. Then, behold, a great ball of fire arose and consumed Loross in flame. The fire wreathed about him and burned hot, flaming white and consuming the flesh of Loross. After the flame receded, nothing remained of Loross but a few bones amidst a pile of ash. The people stood in terror at the fate of Loross and the might of Galban, and the servants and armed men of Galban cried out, "Bow before Galban, your lord and god!" Then all the people collapsed upon their faces and paid homage to Galban, calling him lord and god. But Galban carefully took up the ashes and bones of Loross and interred them in a case. Then he threw the case into a blacksmith's furnace and burned the case with its contents down to ash. Then he took the ash and had it mixed into a mincemeat pie and fed to his dogs. When he had fed the pie to the dogs, he had them killed and burned their bodies. When their bodies had been burned, he gathered up the ashes and ground them into cornmeal. When he had mixed the ashes in the cornmeal, he gave it to a hog to eat. When the hog had eaten, he slew the hog, had his servants prepare it, and then ate it. After Galban ate it his belly was troubled sorely, and he went to relieve himself. After he relieved himself, he gathered up the dung and burned it. After he had burned the dung, he gathered what little ashes remained and smeared them on the head of a cat. After saying incantations over the cat, he took it out and drowned it in the river. Then he dismembered the cat, sealed it in a sack and hurled it down a deep pit. When he had done this, he ordered his servants to work through the night filling the pit with dirt and stone.

But by this time it was nearly morning and Galban returned to the commons to await the dawn, for he recalled the words of Loross who had said, "You will go to the netherworld before the sun rises again." When Galban came to the commons he found it already thronged with people, though the night was not yet passed, and the eastern sky had only begun to glimmer pink beyond the horizon. Galban roved about, searching for any sign of Loross, but saw him not. Then suddenly Loross was present, for Galban heard the people crying, "There is Loross! He has returned a third time from the dead!" Galban stared in horror and beheld the form of Loross coming up across the green, followed by a throng of people. Again, he was whole and unharmed, yet this time his eyes glared with fire and there was authority in his steps. Galban trembled and called for his men, but his servants melted away before the sight of Loross, the thrice-risen one.

Galban tried to speak to cast some spell or hex, but Loross opened his mouth and spoke with power, for his words were like a two-edged sword. He said, "Silence, rogue!" Then Galban found he had gone mute. Loross said, "Trouble these people no more! Behold, we have seen the power of your witcheries. We see that they are nothing before the might of Manissa, She Who Hurls the Spear. Behold, her spear is trained on you! Your evil has been defeated and has no more power over me nor over any of us. Now let us see if your demons will deliver you!" At this the mob rose up and seized Galban, for he now appeared contemptible and frail. Galban tried to gesture and summon his magic but found that he was rendered powerless. Thus the people of Anentora bound Galban hand and foot and hanged him by the neck from a nearby tree until he died. Then they cut his body down and burned it in the commons. After this, Loross proclaimed, "Thus shall be done to every wizard, every medium, and every patron of a foreign god who does not remove himself from this city within three days' time!" Thus all the mages and worshipers of the gods of Caeylon and Illyrana fled from the city, leaving it solely in the possession of the Manissans. As for Galban, the people of Anentora loitered about the place where he was burned for some time to see whether he would rise again. But Galban did not rise.

Then in those days was Loross hailed as a hero and wonderworker, a true paladin and son of Manissa. He took to wife a maid of Anentora called Terea and raised up many sons by her. Never again did he do any such marvels as he had done in his encounters with Galban, nor did he have an answer for those who asked how he had returned to life, save to say, "The powers of darkness and deception cannot prevail over the light." Thus the hair of Loross eventually turned to gray as that of all other men, until finally he expired, being about eighty years of age. He was buried with great pomp and ceremony in the city commons at Anentora and a great shrine was erected over his tomb dedicated to Loross the Undying, who is also called *Loross Triaxus*, which means "Loross the Thrice-Raised."

Ithaross

**n the days when the Manissans waxed strong and put
all Elabaea under their power, it came to pass that the
paladin Ithaross, a warrior of the house of Perior, came
into the lands of old Epidymia and made war on the Elamites
who dwelt in the northeast. Elam is a land of arid wastes that
ascends going north into the highlands of Lamlash, a rugged and
stony country populated by folk both hardy and daring. Yet
Ithaross was a tall man, mighty in war and of the noble house of
Perior, not to be bested by the warriors of Elam. After fleeing
before Ithaross and fighting many bitter battles against the
Manissans, the Elamites sued for peace, agreeing to accept the
lordship of Ithaross and to take Manissan priests into their lands
to teach their sons the ways of Manis. Because he had found
glory in the wars, and slew many Elamites, the King of Manis
confirmed Ithaross in the lordship of Elam, granting him
extensive lands in the north, where the grassy plateaus and
shrub-dotted highlands spread out beneath the shadows of
Lamlash. Thus Ithaross retired to Elam and built for himself the
mighty fortress of Tilmindor, from which he ruled the lands
roundabout and kept the Elamites in subjection.*

Then he took as his wife a young woman of that land
and rejoiced in the love of his youth. Sweet were those years for
Ithaross, when the glories of war, nimbleness of young age, and
the wife of his desire made his heart light and his rule moderate.

Of especial joy to him were the sprawling gardens of Tilmindor, which were the envy of all men, Manissan or Elamite. He and his bride were known to walk there in the morning and at the setting of the sun, taking delight in the myriad of glorious colors brought forth when the sun rose over the flowers of Tilmindor. Thus there was happiness in the house of Ithaross.

But after some years it came to pass that the wife of Ithaross died, still in the flower of youth and without bearing any children to him. Thus was Ithaross plunged into grief, and Tilmindor became a place of sadness. After his wife was buried and the days of her mourning past, Ithaross was slowly transfigured, becoming a cold and bitter man, demanding of his servants and cruel to the Elamites under his governance. He was especially strict with regards to Tilmindor's gardens, of which he demanded the most exacting perfection from the gardeners. He would tolerate not the least deviation, for if Ithaross came through his gardens in the cool of the morning and saw any flowers wilted, or weeds pressing up through the soil, he at once bound his gardeners and whipped them soundly, berating them and threatening them with worse punishments if they should not trim the garden to the perfection he demanded. Likewise, if Ithaross came through his gardens at the haze of dusk and saw any of the grasses growing too long, or anything out of place, he would seize the gardeners and beat them about the back and legs with iron rods, threatening them with worse punishments if so much as one pebble or blade of grass should be found out of place again. Ithaross carried on this way for many years, so that the servants of his manor were quite miserable, but especially those assigned to keep the garden.

Occasionally other Manissan lords would pass through his lands and call upon him at Tilmindor; when they beheld how roughly he treated his servants, they said, "Lord Ithaross! It is not fitting for you to treat your gardeners so, for you have the most splendid gardens in all the kingdom of Manis! What is it you have to be so wrathful about?" But Ithaross scowled and said, "If the flower be not perfect, what joy shall I find in it? No flower of my garden shall ever wilt or fade again!" So he continued treating his gardeners harshly.

It came to pass one day that Ithaross awoke early in the morning and came to examine his gardens, as he was wont to do. But when he entered the courtyard of Tilmindor and came into the gardens, he beheld everything in great disarray, for many of the flowering bushes were mangled or torn up. The grass was trampled, and stones were scattered here and there throughout the place. Infuriated, Ithaross burst into the servant's chambers and dragged the gardeners out into the courtyard demanding an explanation, but the gardeners only stood mute. Therefore he strung them up and had them flogged severely before the entire manor. After he had done this, he commanded all the servants to repair the damage and tell him who had so spoiled his gardens. The servants worked feverishly throughout the day and night repairing the gardens but could in nowise discern who had so ravaged them and could give no answer to Ithaross's inquiry.

On the following day Ithaross awoke and found the gardens again in a state of disarray, and again he dragged out the servants and flogged them, but the servants cried, "Master Ithaross, by our gods and all we hold dear we swear that we have neither disrupted the fair order of your garden, nor do we know who has done this thing!" But Ithaross only flogged them all the worse, for he said, "If you made it your business to know these things and it would go better for you!"

Some of the servants stayed up all night in vigil over the gardens of Tilmindor, but to no avail, for the gardens were always in disarray in the morning, day after day. Finally Ithaross said, "But one night more will I bear with you wicked and lazy servants!" Then he decreed that if the gardens should again be disrupted during the night that all the servants of the fortress should be burnt to death the following day, the gardeners and the field hands, the housemen, and the scullery maids. When the servants heard this they quaked with fear, for they had tried to keep vigil in the gardens night after night and were at a loss as to how the gardens were continually disrupted; some even began to say it was the work of an evil spirit. Many of the servants came and fell down trembling before Ithaross, saying, "Lord Ithaross, be not wroth with us! Have mercy, O lord! Before you should resolve to burn your servants to death for these outrages, let our lord himself keep vigil in the gardens by night and see for himself the origin of these mysterious occurrences." Ithaross pondered their words and said, "Let it be as you have said. I myself shall keep vigil tonight and see who has, these past seven days, thrown my garden and my house into disarray!" So the servants were relieved for a time.

Thus it was on the eve of the eighth day that Ithaross kept vigil in a tower overlooking the gardens, watching them intently for any sign of trespass.* Though his eyes were fixed attentively on the garden, the night passed uneventfully, and Ithaross soon fell off into sleep, despite his anger and his resolutions to the contrary. He slumbered in the tower through the night but was awakened early in the morning before the sun had fully risen, when the mist was still lying heavy on the land, for he heard a disturbance down in the gardens. Leaping up, he strained his eyes to see through the mist and beheld naught but small black goat tramping through the garden, eating flowers, stomping the grasses, and causing great disorder. When Ithaross saw the goat he laughed to himself and said, "Are all my troubles due to this goat? I will make a feast of him tonight!" So he took up his cloak and hunting spear and went down to slay the creature.

Yet when he confronted the creature in the gardens he found it to be swifter than he had imagined, for it easily dodged every cast of his spear. "You are a spry little spirit," said Ithaross, "but you will not elude my shaft for long!" But no matter how Ithaross lunged or thrust his spear the goat ever seemed to be ahead of him and always able to remove himself from Ithaross's vengeful reach. By this time many of the servants awoke and marveled to see their master sparring with the goat in the gardens. Ithaross grew more enraged, lunging madly for the goat, but found he could by no means strike it. Seeing Ithaross's rage, the goat trotted out of the gates of the keep and up the road towards the countryside. Ithaross roared, "You will surely die for these outrages, foul beast of the highlands!" Then he stormed out of Tilmindor, following closely behind the beast in a fury. His servants stood back stunned, saying to one another, "Has Ithaross gone mad? He makes war on the goat as fiercely as in the days when he subjugated all of Elam with his unbreakable spear!"

Ithaross was led out of Tilmindor by the goat, which ran briskly and stayed ever in front of him, sometimes galloping farther ahead to dodge the angry Manissan's blows, sometimes doubling back and staring blankly at Ithaross when the latter stopped to rest by the roadside, as if challenging the paladin to pursue him further. This would only enrage Ithaross all the more, who would then rise to his feet and renew his pursuit, but always in vain, for he could neither overtake the goat nor hit it with his spear.

By and by the goat led Ithaross far into the wilderness, over the dust covered heights of Lamlash going up towards Mount Hellas, which towers over the desolate plains of that region like a hulking giant of old.* Ithaross beheld the goat leaping blithely over the rocks and bushes that crowd the foot of Hellas and said, "Even if I have to pursue you up Hellas's wearying heights, by the gods I will have thee!" So he pursued the goat to the ascent of white-crested Hellas, breathing threats and curses all the while.

The goat, however, was nimble and fleet-footed on the mountainous terrain of Hellas, while Ithaross was tired and slow in his pursuit; gradually the goat receded farther from his sight and disappeared up the mountainside, vanishing into the mist. Ithaross roared, "You will not elude me, you deceitful beast!" and clambered up the mountainside in tired pursuit. Yet after some time he came to a place where the ground beneath his feet was as sliding gravel, and his knees ached and burned with each succeeding step. Finding himself shrouded in a thick mist, with treacherous precipices all about him and the goat nowhere in sight, he began to regret that he had ever ascended Hellas and repented of his foolhardy pursuit of the animal, for now lost in the mist and desolation of Hellas's slopes, the height of his grasses or presence of weeds in his gardens seemed of small account.

Thus Ithaross stumbled about in the thick fog, now looking only for some way to come back down the ascent safely. Then it was that he heard the sound of the goat quite near him, though he saw it not. It bleated and neighed about him, and then charging out of the mist, bucked Ithaross from behind with its horns. The blow knocked Ithaross from his feet and sent him over the side of a nearby precipice. Though the fall was not exceedingly far, he was caught unawares and tumbled awkwardly so that he dashed himself against a large and jagged boulder. He wailed and cried out in pain but could not move himself, for his legs were shattered by the fall. Thus did he weep and lament upon the barren stone-ridden slopes of Hellas, crying out, "Accursed fiend! What wretched demon of the netherworld has sent you hither to torment me so? Thou art no goat but an evil spirit!" But the goat stood upon the height of the precipice from whence Ithaross had fallen and only stared at him, its eyes glistening red in the dim pall of the mist. Then it turned and bounded away up Hellas's desolate peaks and was seen no more.

For some time did Ithaross languish in misery before his servants came and found him, for they had followed him when he raged out of Tilmindor seeking the goat and had tracked him to Hellas. They bore him up and carried him back to Tilmindor, and though his wounds were treated and he returned to health, Ithaross found that he had lost the use of his legs and was ever after a cripple. He raged and cursed Fate for his condition, but the servants were no longer intimidated by him, for they knew he could in nowise carry out his threats against them any longer. So Ithaross became melancholy and brooded about the dim halls of Tilmindor.

Yet he found one joy, for in the cool of the morning his attendants would seat Ithaross in a great chair and bring him out to sit and gaze upon the flowers of the gardens. Instead of scrutinizing them for faults and defects, he came to appreciate their delicacy and the wonders of their look and fragrance. So he began to again find favor in the flowering blossoms and tender grasses that grew therein, marveling at every shrub and movement of the wind upon the leaves. Then was the soul of Ithaross reawakened by wonderment and was contented. And peace returned to Tilmindor.

As for the goat, it was never seen in Tilmindor or its environs again. Ithaross never spoke of it, though the servants of his manor said that it was a *puzi*, a sprite of mischievous demeanor and mysterious power which is sometimes known to prey on the arrogant and the foolish, though this is only the opinion of the Elamites.* But the place from which Ithaross was thrown down was ever after called *Lolúrath* in the Elamite tongue, which means "Goat Fell."

Appendix A
Paladologies: The Tragedy and Redemption of Manissé

☙❦❧ ☙❦❧ ☙❦❧

aladologies is the family history of the Manissan people during the formative years of their development, filling a span of around 1,100 years after the conclusion of Manissa's reign.

Assessing the *Paladologies* is a challenge because of the breadth of the work. It is best to begin by holding fast to a fundamental interpretive key that scholars of the *Paladologies* have always insisted on: that the work, though written primarily as history, has been understood by the Manissans as a religious text. Its stories, though preserving a historical account of the first millennium of the history of Manissé, are rife with symbolic and allegorical meanings that have been endlessly commented upon over the centuries. Thus, *Paladologies* has become much more than a work of history; Manissans find within it lessons on morality, ritual, mysticism, and even eschatology. In this it is quite different from the *Tale of Manaeth*, which, though later utilized in certain religious contexts, was always treated by the Manissans as a historical war epic.

The *Paladologies* were written by at least twenty different authors over a period of more than seven hundred years. The authors are almost all unknown, the exceptions being the paladology of Cyllinus (written by the scribe Isrán) and that of Ezion, which a unanimous tradition ascribes to the priest Sotera. The *Paladologies* were not compiled into a single written account until the time of King Lesalius II, roughly 869 years after the events of the latest story narrated in the *Paladologies* (the building of Tereldian under King Palereus). It is a much younger work than the *Tale*, but also vastly more complex. The *Paladologies* purport to tell the story of the divergent fortunes of the descendants of Manissa and their various houses, detailing the expansion of Asylian power and the development of their religion along the way.

The work is divided into three principal sections, the first being the *Inión éla Hadrior* ("The Chronicle of the Days of Hadrior") and is historical in nature, telling the story of Hadrior's conquest of Cyrenaica in the first years of his reign and his vengeance upon Endumion, who had cast him into the pit of Ochu in the *Tale of Manaeth*. The second work, the *Nöm etha Manissé* ("The Deeds of the Sons of Manissa") presents us with biographical information on the children of Manissa, much of it historical and dating from the time of Anaxandra, but some more mythical in content. The third division of the *Paladologies* is the *Anridion*, the paladologies proper, which tells of the marvelous exploits of the descendants of Manissa, covering the period of almost a thousand years from the founding of Halicor to the reign of Palereus. The *Anridion* are further subdivided into the twelve Major Paladologies (*Anridion Aior*) and the Minor Paladologies (*Anridion Inoré*), the latter of which are simply brief tales of obscure persons somehow connected to the Houses of Manissa and sometimes of a legendary character. *Paladologies* is thus a nuanced word: it can refer to the collection of all three books, or just the third book proper (*Anridion*); it can also be used to denote any individual story within any of the three books (e.g., "the paladology of Belar," or "the paladology of Ianthë").

The three overarching themes of the *Paladologies* (if such a diverse collection of writings can be said to have any definitive themes) are the spread of Asylian power, the development of the Manissan religion—with its gradual deification of Manissa—and the betrayal and persecution of the house of Manissa throughout much of the period covered in the story. It is a tale of disinheritance and redemption, played out through a multitude of stories involving hundreds of characters spanning over a thousand years.

e must necessarily begin any discussion of *Paladologies* with *Tale of Manaeth*, as the last days of Manissa cast a shadow over the opening scenes of *Paladologies. Tale of Manaeth* ends with the grief of Amyntas, husband of Manissa, at her disappearance upon the slopes of Zurlina in pursuit of the Lamassu of Agenor. This event is of pivotal importance for the Manissan peoples and is never viewed in other than a religious context. It goes by various names: the *Ilethiar* ("Taking"), her *Riróthiar* ("Rising"), and the *Embloth* ("Ascent"). Her departure is never conceived as a mere disappearance; it is an apotheosis, an exodus from the world of mortals. The Lamassu in the cultic traditions of Manissé functions as a guardian spirit who draws Manissa into the immortal realm and guides her across the threshold. In the paladology of Mariammné, one of the earliest paladologies, we read of Mariammné that "she was but a girl when her mother was *taken*," in Asylian, *ilethi*. It represents the moment of Manissa's exaltation from mortal queen to immortal protectress of Manissé, of which more shall be said presently.

As we move from the *Tale* to the *Paladologies* we are immediately confronted with a glaring problem—the omission of what occurred in the interim between the taking of Manissa and the vision of Hadrior in the Temple of Mironna, a period of about two years. The *Tale* ends abruptly by telling us that the Asylians mourned "for forty days, until the time of mourning for Manissa Queen of Elabaea was ended." Then *Paladologies* picks up in an equally abrupt manner with—

> It came to pass in the days when Hadrior was king of Asylia reigning from white-walled Cadaras, the City on the Plains, the whole kingdom being at rest, that the king went forth in the second year of his reign to the Temple of Mironna in the Citadel to offer the yearly sacrifice for the well-being of the peoples of Asylia and Cadarasia...

We are thus left with a two-year interim of which there is no information; as we shall see that two-year period is of utmost importance for the subsequent history of Asylia, the house of Manissa, and an understanding of the events described in the *Paladologies*.

Related to this question is a fundamental curiosity that is never addressed in the *Paladologies*: what happened to Amyntas, husband of Manissa? The *Tale of Manaeth* leaves us with Manissa wed to Amyntas, Lord of Kerion and hero of the war against Maruda. We know that she bore seven children by him, all of whom feature prominently in the *Paladologies*. The last sentence of the *Tale* presents Amyntas as returning to Cadaras and mourning for Manissa's passing. But, as mentioned, when *Paladologies* opens, there is a two-year interim of which nothing is told. This two-year period must relate to Amyntas, since whatever became of Amyntas clearly happened within that missing timespan, for he is not mentioned whatsoever in the *Paladologies*. He is not mentioned by name as Manissa's husband, nor as the father of any her children (the children of Manissa are referred to her only, as "Hazer, son of Manissa" or "Baldor, firstborn of Manissa") which is extremely odd, the only instance in ancient Asylian literature of any person being named by their mother's lineage exclusively. Not only this, but it is never insinuated anywhere in the *Paladologies* that any of Manissa's children even had a father. Obviously they did, but no reference to anything close to a father is made with regards to them. It is as if, as far as *Paladologies* is concerned, the father of Manissa's children is of little importance; they might as well not have one. The one and only allusion to Amyntas in *Paladologies* is this sparse and depressing line from the tale of Giannor: "Kerion and Paros, where stood the hearths of hot-blooded Arrax *and other men of renown*, were no more and became as ruins."

It seems quite odd, of course, that a character so central to the *Tale* as Amyntas should simply be left out of the *Paladologies*, especially when Naross, Arrax, Eridax, and even Gygas the Betrayer are all mentioned. This has led some interesting historical and literary theories, the most prevalent being that the absence of Amyntas in the *Paladologies* was not an original feature of the text; rather, his presence was expunged by an outside editor at a later date. According to this theory, the *Tale of Manaeth* and "The Chronicle of the Days of Hadrior" were originally one work, the first ending not with Manissa's sudden disappearance but with the enthronement of Baldor in Asylia. This means the actual ending of the story would not be the abrupt cut-off in the *Tale* but rather this line from "The Chronicle of the Days of Hadrior":

> In Western Asylia, in the realm of Baldor, there was
> peace and prosperity, for every Asylian was secure
> in his field and among his flocks and Baldor ruled
> with justice and mercy.

This gives us a much more satisfactory ending to the whole saga, though it still leaves Manissa's disappearance and Amyntas's omission unresolved. But if the two works were originally one, then it should have included a section on the two missing years. If so, the chronicle of the two-year interim between the end of the *Tale* and the first book of the *Paladologies* must have been expunged at an early date, for no existing manuscripts contain anything other than the *Tale* with its current ending. This would also explain how the *Tale* and "The Chronicle of the Days of Hadrior" became two separate works. But why would such a critical piece of history be expunged, and by whom?

The missing portions would presumably detail not only the passing of Amyntas, but also the rise of Hadrior to the kingship, which we must view as somehow connected. If, in fact, Amyntas had been intentionally removed from the *Paladologies*, it was perhaps to obscure his fate, or reduce his importance. This suggests that his end was not honorable, and we know from the *Paladologies* that Hadrior, especially in his latter days, was not an honorable man. Therefore, it is not implausible to suggest the following scenario, which is pure conjecture:

Following the loss of Manissa, the people of Asylia and Cadarasia were left with the sudden and unexpected task of choosing a successor for her, she whom everybody had expected to be on the throne for several more decades. Given that her youngest son, Baldor, was only a teenager and had never been to war, there was probably a sharp dispute in the council over his fittingness to reign, the same sort of dispute we see narrated in the paladology of Secum. The two obvious choices would have been Amyntas or Hadrior, both of whom would have strong claims. Some parties argued for Amyntas while others pushed for Hadrior (Arrax possibly being dead by then, or if not, perhaps disqualified following his rash vow in the *Tale* to never take up arms again). Seeing Amyntas gaining ground, Hadrior resorted to treachery, and tricking him somehow, managed to catch him with his guard down and kill him. We can presume that he also managed to kill the supporters of Amyntas, for when *Paladologies* begins we see men loyal to Hadrior in every important position in the kingdom, especially Toranoss of Cadarasia and Arummnax of Orioön, who presumably would not have occupied those positions or been so indebted to Hadrior had the lords loyal to Amyntas remained alive. We also know that Hadrior was the sort of man to resort to murder, for only two years into his reign, the "Chronicle of the Days of Hadrior" relates how he conspired to murder Erogel, son of Arrax.

Later in Hadrior's reign, perhaps when early versions of what would become the story of Baldor's battles before Thán were going around, Hadrior could have intervened to expunge any references to Amyntas or his fate, perhaps forbidding it by royal decree. What was forbidden to sing about later vanished from the written accounts as well, partially because the original oral portion was lost or forgotten, and partially because it may have been too shameful for the nation collectively to recall the murder of Manissa's husband by its second king. At any rate, within a generation of the death of Hadrior, whatever may have originally been told about that two-year interim was forever lost, and apparently no poet or bard ever attempted to interpose a fictionalized account in its place, perhaps by virtue of the solemnity of the mystic events surrounding Manissa's passing and the tragedy of Amyntas's murder. This is only a theory, but a plausible one. It explains the missing chronology, the sudden end to the *Tale*, the apparent distaste of Baldor in the *Paladologies* for the court of Cadaras, the disappearance of Amyntas, and it is in keeping with what we know of Hadrior's character in his latter years.

There is another theory, however, which, though a minority position among scholars, deserves discussion. That is the thesis that Amyntas was not expunged from the *Paladologies*, but rather that he never existed to begin with. This theory began with the priesthood of Cadaras and was promulgated by the various clerics of Manis during the reign of Ezion. This theory holds that the reason Manissa's children have no father mentioned in *Paladologies* is because Manissa conceived them virginally. Amyntas is thus a fictional character written back into the *Tale of Manaeth* to account for the existence of Manissa's offspring. There are usually pious explanations given for this that reflect the influence of the cult of virgins that sprung up in Cadaras after the time of Elora. Most scholars reject this thesis, however.

egardless of these academic speculations, the *Paladologies* went on to become the most important text for the Manissan peoples after the *Tale*. But whereas the *Tale of Manaeth* was primarily a national epic, the *Paladologies* came to be considered as a religious text, especially following its compilation into a single book sometime during the long reign of Lesalius II, around the year 1500 in the Arza calendar (consult Appendix C on calendars in Manissé for the Arza reckoning, which counts down backwards). We know that the *Paladologies* and the *Tale* were primary reading in all the lower schools of Manissé from 1700 on, and that portions of the *Paladologies* were read solemnly in temple liturgies in the capital by the High Priest by Arza year 1550. Thus, by the mid-second millennium after Manissa, the *Paladologies* had went from being the sordid history of a single house to a kind of national-religious history, something that confirmed the destiny of the ever-expanding Manissan domains and became the sacred books of a cohesive civic religion, such as the cult of Manissa would become in the centuries following.

The *Paladologies* presented the Manissan peoples with a model of what a virtuous man should look like: following the examples of figures such as Baldor, Pilux and Oros (the *paladins,* and the tales about them being the *paladologies*), he was expected to be a fearless warrior, devout in the service of Manissa, and willing to lay his life down for the faith of his ancestors and the glory of Manissé. From around the year 1000 on, the *Paladologies* passed into the common lore of the Manissan peoples, no longer restricted to the educated scribal class. Glosses and commentaries on the *Paladologies* proliferated (some of which are included in this in Appendix B). It was a golden age of scholarship. Scribes such as Marialus, Numo and (later) Lucan of Anentora established rich allegorical and mystical interpretations of the *Paladologies* that became standard for centuries after.

It was not until the two millennia after the time of Manissa that this compilation of stories, poems, and religious images was given the name *Paladologies*. Sometime in the period of Lesalius II, it became standard to refer to these glorious descendants of Manissa as *paladins*, which comes from a phrase of the Enlilim, *pal eldian*, meaning "sons of glory"; in Asylian the word was *Anridos*, which simply meant "wonderworkers" but is considered equivalent to *pal eldian*. Why was a foreign word used to designate some of the most central figures in Manissan history? It is possible that the turmoil and decadence of the latter part of Lesalius's long reign led the Manissan peoples to reflect upon the glorious deeds of their ancestors, and that due to the Enlilic influence of Lesalius—who was a half-Enlilim—a phrase of his people was used to denote the legendary and somewhat miraculous accomplishments of the house of Manissa in ages past. It is also likely that these paladin stories were raised to a special dignity during this period because it was during the 19th to 13th centuries that the direct bloodline of Manissa grew thin; the miraculous powers of the paladins had already become rare by the time of Mantarax (c. Arza 2500), as his paladolgy tells us. Many would come forward in future centuries claiming to be of one of the houses of Manissa, but all of them were somewhat dubious. Only the kings of Manis maintained their pedigree through Perior with any certainty, and even this bloodline was substantially weakened. Thus the last period in which the houses of Manissa could be identified with any certainty was the same in which the deeds of the paladins became especially important to the kingdom. Though the word "paladin" shows up in the *Paladologies* a few times, it is certain that these are redactions from a later period, for there were no words of Enlilic etymology in the Manissan tongue prior to the time of Lesalius II.

As literature, *Paladologies* is much more of a challenge than the *Tale of Manaeth*, and of somewhat inferior quality in several places. While the *Tale* is a single story with a few recurring characters, the *Paladologies* are an arrangement of at least twenty-four different cycles of stories with a dizzying number of characters, many of whom never recur at later points in the saga. Place names change throughout the work: for example, we are first introduced to the "Asylians and Cadarasians," who are a little later referred to as the "men of Manissé" and finally as "Manissans." There are subtle distinctions: "Manissans" is a political term encompassing all the groups conquered or assimilated by the Asylians and Cadarasians, such as the Tabians, Badoan, and Dretians; indeed, the whole kingdom is finally referred to simply as "Manis" by the time of Ezion. The word "Manissé," on the other hand, is a cultural-geographical term denoting all the lands where the culture of the Manissans is dominant; it can be understood as akin to our word "Christendom." Within Manis or Manissé, groups like the Asylians, Cadarasians, etc. reflect ethic distinctions. Another point of possible confusion of place names is with the city of Cumala on Dretia Island. The city is first introduced as Cumala in the tale of Oros. Later it is referred to as the "Great City of Manissé," sometimes simply as the "capital" or the "court," and later as the "City of Manis."

Another literary trait of *Paladologies* is its tendency to return to a particular story again and again in different segments: an excellent example is the tragic death of Belar, Baldor's son. This is given a passing mention in the first book of the *Paladologies*, the *Iniốn éla Hadrior*. The story is told again in more detail in the *Nöm etha Manissé*, the second section of *Paladologies*, where we are now informed that Belar had a dispute with his father Baldor about Hadrior's war in Lugaria and that he died in battle estranged from his father. Finally, in the third book, *Anridion*, we are told that Belar was not only killed on the Lugarian campaign, but that he was murdered by Arummnax of Orioön and that King Cygnus actually attempted to preserve his life. This is a prime example of the way the *Paladologies* can return again and again to a single event, each time dwelling on it further and revealing more.

This is also the case with the story of Elifanora, for in the tale of Elphas in the *Nöm etha Manissé* we are introduced to the war of Anaxandra against the Illyrs and told that "the King of Emeric had been guilty of a great crime against the house of Manissa." Later, in the *Anridion*, we are told more about this crime, which was the attempted rape of Elifanora and her subsequent suicide. This literary technique of revisiting past events may be tedious and complicate any natural chronological flow to the stories, but it does serve admirably to better acquaint the reader with the persons and events involved and as a reminder that the *Paladologies* were written by scores of people and compiled over hundreds of years.

The three-fold division of *Paladologies* is the closest thing to any chronological progression in the book. The first book, "The Chronicle of the Days of Hadrior" (*Iniốn éla Hadrior*) is concerned with the campaign of Hadrior in the north against the city of Cyrenaica and its king, Endumion, who is a returning character from *Tale of Manaeth*. The book focuses extensively on the earliest days of Hadrior's reign and attempts to explain both the disinheritance of the house of Manissa from the kingship as well as the origin of the miraculous powers attributed to Manissa's children. The latter parts of the book tell of Hadrior's corruption, his disastrous defeats in Lugaria and Ituria, and his pitiful death.

Book two, the "Deeds of the Sons of Manissa" (*Nöm etha Manissé*) consists of five tales of the lives of Manissa's children, plus the somewhat out of place inclusion of a great census of the kingdom taken sometime around 3590 to 3585 Arza, as well as a brief tale on the vengeance of the sons of Perior, which serves as an epilogue. One can notice two distinct emphases in this book: the tales of the epic deeds of Manissa's house, which form the central plot of the stories; then behind this main plot, we see also the tale of the pitiful decay and dissolution of the healthy and powerful kingdom forged by Manissa. Baldor, Hazer, and Perior may be the main characters, but behind them are the paranoid Egol, the murderous Pirox, the dissolute Irglax, and the vengeful lords of Cadaras, men such as Calcax, Thrasos, and Indrior. Though the powerful and sometimes supernatural sons of Manissa dominate the stage, behind the scenes we witness the unraveling of the kingdom through the machinations of the ever fickle and suspicious nobility.

It is in the cycle of the Perior stories that the ambition of the nobility and the claims of the house of Manissa finally come into violent and irreparable conflict. Thus the Perior story has been called the most important of the *Nöm etha Manissé*, for the other stories of the book are all given closure in this one, and the stage is set for the tragic decline of Asylia that is chronicled in the *Anridion*.

The *Anridion* is the *Paladologies* proper; indeed, "Anridion" is simply the old Asylian name for *Paladologies*, which itself is an Enlilic word, as mentioned above. The *Anridion* is subdivided into two additional books, the *Anridion Aior*, or "Major Paladologies" and the *Anridion Inoré*, "Minor Paladologies." The first half of *Anridion* is much longer and involved while the *Anridion Inoré* consists of several entertaining short stories with little or no connection to one another. It is in the *Anridion* that we witness the fortunes of Manissa's later descendants, who are referred to in the story as *paladins*, the "sons of glory." In the beginning of the *Anridion* we see the tragic rejection of Manissa's house by the lords of Cadaras and Asylia, who harbored a special hatred against the descendants of Manissa since the overthrow of Cadaras by the sons of Perior. Following their definitive exclusion from any share in the rule of Manissé—and especially the savage attacks upon them by the villainous Sammas—the descendants of Manissa become wanderers upon the earth, traveling to distant kingdoms to find rest (as exemplified in the tale of Erixus), establish the cult of their glorified ancestress, and do marvelous works. It is these disinherited, wandering warrior-preachers who are best described as paladins, though the phrase was later used to refer to any direct descendant of Manissa.

The *Anridion* covers an astonishing amount of time, over twelve hundred years, but most of this time falls within the period from 3600—2900 Arza, an era generally called the "Manissan Dark Ages," and of which the *Paladologies* is the largest surviving document. While the first part of the *Anridion* reveals the unspeakable crimes against the house of Manissa by the nobility, the latter *Anridion* brings us, by many detours, to the final triumph and vindication of Manissa's house by the ascension of Ezion to the kingship, the first direct descendant of Manissa to secure the throne. This lengthy period—from the passing of Manissa, through the Dark Ages, to the enthronement of Ezion—marks the transition of Elabaea from a semi-barbaric alliance of tribal confederations to the unified and civilized Kingdom of Manis. It thus becomes much more than the story of one family, but the story of the nation. Ezion is a kind of latter-day Manissa, and many commentators have noted that the events of his life parallel those of his divinized ancestress (slaughter of parents, retreat to the wilderness, taking of Cadaras, etc.). What unravels after

Manissa's disappearance is put back together in the person of Ezion, in whom all the misdeeds done against the houses of Manissa are rectified and all the errors of the past put right.

Perhaps the most interesting theme in the *Paladologies* is the deification of Manissa. When we leave Manissa in the *Tale*, she is a regular mortal, albeit with some unusual qualities. In Book VI of the *Tale*, she seems to take on a supernatural character after her coronation when she grows in splendor and power before the assembly of the Asylians:

> Manissa stood tall upon the stone and seemed to grow in stature and grandeur, so that even Arrax was fearful of her might. And the sun fell upon her and lighted on her, that she seemed at that moment to become exceedingly beautiful and glorious, like one of the Mighty Ones of old. And many of the men there bowed their faces to the ground and said, "The beauty of Orianna and Osseia lives in Manissa, and the might of Manx and Orix her forebears!" Never had Manissa appeared so fearsome or beautiful as that day she stood upon the Stone of Cruachan when the Asylians proclaimed her queen.

Lest one think that this is only a literary device for describing Manissa's beauty and not a factual account, we are quickly reminded that this was an objectively real manifestation, for the author of the *Tale* writes that "many of the men there bowed their faces to the ground," a gesture that was not common among the ancient Asylians and would have only been performed in the presence of something of supernatural or of unexplained origin. The Manx legend regarding

Manissa's forebears may offer some explanation as to this phenomenon, for it is seen in her uncle, Arrax, as well, when in Book XIII we are told of his supernatural protection in battle:

> Some Marudans hurled spears and javelins at him, but these struck his rugged flesh harmlessly, like so many sticks, and fell to the earth. The Marudans cried, "He is possessed by some god," and fled before him.

Considering the Manx and Orianna legend, the house of Ioclus *already* had a hint of the divine within its blood by virtue of their descent from Manx even before the rise of Manissa.

Of course, it is Manissa's encounters with the Lamassu of Agenor that are the most mysterious events narrated in the *Tale*. The sighting of the stags, Naross tells her, is a great portent, and to see one three times in a lifespan was unheard of. Whether the stags were drawn to Manissa because of an existing supernatural quality about her or whether she gained her special character because of the stags is unknowable, but the sightings of the Lamassu are intimately bound up in her mysterious and mythic character, giving credence to the notion that even within her own life she was already revered as blessed. Besides Manissa, only Erixus and Elphas are described as seeing a Lamassu. Both had miraculous ends, as well: Erixus was "taken" from the world like Manissa, while Elphas lived for an extraordinarily long time, outliving even his descendants (the *puzi* mentioned in the tale of Ithaross functions as a kind of lesser, descanted version of the Lamassu that provokes the pursuit of Ithaross, but from rage rather than wonder).

In the first book of the *Paladologies*, we see that Manissa has already become a kind of heavenly messenger or intercessor, for in the very first passage we hear of the vision of Hadrior in the temple in which Manissa comes in glory to command war on the Illyrs. Elsewhere Hazer sings hymns to his mother on Ar Pelaroth, and Necho prays to the gods and invokes Manissa's protection three times a day. Most telling are the words of Baldor, whom after the appearance of the constellation Laoön in the Rua Calidé, tells Hadrior that the appearance of the new constellation is a sign that Manissa is "among the immortals" where she "ever lives." This is the closest we get to a description of where Manissa went, and Baldor does not elaborate on what "among the immortals" means, but the clear implication is that the lost Queen of Elabaea is not only still alive but in some glorified or transfigured state. Secum refers to Manissa as "she who broods behind the clouds." In the paladology of Cyllinus, the narrator has a vision of Manissa residing in some sort of exalted hall with the other heroes of Asylia, and in the company of Manx. Despite the vibrant imagery of this episode, we cannot take it as anything more than a vision, and in that sense it confirms what was already revealed by Baldor: that she is "among the immortals," wherever and whatever that may mean. Manissa herself tells Cyllinus that the elaborate apparition is just that, "vision and similitude." The only other clue to Manissa's precise whereabouts is the esoteric cry of the Periorid Erixus, who in the passion of hunting a Lamassu, cries out that he wills to come into "the domains of light, to the resting place of my Lady and the everlasting hills." Cyllinus also gives us the doctrine that Manissa is "appointed" to be the supernatural guardian or protectress of her people: not a divinity or a god in her own right, but exalted, glorified, and given divine powers from on high for the purpose of ruling and guiding the Manissans through the ages—a kind of patron saint of the Elabaean peoples.

By the middle of the *Paladologies* we see Manissa being prayed to and men invoking her name against evil (as in the story of Giannor, who drives out the spirit of Gygas from Nimru by invoking Manissa). In the paladology of Casias and

Lyrgoné she has her own order of priests (perhaps an outgrowth of the order of virgins that began in the time of Elora) and her cult is the focal point of Asylian religion. Most striking is her apparent theophany in the story of Oros and the taking of Cumala, where she appears in the flesh, spear in hand, to save the Manissans and bring doom to the Dretians. By the time of Ezion her cult has a centralized high priest officiating from a grand temple in the City of Manis. If all these elements are taken together, we can see a clear development throughout the *Paladologies* of a gradual deification of Manis's first queen as she evolved from a human heroine to a supernatural being.

Despite this, the Manissans never seem to lose the fundamental truth that she is not an end in herself or supreme in any absolute sense; she is rather an intercessor, a mediatrix and eternal patron of the kingdom. Even Manissa herself is powerless against the power-beyond-power, which the Asylians call "Fate" and the Cadarasians refer to as Mironna (*Merona* in later Manissan vernacular) and which is a personification of the inscrutable Providence which governs all things. This truth is depicted in the vision of Cyllinus and the light beyond the sea, where Manissa alludes to a power greater than herself, something that has "entrusted" her with the guardianship of the Manissan peoples.

From a political perspective, the two most important events of the *Paladologies* are the capture of the Island of Dretia by Oros and the reign of King Ezion. We shall consider each in turn.

One of the central stories of the *Anridion* is the paladology of Oros, telling how a coalition of Manissan lords marched over the Bados Mountains to the coast of the Bay of Norn and conquered the island of Dretia. Once they seized the island from the native Dretians, the Manissans occupied the Dretian fortress of Cumala and dominated the island from this location. So important does this impenetrable fortress become to the Manissans that almost immediately it functioned as a second capital of the kingdom. Sometime after the conquest, the Manissan kings translated the court from the Cadaras to the Isle of Dretia, probably due to its more centralized location. Thereafter, the kings of the Manissans will rule from Dretia, not Cadarasia, the capital being the "Great City" (called the City of Manis in Ezion's tale), and no longer Cadaras. This translation of the court from Cadaras to Dretia is a major hinge in the *Paladologies*, marking the point when the Manissan peoples began to climb forth from the chaos and instability that marked so much of the previous centuries, paving the way for the reforms of Eumaios and culminating in the glorious reign of Ezion the Periorid.

The capture of Dretia by Oros took place in the midst of a period ancient scribes called the *Scathéla*, the "shadow times"; later historians called them the Manissan Dark Ages. The Scathéla began after the death of Anaxandra, around 3598 in the Arza calendar, and lasted almost nine hundred years, till the reign of King Eumaios. The campaign of Oros occurred almost in the chronological center of this period, around 3150. The date is a rough estimate; scholars agree dates as early as 3250 and late as 3000 are also plausible.

The conquest Dretia was part of a larger migration of Manissan peoples westward from the northern plains about Engor, Halicor, and Anentora, in alliance with the men of Badoa and Corbalund. Their expansion came at the expense of the Dretians, a hardy folk who had inhabited the coastal mountains since primeval times. The coalition that formed under Oros was unique in Manissan history in that it was not organized under the banner of any king; it appears to have been a spontaneous mass movement bent on making an end of the

Dretians after years of strife in the foothills. It has the feel of a popular movement, not a royal campaign.

The Dretians took their name from the Isle of Dretia, their eponymous homeland in the midst of the Bay of Norn. The capture of Dretia will signify the shifting of the political power of Manissé from the north to the midlands. Dretia was an ideal capital: as an island flanked by the Cliffs of Ardilla on the east, it was vastly more defensible that Cadaras; it possessed a central location, allowing for easier administration of the northern plains and the expansion of Manissan power further south into Corbalund. The establishment of the new capital— simply called the "City of Manis"—would signal the end of the long Scathéla and the beginning of a Manissan golden age. As such, later generations of Manissans regarded the taking of Dretia by Oros as an event of profound national significance, of almost religious import. The paladology of Oros is lush with symbolism stressing the importance of the island as the new center of Manissan power, a theme thoroughly explored in the glosses of Appendix B.

The movement of the capital to Dretia sets up the second great political event of *Paladologies*, the reign of Ezion of the Glorious. Ezion's reign is incomparable in its importance to Manissan history. The reign of Ezion the Periorid was the first time a direct descendant of Manissa ruled a united Manissé; it was also the first time a king was able to establish effective centralized control over the kingdom. Ezion was graced with long life, living for 119 years and reigning for 94 of them. Ezion and Eumaios reigned for a combined total of 116 years, a period of complete transformation for the Manissans. Ezion's reign would see the Manissan peoples emerge into the light of high civilization, with literary, political, and cultural achievements unparalleled before or since in their history.

Almost none of this is chronicled in *Paladologies*, however. While *Paladologies* does contain brief foreshadowing of the glory to come under Ezion, it is more concerned with

Ezion as a fulfillment of past prophecy and aspiration. In Ezion, all the promise forfeited by Baldor, Perior, and all the other paladins is realized. Ezion is the child hurled to earth by Manissa in Elora's vision and plucked from the flames by the wolf in the dream of Eldax. The Manissans saw in him a chosen vessel destined by Fate to restore the fortunes of Manissé through the reconstitution of Manissa's bloodline upon the throne. In him, Manissé is ruled as Manissa originally intended. The shame and disinheritance of the age of the paladins is ended—an end that corresponds with the decline and disappearance of the paladins themselves.

During the reign of Ezion, the priestly commentator Gennax wrote, "What can be said of the *Paladologies* that has not already been written by men more learned and wise than I? For in them is the history of Manissé told, the lessons of brave and noble persons shewed forth, and the mysteries of our holy faith made resplendent in deed and symbol." This is an admirable summation of the work that was so pivotal to the identity of the ancient Manissans, a text through which they interpreted their history and contextualized their future. As the great Dionus of Lygon said, "Among the Manissans, the past and future are hardly distinguishable, for they run constantly one into the other, bound in an endless knot woven by Fate which no man of Manissé can untangle."

Appendix B
GLOSSES AND COMMENTARY

ভ᛭ঙ ভ᛭ঙ ভ᛭ঙ

Of the Murder of Erogel

If you do this, victory shall never flee from you. Later generations of Manissans saw in Hadrior's failure to obey Manissa's instructions to invade the south as the source of the all the troubles of his later reign. Kaldor (1104 AZ) says, "Inasmuch as our Lady promised blessing for obedience, what can be inferred from the disobedience of Hadrior other can cursing?"

Arummnax of Orioön. Arummnax had been a young man during the war with Maruda and made a name for himself by dashing through enemy lines to retrieve the Spear of Ioclus after Manissa hurled it at a Caeylonic captain at the battle in the forest. He was rewarded for his efforts by three mares from the royal stables (*Tale of Manaeth*, 13).

Erogel son of Arrax and Baldor son of Manissa...were given but small commands. Here we see the first attempt in the *Paladologies* of evidence of an effort on the part of the kings to supplant the place of Manissa's house.

Thus Toranoss had them speared to death as they came forth. An obvious allusion to the similarly treacherous killing of the sons of Ioclus by Arahaz (*TM*, 4).

Of the Siege of Thán

Hadrior swore an oath to Baldor...entering into covenant with him. Manissan tradition sees this as the beginning of the woes of the house of Manissa; Perior later rebukes Baldor for not at that time slaying Hadrior for his treachery; later Manissan sentiment has followed this opinion. Lucan of Anentora said, "If you seek to find examples of what evil befalls those who placate the ravenous desires of evil men for power, look no farther than our own histories and see what disaster befell the house of Baldor after he entered into covenant with Hadrior, though the latter had killed his own kinsman, Erogel."

Eiriniétha. The location of Eiriniétha was soon forgotten and was unknown even by the latter reign of Anaxandra, perhaps symbolic of the transitory peace established there, which was paradoxically built in the aftermath of a brutal series of killings.

Achanor. In Cyrenaican, "He who triumphs over the beast" (*TM*, 11).

Then came forth Baldor, son of Manissa, and a great trembling and a rage fell over him. The first such example in the *Paladologies* of the legendary powers and abilities that subsisted in the house of Manissa for many generations.

[H]ad it filled up with stone and mortar. The pit of Ochu has never been excavated and its location remains unknown, though there is a ditch near the old section of Thán that the locals claim to this day to be Ochu's pit.

Any man who would kill the son of Manissa in order to have her spear is not worthy of it. Marialus (965) writes, "In this statement of Baldor we see that the authority of the house of Manissa, symbolized by Ioclus's royal spear, will be removed from Elabaea until such a time that the people of that land are ready to acclaim and accept the rule of her sons."

Of the Rua Calidé

[H]er spear has appeared in the heavens. "The appearance of the spear signifies the twofold truth that Manissa ever lives among the immortals, and furthermore that from her celestial abode continues to watch and guide the destiny of her people, though the physical sign of her authority, namely, the Spear of Ioclus, was lost" (Norox, *Antiquities of Asylia*, 53, c. 1499).

The Final Days of Hadrior

Are they not all written in the Book of the Deeds of the Sons of Manissa? Since it is almost certain that the "Chronicle of the Days of Hadrior" was compiled before the paladology of Belar, this statement is most likely a gloss dating from a later age, possibly the period of the early Dretian kingdom (Arza 3150-3000).

But these things are written of in another place. In the paladology of Mariammné and Baldor in the *Nöm etha Manissé*. See Appendix C for dating and chronology.

Mariammné and Baldor

Then the sons of Manissa began to be great upon the earth. This clause and the following paragraph introduce one of the main themes of the entire *Paladologies*: the exceptional (and sometimes frightening) powers of the descendants of Manissa.

When the virgins go forth in flowered troupes. A reference to the ancient Asylian celebration of Trillia, which predates Manissa by at least a century.

[She] was therefore considered altogether lovely. Demonstrating that the ancient Asylians valued a woman who could fight as well as

keep a home, in contrast with later generations of Manissans who looked down on women who took up the sword.

In former days it was said that you were the cleverest of all men of Asylia. "In this greatest sin of Hadrior we see how lust and wickedness rob a man not only of virtue but of wisdom as well" (Marialus).

Baldor made known to them the vision. "Is it not written in the ancient tales how even Baldor exercised the gift of second sight? For he knew and told others after the battle of Enna of the vision of Hadrior in the Temple of Cadaras, though Hadrior himself had as of yet told nobody" (Dionus of Lygon, *Commentaries,* c. 1345).

Hazer

Only that it comes as a sign, as do the deeds done by all the children of Manissa. Norox: "As strength was given to Baldor, so healing song to Hazer, beauty to Ennus and so on, for in the paladins exist the powers of the immortals, though as it were broken up and distributed over the many, so that one possesses this power, another that, but so that all in all they collectively wield power divine" (*Antiquities of Asylia,* Chap. 33).

Many of the songs of Hazer are recorded in the Temple of Mironna. Forming the basis for the collection of sacred hymns later known as the Hazeritic Oracles, of which approximately about half are said to come from the mouth of Hazer, the rest from his descendants.

And as much as the land had been blessed before by his singing was it now cursed. An allegory for the tension between the blessing the sons of Manissa are capable of bringing to the land and the bane that they can be to king and people when their powers and knowledge are abused.

Iyla...bore to Hazer his third son, Asaph. The chronology does not work here, for in order for Asaph to have been at the court of Belabret in Epidymia, he could not be the son of Hazer. The scribe Kaldor attempted to resolve the problem by speculating that Asaph had an extraordinary long lifespan; others, namely Lucan of Anentora, settle the issue by saying that Asaph was actually the grandson of Hazer. See the first note for Asaph and Elora.

Ever after was it a destination of pilgrims. Since the shrine did not remain "ever after" but was destroyed by Sammas around 3504, this passage gives the Hazer paladology a relatively early date, perhaps Arza 3580-3530.

Necho and Elphas

[P]rovoked Anaxandra into war. It is interesting that elsewhere the death of Elifanora is declared to be the cause of the war; yet here, no mention is made of her. This has led the historian Bartellian to famously claim that Elifanora did not exist but was invented after the fact as a myth to justify the ensuing Asylian massacre of the Illyrs. But the more ancient tradition, as found in the works of Dionus and Norox, state that Elifanora is omitted here because her story was so well-known in ancient Asylia that to mention it here would be redundant, which is plausible.

The King of Emeric had been guilty of a great crime against the house of Manissa, as is told in other tales. A veiled reference to Elifanora, which Bartellian sees as a later gloss, but which older commentators take as authentic. See above note.

Tales of Manissa and their peculiar devotion to her. Apparently homage to Manissa was still viewed at this time as an eccentricity of the existing Asylian religion and not the distinct religious system it would later become.

[He] saw not the stag as it had previously appeared, but now a creature glorious and full of splendor. Lucan says: "The Lamassu,

though in the form of a stag, was yet not a stag but a creature of even greater splendor and radiance, one of the creations of the Titani of old. The glory of the Lamassu became veiled in proportion to the decay and corruption of the world, and as such have not been seen among us now for over a millennium, but some say that at the end the Lamassu will rise again with the Titani on their day of vindication" (*On the Titani*, 200).

And he carefully picked the bloody grass and kept it as an heirloom. For millennia afterward a patch of withered grass called the Grass of Elphas was displayed in a shrine at Anentora for the veneration of the locals.

Secum

So they spoke ill of Hazer and the sons of Manissa. A foreshadowing of the hostility that the lords and nobles of Cadaras will bear towards the House of Manissa.

[L]et there be a vote taken...let whomever the lords choose be our king. Lucan says, "The debate between Egol and Elphas concerned the manner in which the kingship of Asylia was passed on in the ancient days. From this dialogue, and from what we know from Manissa's life, it seems that the tradition of antiquity was that the throne should pass from father to son by right. Yet, when the sons of Ioclus were slain and the kingdom deprived of its princes, an irregularity was introduced that necessitated the calling of the Council of Cruachan, which subsequently gave the throne to Manissa. This nominating council, which was called only as an exception in the case of Manissa, became an institution with regards to the elevations of Hadrior, Anaxandra, and many succeeding kings. Thus, Secum and Gilgax are shown to favor the more antiquated method, Egol the novelty of the council."

Is the tomb of my mother among the Cadarasians? "By this verse some impious madmen have dared to speculate that our Lady was not taken from the earth as is told in the *Tale* but rather that she died and is buried. Let such speculation be considered the most abhorrent blasphemy, for Baldor says not that her tomb is to be found elsewhere, only that it is with certainty not among the Cadarasians" (Norox, *Antiquities,* Chap. 68).

The spirit of wisdom left him. An expression of the ancient Asylian belief that wisdom and personal virtue are inseparable. See the sixth gloss under Telux and Andrior.

Secum opened his mouth in the vineyards. Many derivations of these sayings can be found on an ancient Epidymian pillar in the region of Anorel bearing the title, "The Teachings of the Sage Sekuma." The pillar dates from around 3450 AZ, almost two centuries after Secum.

The Council of Lords and the Great Census

Let us be done with kings! For the confusion over the regal tradition, see note two for Secum.

The first act decreed by this Council of Lords was a census. Presumably to clear up, once and for all, much of the confusion attendant upon the union of the kingdoms of Asylia and Cadarasia in the person of Manissa and the unresolved matters of jurisdiction.

Peredoss ruled Cyrenaica as a king. "Thus is it written that the kingdom was not finally united until the reigns of Eumaios and Ezion, for though Cyrenaica had been taken by Hadrior, its lords acted in all ways like kings from the time of Peredoss until the ascent of Ezion" (*Chronicle of Ezion*, Caput XIII).

Three hundred and forty-seven thousand persons. Counting women and children, this brings to total population of the Manissan dominions near 1.5 million at the time of the census.

For which they were to be justly punished. A redaction from a later scribe attempting to demonstrate the connection between the evil of the lords and the wrath executed upon them by the Perior.

Perior

[T]hey ran out of stones to throw. "In this passage we see presaged the truth that, though the other houses of Manissa would falter, the house of Perior would remain ever vital, for just as there was no stone which Perior could not throw, so there would come not obstacle or persecution which the house of Perior would not endure and triumph over, as we see in the establishment of Ezion the Periorid and King of Manis in the latter days" (*Chronicle of Ezion*, Caput V).

He pulled up the two great posts of the Hall of Orix...and carried them on his shoulders. "Even as the posts of the Hall of Orix, that is, the authority of kingship, rested on the shoulders of Perior, so would the throne of Manis pass to Perior's descendants" (Norox, *Antiquities*, 87).

A cruel race of hill giants. According to most authorities, these giants were the foes of the sons of Anak, remnants of that ancient brood which had made war on Agenor at the dawn of time.

Rowan trees. "Ever have the nymphs of Adarwood been delighted by the bright rowan berries, so much so that groves of rowan are still said to be frequented by the nymphs, for their branches signify power, and their berries life" (Kaldor).

A curse upon those who would seal the gates of this city against me. Marialus says, "Inasmuch as Perior pronounces curses upon those whom Hazer had blessed, the cursing which Perior intended for his foes returned and fell upon him instead." Some dispute this, however, based on Hazer's words later in the story that his singing can have "no effect on him for either good or for ill."

It is sealed from me. Regarding the stars, Dionus of Lygon says, "As stars guide the mariner by night along his appointed route, so the meaning of the vision of the stars is that the sons of Manissa and their houses will serve as guides along the years, leading the Manissan peoples back to strength and prosperity" (*Commentaries*, 44)

[T]hough the shrine has long since vanished. Indicating that this tale was penned after the destruction of the shrine by Sammas two generations later.

Sons of Perior

[A]re they not sung of in the lays of the sons of Perior? A reference to the later work also called *Sons of Perior*, which chronicles the adventures of Perior's children. Originally composed in verse, it was transcribed to prose during the reign of Ezion. Only fragments of the original metrical verse have ever been found.

Belar

But Belar his son opposed him to his face. Suggesting that there may have been many in Asylia and Cadarasia who were not sympathetic to Mariammné and who may have seen Hadrior's actions as necessary for the raising up of an heir and the prevention of civil war.

Elifanora

Kingdoms of Illyrana and Emeric. Throughout this story the kingdoms are sometimes referred to separately, sometimes as one people. Apparently, the cities of Emeric and Illyrana were distinct kingdoms, but the people of the two kingdoms were both ethnically Illyrs. Thus the two kingdoms are sometimes referred to simply as "the Illyrs."

[T]he Zhinkanthians had oppressed the Marudans and made them slaves. See *Tale of Manaeth*, pg. 35, the speech of Arrax.

King of Emeric. Though this lusty king remains unnamed in the tale, tradition calls him Birguk, a word of Caeylonic origin meaning "rapacious."

Asaph and Elora

Iyla... gave birth to Asaph. This is the only story in the *Paladologies* that presents a clear historical problem. Asaph is supposed to have been the third son of Hazer, and, given what we know of his life and the manner of Hazer's death, this would place Asaph's own death somewhere around 3540 in the Arza reckoning, give or take a decade. Yet the story is supposed to parallel the reign of the Epidymian King Belabret, who was most certainly killed in Caeylon in 3510, contemporary with the reign of Sammas in Cadaras. There is no way Asaph could have been contemporary with Belabret if he is to be the son of Hazer. Furthermore, a very strong tradition has it that Elora, daughter of Asaph, was elderly at the time of Sammas and was persecuted by him; yet, if Asaph was contemporary with Belabret, Sammas would have taken the throne of Cadaras three years before Elora was even born! In addition to this, Elora's vision clearly portrays Sammas's tyranny as something still in the future, not yet already existing. Two theories have been suggested to resolve this chronological difficulty of this tale (1) the Epidymian portions of the Asaph story are legendary accretions which, over time, replaced the authentic biography of Asaph. Thus, most of the story, at least the parts about Asaph in Epidymia, are mythical (2) Asaph was actually the grandson of Hazer rather than the son, the mistake in the *Paladologies* being attributed to a scribal error in translation the Asylian word grandson (*anomé*) that became simply "son" (*nom*). This would allow for the historicity of the tale and explain the problem of chronology, though it would not explain the problem with Elora's age. This latter difficulty is explained away by saying that Elora was no relation of Asaph at all and that her designation as the illegitimate daughter of the Hazerite prophet is legendary. Most scholars, ancient and modern, have adopted the latter solution, making her a Hazerite but of unknown lineage.

The Erriad... branched out into seven courses. "Is it not clear that the seven rivers of Asaph are the seven houses of Manissa?" (Norox)

The priesthood is reserved to males alone. Inorax refers here to the priesthood or Mironna (Merona), which was distinct from the priesthood of Manissa that developed later, though the latter priesthood also refused to admit females, which they saw as a vile, pagan custom of the Marudans.

She had a great vision. Though interpretations of the dream of Elora abounded in ancient Manis, we will follow here the schema developed by the Lygonian sage Eratus (c. 2200 AZ), whose interpretation of Elora's apocalypse became standard in the 2nd millennium of Manissé. Eratus, in his work on Manissan prophecy, sees most of Elora's vision fulfilled in the tyranny of Sammas and the ascent of Ezion to the throne. He gives the following explanations:

> *Hill of Cruachan overgrown*: the woeful state of Manissa's house
> *Pricked her fingers*: those who tried to restore Manissa's house were slain
> *Herd of deer*: the seven houses of Manissa
> *Troupe of riders from the east*: the hordes of Sammas
> *Single doe*: Mariammné's house
> *Solitary buck*: the house of Necho
> *Fiercest of all the bucks*: the house of Perior
> *Black sludge*: foreign cults
> *Hideous frogs*: foreign gods/demons
> *Whirlwind*: Providence or Fate
> *Twelve gloriously armed warriors*: the Paladins; the number is generic for fullness
> *Riding to the north*: preparing for the coming of Ezion/retreat of the Periorids

> *Tall mountain*: Mount Sligo in western Cyrenaica
> *Hidden child*: Ezion's youth spent in hiding among the
> Periorids
> *Hurled him to the earth*: the sudden and unexpected
> exaltation of Ezion
> *"I will be ever with my people"*: the final triumph of
> Manissa's house and destruction of the foreign cults

Though this interpretation has been commonly accepted, one ought to bear in mind that the visions of Cyllinus (which ought to be read alongside those of Elora) portray things in a much more eschatological context, as opposed to the historical one given by Eratus. Thus the fulfillment of Elora's prophecies could be either in or outside of history—or perhaps both.

Sammas

Rugged shepherds and farmers. Suggesting that the kingdom did not as of yet possess any significant standing army.

Left-handed. This taboo is not mentioned anywhere in ancient Manissan lore outside of the paladology of Sammas and Apollus, indicating that it was most likely confined to the regions around Cadaras and An Hered.

But you are half-Asylian. The comment of Zimrah makes little sense, given that the father of Sammas was from An Hered, a region associated with Cadarasia, not Asylia. One can only suppose that the errant statement was due to her unfamiliarity with Elabaean tribal divisions and was using the word "Asylian" to refer to all the Elabaean peoples collectively.

They found it very wild and overgrown with many thorns and brambles. Marialus says: "But a darkness of ignorance had fallen on all the peoples of that age, for had they remembered the visions of the prophetess Elora, they would have called to mind that the vision of Cruachan covered in brambles served to announce the beginning of miseries. Thus they were greatly deceived."

[V]ile ceremonies of the Nergalim. Also spelled "Nirgalim," Dionus of Lygon in his *Commentaries* says these rituals to the god Nergal consisted in "the vile sacrifices of chickens, dogs and other beasts unfit for divine worship." (Chap. 54)

Scylax. Though he does not appear in the *Paladologies*, many great tales come down in song of the deeds of Scylax, grandson of Baldor.

Slay...the young with the old, the men with the women, the mother with the suckling babe. This formula, which shows up more than once in the tale of Sammas and Apollus, was employed in Caeylon by the kings of the Mordic dynasty when ordering the utter annihilation of a rival people. The Caeylonics called it the *Nurbadir*, the "Black Order."

So that the city should not be defensible anymore. "After the coming of Javad the Marudan, the city of Asylia became greatly diminished, and its lords of were little account thereafter." (Norox, *Antiquities*, 109)

Sammas was intent upon wiping out the houses of Elphas and Necho. Most scribes and commentators agree that this paragraph is out of sequence and should be placed before the one prior to it.

[H]ow he persecuted the holy virgins. This may refer to an apocryphal story, mentioned by Kaldor, Norox, and Dionus, that Sammas, upon taking the throne at Cadaras, was aroused to fury by the rebukes of the elderly Elora and attempted to have prophetess burned to death, only to see her ascend from the flames and fly away to Mount Eriar before his eyes. More recent authorities (Lucan, Numo) say Elora died during Sammas's sojourn in Maruda and that this passage refers to another apocryphal episode in which Sammas allegedly disbanded Elora's order of virgins and forced them all to take husbands on pain of death. The strong tradition

that Elora and Sammas were somehow contemporaries is complicated by the problems with dating the paladology of Asaph and Elora, as mentioned above in note one. Regardless, all traditions attest that Sammas persecuted the virgins of Cadaras, whether Elora was personally involved or not.

Giannor

Some even forgot the language of Asylia. From this time on the ancient Asylian tongue began to be altered by heavy borrowings from Cadarasian and Marudan; by the time of Ezion about a thousand years later it will have morphed into the so-called "common" of Manis.

Old Asylia waned. See note eight for the tale of Apollus and Sammas.

[E]vil spirits and vile creatures came forth and troubled the people of the land. Numo: "In those days swarmed the *vogi* [vile ones] who took advantage of the disarray in Elabaea to creep forth from their abodes to trouble the land." (*Inquiries*, Book II)

Lothar

Slavery in Caeylon. An indication that the early Manissans did not practice slavery.

This was erected in the days of King Sammas. Though Sammas was overthrown and slain, it appears that the foreign cults he established remained in the land for quite some time, not being driven out until the time of Lothar (at least in Cadarasia).

Frenzied words. Norox: "The religious rites of the Illyrs, like the Zhinkanthians before them, were carried out amidst inane babbling and frenzied crying from the priests and those officiating, so much so that those in attendance were cowed into terror by the fearsome noise, which sounded not so much like human utterance as the very chaos of the underworld." (*Antiquities*, Chap. 100)

Prove...by some ordeal or trial. It is uncertain when trial by ordeal first entered Manissé, though from this passage it is clear that it was already established in the time of Lothar and Alcidus. Though trial by ordeal had vanished by the time of Ezion, it lived on in the practice of gladiatorial combat which passed to the Kingdom of Vygarrd by way of Manis.

Son of glory. In Enlilic, *pal eldian*, or "paladin" in later Manissan common.

Shall I be ordained... and then condemned because I did what was ordained? The classical Manissan dilemma regarding their approach to Fate, which is personified and deified as Merona (Mironna in old Asylian).

[T]o atone for the blood of Dimmoth and Vinos and for the sins of Eira. Most Manissan commentators see the continence of Lothar as being chosen to counter the particular sins of his house. For example, Dionus of Lygon: "The penance of Lothar was efficacious in atoning for the sins of Eira inasmuch as his perfect continence during his three years in Corbalund cancelled out the excesses of Eira. Moreover, only continence could accomplish this, for since paganism is akin to lust and infidelity, so continence, by the fidelity of its adherents to its practice, is able by purity to perfectly cancel out the impure vices of paganism." (*On the Mysteries*, Book II:33)

She is still seen roaming...at night. To this day the shade of Eira is reported to haunt the barren ridges that surround the ruin of Halicor.

Casias and Lyrgoné

Sing in me, O spirit of song. The tale of Casias and Lyrgoné is the only paladology that was most certainly composed first as an oral ballad set to music. This explains the invocations to the "spirit of song" and throughout the story as well as the literary style of the writing, as contrasted with the purely historical "chronicle" style of the paladology of Oros, for example.

Teach them of the religion and ritual handed on to us by our forefathers. Here we see the expression of the "evangelical" spirit of the Manissans in assuming that alliance with other peoples of Elabaea is not possible unless there is a shared "ritual" to the glorified foundress, Manissa. This evangelical element was always present but was especially so in the five centuries between Casias and Ezion.

Uncertain lands. In the paladology of Ezion, this region is called Albia.

Succo...Manes and Silent Watchers. Succo is called Succoth in later Tabian tradition. Little is known of the Manes, though the Silent Watchers are believed to be wraith-like creatures that haunt the wilderness at night and secure the desolate highways against thieves and robbers. Their ire is said to fall on any solitary man found on the road after dark.

Vâlcea Bridge. Of the many architectural marvels attributed to the Tabians, the Vâlcea Bridge alone has survived the centuries. The Caeylonic traveler Damasur, writing around Arza 2525, said, "The rigors of the Manissan wilds and all the perils that beset a traveler coming west from the highlands are all as nothing compared with one moment's vision of the setting sun beyond the sea as viewed from the placed called Vâlcea on the Soldara in Tabia" (Damasur, *Journeys and Adventures*, 28). The bridge later fell into disrepair and collapsed in 1717, though its ruins can still be seen.

As he spoke, the heart of Casias was enflamed with desire for Lyrgoné. Numo says, "What shall we say about love? Does it proceed from knowledge, as some of the sages say, or ought we to rather value the opinion of the ancients, that love is as random as lighting and does not follow knowledge but rather precedes it, for a man does not seek to know that which he does not love? Consider, in the sacred writings, what is told of brave Casias and light-footed Lyrgoné, for the heart of Casias was enraptured with love for the maiden before he had yet known her name or her lineage. This seems evidence that the view of the ancients is vindicated, though it has also been said that, in this case, the will of Fate had a hand in the meeting of the lovers. If Fate is to be invoked in this inquiry, then further speculation is futile." (*Inquiries*, Book IV:177).

If it be not so, may I suffer an ignoble shame! A rash oath on the part of Casias that does in fact lead to shameful consequences for the otherwise noble paladin.

Drowned in the depths of the merciless sea...as was custom. "Among the Tabians there was known from ancient days of a vile and brutal custom and drowning women suspected of infidelity in the depths of the sea. These poor wretches, bound securely to a great stone, were cast into the waters from a great precipice with many incantations to their god Succoth. Nor did this custom end with ease, for it was not until sometime after the Manissans took the region of Tabia that they could compel the people there to stop drowning their women, and this only with great difficulty and the threat of punishment behind it." (Norox, *Antiquities of Asylia*, Chap. 202)

Then she cried forth a torrent of tears. In Lygon to this day there is a peculiar devotion to the "Four Sorrows of Lyrgoné," she who, according to Dionus, "Suffered more than any other maiden in the history of Manissé, her tears as precious and life-giving as those of Ornis." (*History of Lygon*, Book III:7)

Hymns and dirges...written by Hazer, son of Manissa. In the hopes that the blessings and curses contained in these compositions would be mystically transferred to the Manissans, or their foes, depending on the situation, just as Hazer himself had the power to bring blessing or cursing to those who heard him sing.

Manissa Dylydia...the Avenger. A title of Manissa common among the Periorids in invoking her to undue the injustices done to the houses of Manissa throughout the centuries.

But the place...he called the Lygonea. The hillside shrine of Lygonea became the camp of the Manissans in the campaign against the Tabians and later grew into the city of Lygon. The Lygonea, the original hill wherein the two lovers are buried, stands in the very heart of the great city. It is now enriched with many shrines and edifices of marble and stone.

Oros

Reckoned among the Manissans. Meaning that their peoples, though not ethnically related to the Asylian or Cadarasian tribes, had pledged fealty to the king at Cadaras and were subsequently accepted as Manissan allies.

All of whom had scores to settle with the Dretians. "Never were there two peoples more opposed than the Badoans and the Dretians, for the Badoans did ever make war on the Dretians to drive them out of the hill country into the western mountains, and the Dretians likewise ever sought to press the Badoans eastward into the plains. Thus they constantly raided one another and were settling vendettas perpetually." (Norox, *Antiquities*, 29)

The birds were slain, the auguries taken. The first mention of augury in Manissan history. In ancient Elabaea, it was the Cadarasians who were known for their auguries. The practice was probably adopted through Asylian exposure to Cadarasian customs.

The men elevated Oros upon their shields. "In elevating Oros upon the shield, a gesture typically reserved for the coronation of a new sovereign, the soldiers of Manissé prophetically show forth that the royal authority will be transferred from Cadaras to the City of Manis in the person of Oros." (Dionus of Lygon, *Commentaries*, 203).

O isle of pleasantness, haven of rest. Later to become a famous Manissan anthem, the *Orosia*.

Oros spoke with the very fire of Manissa in his bosom. Based on this phrase, Manissan tradition considers these words of Oros as inspired by Manissa. Thus says Marialus, in his sixth book on Manissan history, says: "The taking of Dretia was not in accordance with human planning and stratagem, for it was Blessed Manissa herself who decreed the handing over of the sacred isle to the Manissans when she spoke to the men assembled by Norn's waters through the mouth of Oros."

[T]he heart of Dindar was arrogant. Numo says, "And what man will say that arrogance is not a detestable vice? For arrogance, besides being the most unpleasant of all qualities that can be found among men, is also destructive and is the mother of folly. Have you not read what folly arrogance led Dindar to in the days of Oros and the taking of Dretia? Were it not for his exceeding arrogance, he would not have foolishly gone to his death over the treacherous cliffs upon Norn's clear waters, nor led others to doom as well. Oros and Dindar are distinguished in this most of all, that the former was humble, but the latter was full of foolish pride." (*Inquiries*, Book VI, 59)

This past night a vision came to me. It is often forgotten that Oros, besides being a military commander, was also a prophet. Thus is he listed among the prophets in the temple litanies that are still sung in the regions around Bados and along the coasts of the Norn to this day.

Oros remained in his tent. "In this tale, the great Manissa acts in the person of the captain Oros. Manissa speaks her words through him; when he is absent, things go afoul, as when he refused to come forth from his tent to witness Dindar's attempt to scale the cliff; when he is present, things are blessed. Nor is it improper that this should be so, for to Oros alone of all the paladins was it given to seize the sacred city from the pagans of Dretia. Therefore, it is fitting that our Lady should be so intimately concerned with his effort, as is chronicled in the paladology that bears his name." (Norox, *Antiquities*, Chap. 103)

Buturlüe. Ever since the time of Oros there has been a yearly pilgrimage from Bados, the site of to Betulia, commemorating the weary march of Oros's men. The route goes from Bados (old Ardilla), north through the mountains and the desolate region of Galmura to Betulia and takes between three and four weeks to complete. A shrine in Betulia is the end destination of the pilgrimage.

Adlor. The archaic *-or* suffix was later dropped from the place name, becoming Adlo by the time of Lesalius.

Corax...threw himself at the feet of Oros. The *Chronicle of Ezion*, as well as later tradition, see in this passage a statement about the submission of the city of Cadaras to the new City of Manis. The *Chronicle* says: "Is any in doubt that the authority of Cadaras is inferior to that of Manis? Behold how, in the tale of Oros, Corax, who represents Cadaras, throws himself at the feet of Oros and does homage to him, he who represents in his very person the City of Manis which he founded. For the sacred writings speak of Corax serving Oros as a vassal, even as Cadaras is to this day in vassalage to the great City of Manis, the first of all cities of queen of the dominions of the Manissans" (*Chronicle of Ezion*, Caput XXXV).

Manissa Tualitha. Still the greatest religious celebration of the year upon the Isle of Dretia.

The deeds of Manissa were read aloud. The first reference to a written copy of the *Tale of Manaeth*, as noted by the use of the verb "read."

They perceived that he had uttered a prophecy. This famous prophecy was fulfilled nearly three thousand years later, when the City of Manis was again besieged, this time by the hostile Bavor federation in the time of the last Periorid king. Manissa again appeared before the walls of the city, though then as a portent of doom, for the city soon after fell to the ravages of the Bavor, and the Periorid line was extinguished forever.

Durmius...swore no oaths to Oros. "Can it be doubted that it was because Durmius failed to swear fealty to Oros that his lordship, that of Halicor, fell into insignificance and destitution shortly after the time of Oros' conquest?" (Marialus)

Fragments of Adrius

Old stones, remains of tumbled down pillars. "Of old the Lugarians were known to patronize the location, believing the spring to have healing properties. In ancient times was their god Vinus placated there with offerings of wine and obscene rites carried out within the veil of the glade." (Kaldor)

Ezion

Most of the commentary on the tale of Ezion comes from the *Chronicle of Ezion,* compiled around Arza 2500 by scribes of the Manissan court. The *Chronicle,* though distinct from the earlier paladology of Ezion, takes most of its material from the paladology, its other sources being oral tradition and records from the court, which were at that time scant.

Eumaios summoned the great lords. We are told in the *Chronicle* that this council, though postponed due to Eumaios's sudden death, was in fact summoned during the reign of Ezion for the purpose of "consolidating the work of our illustrious predecessor Eumaios in the efficient and just management of the affairs of the realm." (*Chronicle of Ezion,* Caput IV).

This place has become my Lissus. The first of many such parallels this paladology draws between the lives of Ezion and Manissa.

Roused by a great wolf. The ancestral symbol of the house of Perior.

Mount Sligo. The "tall mountain" Elora saw in her vision. See the Note 4 in the gloss for Asaph and Elora.

Thalon sought to install one of his own companions as lord. This was one of the means by which Eumaios, and later Ezion, also sought to centralize power in the throne. The fact that the people of Cadaras resisted Thalon's efforts suggested that they had considered this a privilege allowable to Eumaios alone rather than a permanent prerogative of the court, as it later became. And certainly Thalon's appointment may have been more acceptable to the Cadarasians had the appointee not been an inept youth.

May your throne endure forever! This is the tradition sevenfold-blessing, the *Septoria*, which from the time of Ezion on was proclaimed at the coronation of every Manissan king (*Chronicle*, Caput X, XIV).

[T]he men arose and fled east to Caeylon. The *Chronicle of Ezion* tells us that this dispatch was made of two men called Marsius and Erior, who later returned to Manis in the days of Ezion's ascension: "After hearing of the glorious triumph of Ezion, and of his exceedingly great mercy, the servants, Marsius and Erior, returned from Caeylon and prostrated themselves before the throne of Ezion, begging his pardon. Gracious Ezion raised them up, and with many kind words, restored them to their lands with many gifts. Till the end of their days were no peers of the king to be found in all the land who were more trustworthy or dependable than Marsius and Erior." (*Chronicle*, Caput. XII)

Spending many days receiving delegations from the south. Again, the *Chronicle* gives us insight into the reasons behind Thalon's delay: "At the time when Thalon was mustering his armies at Engor, a delegation arrived from the Kingdom of Elgard in the south, seeking the king's mediation in some dispute between the men of that country and the Enlilim over certain rights and prerogatives of the two orders. The king's father was greatly put out at this, for the issue concerned not the Kingdom of Manis. But Thalon heard the delegation with eagerness, hoping thereby to perhaps secure the good will of the men of Elgard in an alliance against Ezion. It was only with much persuasion that Argoss was able to convince Thalon to arbitrate the dispute after Ezion was dealt with, for Thalon would have gone south to Elgard at that time and happily left the battle with Ezion to his captains." (*Chronicle*, Caput XL).

Iontaré. It's Asylian name, An Parthas, means "Paradise."

[T]he army of Ezion attacked Engor and overthrew it. This was the final overthrow of Engor, for the city was never rebuilt after its destruction. The *Chronicle* tells us: "Ezion, fearing Engor as a seat of treachery because of its affiliation with the house of Thalon, refused to allow the city to be rebuilt, but instead settled the survivors upon the Island of Dretia or in Corbalund." (*Chronicle*, Caput L)

Silius was thrust out...in his place Ezion installed Pontus. It is noteworthy that, while Ezion regards Silius as an impostor for being appointed by the king from among his friends, Ezion does the exact same thing in the appointment of Pontus. It is believed that this was the origin of the custom of the High Priest of Manissa's temple in the capital obtaining his office through royal appointment.

He decreed a holy day. The celebration of the translation of Perior's bones is celebrated yearly in Cadaras on the fifteenth day of the eighth month.

Mantarax

Four hundred and fifty years. A crude approximation, since nobody knows the exact date of Oros's conquest of Dretia.

[T]he great city of Thon. More of a permanent encampment than a city, as the Iturs were a semi-nomadic people.

Tereldian. The Shrine of Mantarax was frequented by pilgrims for over fifteen hundred years until it was mysteriously (and some say miraculously) lost in the year 922 AZ. The details are related in Book VIII of Numo's *Inquiries*.

Pilux

A fearsome beast. An ogre of Corbalund. Such creatures were frequently found in the regions south of Corbalund during the time of Pilux, as the *vogi* were still dwelling in the lands south and east of the Enlilim.

Signs and letters that Pilux did not recognize. Probably of Enlilic origin, or perhaps Marudan.

Ennus

Born to the house of Baldor. This places the tale of Ennus somewhere between the time of Hadrior and the reign of Sammas, a window of about one hundred years. Some commentators consider this story mythical, an allegorical statement on the reckless nature of love.

This has been the custom in Cadarasia from time immemorial. Norox: "No man of Cadaras, no matter how virtuous or wealthy, would be suffered to wed any of the noble maidens of that city unless he should prove his worth by winning victory in war, slaying some foul beast, or doing some other feat of daring. This was an ancient institution of the Cadarasians for the purpose of insuring that the lords of that region came only of the most noble and illustrious stock and that their men folk would never want for courage." (*Antiquities*, 100)

Trianta. Numo says in the fourth book of the *Inquiries*: "And what of the glistening trianta, those splendorous white roses which are known to blossom only upon the banks of the Cadar in fair

Cadarasia? Tradition tells us that in the ancient days, when Laban and his sons came west to settle fair Elabaea, that the wife of Laban, Uta, passed by the Cadar and napped by its lapping banks in the cool of the day. When she awoke, she found that a bed of the most lovely and delicate roses had sprung up about her, and thereafter they spread west along the banks of the brook, as if following Laban and Uta in their journey. I know not whether this tale holds any veracity, but to this day the trianta will not bloom in any other locale, though many have attempted to transplant them."

Ianthë

Bequeathed to the house of virgins. Bequests to the orders of virgins were common in the first millennium and a half of Manissan history, as is evidenced by the tale of Ianthë, as well as Elora. A girl could be given up as young as age five and made solemn vows of perpetual virginity at age thirteen. Beginning during the period of Lesalius, royal law made the procedure more difficult by raising the minimum age of bequest to nine and requiring the consent of the girl being handed over. The practice was outlawed entirely by royal decree in 1109 but continued nonetheless until around Arza 500.

Prayers from the virgins there for the welfare of the kingdom. The fact that Tullus is seeking prayers for the well-being of his house suggests that the story takes place not long after the transfer of the throne from Cadaras to the City of Manis, for the house of Tullus does not appear to be long established. Note also that the wealthy prince of the tale, Phantos, is not from the City of Manis but Cadaras.

Not in many years had such a mighty lord visited old Asylia. At the time of this tale, the city and region of Asylia had lost much of its importance to Cadaras, just as Cadaras at that same time was losing prestige to the newly founded City of Manis upon Dretia Island.

[He] took in her fair form with his eyes, withholding nothing from them. "The sin of Phantos began in the eyes, as does every

adulterous affair and union of fornication. But if the eyes be kept pure, then these vices are likewise kept at a distance" (Agrius the Sage, *Hectarion*, Book III, c. 2100 AZ).

Stroking his grizzled beard. An ancient Asylian gesture signifying the swearing of an oath.

Amatós

Like the tale of Ennus, the story of Amatós is believed to be mythical in nature, a moralizing tale to young Manissan boys about the perils of venturing too far into the deep woods (see the note below). However, those dwelling in the region of Eidyllion have always insisted on the tale's historicity.

Asylians feared all the nymphs. Marialus: "But the Asylians kept ever before their mind the fact that they were in nowise the first inhabitants of the land, recalling that it was inhabited by the nymphs and spirits before them, and in turn by Agenor and the Great Ones prior to that. Thus they avoid the woods if it can be helped, for these are said to be still under the dominion of the ancient powers." (*The Elements*, 40)

Iassos

There are no textual references to Iassos outside of this paladology, but there are several place names around Lygon that are named for him, suggesting a strong local memory of his presence.

Irglax, a worthless fellow. Nothing is known of this Irlgax from history. His sole mention is in this paladology of Iassos.

Erixus

Word came to Erixus from the king. Between the time of Oros and Eumaios, only the name of one Manissan king is known with certainty, Tullus, he who is mentioned in the tale of Ianthë. Even so, only a few fragments remain attesting to his rule. All the others are lost to history, as is the anonymous king of Erixus's tale.

Erixus...was never seen again among the world of men. "Where, then, did Erixus vanish to? It is as difficult as asking where our Lady went when she climbed Zurlina's foggy slopes. Yet it seems not unreasonable to suppose that, like her, he went on to those realms of glorious light inhabited by the *titani*, the sons of Anak, and there he lives still. This is what is signified when the people of Beru name their westernmost constellation after him, saying it depicts his pursuit of the Lamassu." (Lucan, *On the Titani*, 28)

Cyllinus

[B]y the sign of the spear you shall understand that the authority of Manissa shall be restored; even now she hastens to bring justice to the land. See Note 1 for Rua Calidé.

The remedy of mortality. Lucan: "It is even told in marvelous tales and visions that men of flesh and blood were fed the blessed food of the Mighty Ones of Old; thus was the visionary Cyllinus nourished by the bread of the Anakim, as is told in his tale." (*On the Titani*, 3).

Radiant, shimmering and full of power and virtue. Drawing upon the ancient Asylian ideal that virtue translates to glory and radiance; for example, the radiance of Manissa on the day of her coronation. (*TM*, 5)

These are the souls of the just who sing forever. Taken from a well-known but apocryphal saying of Manissa: "The soul of the just man is among mankind as gems and precious jewels among the stones of the earth, equal in splendor and in rarity." Quoted in the *Chronicle of Ezion*, Caput II.

Be opened, gates of gold, for thy master, Orix, bids thee! Of this passage Kaldor says, "Inasmuch as the Hall of Orix with its wooden gates was thrown down by the Marudans, so blessed Orix's reward is to have dominion over the splendorous gates of gold that adorn the hall of the fathers."

I could not tell at which side of the table the history began and at which side it ended. Some commentators say this means that the ultimate destiny of the Manissans is unknown, while others interpret it to mean that the final destiny of the Manissans is to be like that of their beginning.

[E]ach flower wrought a great mystery. Norox: "Each flower stands for a different virtue–the one Cyllinus records being the virtue of courage."

Thus land and people were purified. Older commentators, following ancient tradition, see in this passage and the following vision of the man grabbing the spear the promise of the return of the kingdom to the house of Manissa in the person of Ezion. Lucan of Anentora, however, sees the former vision fulfilled in at the end of time, with only the succeeding paragraph of the man grabbing the spear as applying to Ezion.

For a purpose was I exalted among all Asylians and peoples of the west. This passage is central to the understanding of the religion of the Manissans as it developed in the divine honors it pays to Manissa. All commentators, both ancient and modern, make it the centerpiece of their thought on the role of Manissa in the destiny of the nation. The summary of their thought can be summed up in three points: (1) Though not a god by nature, Manissa has been exalted and given celestial powers over the lives and destiny of her people. (2) Therefore, since this has been arranged by some divine providence, it is fit and just that Manissans pray and petition to Manissa, and only her. (3) Therefore, no foreign cult or deity can be permitted within Manissan lands. This means that they are to be actively suppressed or rooted out, thus giving the religion of the Manissans its "evangelical" or missionary nature in all lands where it becomes dominant.

He is a great power, one of many. "By this passage we understand that Manx, though worshiped as a god in ages past, is accounted among the *titani*, whom the Marudans call the Anakim and the old Asylians called the Mighty Ones. It is these sons of Anak who, though might in days of old, now sleep and entrust the governance of the world to the power of men." (Lucan of Anentora, *On the Titani*, 121).

My Lady laughed. Reflecting the traditional Manissan uncertainty and carefree attitude towards afterlife save for the conviction that the righteous are rewarded.

Pelinós

This tale, a relatively late addition to the *Paladologies* (c. 2500 AZ) was a favorite among the Manissans in the following millennium and was more frequently depicted in art than any other story from the *Paladologies*.

Thus has it been even unto this day. The hereditary stewardship of the descendants of Lapax lasted until Arza 1998, when the last steward of the line, Turrius, was disinherited after a failed attempt on his master's life. The House of Pelinós retained their lordship until the time of Lesalius II (c. 1720) when they were deposed and replaced by other descendants of Mariammné by Lesalius. The line of Pelinós has since vanished from history.

Telux and Andrior

According to Agrius the Sage, the tale has an allegorical aspect: "In the narrative of Telux and Andrior we are told how two twin brothers sought to bring philosophy and architecture into Asylia. However, the tragic death of one of the brothers leaves Asylia with only architecture deprived of philosophy. In this we see an image of the dilemma of mankind in being adept at the marvels of practical philosophy, sometimes called science, while at the same time remaining ignorant of the ultimate causes of things, which are deduced by speculative philosophy." (*Hectarion*, 36)

Enlilim. The ancient race who inhabited the lands beyond Corbalund from ancient times. In old Asylian the word means "Children of Enlel," a derivation of the Enlilic word *Elíl*, "The One."

Of the origin of all men...and the lore concerning the Enlilim and the Anakim he was instructed. "Would to the gods that the knowledge of Telux might have been preserved! In ten thousand years we could never, by own our study, come to attain to that level of wisdom which Telux attained in a single year!" (Lucan, *On the Titani*, 22)

He was also instructed in the music of the Enlilim. "Let it not be lost on you, who would study the wisdom of the ancients, the great connection perceived between wisdom and music, between beautiful melodies and beautiful souls; for thus when Telux, after he had mastered the lore of the Enlilim, sought to make this knowledge ever more resplendent by adding to it the beauty of the sacred scales and harmonies, thus transforming knowledge into virtue and wisdom into power." (Norox, *Antiquities*, Chap. 100)

[T]here was war in the regions of Engor and Corbalund. Presumably to do with the house of Scius.

Why...with all thy knowledge and wisdom didst thou covet my place beneath the tree? An example of the truth, taught by the ancient Asylians, that wisdom was always susceptible to corruption through pride or envy.

The Pillar of Andrior, which remains there...to this day. The *Chronicle of Ezion* relates the pillar still standing and discernible in 2650 AZ when the king made a notable pilgrimage to the place. Norox says in his day, over a thousand years later, several formations were believed by locals to be Andrior's pillar but that it was uncertain which.

Fála and Miross

The shield rang out clearly. According to many ancient authorities, the voice was that of Iolcus himself; the invisible arms those of the spirit of Elphas.

[T]he shield of Ioclus remained fixed in Fála's hall...for many generations. In fact, the house of Corinos went extinct shortly after Fála's time (c. 3300?), at which ownership of the shield passed to the lords of Cyrenaica. The precious relic was translated to the City of Manis in the generation after Oros (c. 3050) but was lost by the time of Ezion. There are no records of what became of the sacred shield; some say Thalon bore it at the battle of Iontaré, and that after he was slain, it was spirited away by Eldax and given into the custody of the Periorid clan of Antyas, who hide the shield among the vales and hillocks of An Erras to this day. The Periords themselves maintain this, though even among them it has long since become more of a legend than a seriously asserted fact of history.

Loross

[M]y verse alone...preserves any semblance of goodness. As in the paladology of Hazer, the song of Loross is so powerful as to be confer blessing; this is seen most radically in Loross's triple resurrection, in which is music is seen to be not only a blessing, but a source of life as well.

The Immortals who ever guide Asylia through their chosen one Manissa. Signifying a familiarity with the doctrine set forth in Cyllinus, that Manissa is a mediatrix of the greater powers, the "Immortals," who have entrusted governance and judgment of the Manissan peoples to her alone.

Ithaross

[T]he mighty fortress of Tilmindor. Formerly the Elamite capital of Ambré.

Eve of the eighth day. The priest-commentator Numo (c. 500 AZ), in his work *Inquiries*, says the number eight held a mystical meaning to the ancient Manissans: "For inasmuch as the week is apportioned among seven days, which corresponds to the span of time from the beginning of the world to its ending, so does the eighth day (which is also the first day) stand for a new beginning–a new creation. Thus in the tale of Ithaross, the paladin's great conversion is inaugurated on the eighth day, symbolizing thereby a new man or a new disposition of heart." (*Inquiries of the Ancients*, Book X, 55).

Like a hulking giant of old. Lucan of Anentora: "Among the Elamites and Lysonians of Caeylon it is said that of old the titani came west and made for themselves a glorious fortress which in later days became called Hellas in the Manissan tongue." (*On the Titani*, 18)

Puzi. Norox: "To this day, when travelers lose their way on some desolate Elamite road, or when crops fail inexplicably, the denizens of those regions are apt to blame the puzi and propitiate them with sacrifices at the local rivers and crossroads." (*Antiquities*, 110)

Appendix C
CALENDARS OF MANISSÉ

꧁꧂ ꧁꧂ ꧁꧂

The Manissans used five different means of chronological reckoning. Each is described below with tables to demonstrate how the chronologies align with one another.

The Orlux Calendar

The most ancient was the Orlux Calendar. The word *Orlux* is of uncertain etymology; it may be derived from the proto-Elabaean dialect that was the parent of Old Asylian.

The Orlux Calendar is a lunar calendar with twelve months of thirty days and an additional five-day festival tagged on to the end of every year called the *Annux*. The observance of the Annux fell into abeyance within a few centuries after Manissa, however, corresponding to the general decline in the use of the Orlux Calendar.

The epochal year of the Orlux reckoning is the coronation of Manissa, which is year 1. This calendar was used first by the Asylians and then (except for the Cadarasians) by the peoples brought under Asylian domination: there is evidence of its use in Cyrenaica, Badoa, Tabia, and possibly Epidymia after that region's assimilation by the Manissans. As it is essentially a regnal calendar, the Orlux reckoning infers pre-Manissan calendars were anchored to regnal dates as well. The notation for Orlux reckoning is the letters OR followed by the numeral. So, the final year of Manissa's reign would be written as OR 18.

The Orlux is an interesting calendar because it continued to be utilized for ceremonial purposes long after it had ceased being used as practical means of timekeeping. Its importance waned with the decline of Asylia as a regional power; by the time Oros seized Dretia around the year OR 495, nobody outside Asylia was using the Orlux reckoning for practical timekeeping. It endured, however, in the temple complex of the City of Manis for calculating the days of religious festivals and the anniversary celebrations of the paladins. The continued use of the old calendar provided a tangible link to the foundational events of Manissé. By the reign of King Eumaios (OR 939-961) it was viewed as an exclusively religious calendar used and understood only by an elite class of clerics.

The Cadarasian Annals (Cadara Corú)

The Cadarasian Annals are undoubtedly the most ancient of the calendars ever used in Manissé. The Cadarasian Annals use an *ad urbe condita* reckoning, counting years from the founding of the city of Cadaras. In the ancient version of the Annals, the first year of Manissa's reign is recorded as the 273rd year of the city of Cadaras, implying a foundation of Cadaras 273 years prior to the crowning of Manissa.

As a calendar proper to Cadaras, the Cadarasian Annals were never used outside of Cadaras and its environs (Avlos, Elos, and Molossia). Since, however, Cadaras functioned as the titular capital of the Manissan kingdom for over 545 years, it assumed a special significance. Within Cadaras, all records were kept in according to this reckoning, called *Cadara Corú* (CC), which meant "Cadarasian Counting" in the Old Cadaran dialect. Decrees sent west of the Erriad were issued in issued in both Cadara Corú and Orlux.

In the beginning, the Cadarasian Annals were not a calendar but an actual history, as the name suggests. Historical events connected with the city of Cadaras were recorded annually (none of these records survive, save in the convoluted legends of old Cadaras). The practice of annual counting, however, endured and became the Cadara Corú; an event recorded according to this reckoning was said to have occurred "according to Cadaran counting."

The Cadara Corú reckoning of the Annals was notoriously imprecise and unwieldy. This was due to the variable length of the Cadarasian year, which lasted between 353 and 415 days. This in turn was because the Cadarasian new year itself was movable, its date dependent upon the priests of Mironna observing specific auguries *and* a certain stellar alignment occurring within the same window. During times of war, sometimes the auguries were not taken at all, and dates had to be retroactively adjusted, sometimes months or years afterward. Later generations of scholars labored meticulously to reform Cadara Corú by maintaining the overall CC dating scheme but aligning the years closer to the conventional 365-day solar year, as used in Arza reckoning. This reformed system was known as *Cadara Corú Pel*, "New Cadaran Counting." In the reformed calendar, Manissa took the throne of Asylia in 268 CC.

Meaningful use of the Cadarasian Annals requires the reader to understand primitive Cadara Corú, align it with the reformed dates of Cadara Corú Pel, then further align Cadara Corú Pel with the universal Arza calendar. Cadara Corú was abandoned around five centuries after Manissa's reign; the final entries in the Cadarasian Annals are dated 663 CC and relate the deaths of Casias and Lyrgoné. For ease of use, dates in the tables of this appendix are in Cadara Corú Pel.

Arza Reckoning

Arza reckoning was one of two calendars used by Caeylon. It originated during the Marudan period and was used wherever the Marudans went, eventually gaining broad acceptance in many lands due to its universality and ease. It gradually displaced all other calendars in Manissé to become the dominant reckoning in the west. Dates in Arza reckoning can be denoted either by the word "Arza" ahead of the numeral, or else the letters AZ afterward (e.g., Arza 2500 or 2500 AZ). In common usage, however, this is seldom necessary; since Arza is the most common reckoning, all dates are generally assumed to be in Arza unless otherwise stated.

Arza is unique in that it counts down instead of counting forward; in other words, it counts "backwards." This reflects its origins in the priestcraft of the scribes of the En'Thoth temple in Caeylon. To understand Arza, a brief detour through ancient Marudan cosmology is required: The word Arza is derived from the old Marudan word *arzawa*, which is generally taken to mean "creation" but may also mean something like "establishment" or "ordering." Arza purports to date backwards from what the ancient texts called the *geba arzawa*, the "creation of the world" according to Marudan mythology. The Marudans held that the world is divided into four epochs called *renpu*. Each *renpa* consists of one thousand 365-day solar years (with a leap year every fourth year). Mankind is allotted four *renpu*, at the end of which will come *tutaheka*, the apocalyptic ending of the world in the final war of the gods. The Marudans thus bracketed the age of men between the *geba arzawa* and *tutaheka* with four thousand years between, divided into four *renpu*.

It should be noted, however, that the idea of *geba arzawa* as the creation of the world was not uncontested. Given the varied meanings of *arzawa*, some Marudan scribes took it to mean not the creation of the world but the *reconstitution* of the world, or the *reforming* of the world—the fashioning of the current form of the world after a primordial period of war and chaos that stretched back indeterminately into the past. This represents a later interpretation, however, probably reflecting the influence of the Enlilim, whose history was vastly more ancient than the Marudans.

Fascinating as the mythos behind this is, we are concerned mainly with Arza as a calendar, not a cosmology. The epochal year of the Arza reckoning is 4000, denoting the creation of the world. The final year would be year 1, at the completion of which will occur the *tutaheka.* In the Arza reckoning, Manissa became Queen of Asylia in 3645 and reigned until 3627; Oros conquered Dretia around 3150, and Ezion reigned from 2675 to 2581.

The Arza calendar was a priestly system first devised in the Temple of En'Thoth in Caeylon, likely by the priests of Shamash who, of all the ancients, were more skilled in the craft of reading the heavenly bodies. The Arza calendar existed side by side with the regnal dating of the Marudan king lists, but eventually became the dominant calendar due to its accuracy, ease, and universal scope. It came into use in Manissé through the Anentorans (who once were joined to Caeylon), gradually displacing Cardara Corú in Cadaras by 3200 and spreading throughout Manissé in the centuries after. It should be noted that though the Manissans adopted the Arza reckoning for its utility and accuracy, they did so without affirming its underlying mythos or apocalypticism, which most Manissans remained entirely ignorant of.

During the renaissance under Ezion, the Manissan court was alarmed at the dominance of a foreign calendar in Manissé and attempted to stay its spread by creating the Ezionic Calendar. This proved futile, however, and Arza reckoning was universal by 2450.

The Marudan King Lists

The Marudan king lists are the second of the two calendars used in ancient Caeylon. As the name suggests, the Marudan king lists were based on the regnal year of the Marudan monarch. For example, Manissa's victory over Adaran in the Arcorian Wood took place in the fourth year of King Belthazre; Sammas took the throne in the forty-ninth year of

King Bakku, and the reign of Ezion began in the third year of King Tahrus V. The events of *Paladologies* align with the reigns of twenty-three different Marudan kings, as shown in the table.

Marudan regnal dates were used for all civil acts in Caeylon. The kings preferred regnal dating as it asserted their own power against the growing influence of the priesthoods, who used the Arza calendar. Marudan king lists were never extensively used in Manissan lands. Before the accession of Manissa, they were used in Cadarasia during the reigns of Dathan and Belthazre alongside Cadara Corú. After the expulsion of the Marudans, they were seldom used save in An Hered, Ganas, and the borderlands, where Manissan merchants needed to deal with Marudan law. By the time of Ezion, however, even the Kings of Caeylon themselves had ceased using the regnal dating, yielding at last to the universal supremacy of the Arza calendar.

The Ezionic Calendar

Unlike the other calendars discussed, the Ezionic Calendar was created by royal fiat for the specific purpose of providing an alternative to the Arza calendar.

As we may guess, the Ezionic Calendar centers on the reign of King Ezion. Manissans have tended to view Ezion's reign as a golden age—a renaissance in which the culture and political influence of ancient Manissé reached its apex. Manissan literature refers to Ezion's reign as the "Golden Reign." Part of the glory of Ezion's reign was the birth of a truly national consciousness; it seemed, for the first time, that the peoples of Manissé were able to put aside the dynastic and provincial squabbles that had characterized the first millennium after Manissa and begin to think of themselves as simply *Manissans*.

As part of this new patriotic sensibility, Ezion sought to curb foreign influences he believed were detrimental to the Manissan spirit. This included the Arza calendar, which by Ezion's time was ubiquitous throughout Manissé. To that end his government fashioned what has become known as the Ezionic Calendar, taking the date of Ezion's accession as its epochal year. The Ezionic Calendar mimicked the Arza in its measurements (as it was not possible to improve upon it); it also borrowed Arza's "backwards" counting: dates prior to Ezion's reign were said to be "Before Ezion" and counted down to his accession, while dates after his accession were "After Ezion" and moved forward. These are typically designated BE and AE. For example, in the Ezionic system, Manissa became Queen of Asylia in 970 BE; King Palereus, who came after Ezion, built Tereldian in 206 AE.

Ezion mandated the Ezionic Calendar in all his domains by royal decree (though he did not call it the Ezionic Calendar; he simply referred to it as the "New System"). The Arza reckoning was too well entrenched to be so easily swept aside, however. The Manissans did not adopt the new system willingly; the only ones who did were royal officials and others whose professions connected them with the court. Others complied only half-heartedly, and many regions never adopted it at all. It was the insistence of Ezion alone that kept his calendar alive. After his death it was retained only on the Isle of Dretia and even there was abandoned entirely after a few generations.

The following two pages contain tables showing the alignment of important dates according to the various calendars.

	Arza	Ezionic	Orlux
Ioclus murdered; Manissa ascends the throne	3645	970 BE	1
Reign of Manissa	3645-3627	970-952 BE	1-18
Manissa's triumph in the Arcorian Wood	3641	966	4
Manissa vanishes pursuing the Lamassu	3627	952	18
Reign of Hadrior	3627-3612	952-937	18-33
Hadrior's conquest of Cyrenaica	3625	950	20
Hadrior's defeat by Cygnus; killing of Belar	3613	938	32
Reign of Anaxandra	3612-3595	937-920	35-50
Lamentations of Hazer	3610-3600	935-925	35-45
Death of Elifanora	3610	935	35
Conquest of Illyrs by the sons of Manissa	3607	932	35
Joint reign of Gilgax and Egol	3595	920	38
Reign of Egol	3595-3590	915	50
Killings of Secum, Pirox, and Irodel	3590	915	55
First Council of Lords	3590-3580	915-905	55-65
Pilux comes to Corbalund	3582	907	63
Sons of Perior destroy Cadaras	3579	904	66
Ennus in Cadaras	3530 (?)	855	115
Sammas takes the throne at Cruachan	3513	838	132
Sammas's wars against the Manissan houses	3504	829	141
Giannor exorcises the spirit of Gygas	3495 (?)	821	149
Lorion founds Halicor	3484	811	161
Death of Lorion; Eira controls of Halicor	3466	791	179
Lothar flees to the court of Alcidus	3460	785	185
Lothar inherits Halicor	3455	780	190
Lothar's penance in Corbalund	3450-3447	772-772	195-197
Amatós	3400 (?)	725	245
Telux and Andrior in Islindia	3350 (?)	675	294
Ithaross conquers Elam	3300 (?)	625	345
Deaths of Casias and Lyrgoné	3250 (?)	575	395
Iassos and Irglax	3200 (?)	525	445
Loross the Undying in Anentora	3190 (?)	515	455
Oros conquers the Isle of Dretia	3150 (?)	475	495
Translation of the capital to the City of Manis	3100 (?)	425	545
Ianthë carried off by Phantos of Cadaras	3050	375	595
Adrius founds the Oracle of Orale	3000 (?)	325	645
Erixus vanishes in Adarwood	3000 (?)	325	645
Visions of Cyllinus	2950	275	695
Reign of King Eumaios	2706-2684	31-9	939-961
Tyranny of Thalon; Ezion in hiding	2684-2675	9-1	961-970
Golden reign of Ezion the Glorious	2675-2581	1-94 AE	970-1064
Mantarax conquers the Iturs	2520	155 AE	1125
Killing of Mantarax in Hamach	2470	205	1175
Palereus reconquers Iturs, builds Tereldian	2496	206	1176

	Cadara Corú (Pel)	Marudan King Lists
Ioclus murdered; Manissa ascends the throne	268 CC	Belthazre Year 1
Reign of Manissa	268-286 CC	Belthazre Year 1-18
Manissa's triumph in the Arcorian Wood	272	Belthazre Year 4
Manissa vanishes pursuing the Lamassu	286	Belthazre Year 18
Reign of Hadrior	286-301	Belth. 18 - Arctos (I) 9
Hadrior's conquest of Cyrenaica	288	Belthazre Year 20
Hadrior's defeat by Cygnus; killing of Belar	300	Arctos (I) Year 8
Reign of Anaxandra	301-318	Arctos (I) 9 - Luruk 5
Lamentations of Hazer	303-313	Arctos (I) 11 – Luruk 1
Death of Elifanora	303	Arctos (I) Year 11
Conquest of Illyrs by the sons of Manissa	306	Arctos (I) Year 14
Joint reign of Gilgax and Egol	318	Luruk Year 5
Reign of Egol	318-323	Luruk 5 – Bathaal 4
Killings of Secum, Pirox, and Irodel	323	Bathaal Year 4
First Council of Lords	323-333	Bathaal Year 4-14
Pilux comes to Corbalund	331	Bathaal Year 12
Sons of Perior destroy Cadaras	334	Bathaal Year 15
Ennus in Cadaras	383 (?)	Bakku Year 32
Sammas takes the throne at Cruachan	400	Bakku Year 49
Sammas's wars against the Manissan houses	409	Laman Year 6
Giannor exorcises the spirit of Gygas	418 (?)	Laman Year 15
Lorion founds Halicor	429	Pazu Year 1
Death of Lorion; Eira controls of Halicor	447	Pazu Year 19
Lothar flees to the court of Alcidus	453	Pazu Year 25
Lothar inherits Halicor	458	Pithis Year 1
Lothar's penance in Corbalund	463-466	Pithis Year 5-8
Amatós	513 (?)	Parsaniah II Year 11
Telux and Andrior in Islindia	563 (?)	Keshuru Year 30
Ithaross conquers Elam	613 (?)	Arzerus Year 17
Deaths of Casias and Lyrgoné	663 (?)	Palian Year 7
Iassos and Irglax	—	Nephaliah Year 3
Loross the Undying in Anentora	—	Nephaliah Year 13
Oros conquers the Isle of Dretia	—	Daran Year 12
Translation of the capital to the City of Manis	—	Durunda Year 1
Ianthë carried off by Phantos of Cadaras	—	Gazzat Year 17
Adrius founds the Oracle of Orale	—	Ereshk Year 6
Erixus vanishes in Adarwood	—	Ereshk Year 6
Visions of Cyllinus	—	Vamir II Year 11
Reign of King Eumaios	—	Tahrus (IV) 2-23
Tyranny of Thalon; Ezion in hiding	—	Tahr. (IV) 23-Tahr. (V) 3
Golden reign of Ezion the Glorious	—	Tahrus (V) 3 – Doriah 4
Mantarax conquers the Iturs	—	Yusef (II) Year 29
Killing of Mantarax in Hamach	—	Yusef (IV) Year 12
Palereus reconquers Iturs, builds Tereldian	—	Yusef (V) Year 3

Appendix D
READING PALADOLOGIES CHRONOLOGICALLY

꧁ ꧁ ꧁

Below is a sequence for those interested in reading the *Paladologies* in chronological order. Titles appearing in *italics* are from the Minor Paladologies.

Of the Murder of Erogel
Of the Siege of Thán
The Spear of Ioclus
Of the Rua Calidé
The Final Days of Hadrior
Mariammné and Baldor
Belar
Necho and Elphas
Elifanora
Pilux
Hazer
Secum
The Council of Lords and the Great Census
Asaph and Elora
Fála and Miross
Perior
The Sons of Perior
Ennus
Apollus and Sammas
Giannor
Amatós

Lorion and Eira
Lothar
Telux and Andríor
Ithaross
Casias and Lyrgoné
Pelinós
Iassos
Loross the Undying
Oros
Ianthë
Fragments of Adrius
Erixus
Cyllinus
Ezion
Mantarax

Glossary of Important Persons
and Place Names of *Paladologies*

Adlor: The Manissan fortress in the region of Greystone, later the city of Adlo (Asy: "Defense").

Adrius: Son of Malech who lifted the curse of Adurax by slaying his father and founding the Oracle of Orale.

Adurax: Father of Malech and grandfather of Adrius; he incurred a curse upon his house for the slaying of a priest of Manissa, for which he himself was struck with leprosy. He is sometimes called 'Adurax Gorgos', "the Leper."

Aella: One of the names given for the nymph who carried off Amatós.

Aiareth: A grandson of Necho and Lord of Engor.

Aïross: A son of Necho who slew Zupha.

Albia: The narrow land between north Adarwood and the sea.

Alcidus: King of Cadaras in the days of Lothar and Eira.

Amatós: Carried off by a lovesick nymph in Eidyllion.

Amela: Princess of Badoa, wed to Pilux.

Amira: A Caeylonic captain who fought for Sammas at Cruachan.

Amoroth: Chief of the clan Erytas, killed at Iontaré fighting for Ezion.

Analissa: Mother of Anaxandra and wife of Erogel.

Anaroth: A city of Epidymia where Secum took refuge from Egol.

Anax: A chief of the hillmen of Bados who helped Oros in the war against the Dretians.

Anaxandra: Granddaughter of Arrax and Queen of Elabaea.

Ancyrus: Father of Ioclus, Naross and Arrax.

Andelor: Tabian captain slain by Casias.

Andor: Grandfather of Ioclus.

Andríor: Twin of Telux; learned architecture from the Enlilim and brought his skill back to Asylia.

Andross: Husband of Iyla; slain by Hazer.

An Erras: A valley just west of the Erriad where Hazer dwelt.

Annete: Companion of Queen Anaxandra.

Anorel: A fertile plain in central Epidymia, once home to both Secum and Asaph.

Anrothan: Ancestor of Manissa.

Anthalus: Birth name of Sammas.

Antyas: One of the sons of Perior.

Antylos: Brave lord of Asylia killed fighting for Oros in the mountains of Bados.

Apollus: Heir to the chair of Baldor; chief opponent of Sammas.

Araímsir: "Hill of the Stars," where Indor first sighted Laoön.

Ardilla: The great fortress of the Dretians, taken by Oros and later renamed Bados.

Argoss: Lord of Engor, brother of Eumaios and father of Thalon.

Arialor: The Asylian name of Halicor.

Ar Pelaroth: "Hill of the Poplars," the abode of Hazer and later site of a shrine to Manissa.

Arrax: Brother of Ioclus and uncle of Manissa.

Arrax the Younger: One of the sons of Perior; also, uncle of Manissa renowned for his strength.

Arummnax of Orioön: Lord of Asylia and ally of Hadrior; killed Belar, son of Baldor, at Enna before being slain by Cygnus.

Arytos: King of Cadaras at the time of Casias and Lyrgoné.

Asaph: Prophet and third son of Hazer.

Assio: A son of Elphas slain by Egol.

Athoss: War chief of Anaxandra, slain by Elphas.

Athyrac: "Silver demon," the sea serpent slain by Pelinós. Also called Rahan.

Attus: Manissan noble who defected from Thalon to serve Ezion.

Azael: Last King of Epidymia and successor of Belabret.

Bakku: A King of Caeylon.

Bassio: Son of Endumion of Cyrenaica, slain by Baldor.

Belabret: King of Epidymia whose wife committed adultery with Asaph.

Belar: Firstborn son of Baldor; killed in Enna by Arummnax.

Beru: A wild region of western Cyrenaica associated with the wanderings of Erixus.

Beruah: One of the lords who accompanied Oros in the war against the Dretians.

Betulia: A pleasant land in southeastern Greystone near Galmura (Mog: Buturlüe).

Calanthé: Daughter of Baldor and wife of Gilgax.

Calcax" Lord of Avlos who led the killing of Perior at Ar Pelaroth.

Canakkalé: "Ditch of Blood," the site in Migdalim where Sammas destroyed the armies of Engor

Carius: Mentioned in the tale of Casias and Lyrgoné as the father of Casias.

Carus: A Manissan captain who fought with Oros on Dretia isle.

Casias: A warrior of the house of Mariammné who fell wed Lyrgoné of Tabia and brought down the wrath of the Tabians upon him.

Cassos: One of the sons of Perior.

Cayla: Daughter of Cerbel, Lord of Lygon, and wife of Pelinós.

Celina: Wife of Ezion and Queen of Manis.

Cerbel: Lord of Lygon in the time of Pelinós and father-in-law of the same.

Cerdos: One of the sons of Perior, the only who refused to make war on the lords of Cadaras.

Cerigo: Eunuch of Inaya who killed Asaph.

Cerinthar: Priest and guardian of the Temple of Manissa in Asylia.

Cilla: Epidymian wife of Secum.

Ciphoné: Nymph of Arcoria who became the wife of Perior.

Corax: One of the lords who accompanied Oros in the war against the Dretians.

Corinos: A Periorid family of the house of Aïos.

Council of Lords: Ruling body of Elabaea from the death of Pirox to the ascension of Sammas.

Crastor: One of the sons of Perior.

Croas: Crossroads about a day east of old Asylia.

Crodurus: "Crossroads of Doom"; the place on Dretia Isle where the Dretians massed to advance upon and destroy the army of Oros.

Cruachan: Hill where Asylian monarchs were proclaimed and where the bones of Perior were hidden.

Cygnus: King of Lugaria and husband of Mariammné.

Cyllinus: Periorid visionary.

Dakor: A vile sun god worshipped by the followers of Malech in the city of Molcha.

Danathor: The valley outside of Cadaras, a corruption of the old Marudan "Danath Hered."

Danion: Fierce chief of the clan Antyas and ally of Ezion.

Dario: Trusted counselor of King Eurastes of Tabia.

Darion: King of Badoa, father of Amela.

Dimmoth: A wicked son of Eira, slain by Lothar.

Dimmura: Oak in An Erras where Ezion mustered his armies.

Dindar: Arrogant chief from Cadaras who accompanied Oros into Dretia and was slain while attempting to descend the cliffs on the coast of the Norn.

Díndumon: Plains in the southern district of Cadarasia.

Diptos: A servant of Thalon who was killed trying to deceive Ezion.

Dretians: A tribe of rugged mountain folk who dwelt in the Bados Mountains before being displaced by the conquests of Oros.

Durimor Pass: The main pass into the Bados Mountains from the plains around Engor.

Durmius: Lord of Halicor and co-leader of the campaign to conquer Dretia.

Dyans: The first King of Epidymia.

Dylydia: A title for Manissa meaning "Avenger."

Eamon: Father of Orianna.

Eburax: Son of Arummnax who slew Belar.

Echol: One of the sons of Perior.

Egol: Descendant of Eridax and King of Elabaea following Anaxandra's death.

Eidareth: Lord of the house of Necho and contemporary of Ornax.

Eira: The witch of Bados and mother of Lothar by Lorion.

Eiriniétha: The place on the outskirts of Ituria where Baldor swore a covenant with Hadrior.

Elam: A kingdom of half-Caeylonic Elabaeans in the extreme northeast of Elabaea; conquered by Ithaross.

Eldax: A Periorid of the clan of Antyas and protector of young Ezion.

Eldorus: Third son of Ezion.

Eleftaia: "Last Hope," the hill where Casias fell to the Tabians, later the shrine of Lygonea.

Elgerian: Old Enlilic name for the land of Elgard.

Elifanora: Maid of the house of Naross, whose rape by the King of Emeric prompted the war against the Illyrs.

Elios: Son of Ezion and King of Manis following his father's death.

Eloë: Daughter of Eumaios who bore Ezion by Embor the Periorid.

Elor: A small brook near the city of Asylia where Perior slew Indor.

Elora: Daughter of Asaph, prophetess and first consecrated virgin.

Elphas: Son of Manissa and twin brother of Necho.

Emeric: One of the two southern kingdoms destroyed by Anaxandra's armies.

Embor: Father of Ezion; slain on Thalon's orders.

Engelé: Wife of Necho and mother of Pilux.

Enlilim: The ancient magical race who dwells south of Corbalund.

Ennus: The most beautiful of all the descendants of Manissa, killed by a trianta rose.

Entharion: Son of Endumion of Cyrenaica, slain by Baldor.

Enusath: One of the sons of Laban, ancestor of the Elamites.

Eranor: A Lugarian prince and descendant of Mariammné; slain on Cruachan by Sammas.

Eriar: Mythical mountain at the top of the world; abode of the immortals.

Eridax: Created lord of Cadaras by Manissa.

Erius: Son of Eumaios, lost at sea.

Erixus: Periorid who vanished in Adarwood pursuing a Lamassu.

Ermarius: Prince of Badoa, son of King Panastes, companion of Oros.

Erogel: Son of Arrax, murdered by Hadrior.

Erras: First son of Hazer.

Errion: Second son of Ezion.

Eryice: Wife of King of Eurastes of Tabia.

Erytas: Eldest son of Perior.

Esmer: The fords where one crosses over the Erriad into Epidymia.

Eumaios: King of Manis and grandfather of Ezion.

Eurastes: King of Tabia at the time of the coming of Casias and Prastor.

Evlas: Site of the Manissan encampment near Ardilla in the Bados.

Evlos: Village in the vicinity of Cadaras.

Eydor: Son of Eumaios, lost at sea.

Ezion: Periorid of the house of Antyas; grandson and heir of Eumaios who became King of Manis after the usurpation of Thalon.

Fála: Widow of the house of Corinos who possessed the shield of Iolcus.

Galban: Powerful mage who controlled Anentora until his defeat by Loross.

Gallo: Companion of Prince Lysias of Tabia and brother of Lyrgoné.

Galmura: Rugged land on the northern shores of Norn north of the Bados.

Gemurath: Oak tree in Engor sacred to the houses of Necho and Elphas.

Gennasius: Ally of Ezion and chief of the clan of Arrax.

Giannor: A descendant of Mariammné who cast out the spirit of Gygas from Nimru.

Gilgax: Companion of Baldor and briefly King of Elabaea.

Goar: Hill giant slain by Perior.

Greystone: The name of a city and a peninsula in the extreme west of Elabaea.

Gura: Oak in Ituria where the Iturs swore obedience to King Palereus.

Gygas: The betrayer of King Ioclus whose spirit was cast out of Nimru by Giannor.

Hadrior: King of Elabaea following the departure of Manissa.

Halicor: The hall of Lorion in the foothills of the Bados.

Hamach: The shrine and city founded by Mantarax in Ituria.

Hazer: Second son of Manissa whose words had the power to bless or curse.

Hellas: A lonely and desolate mountain in the heights of Lamlash.

Hembraean: An antiquated Enlilic name for Hammer Bay, where sits Islindia.

Ianthë: A virgin of the Periorids; carried off by Phantos of Cadaras.

Iassos: Descendant of Mariammné who killed himself rather than aid King Irglax.

Idoreth: Hazerite, head of the house of Erras, slain by Sammas.

Ilos: Companion of Mantarax.

Illyrana: A great southern kingdom destroyed during by Anaxandra.

Imbrossé: Eldest and most powerful of the sons of Endumion of Cyrenaica; slain by Baldor.

Imloss the One-Eyed: Captain of Oros slain on the isle of Dretia.

Inaya: Beautiful wife of King Belabret whom Asaph lusted over; mother of Elora the Prophetess.

Indor: Faithful servant and comrade of Baldor; slain by Perior.

Indrior: Cadarasian lord slain by Perior.

Inorax: Priest of Mironna who established Elora as a consecrated virgin.

Iontaré: The flowery meadow near Engor where Ezion defeated the armies of Thalon.

Irglax: The wicked and dissolute King of Cadaras in the days of Iassos.

Irodel: Companion of Elphas, slain by Pirox.

Isrán: Scribe mentioned in the tale of Cyllinus.

Issos: Powerful lord and father of Anthalus-Sammas.

Ithaross: Paladin of the house of Perior who conquered Elam.

Ixindor: A captain of Hadrior.

Iyla: Cadarasian wife of Hazer.

Javad: Commander under Sammas.

Juna: A King of Epidymia.

Jura: A garden in Tabés where Myrax was murdered.

Kadmeia: One of the names given for the nymph who carried off Amatós.

Kaganus: The only crewman of Pelinós to be lost, due to his fear.

Koharth: City of western Epidymia near the Erriad.

534

Laios: Son of Eridax, slain by Bassio son of Endumion.

Laius: Servant of King Tullus who attended upon him at his death.

Lamlash: A rugged, mountainous region of eastern Elabaea bordering Elam on the north.

Lana: Nursemaid of Perior in the court of Asylia.

Lapax: Faithful companion of Pelinós who helped him slay Rahan and later became hereditary steward of his house.

Laoön: Constellation of the spear, first sighted by Baldor.

Lapidoth: "Stone of Gazing," the stone in Cyrenaica where Baldor first descried the constellation Laoön and where Sammas killed the Secumites.

Ligar: The sea port the Manissans constructed for the city of Lygon.

Limnos: Father of Loross.

Lolúrath: (El: "Goat Fell") The place on Mt. Hellas from which the paladin Ithaross fell.

Lorion: A descendant of Mariammné and father of Lothar by Eira.

Loross: Paladin of the house of Necho who rose from the dead three times.

Lothar: Noble son of Lorion who slew his wicked brothers.

Lygon: Great western city of the Manissans which sprung up around the tomb of Casias and Lyrgoné.

Lygonea: The tomb of Casias and Lyrgoné on the hill of Eleftaia.

Lyrgoné: Beautiful Tabian maiden who fell in love and eloped with Casias.

Lysias: Son of Eurastes and Prince of Tabia, killed by Casias.

Machor: One of the sons of Laban.

Malech: Father of Adrius and son of Adurax, slain by Adrius.

Glossary

Makur: A god of the Illyrs worshipped by Eira.

Mamura: Father of Mantarax the paladin.

Manissa: Foundress of the Manissan kingdom and deified ancestress of the seven royal houses of Manis, from whence the paladins spring.

Manissa Tualitha: A title of Manissa; "Manissa Who Delivers."

Mannax: Giant captain of the Crastorids and ally of Ezion.

Mannoth: Companion of King Ancyrus, executed for usurping the king's powers.

Manruthim: Nomadic descendants of the Marudans who dwell around the Cyrian Highlands.

Mantarax: The last paladin; conqueror of the Iturs.

Manx: Asylian god who is said to live upon Mount Eriar.

Marax: One of the elder sons of Perior.

Marí: Son of Lothar and Ornis.

Mariammné: Eldest child of Manissa and wife of Cygnus of Lugaria.

Marius: Fourth son of Ezion; also the name of a scribe mentioned in the tale of Cyllinus.

Marmella: Regions of southern Asylia near the forest of Eidyllion and Enna.

Marmelos: A chief of the Iturs offended by Hadrior.

Menthor: Father of Amatós and Pipos.

Migdalim: Fertile and sloping farmland between Engor and south Cadarasia.

Mimmoth: Hill outside Engor where Necho was slain.

Mirana: Mother of Amatós and Pipos by Menthor.

Mironniur: The Manissan name for the city of Emeric following its overthrow by Baldor; it means "Fate is just."

Miross: Thief who tried to steal the shield of Ioclus from Fála.

Moguls: A primitive people who once inhabited the Greystone Peninsula.

Molcha: City founded by Malech where the god Dakor was worshipped by human sacrifices; destroyed by Adrius.

Myrax: Companion of Casias murdered by Lysias and Gallo.

Narmoros: Father of Ianthë and unwitting slayer of King Tullus.

Necho: Son of Manissa, twin brother of Elphas; founder of Engor, slain by the Marudans.

Nelus: Father of Oxanna, wife of Baldor, and companion of Manissa.

Nico: Lord of Kerion who gave Perior the sword and armor of Belar.

Nimrah: Caeylonic mother of Sammas.

Ninós: Cadarasian captain who slew Sammas.

Noria: Wife of Elphas.

Norn: The great bay in western Alabama in which sits the isle of Dretia.

Nuba: Epidymian champion slain by Elphas.

Nubio: Official recorded as a witness to the transcription Cyllinus's vision.

Númerian: An Enlilic lord who took in the brothers Telux and Andríor and granted them their gifts of wisdom and artifice.

Oracle of Orale: Sacred spring of Lugaria, established as a Manissan shrine by Adrius.

Oria: The maid of Elifanora who brought news of her death to Cadaras.

Orianna: Ancestress of Manissa taken to wife by Manx.

Orix: Son of Orianna by Manx; first King of Asylia.

Orius: Only son of Secum.

Ornax: Lord of the house of Elphas, slain at Canakkalé.

Ornis: Wife of Lothar who did penance with him seven years in Corbalund.

Oros: Descendant of Necho who conquered the Isle of Dretia.

Oruseth: A captain of Hadrior.

Oxanna: Wife of Baldor and mother of Belar and his brethren.

Panastes: King of Badoa mentioned briefly in the tale of Oros.

Pelarus: Second son of Hazer.

Pelinós: Kinsman of Casias who slew the serpent Rahan.

Periath: The region in westernmost Cyrenaica bordering Adarwood.

Perior: Youngest and strongest son of Manissa.

Phantos: A Cadarasian lord who carried off Ianthë.

Pictor: Lord of the Periorids who fought Sammas on Cruachan.

Pipos: Brother of Amatós.

Pirox: Briefly the King of Elabaea who killed Irodel and Secum.

Pontus: Good shepherd of Enna whom Ezion made high priest.

Prastor: Manissan priest and head of the delegation of Arytos to Tabia.

Prato: Chief of the clan Marax, killed at Iontaré fighting for Ezion.

Puzi: A mischievous shape-changing sprite of Elamite folklore that deceived the paladin Ithaross.

Rahan: (Tab. "Tumult") The Tabian name for the beast Athyrac.

Ramah: One of the sons of Laban.

Rammol: A descendant of Eridax and Lord of Cadaras.

Rhianna: Foolish lover of Ennus.

Glossary

Rommoss: Son of Pelarus and grandson of Hazer.

Sammas: Wicked king who put to death many of the descendants of Manissa.

Samnor: One of the sons of Laban.

Scius: A lord of Engor, opponent of Telux and Andríor.

Scylax: Father of Apollus and grandson of Baldor.

Secum: Son of Manissa, counselor to Anaxandra, Baldor, Gilgax, Egol and Juna of Epidymia.

Semnos: One of the sons of Perior.

Servius: Father of Eranor and grandson of Mariammné.

Silius: A companion of Thalon made high priest when Ezion was exiled; later deposed by Ezion.

Sinnechan: The place on Mimmoth where Elphas spent his last days.

Sirmius: A captain who fought with Oros on Dretia isle.

Sligo: A mountain in Periath where Ezion hid from Thalon's spies.

Solax: A minor captain in Oros's army; helped take Cumala.

Soldara: A river that winds through the city of Tabés westward to the sea.

Succoth: The god of the Tabians.

Tabés: Royal city of Tabia; burned by the Manissans in vengeance for Casias' death.

Tabia: Kingdom in the westernmost regions of Elabaea.

Tanus: Lord of Engor who aided Oros in the conquest of Dretia.

Telendor: The name taken by Lothar when he came to Cadaras in hiding.

Telux: Twin brother of Andrior; learned all the wisdom of the Enlilim but died before he could bring it back to Asylia.

Glossary

Temenids: The ruling family of Cyrenaica after the fall of the house of Toranoss.

Terea: Wife of Loross.

Tereldian: The lost tomb of Mantarax in Ituria.

Teruel: Brook in the foothills of the Bados where the Manissan armies mustered before setting forth to conquer Dretia.

Thalon: Cousin of Ezion and pretender to the throne of Manis.

Thalus: An obscure king of Cadaras, mentioned only once in the *Paladologies* as reigning at the time Cyllinus had his famous visions.

Thrasos: Lord responsible for the poisoning and death of Perior.

Tilmindor: The fortress built by Ithaross after his conquest of Elam.

Temoras: The manor of Calcax of Avlos, burned by the Periorids.

Toranoss: An Asylian lord, placed over Cyrenaica by Hadrior and later slain by the Lugarians at Enna.

Tricodiad- (Asy: "Thrice-Raised") A title for Loross the Undying.

Tullus: A King of Manis, one of the first to rule from Dretia.

Tythodii: "Gods of the West," a title of the ten sons of Perior.

Umba: A large Dretian chief slain by Durmius of Halicor.

Urbus: A chief of the hillmen of Bados who helped Oros in the war against the Dretians.

Urilla: "The Worm," the chief deity of the Illyrs.

Urmax: Captain of Oros slain on the isle of Dretia.

Uta: Wife of Laban and matron of the Elabaean peoples.

Vâlcea: Bridge in Tabés where Casias first met Lyrgoné.

Varius: Grandfather of Mantarax.

Vinos: A wicked son of Eira, slain by Lothar.

Yellow Forks: The site of a disastrous defeat for Hadrior at the hands of the Iturs.

Zinzarel: Epidymian nobleman in the court of Belabret aided by Asaph.

Zupha: Marudan captain who slew Necho and was subsequently

www.ingramcontent.com/pod-product-compliance
Lightning Source LLC
Chambersburg PA
CBHW031022030726
47497CB00004B/964